Praise for the work of
Charlotte Featherstone

"A wonderf[...] very heart of
this novel. [...] its damaged
hero, it [...] nal clout."

"Ms. Featherstone, will you be writing about
any of the other characters in future novels? I hope so;
the characters you've built in *Addicted* have very likeable,
very human personalities… Your novel was
an easy and an especially enjoyable read."
—*Night Owl Reviews* Top Pick!

SINFUL
"Pairing a tortured hero and a strong-minded heroine
creates a dynamic conflict and off-the-charts sexual tension.
Throw in lots of witty dialogue and a nontraditional
happy ending, and you've got a keeper."
—*RT Book Reviews* Top Pick!

"[Featherstone] manages to weave an interesting tale,
combining sizzling sex scenes with characters deeply rooted
within their sexual identities… I'm impressed with what
[Featherstone] has to offer in the romance world."
—*Dear Author*

LUST
"Featherstone knows how to write sexy
in this unusual tale of the fey. Thane's seduction of Chastity
is titillating and is complemented by the other well-written
characters and their relationships."
—*RT Book Reviews*

"This was the first time I have read a Charlotte Featherstone
book; I can safely say that it will not be the last…
Now I just have to be patient and wait for the next
Sin to find his Virtue."
—*Forbidden Reviews*

**Also available from
Charlotte Featherstone**

*LUST
SINFUL
ADDICTED*

Anthologies

*THE PLEASURE GARDEN
WINTER'S DESIRE
THE WEDDING OF THE CENTURY & OTHER STORIES*

CHARLOTTE FEATHERSTONE

SEDUCTION & SCANDAL

HQN™

Recycling programs
for this product may
not exist in your area.

ISBN-13: 978-0-373-77587-3

SEDUCTION & SCANDAL

Copyright © 2011 by Charlotte Featherstone

This book is dedicated to my granny MacAlpine, and all the ancient Scots who weaved their stories and shared them, passing them down for the next generation to enjoy and share.

Had it not been for Janet and Death's story, told to me when I was a child, this book would never have been written! I made it my own, Gran, and hope you won't mind that Janet is Isabella, and that instead of moving Death to tears with her song, she does so with her words.

Till we meet again....

And to Beth, from the Pussycat Parlor, for that oh so inspiring picture of Lord Black! You're the best!

I am the fog, mist and rain, the shadows that creep across your windowpane.

I am darkness and disease, the entity whom all fear to see.

I am hate, dread, rage, all humans pray to keep me at bay.

I am sorrow and loneliness. Emptiness and despair.

I am, and will be, your last breath of air.

In the end it is you and me, and our walk of darkness where I will set you free.

Side by side we will go, we'll touch hands, mine will be cold.

You will look at me, and say, "Please, Lord Death, don't take me away." And I will reply, as I always do, "Nothing can sway me, pray do not try, for I have seen millions cry. Their tears, while soft, cannot break through this iron heart."

I am Lord Death, bound by command, to steal life from those souls who have reached their end. I am Lord Death, a shadow of fear, a man say some, a demon cry most.

I am Lord Death, and this I will say, one day you and I shall walk the path of eternal darkness.

CHAPTER ONE

London, 1875

The first time I met death, it was at a ball and we danced a waltz. Beneath the glittering chandeliers, and amidst the swirls of ball gowns, their silk trains decorated with pearls and lace, Death guided me in sweeping circles until I was dizzy and breathless and all the other dancers had seemed to melt away, leaving only Death and myself whirling on the dance floor.

I should have feared him and his steely embrace, but I did not. Death had been by my side for so many years that I felt a kindred spirit in him. I have seen Death. He is beautiful in his severity, heartrending in his coldness. A dark, shadowy specter whose web draped like an ethereal veil over the mortals he would one day lay claim to.

A man in every appearance, whose isolation and loneliness he could not hide. It shone in his eyes, which were a mesmerizing dichotomy of coldness and warmth. His irises were a light shade of blue with the faintest chips of pale green, reminding me of the turbulent, chilly waters of the North Sea. But his lashes, thick and luxurious, and black as a raven's feathers, put me in mind of a sable wrap, warm and comforting and soft—so supple and inviting. His hair was just as dark, inky and shining as it hung to his shoulders, like a pelt of fur. I yearned to run my fingers through the long strands, burying them in the thick suppleness and warmth.

"Do you know who I am?" he asked me, his voice deep and velvety. It slithered along my pores, awakening a deep feeling inside me—not fear, but something else. Something that made me warm and languorous, and as though my will were no longer my own.

"Lord Death," I replied in a breathless whisper.

"And do you not fear me?"

I looked up, held his icy blue gaze steady. "No. I do not."

He pulled me closer, till our chests meshed and our bodies danced, pressing and moving as if as one. It was indecent. Hedonistic. Exhilarating. My pulse raced, heating my skin. He found the frantic beating in my throat, his gaze lingered there and I knew then that he could snuff the warmth that was climbing steadily inside me.

"Have you come to claim me, Lord Death?"

His gaze slowly lifted to mine, and the thick, onyx lashes lowered, casting a hood over his eyes. "I have. Will you come with me now?"

We finished the turn and he took me by the hand, threading his fingers through mine, guiding me toward the French doors and the velvet blackness beyond.

I followed him willingly, his beauty beckoning me, and like a sleepwalker, I trailed beside him, compelled by something I could not name.

"Am I to die?" I asked, and he stopped, raised

*our joined hands to his mouth and gently kissed
my knuckles.*

*"You are, my love, and in your sleep, you will
become Death's bride."*

"And that is it?" cried Lucy as she threw a pillow at
Isabella. "You fiend!"

Lucy rushed to the dressing table where Isabella sat
and pulled the black leather journal from her hand. Flip-
ping through the pages, Lucy searched frantically for
more.

"I told you, Luce, that I had only just begun the story."

Lucy looked up from the book, her cheeks flushed with
excitement. "I was just about to swoon when you ended
it. I vow I am in love with Death!"

A tremor of pride curled within Isabella as she accepted the volume back from her cousin. "Do you think
it's that good?" she asked, feeling nervous as she gazed
down at the words she had written. "I will admit it is a
rather strange concept."

"Good? Gracious, Issy, you've outdone yourself with
this one. Not even Mr. Rochester is as gloriously brooding as your Lord Death."

Smiling, Isabella tucked her journal and pencil into the
seed-pearl reticule she was using for the night. "I could
never outdo Mr. Rochester, Lucy. Charlotte Brontë has
penned an unsurpassable hero with him."

"Death, with his black hair and pale blue eyes…" Lucy
murmured, closing her eyelids as she began to dance
around the room, as though she was waltzing. "He is
every maiden's dream. To be swept up into the arms of
a man focused solely on you… Issy," she said, stopping
before her. "It's perfection."

"I must confess, I do rather like the opening."

"Oh, don't be so modest," Lucy ordered as she glanced
in the mirror and replaced a few wayward auburn ringlets,

"it's only me. You can say you think it's a smashing opening, and I will wholeheartedly agree."

Hiding her grin, Isabella turned on the little stool and
straightened the amethyst-and-diamond necklace that
adorned her throat. It had been a gift from her uncle,
and she wore it whenever possible. Never could she have
imagined wearing something so beautiful—and expensive.

Her hair could use a fixing, she noticed, but there
wasn't much that could be done with the riotous flaxen
curls that enjoyed springing from their pins. She had been
able to cover up most of her past, to bury her common
roots and essentially make a silk purse out of a sow's ear,
but her hair, it seemed, had other plans. It would not obey
and she hid her smile, realizing that bit of tough Yorkshire
stubbornness would not be stretched, ironed or pulled out
of her. At least not yet.

"Tell me about your heroine, Issy, the woman who is
to capture Death's heart."

Isabella frowned. That was the strange part. She hadn't
really put much thought into the woman who was to be
Death's bride. The opening had come from someplace
deep inside her, the words spilling out from her soul. She
did not want to look too deeply there, afraid of what
she might see of her past—or perhaps it was the future
she feared?

Lucy caught her scowl, and lowered her head, so their
temples were touching as they looked at their reflections.
"Or are *you* Death's heroine, Issy?"

Isabella's mouth fell open and Lucy laughed as Isabella
flushed furiously. "Don't be silly, Lucy."

Her cousin gave her a dubious look. "You naughty little
girl, penning such a thing."

Had it been her in that opening? Had it been herself
she'd envisioned, had written about dancing indecently
with Death?

She was no stranger to him, that was for certain. But to write him as a hero? As someone who could lure and seduce...someone to be desired, and not reviled...

"You know I'm only teasing," Lucy said. "For heaven's sake, Issy, do not be so temperamental. I can't abide that in artists. That's why I broke off my flirtation with Eduardo. He was too moody for my tastes."

"Well, what did you expect?" Isabella mumbled, finally recovering from her shock that she might possibly be the heroine in her story. "You met him at a séance."

Lucy's emerald-colored eyes flashed with excitement. "And there's going to be another one in a few days. Say you'll come, Issy."

It wasn't as though she didn't have loved ones she'd dearly love to connect with in the spirit realm. Her mother, grandmother and now her aunt. They had all been taken from her, and each time she had felt Death's shadow, standing quietly in the corner, waiting to take them.

Perhaps it was just her overactive imagination, but each time she had fancied that she had seen Death with her own eyes. Of course, she had never dared to admit such a thing. For who would believe her? Still, a part of her feared she really could see Death, and that part absolutely refused to attend a séance with Lucy, for fear the Grim Reaper would present himself.

"Well?" Lucy prodded. "If nothing else, it's a good night away from balls and soirées. You might even think of it as research for your book. Bring Mr. Knighton if you wish."

"I don't think the curator of medieval studies at the British Museum would be very interested in a séance, or chair tipping, or communicating with spirits while using a talking board."

Lucy huffed as she pulled on her long leather gloves. "What you see in that stuffed shirt, I'll never understand."

"He's very kind. And...and I think him handsome."

"I'll give you those two, but I would like to remind you that he's rather boring in his conversation, and that he's probably not going to look upon your dream of being a lady novelist with a kind eye. The academic sort never do," she reminded her. "Knighton is a scholarly fellow in a scientific, hard-facts sort of way. Novels are made up stories, after all. I doubt Knighton could wrap his rather well-formed brain around that fact to grasp the delight to be found in them."

"What is it you are trying to say, exactly, cousin?"

Lucy's gaze softened. "That he is likely not going to be able to understand your brilliant mind, Isabella. He deals in facts, and you delight in fantasy. You're opposite in every respect."

Isabella dropped her gaze to her hands, where they folded primly in her lap. The jet bracelet that held the key to her journal caught her eye, and she brushed her thumb over the shining black stones. "It would do me well to give up this fantasy I so enjoy. Perhaps that is what I need, Lucy, a man who keeps me planted on earth, not in the ethers of some magical realm." Shrugging, she glanced up to see her cousin watching her with what Isabella imagined was sympathy. "It hardly matters. The chance I will be published is very slim, Lucy. It's really only a hobby."

Lucy lifted Isabella's chin with her slim fingers and gazed down upon her with her brilliant green eyes. "Repeat after me. I, Isabella Fairmont, will finish this book and submit it to every publisher in London—"

"And New York," Isabella reminded her.

"And New York," Lucy added. "And I will not rest until I see it published. I will not give up on my dreams."

Isabella stood and hugged Lucy who, although she was her cousin, was more like her best friend. They were sisters of a sort, now that Isabella had come to live with Lucy and her father. "I promise you, Luce. I will finish it, and it will find a home. And I will make Mr. Knighton a devotee of the fictional world if it's the last thing I do."

"And you must promise to read to me, every night when you've written something new."

Isabella flushed. "You only want the parts that speak of breathlessness and heaving bosoms."

"Well, of course," Lucy drawled. "Why else does one read a novel? Now then." Lucy sighed. "Let us go downstairs. We're already late and Papa will be snorting with indignation. We must not keep the Marquis of Stonebrook waiting." Lucy shook her head, although she was grinning. "Papa is such a pompous aristocrat."

Yes, the old marquis was rather self-important, but he was a good man. He had taken Isabella in, his niece by marriage, despite the scandal of her parents' nuptials. He had clothed her, protected her and Isabella loved him like the father she never knew. He had saved her from an uncertain future and from herself. She owed her uncle more than she could ever repay. Still, she missed the comfort of her mother's stories, and her grandmother's arms. She missed Whitby with its dark and forbidding abbey, and the mist that rolled in from the sea. She missed the heather-covered moors, and the rocky cliffs that stood tall and proud against the foamy, turbulent waves of the North Sea. She missed home, and everything about it.

She missed *them*.

How dearly she longed to see her mother and grandmother again, and Isabella felt her eyes begin to well with tears. Thankfully Lucy's voice drew Isabella out of her thoughts. "My feet ache already just thinking of the night ahead of us. Dear me, Issy, I'm tired of the social whirl."

Whitby forgotten for now, Isabella strived for composure. "I am as well, Luce. I would pay a very high price for a chance to stay in my room and sit at my desk and write until my fingers are blackened with ink."

"As much as I'd like more of Death, Issy, it's pertinent we make an appearance at my father's ball."

"You know, when I was a young girl, I envied you your life, the gowns, the balls, the suitors… Now, I'm not so certain you had it better than I."

Lucy tossed her a cheeky smile over her shoulder as she headed for the door. "*I* always envied you your cozy cottage and the meadow and woods where you and the other children from the village ran and played without any concern for deportment. You had a childhood, Issy. Something I never did." Lucy tipped her head and smiled. "I've always been envious of *that*. And here we were all this time, feeling resentful of the other. It's ironic, isn't it?"

"It is, indeed, for I'm sitting here loath to go to a ball, something I've always dreamed about."

"Chin up," Lucy ordered. "There could still be light at the end of the tunnel for this night. Perhaps you can write more of your book. Our ballroom has many private corners, you know."

"And of course that will have the suitors flocking to my side," Isabella muttered ungraciously. "Men adore lady novelists."

"I bet Lord Black does."

Isabella sent her cousin a glare before she reached for the ivory gloves that sat atop her dressing table. "How could you suppose such a thing, Luce? Lord Black never comes out of that mausoleum he calls a town house."

Lucy stopped at the threshold, and slowly turned, the salmon-pink silk of her gown's elaborate train wrapping around her legs. "I saw him last night."

"*Fibber!* You did not!" Isabella challenged.

"I did, I swear it. I couldn't sleep after the Anstruther soirée. I was sitting on my window box, gazing out at the stars when I saw those massive iron gates swing open. A carriage, black and shining and led by four black horses, came clattering out of the drive. The conveyance lingered for a moment, and then I saw it, a shadow that was illuminated by the lanterns. It engulfed the interior, like spilt ink, and then I saw him, his pale face appeared in the window, and he was looking up, and I swear his gaze lingered on the window beside mine—*your* bedroom window, Issy."

"Nonsense," Isabella scoffed.

"It's the truth."

"I think, Luce that you should take up novel writing with me. You've the imagination for it."

"Think what you like, Isabella, but I know what I saw. And you mark my words, our neighbor will be here tonight. The Marquis of Stonebrook will have it no other way, I assure you."

THERE WAS ONE THING that had surprised Isabella after coming to live with her uncle, the Marquis of Stonebrook, and that was the strange fact that she rather despised balls.

For most of her girlhood, she had sat on the weathered window bench of the small cottage her mother rented, thinking of her beautiful cousin, laughing and flirting and dancing around the Stonebrook's glorious ballroom, wearing an outrageously expensive gown. Her young heart had ached with longing. She had wanted to attend a ball. To wear a stunning gown. To have a handsome suitor.

It was rather satirical that now, after she possessed all three, she had no taste for it. She would have much preferred curling up before the large hearth in her room, wearing her old flannel nightrail, writing her stories— just as she had before Stonebrook and Lucy had come to Whitby to bring her back to London.

The wonder and novelty of town life had soon worn thin. There had been so many balls this past week, despite it being October. It seemed that the aristocracy no longer found it necessary to depart for their country estates at the end of the season as they did in the past. Perhaps it was because the nouveau riche rarely ever left London. An aristocrat could hardly marry off his titled daughter to a wealthy businessman if he was up in Yorkshire with sheep and trees.

No, the marriage mart had extended well beyond the traditional season. And this season, it was no secret that the Marquis not only wanted to marry off his daughter, but his niece, as well.

Isabella had been taken with the idea at first. The romance of a courtship, rides in the park, the soirées, the balls, the musicales. It had not taken long before she realized that the thought of going out yet another night provoked her to distemper. Not even Lucy who had been born and raised in this way of life enjoyed the endless parties.

They were a fine pair, Isabella thought, as she slipped the delicate silver strap of her reticule higher onto her wrist. Lucy was content to pursue her interest in the occult, and Isabella was happy writing the stories that constantly filled her head. Both of them were originals, and nothing like a young lady of good breeding should be. Perhaps both of them had inherited Isabella's mother's taste for shunning the ideals of what made a woman a proper lady. Lord knew her mother had been nothing like her sister. Aunt Mildred had always been frightfully proper—haughty, even. So unlike Isabella's mother who shunned society's rules. Lucy, Isabella thought, very much reminded Isabella of her own mother—both in looks and temperament. She wasn't the only who had thought so, either. Aunt Mildred had despaired of Lucy becoming just like her "fallen unfortunate sister." That fear had been so great that upon Lucy's tenth birthday, Aunt Mildred had refused to come to Yorkshire to visit them. They had been kept separate after that, lest Lucy catch the wanton, wild streak Isabella's mother had never outgrown.

There hadn't ever been any fear that Isabella would end

up like her mother. She had learned a hard lesson, from a very young age. She would *not* follow her mother's footsteps.

"My toes are already pinched," Lucy hissed into her ear as they stood and watched the swell of dancers waltzing around the overly hot room. "And I fear my forehead is glistening."

Isabella studied Lucy. "Only a titch. Can you discreetly wipe it?"

"Not likely. I feel like all eyes are on us."

"Not us, *you,* sweetie," Isabella murmured. "I think they're waiting to see if the Duke of Sussex will come up to scratch tonight."

"Good Lord, let us hope not," Lucy moaned as she furiously beat the air with her fan. "I cannot for the life of me imagine His Grace at a séance."

Hiding her laugh behind her hand, Isabella stood on tiptoes, searching for the duke who had become increasingly more ardent in his pursuit of her cousin. He glanced their way, and immediately his expression changed from feigned politeness to brooding. Sussex certainly could brood, and he looked immensely handsome while doing so. Why her cousin could not see this, Isabella had no idea. The way he stared at Lucy was positively worthy of a dramatic swoon.

"Do you like him, Luce?"

"He's handsome. Rich. Titled. He has at least four estates spread throughout the kingdom and I hear he's a bit of philanthropist to boot—belongs to all sorts of charities and committees to better the ordinary man and those less fortunate. A virtual paragon," Lucy muttered as she glanced away from Sussex's prolonged stare. "Of course I should like him, but I confess that I do not feel much more than friendliness toward him. He's too shiny," she said, her tone turning thoughtful. "Rather like an immaculate archangel. I admit—but only to you—that I have a taste for more of the fallen angel. With those black curls and his beautiful face, you would think him one of the fallen, but no, he's not the least bit dangerous, but one hundred percent glowing and pure."

"Dangerous men prove only useful in selling books," Isabella muttered as she watched Sussex conversing with his friends. "In real life they serve to be more of a handful than what they're worth. Trust me, I am the product of a dangerous rakehell and a naive, overly passionate woman."

Lucy let out a most unrefined snort. "Issy, there is no woman on earth who can pen a more compelling, delicious rakehell than you. Pray do not pretend that you do not also covet a bit of danger in your life. Your writing is an extension of your soul. A glimpse deep inside. No," she said, slapping the tip of her fan over Isabella's hand. "Do not deny it. Admit it," Lucy whispered, "there is someplace inside that wishes for a dangerous man to come and sweep you off your careful, proper feet."

"No. I do not. Of that I can safely say you're wrong, Lucy. If I were ever to encounter a dangerous man I would run screaming in the opposite direction."

Lucy laughed, and Isabella scanned the dark-haired man from across the room. Sussex was tall, well formed, extremely well dressed and possessed a light, jovial personality. He enjoyed a laugh, as did her cousin. Isabella had thought it a perfect match when the duke had sought an introduction to her cousin, by way of Isabella's suitor, Wendell Knighton. Unfortunately, her cousin remained utterly obtuse to the duke's merits.

At the thought of her suitor, Mr. Knighton suddenly appeared beside the duke. She felt the slight lurch of her heart at the sight of him. Her pulse definitely leaped when his dark brown gaze found hers from across the room. He smiled, and Isabella returned it, along with the delicate beginnings of a flush. "Your Mr. Knighton is obviously smitten, Issy."

Her flush grew to a full-out blush. "I like him very much."

Lucy tipped her head and studied her. "And yet I still feel, as I always did, that he's not the right man for you. You need someone different. Deeper. More complex. Someone who understands who you really are, Issy."

"Nonsense," Isabella scoffed as she watched the dancers. "You make me out to be a mystery when I am nothing but a simple Yorkshire country girl."

But that wasn't true. After the *unfortunate event* of last spring, everyone knew she was different. Neither she nor her family talked of it, but it was there, always lurking, threatening to come out.

"Oh, look," Lucy murmured. "He's come."

"Who's come?" Isabella tried to peer over two ornate feathered headdresses, but could see nothing.

"To the left, on the balcony."

The crowd quieted, sensing something was about to happen. All heads turned in the direction of the balcony where the butler stood and pronounced, "The Earl of Black."

The cacophony of music and laughter faded as the guests pressed forward, waiting for a glimpse of the man whose name had just been announced. The room went perfectly quiet as all interest was now focused on the crab-shaped staircase. Like a magus arising from a cloud of smoke he appeared, looking down upon the faces that peered curiously up at him.

Hair as black as night fell in loose waves to his shoulders. Skin, pale and smooth, glinted beneath the blazing chandeliers. Eyes, a haunting shade of turquoise, scanned the crowd with unconcealed interest. Black brows, perfectly arched, enhanced his eyes, which had a slight upward slant.

His fingers, long and elegant, ever so slightly rapped against the balustrade as he surveyed the scene below him. He was very tall and immensely broad in the chest and shoulders. His black dress clothes and white cravat were impeccably tailored. Bow ties were the fashion now, but the elegance of the old-fashioned cravat suited him, giving him an aristocratic allure. So, too, did his black velvet jacket, which was styled in the Eastern fashion— mandarin collar with two rows of gold buttons in the military style.

He looked liked an ancient Romany prince—a warrior boyar—as his head moved slowly from right to left, his gaze spanning the entire room and its occupants.

Here was a man of the world, Isabella thought as she perused him from head to toe. A man who was mysterious and experienced, and utterly captivating. There was an air of danger about the man, a thought that was supported by the fact that a few matrons to her right were quietly but rapidly whispering behind their fans. More than one gentleman stiffened, their eyes wary as they watched the commanding earl. Everyone seemed to move in the smallest of increments—as if they were in slow motion. Was it out of fear that their movements might catch the infamous earl's attention?

Warmth spread through Isabella's body as she watched the Earl of Black stroll with negligent ease down the stairs. He was all arrogance and predatorlike grace. Tall and sleek, he resembled the Bengal tiger Wendell had shown her on display in the British Museum. He had the same rapacious look in his eye as she had seen in the tiger's green eyes. He was on the hunt, that was for certain, but for what, or whom, she feared to guess.

Lord Black never emerged from his town house, which was across the street from her uncle's town house. She had only ever caught the odd glimpse of him. His reclusiveness just fueled her imagination, and Isabella felt her breathing grow rapid and shallow, her writer's mind taking over. Her skin had grown taut, itchy beneath the lilac satin of her tight-fitting bodice as she watched him cut a swath through the guests who parted for him as though he were as powerful as Moses, parting the sea. Suddenly he stopped, turned his head and found her amidst the crowd. Isabella felt strangely light-headed as their gazes collided from across the ballroom.

He was all mystery and exoticness and more than a touch hazardous to a lady's well-being as he held her gaze. Needing to break the hypnotizing spell of Lord Black's aqua eyes that were holding her captive, she blinked and forced her body, which now felt overheated and lethargic, to move.

"It's grown rather warm, don't you think?" she asked her cousin in what sounded like a strangled voice. "I do believe I could use some air."

Before Lucy could protest, Isabella backed away and turned in the direction of the French doors that led to the terrace. Reaching for the handle, she glanced back over her shoulder and saw that Black was still in the middle of the dance floor, surrounded by hordes of London's elite. He paid his admirers no heed, but instead stared at her with his piercing eyes. There was a promise in those eyes—a very dark, forbidden promise.

"My dear," her uncle said behind her. She felt his hand lift hers from the door handle, then the feel of his arm threading with hers. "Someone wishes an introduction with you."

She tried to refuse as her uncle steered her to where Lord Black held court. His gaze was still focused solely on her, and she shivered.

"Here now, there's nothing true about what you've heard about Black. It's only rumors."

She hadn't heard anything about the earl, other than his appearance at tonnish events was much sought after, and that he was generally considered a recluse. What rumors could her uncle be referring to?

When she stood before him, when their eyes met, she gasped, unable to disguise the sound. Black did not possess turquoise eyes, but pale blue, with flecks of light green. Tempest-tossed eyes, she thought, like the churning seas in Whitby.

"Your servant, Miss Fairmont," he murmured in a dark, husky voice that was as velvety as a starless night.

"Shall we?" he asked, accepting her hand from her uncle. "I believe a Viennese waltz is next on the program."

As he pulled her to him, she was shocked by the tingle she felt beneath her glove. When the music started and he pulled her close, his hand resting low on her back, the words she had written whispered to her.

The first time I met Death, it was at a ball, and we danced a waltz.

Black looked down at her, his gaze lingering over her in a far too familiar way. "And you were not afraid," he murmured, then swept her up into a graceful turn that stole her breath.

CHAPTER TWO

"I BEG YOUR PARDON, my lord, but what did you say?" Isabella demanded. But the earl ignored her imprudence, and softly turned her once again. Her hand trembled in his, and he squeezed, ever so softly in an attempt to ease her.

"You are nervous, Miss Fairmont."

"I...yes. My apologies."

"I believe you were asking me something."

"Oh, yes. Forgive me, my lord, but I believe you were saying about being afraid when we began our dance?"

Black's pale gaze lowered, and Isabella was positive she saw it linger at the base of her throat where her pulse beat wildly. She swallowed, hard, and her hand began to tremble again.

"Ah, yes, now I recall. Although I do not make it a habit to be out in society, I am able to dance with some degree of efficiency, Miss Fairmont. There's no need to be afraid that I may step on your toes."

All her nervousness was vanquished with the sight of his charming grin. Her writer's imagination had run away with her when she thought he had said something altogether different.

What nonsense, she chastised. She was being silly, believing that his looks, and in fact, this dance, was reminiscent of her own book opening. Good heavens, she had to get a hold of herself and her impetuous imagination.

Lord Black was a distinguished earl from a titled

family that went back to the earliest of times. While a re-cluse, he was only just a man. Not...*death*.

Besides, death by all accounts smelled sickly sweet, and Lord Black's pleasing scent was a mysterious and exotic blend of spice. Eastern spice if she was correct.

"You dance very well, Miss Fairmont."

"Thank you, my lord." She could not hide her smile at his compliment. She'd had a devil of a time learning the waltz. She was quite proficient at country dances, having grown up dancing them, but the waltz was entirely an-other matter. Appearing as though she knew what she was doing while remaining elegant and light on her feet wasn't easy.

"I believe you grew up in Whitby, on the coast?" Lord Black asked as he deftly maneuvered them away from the throng of couples. They were dancing on the peripheries now, where it was quieter and much more conducive to conversation, which the earl seemed inclined to encour-age.

"I did," she replied, not giving any further particulars than what he had asked. Her uncle had cautioned her not to give out too many details of her life. The marquis had paid a great deal of money to bury her mother's scandal.

"You came to London only last year to live with your uncle and cousin, is that not right?"

"It is, my lord."

"And this is your first season out in society."

"Again, you are correct." For a recluse he was remark-ably well informed.

"And how have you found the season, Miss Fairmont?" *Insufferably long and trying.* "Glorious," she lied.

He chuckled and the sound wrapped around her. "As a person who detests society most of the time, you would not injure my sensibilities if you were to tell me the truth. You've found your first season to be tedious at best."

Isabella felt her eyes flare wide with shock. How was it Black could read her so well?

"Your mother was your uncle's wife's sister, I believe."

She swallowed hard at this new line of questioning. "Yes, my lord."

"You look very much like your mother, Miss Fairmont."

She caught her breath in surprise. "You knew my mother?"

"I was a young boy when your mother left London for Whitby."

A very polite and discreet way of informing her that he knew of her mother's scandalous past, and the wicked rogue who was her father.

"Your aunt and mother lived just down the street from here, I believe."

"Yes, they did," she answered, feeling much too unsettled. Just how much did he know about her?

"I used to see them go out for walks. My schoolroom window faced the street, you see, and I found myself staring out of that window more often than I should have."

"Ah." She glanced away from his gaze, which was focused deeply upon her.

"You have your mother's curls and pale hair."

Yes, she did. She also possessed her mother's inclination toward romantic adventures. But unlike her mother, she would only write about them, not indulge in them.

"You were all alone when your uncle came to Whitby to bring you back to London."

Yes. But how had he known that? That fact, and the *unfortunate event* surrounding it was a secret no one save Lucy and Stonebrook knew about. It was impossible that Black would know. Unless, of course, he'd been there that night…

Impossible. She was allowing her fertile imagination to ride roughshod over her sensibilities.

"We are playing quid pro quo, Miss Fairmont. It is your turn to ask me anything you'd like."

"All right," she murmured, her mind racing for something to say. "What brings you to London?"

He pulled her closer to avoid another couple who had decided to quit the dance. She felt her breath leave her body as her bodice brushed up against his jacket. "I'm here on business," he answered.

It was on the tip of her tongue to inquire about what sort of business, but she held her curiosity in check. She did not wish to have others prying into her life, so she extended the same courtesy to Lord Black, whom she assumed guarded his privacy fiercely. Perhaps now he would indulge her with the same civility, and refrain from asking further questions about her past and her family.

"I hope you will visit the museum while you are here, my lord. Mr. Knighton is opening a new exhibit. It's bound to be a smashing success."

"Knighton," he murmured, and Isabella saw Black's gaze find Mr. Knighton through the dancing couples.

"Yes, he's a very good friend of mine, and while on a dig in—"

"He's your suitor, Miss Fairmont."

She missed a step, and slammed up against Black's broad chest. He steadied her, pretending she had not made a faux pas.

"You said he was your friend, but I have been told he's courting you."

She blinked rapidly as she met his gaze. "Yes, well..." She flushed, off balance and not knowing what she should say. Suddenly, the scent of spice was all around her. It toyed with her mind, making her dizzy. He smelled so good...

"You said he was on a dig?"

Isabella tried to rein in her reeling senses. How had

Black known about Wendell Knighton? It had been only a month since Wendell had starting courting her.

"Yes, a dig," she murmured, finding her footing at last, "in the holy city. He's bringing back medieval treasures, and amongst them are some belonging to the Templars. It's going to be an extraordinary exhibit. Do you enjoy antiquities, my lord?"

His lips twisted into a sardonic smile. "You could say that, Miss Fairmont. I have been to many places and have had many opportunities to collect antiques. Even your lovely frock will one day be found on display in a museum."

She laughed and brushed aside his comment. "Nonsense. It is only lilac silk."

"It is a Worth gown, is it not?" Heat infused her cheeks as well as her décolletage when his seemingly expert gaze lingered on the tight bodice and the flesh that was displayed above the deep lace flounce. "Worth will be famous well into the next century for his ability to dress the female form as it should be."

"A gown can hardly compare to a medieval artifact, my lord."

"It can when worn by you, Miss Fairmont."

Butterflies circled like mad in her belly. Wendell had never said anything that caused this mad fluttering. Fighting the urge to fan herself with her hand, Isabella said, "Well, I do hope you will stop by the museum, it is a must-see for anyone who visits London, as I'm certain you are already aware, my lord."

"And will you be there, Miss Fairmont?"

"Oh, yes. Mr. Knighton has promised that when the boat docks, which he believes will be tomorrow, I shall have an exclusive peek into the crates."

"It is not my place to tell you what you should do, but I feel very strongly that you should allow Mr. Knighton to carry on about his business—without you. The docks are no place for a lady." She felt his hand squeeze tightly around hers, forcing her to meet his gaze. "I would be most angry if anything happened to you, Miss Fairmont."

"What could possibly—"

"Not all treasure is glowing and pure. Remember that."

Black pulled her to a stop, and she saw that his gaze followed that of a young lord whose name escaped her. She had seen him before, recalled that he was an acquaintance of the Duke of Sussex. Black's gaze seemed to darken, and his pupils dilated to large, black spheres.

"You will forgive me, Miss Fairmont, but I see someone I am expected to meet."

He pulled away, and Isabella's hand caught in his. As well, her purse tangled with the button of his jacket, opening the reticule. Before she could right it, her journal fell to the floor, opened to her writing. *Blast!* She always kept her journal locked—it contained her secrets and dreams, not to mention the outline for her book. She never wanted anyone to glimpse inside, but tonight she'd been distracted by Lucy's glowing compliments for her story, not to mention their discussion of Black.

Had she had her wits about her, she would have locked the journal, or better yet not put it in her reticule and carried it down to the ball in the first place.

Both of them bent to retrieve the book. Black was quicker, and reached for it. She knew without a doubt that he was reading what was there, despite how rude it was for him to be reading her private words.

A gentleman would have closed the cover immediately and handed it to her. But Black continued to gaze at it as he reached for her hand and raised her up. The book snapped closed, and Isabella jumped at the sound, and the queer intensity she saw in Black's gaze.

"Thank you for the waltz, Miss Fairmont."

And then he left, leaving her with the distinct impression that she had offended him.

"GRACIOUS," LUCY EXCLAIMED as she hauled Isabella off to the ladies' retreating room. "Tell me all about it. Was it divine, dancing with the earl?"

Isabella could hardly think as she dashed off with Lucy to the privacy of the room that had been set up for the ladies to see to their personal needs. Instead of going inside, Lucy hauled her into another room that was lit with only one gas lamp. They were alone, but still, Isabella felt a presence. Her gaze danced to every corner, and she breathed a sigh of relief when she realized they were devoid of any disturbing shadows. But then, she felt a familiar tremor snake its way down her spine, and she rubbed her arms with her palms in an attempt to stave off the sudden chill. She hated the dark—and the shadows.

"Well?" Lucy demanded.

Isabella nodded. "It was indeed divine."

"I knew it," Lucy gushed. "From the very second he found you, he kept his eyes on you. Oh, it was so romantic the way he looked at you. And the picture the two of you made, dancing around the ballroom—"

"You make too much of it, Luce."

"I certainly do not," Lucy grunted. "An earl! Issy, this is a coup for you!"

"I know nothing about him."

"That's what a courtship is for."

"I am already being courted by Mr. Knighton."

Lucy's pretty face puckered into a frown. "Issy, be reasonable. I saw the way Lord Black looked at you, and furthermore, I saw the way you looked at him."

"I did no such thing," she shrieked, mortified by the thought her emotions had been so transparent. She had been taken by him, but to discover that everyone knew it as well was beyond humiliating.

"Admit it, Issy, there's something about the earl that intrigues you."

Of course there was. What woman wouldn't be

intrigued by his mysteriousness, or lured to his handsome face? There was an air of danger about Black that was impossible to ignore—or not be drawn to. It was only natural, wasn't it, for a woman to be fascinated by a man as commanding as Lord Black? He was older than her. Experienced. A man of the world. It was expected that his worldly aura called to her. For heaven's sake, until last year she had been nothing but a rag-taggle country girl in Yorkshire.

This…attraction to Black. It was nothing but innocent female curiosity, that was all. And nothing more would come of it. She had experienced her moment of exhilaration and danger, and that would be all. She would not allow her overly imaginative, impulsive nature to be her ruination.

"Issy," Lucy warned, "you aren't going to deny that you find the earl charming?"

"If I did, we would both know it for a lie. The truth is, I find him very charismatic."

"And handsome."

"Yes."

"And rich." Isabella inclined her head in acknowledgment. "And clearly besotted with you."

"I do not believe the earl capable of being besotted, that is for young men. The earl is a man, Lucy."

"And that scares you, doesn't it?"

Heavens, when had Lucy become so bold? Isabella refused to answer that question despite the truth of it. The earl did frighten her. She had never felt her body respond in such a way. It was terrifying yet exciting. Every cell tingled with awareness, and it made her want to run and hide. Her father had been a charmer. Her mother had told her the stories. She did not want to wind up like her mother, she reminded herself, ruined and alone, barely able to scrape out a living. Passion had its place, and for

Isabella, that place was one of control and moderation. Imprudent recklessness was the kiss of death.

"Do you know what I think? You've realized that it is rather easy to keep Mr. Knighton at bay. But in one dance, you've discovered that it would be quite impossible to sway Lord Black. Black would take what he wanted, not by force, of course, but just the same, he would find a way to obtain what he desired. He wouldn't be deterred like Knighton."

"I do not keep Mr. Knighton at bay, Lucy."

"No, you do not have to. Knighton does that for himself, and you find relief in that because it makes it easier for you to keep your vow of not making the same mistakes your mother did."

Isabella didn't know what to say. Lucy was right. Knighton was not an ardent suitor. He was kind and his affection was all very proper. But Black… Isabella shivered. Black would not be chaste or proper in his pursuit of anything if he wanted it enough. Of that she was certain.

"Mr. Knighton is the sort of life companion I desire, Lucy. I do not require a town house in Mayfair, or a title, or heaps of money. What I wish for is constancy, security and perhaps a little affection."

Squeezing her hands, Lucy smiled. "Dearest Isabella, when will you see that Mr. Knighton's first love is work?"

"I will see it when you finally decide that the Duke of Sussex is worthy of your time."

Lucy arched her brows. "You aim your arrows well, Issy."

"I know you mean well, but I know what I'm doing, and pining after the unreachable Lord Black is not something I'm going to do. He isn't the sort I'd want as a husband. Besides, it was one dance, not a vow of marriage, or anything of the sort. You make too much of it."

Lucy gazed at her knowingly. "I wonder if I do. Time, of course, shall tell us."

"Really, Lucy," she admonished. "You've become far too bold."

"Have I? I do apologize. Well, then, I hear another waltz beginning, and I believe you promised the third waltz to your Mr. Knighton. But I am not done with you yet," Lucy said with a smile, before dropping her voice to a whisper. "Tonight, I want every little detail of your dance with the handsome Lord Black."

With a reluctant nod, Isabella looped her arm through Lucy's as they left the room and reentered the ballroom, which felt warm and stuffy. Instantly she wished for a reprieve. She was not in the mood for idle chitchat. What she wanted was to be alone with her thoughts, and her memories of that wonderful dance in Lord Black's arms.

"Good evening, Isabella."

She stopped and smiled at Wendell, who looked very handsome in his black dress clothes, except for the bit of dust marring the cuff of his jacket. He followed her gaze and stiffened.

"Damnation!" he cried, wiping it off. "Sorry about that. I couldn't help myself, I had to stop by the museum on my way here this evening."

Lucy shot her a pointed look that Isabella chose to ignore. "There is nothing to worry about. I assume you were checking on the preparations for the unveiling of the new exhibit?"

"I was. And…" Wendell flushed as he met her gaze. "I was wondering if you might consider letting me out of this dance. I know it's bad form, but one of the patrons of the museum is here tonight, and I wished to speak with him. Funds, of course. If I don't see to the donations…" He trailed off expectantly, his brown eyes full of hope that she understood his plight.

"Of course. You must go and meet him."

"Thank you. I will endeavor to make it up to you."

"Don't even say it," Isabella ordered her cousin when Wendell had taken his leave. "You of all people should know that I'm not the least bit crestfallen to have to sit out a dance."

"I didn't say a word."

"But you wanted to."

"Sorely," Lucy said around a grin. "But I love you too much. And I'm too much the lady to say I told you so!"

"Ha! This from the *lady* who keeps pestering me to write naughty scenes in my novels."

"I'm merely living vicariously through you."

"Ah, Lucy, there you are. I do believe you promised me this dance."

Lucy pressed her eyes shut at the sound of the duke's voice. "First names are far too personal, Your Grace," she admonished as Sussex came to them. "It isn't at all proper."

"Neither is standing up a gentleman to whom you promised a dance." Sussex's smile could only be described as mischievous as he held out his hand to Lucy. "You will excuse us, Miss Fairmont?" he asked, but he didn't take his gaze off Lucy. "I'm afraid I've been waiting all night for this dance."

Isabella laughed as the duke steered her cousin to the floor. After watching Lucy step into the proper dance frame with the duke, Isabella realized that this might very well be her one and only opportunity to escape. It was hot and stuffy, and she would give anything for a chance to go out onto the terrace and smell the crisp fall leaves.

Careful not to garner any notice, she made her way to the terrace and the French doors. Opening the glass door, she stepped outside, breathing deep of the damp night air. The fog was rolling in from the Thames, blanketing the earth with gray mist. Moroccan lanterns hung from the branches of the trees, the candlelight shining with a muted, hazy glow through the mist. Beyond the terrace and the trees lay a rose arbor whose leaves had begun to turn brown. Beyond the arbor was a maze. There she would find privacy and quiet.

Lifting her skirts, she ran down the steps, thankful that the chilly night had deterred guests from going outside. No one would see her slip into the maze.

Growing up in Whitby, on the sea, had inured her to the dampness. There was nothing like the crisp air to clear one's head. And her head most certainly needed to be cleared. All she seemed capable of thinking about was the enigmatic Earl of Black.

Rounding the corner, she walked deeper into the maze, where the stone bench would lay waiting for her. It was her favorite place, and tonight she needed its familiar comfort.

"Oh," she cried as she saw someone sitting there. That someone looked up and Isabella stopped, her breath frozen in her throat. "Lord Black."

He uncurled his tall frame from the bench and slowly rose. "Miss Fairmont."

"I...I did not mean to intrude upon your privacy. I had no idea—"

"Do not concern yourself. I only needed a moment's reprieve from the stuffiness in the ballroom. And you?"

"The same, I'm afraid."

"Will you join me?"

Inanely she looked to either side of her. There was no one outside. It was black as pitch. It could ruin her reputation if they were to be discovered alone and in the dark. And the orchestra was loud. Even out here she could hear the violins. Would anyone hear her if she screamed?

"I realize it's all rather untoward to be out here alone— with a man you've just met, but I am loath to give up this spot. Rather ungentlemanly of me, isn't it?"

"Indeed it is, my lord."

He smiled at her honesty, and she saw that he had dimples. For some reason she could not stop staring at them—at him. "I'm willing to share this spot. Will that suffice?"

She was sure she could not hide the wariness in her eyes, or the watchful stiffness in her body. She should say no. But her lips could not seem to form the word.

"I will not hurt you, Isabella."

The intimacy of her name, said in his deep voice, made her shiver. How had he known it? But then again, it seemed that Lord Black knew a good deal about her.

"Will you not join me?"

She was being silly. Besides, she could not seem to deny him when he looked at her like that. Like what? she asked herself as she walked to the bench. Like a fox after a hare, was the answer.

"Are you cold?" he asked as she sat down next to him. Her train bunched up, the lilac silk spilling onto his thigh. She went to move it, but he stilled her hand, and instead smoothed the silk over his knee. "Shall I lend you my jacket?"

"I'm fine," she said, shivering. Curious, she wasn't at all cold.

He moved away from her and began shrugging out of his velvet jacket. "No, I insist," he said, covering her naked shoulders. "You might catch your death out here."

She stilled, their gazes collided and he moved, inched closer to her.

"That was not in the best of taste, was it?"

"That depends, were you making a jest of what you read in my journal?"

His gaze flickered over her face, coming to rest on her mouth. "No. I was not referring to your writing. Forgive me, Isabella?"

She looked away, unable to think as once again the butterflies began to circle. The way he said her name was so soft, so lulling. There was something about him that pulled at her, made her will no longer her own.

He captured her chin with his fingers and forced her to look back at him. "I should not have read your journal, but I confess I could not stop."

"Was it so engrossing then?" she asked, trying to make light. But there was nothing light and frivolous about Black. He was purposeful, intense and the way he was gazing down upon her made her shiver.

"I…want to know you. Everything about you."

Her lips parted, yet nothing came out. She was shocked. Mesmerized.

"Would you let me, Isabella?" His voice dropped as he pressed closer, the moment intimate and wildly exciting. "Would you let me learn everything about you? Discover you as I want?"

His gaze, blistering with intensity, burned through her skin, warming her to the very core of her being. Inside, her body seemed to bloom, to open like the petals of a rose in the sunlight. She knew what he wanted, the innuendo of his words. And she admitted that somewhere deep inside her, she wanted to know him, too.

There was a strange, almost magnetic pull between them. They were strangers, yet he spoke to her familiarly—not at all gentlemanly. She should be shocked, outraged. They had just been introduced, yet Isabella felt as though she had known him forever. As if her soul recognized him from another time and place.

Gathering the edges of his jacket around her shoulders, she luxuriated in his scent, which wafted up from the fabric, mingling with her perfume. It made her think very dangerous thoughts—thoughts that did not entail running from him.

This was much too dangerous. She should put an end to it, and opened her mouth, but the words still would not come. Instead, she said, "Quid pro quo, then?"

His smile was slow and sensual, and she saw the glint of victory shining in his eyes. "Very well, you go first."

"What is the real reason you are out here?"

His gaze flickered to hers. "As I said earlier, I needed to clear my head."

"You don't seem the sort to run away from something, which I think was what you were trying to accomplish by coming out here."

His eyes lit with something like admiration. "How in tune we are. Indeed, I was running. I detest society, and much prefer my life as an enigmatic recluse. Is that the answer you desire?"

"I believe it more to the truth than your original answer."

"And what of you, Miss Fairmont, what is your true motive for being here?"

To escape you, and the effect you have upon me. "The same, I'm afraid. I am new to society and have not yet learned to give up the craving for solitude. I am used to being on my own and sometimes the crush of the ballroom is just too much."

He nodded and she saw that he was running his fingertips lightly over the grain of satin. He was watching as his fingers traversed her skirts, and she found the gesture the most romantic thing she could ever imagine.

"My turn." He tipped his head and looked down at her. "How do you do it, suffer through it, the monotony of balls and all the insipid, shallow conversation that reveals nothing of a person's soul but the fact they are vacuous, spiritless followers?"

She smiled and lifted her gaze to a sky that was filled with stars. "I write." Closing her eyes, Isabella inhaled deeply of the damp grass, listening to the sway of the crisp leaves as they rustled in the trees and smelling the acrid odor of coal burning in the chimney. "I pretend I'm elsewhere—*anywhere* else."

She felt him move, his thigh brushing against hers. "Where do you go?" he whispered, and she felt it as a caress along her body. She savored it, that haunting, alluring voice, and the queer sensation it gave her.

"A place where I can be myself. Where no one cares who my parents were, or the circumstances of my past. Where even I can forget."

Her eyes opened as she felt the thrilling shiver of his fingers trace the contour of her cheek. He was looking at her so deeply that she felt the need to put space between them, but she couldn't move, she was immobile, lost in his lovely pale eyes. "You never have to be anyone else than who you are, Isabella. Especially with me."

She swallowed and he rubbed his thumb along her chin, tilting her head, studying her in the moonlight. "If someone doesn't want you as you are, then they aren't worth the time."

He was far too perceptive, and familiar, and she was falling much too eagerly to his experienced, silky tongue.

"I think you are perfect, Isabella."

"My lord—" she warned as he angled his head, lowering his mouth to hers.

"Black," he murmured, his lips brushing her cheek. "Just call me Black."

His breath caressed the shell of her ear; her body went languid and hot all over. She felt his nose against her temple, followed by the satiny smoothness of his lips. Oh, this was temptation!

"Black," she whispered, but didn't know if was a plea to continue or stop.

"Tell me, what do you write about, Isabella?"

Her lashes fluttered closed as she swayed closer to him. "I...I do not care to share my writing with others, my lord."

"You can trust me. I would never betray your confidence."

She sensed that she could, indeed, trust him. "I am a lady novelist."

"Fiction," he murmured, his voice deepening. "For women?"

"Yes," she answered, her cheeks heating with warmth. What must he think of her? First her writing, and now this, sitting here in the dark, allowing him to brush his mouth against her cheek. He would think her fast and immoral. A harlot to enjoy in a dark garden. And why not? She was acting as such.

"An escape from the world so full of rules and restrictions," he whispered, "to a world where you are free to think and feel as you will, regardless of your sex and the convention put upon you."

"Black," she murmured, but this time it sounded like a plea. But a plea for what, she could not tell.

"Tales of love," he drawled as his lips moved along her jaw. Her head tipped back of its own accord, and his fingertips smoothed down the column of her throat, to her necklace, which he traced with the tips of his cool fingers. "Stories of passion, desire…"

She exhaled through her parted lips, her heart hammering heavy in her breast. She could not answer that. To do so would be too damning. She could not admit it, even though it was the truth.

"Will you tell me a story, Isabella?" He pulled her closer, till her bodice was against his chest, and his breath rasped against her ear. "A story of burning passion and forbidden desire."

"Please. I…"

"I know." His fingers toyed with the curls that had begun to cling to her neck. "You mustn't tarry here— with me."

"N-no," she stuttered, reaching for the starched pleats of his crisp white shirt. "I shouldn't."

"I've never been very good at resisting things I know

I should," he murmured as he inched his mouth to hers. "What of you, Isabella?"

She had always been good. Always fearful of ending up like her mother.

"Bella?" He brushed his lips, featherlight, against hers. "Can you resist?"

Her lashes fluttered closed. "I must," she said, and moved away. His jacket slipped from her shoulders and puddled onto the bench. "Good night, Lord Black."

He watched her rise from the bench, tracking her progression. The wind rose, weaving through the branches. An owl hooted, and she chanced a glance back over her shoulder only to find him standing where they had seconds ago sat.

Their gazes locked, and a voice, beckoning and seductive, whispered to her. *The first time I met Death, it was at a ball and we danced a waltz, and I feared him, feared the things he made me feel, made me want. That night I ran from him, but Death was right behind me, chasing me and I wanted him to catch me.*

CHAPTER THREE

Even in death she was beautiful. Her porcelain skin, drained of color, rendered her angelic. Her hair, which was fanned out over black velvet, shone silver beneath the moonlight, reminding him of shimmering silk threads as it dangled over his arm. He lowered his head, inhaling the scent of all that luxurious hair, imagining it gliding along his body, his hands cupping handfuls of curls.

So still she lay that he could not bear it, and slowly he raised his face from her hair to touch the cold alabaster cheeks that were plump, the becoming flush he had seen no longer there. He bent to kiss the lips that were no longer pink. A goodbye. A parting. Their mouths touched, hers cold, his colder. Death's eternal kiss....

Black awoke in a rush. He was sitting up in bed, the darkness shadowing his walls, a scream burning his throat.

He had dreamed of her. She had been lying dead in his arms, her delicately flushed skin devoid of color and warmth. The pliant body he had felt in his arms was stiff, unyielding. The sparkle in her green eyes gone, replaced with an opaque veil that clouded her eyes.

Dead. He couldn't bear it.

Breathing heavily, he threw the bedcovers off and

stood, reaching for the black velvet dressing gown that lay draped over a chair. Shrugging into it, he belted the sash around his waist, covering his nakedness as he went to the window, resting his forearm on the frame. Flickering light illuminated the window in the mansion across the street and his fingers, which had been lax, curled into a fist. It was *her* window—Isabella's.

He still had the scent of her lingering on his fingers. Every time he closed his eyes he saw her as she had been only a few hours before, sitting with him in the maze, her lashes lowering, her lips parting in invitation. She had been a vision there in the dark, in his arms, her softly rounded body melting into his. He had seen desire in her haunting green eyes, had felt it heat the skin he had not been able to resist touching.

The scent of her aroused him, clouded his mind. He'd wanted her. *Fiercely.*

Damning as the admission was, he could not lie to himself. He would have taken things further tonight if Isabella had not pulled away from him. And what business had he, a man of experience, to pursue an innocent virgin?

For the hundredth time that night, he cursed himself for a fool. Asking her to dance had been a mistake. But he hadn't been able to stop himself. For so long he had hungered for her, keeping his distance. For too long he had stood at this very window, blending in with the shadows, wishing night after long, interminable night that he might see her beyond the glass.

It was strange, this feeling. His body actually warmed at the thought of her. It had been years since he had felt anything but coldness—emptiness. His life had become one of isolation, rumor and speculation. He was cursed. He knew it, had accepted it and used that comprehension to erect the ice that now surrounded his heart. Yet one glimpse of Isabella was enough to begin thawing the thick, frigid layers.

He'd only ever had a job to do, duties to see carried out. It was those obligations that had brought him back to London. It was those duties he should have been seeing to this evening when he was dancing with Miss Isabella Fairmont.

But she had looked too damn lovely and irresistible to avoid. In her lilac gown, which was sparsely adorned, she stood out to him from amongst all the fluffy, overly embellished women who had flocked to his side. She had been elegant standing there, her hair pulled up in a loose cascade of curls. He had liked her hair like that, enjoyed the way it allowed him to see the long column of her throat, which had been adorned with a diamond and amethyst choker. He had wanted to kiss the bounding pulse that beat a furious tattoo beneath the skin she had perfumed. He wanted to feel the delicate beat of her heart against his lips. Her body against his—her flesh, flushed with passion, warming him. But that was madness.

So was standing here in the dark, hidden away in his home, waiting for a glimpse of her. He smiled, thinking of her sitting on a settee, her legs folded beneath her as she wrote feverishly in her journal.

He had seen her that way before, scribbling away while the wind blew her hair and mist hovered around her. But that had been another place—another time. He could not allow her to know of that—how he had watched her.

Hers was a fertile imagination. And a considerable threat. There was no telling what might happen if Isabella discovered anything about him. In truth, she was too perceptive, and he had spoken too freely tonight.

Still, he could not regret those moments in the maze, or the hunger for her that suddenly felt insatiable. She was young—an innocent. He was older, experienced, a connoisseur of all things forbidden. He had no right to even gaze at her, let alone kiss her in a maze. Even as he realized the dangers of doing such a thing, he knew he would go to her again—*soon*.

"My lord, you've been summoned."

He had not heard the door to his chamber open, a fact that should have disturbed him, but he could not work up the remorse. He'd been too busy reliving his dance with the delectable and highly desirable Isabella Fairmont.

Billings, one of only a handful of servants he employed, padded wraithlike across the Turkish carpet. "I've sent round for the carriage. Shall I lay out a fresh suit and cravat, my lord?"

"No, thank you, Billings." He gazed to the corner where his brindle-colored English mastiff, Lamb, lay snoring by the hearth. "Take him outside, will you, Billings?" A shadow flickered in Isabella's window, and his gaze was drawn to the spot of movement like a moth to a flame. "No, on second thought, I'll do it."

"As you wish, my lord," his faithful retainer murmured as he backed out of the room.

"I've been summoned by the Brethren, then?"

"You have, milord. Sussex's seal was on the carriage door."

He snorted, hating to leave his spot by the window and a chance he might see Isabella wearing a transparent nightrail with her hair unbound, spilling about her shoulders. "I suppose the carriage is waiting in the street."

"It is, my lord."

"Well then, they shall have to wait, for I have something to see to before I go."

With a snap of his fingers, he awoke his pet and signaled for him to follow. Dressing quickly in a shirt and trousers, Black moved through the darkness, descending the steps of the winding staircase, and headed for the kitchen, and the door that led to the garden. He knew where he was going and what he wanted.

So did Lamb.

Off into the darkness the mastiff loped, chasing a rabbit that had ventured into the garden. Himself, he made his way down the path to a rosebush. One lone rose bloom wavered on a tall stem that waved back and forth in the chill October breeze.

Carefully he snapped it off and brought the delicate bloom to his nose. It was a heady scent, and he stood there for long minutes with his eyes closed, bringing the sweet aroma into his lungs. Isabella had smelled of roses. The scent had been in his head all night, ever since the moment he had captured her hand during their introduction.

There were few things he was certain of, but of two things he was one hundred percent convinced. He wanted her. And he'd find a way to have her.

"Our greatest fear has come to fruition," a voice announced behind him.

"We have feared many things since the Brethren Guardians came to rest in our hands," he replied, savoring the last images of Isabella as they floated away.

"I think you know I'm here on business that cannot be delayed."

Out of long habit, Black flicked his gaze to each of the darkened corners of his back garden. No place was truly safe. "I will meet you at the lodge and we can discuss it there."

"I've already ensured the garden is secure," Sussex snapped. "You will meet with me now."

Irritated by the anger he heard in Sussex's normally controlled voice, Black slowly turned and allowed his guest to see the savagery in his eyes. "What do you want, Sussex? I thought we decided that it's not prudent to be

seen in each other's company. Do you not remember the
rules of the Brethren?"

"Damn you! I know them every bit as well as you do!"

"Then why are you here? I thought we settled our business upon leaving Yorkshire."

"They're gone."

Twirling the stem of the rose between his fingers, he
inhaled the delicate scent as it whirled around him. "What
is gone?"

"The chalice and pendant."

Black's gaze narrowed, even as the hairs on his neck
rose in alarm. "When we took them from Yorkshire, we
hid them away where they could never be found—only
the three of us know of the catacombs beneath the lodge.
How can they be gone?"

"How the hell should I know?" Sussex snapped. "When
I learned that Wendell Knighton had unearthed some artifacts from Solomon's Temple when he was in Jerusalem,
I feared he might have come across some information of
the existence of the artifacts. Naturally, I went to ensure
the chalice and pendant were still hidden beneath the
Templar church. They were not there."

"And what am I to do about it?" Black grumbled. He
had never wanted anything to do with protecting the
whereabouts of the legendary chalice and pendant. But
both Sussex and himself had been charged with their protection, a behest from both their fathers. Sussex's father
had hidden the chalice, and Black's had kept the pendant.
Both artifacts had brought nothing but death and grief to
both families since the time their Templar ancestors had
returned from the Holy Land, carrying them—charged
with the task of keeping them hidden from the world.

*Never tell what you know. Never say what you are.
Never lose faith in your purpose, for the kingdom to come
will have need of you and your sons.*

It had been the mantra—and curse of his family, and

that of Sussex's. Those words had literally been written on his flesh, branded into his soul. He could never forget, because it was who he was. Who he would always be. What his sons would one day become.

"You forget, we vowed allegiance to hide them from the world. And if someone has found them—if they know of what their true purpose is—"

"I'm fully aware of what could happen, Sussex. I just don't happen to believe it." His faith had died years ago—along with any desire to carry on the family legacy.

"Your beliefs are irrelevant. We must find them and make sure that no one discovers their powers. I've already summoned Alynwick. He's coming with the scroll."

"I know, I saw the marquis at Stonebrook's soirée tonight. He's a Highland brute and people were staring. He'll cause a bloody scene and people will begin to talk. If it's known he's associated with either one of us, there could be speculation—especially if Knighton uncovered anything about our forebears in Jerusalem."

Sussex shrugged. "He is part of this, isn't he? It's his knowledge of the old order that we need. He has a right to be here, to help us find the chalice and pendant."

Indeed he was. Alynwick and his forebears had been in charge of keeping the ancient religious text safe, and well away from the chalice and the pendant. The text, which was in the form of an ancient scroll, was the third artifact that had been carried out of Solomon's Temple by their Templar ancestors. The scroll was said to have the power of prophecy and alchemy, and contained the secrets of how to bring the powers of the chalice, pendant and scroll together. It was said that to possess all three, and their knowledge and power, was to rule supreme. Black had never believed, but there was that time, once, when he had held the black onyx pendant with its strange symbols marked in gold in his hand, and began to wonder if what his ancestors had passed down from generation to generation, son to son, was not true. He had felt something…heard something…a voice calling, whispering to him, tempting him with all he might have.

He'd been grieving at the time, Death had surrounded him, come in threes to take those closest to him. He'd assumed what he'd heard had been nothing but grief and despair. But now, ten years later, he began to wonder whether the pendant really had magical properties.

"Those are Templar treasures coming," Sussex reminded him, "and we need Alynwick's help if we are going to be able to keep London safe in the event that whoever has stolen the chalice and pendant discovers their powers."

"Safe," he murmured, gazing at the sky, thinking of Isabella. "Death follows me like a cloud, Sussex. No one is safe from my family's curse."

"We're all cursed," Sussex grumbled. "But that hardly matters now, does it?"

"No, I suppose not."

Sussex raked an unsteady hand through his dark hair. "Tomorrow the ship from Jerusalem arrives. Be there to find out what Knighton has unearthed. Report back as soon as you discover anything. We must be very careful, Black."

"Aren't I always cautious?"

"Tonight you weren't."

He glared at Sussex. "Some could accuse you of the same."

"Just keeping tabs on what could be a very inconvenient discovery of our involvement."

Black laughed, a deep sound of jaded weariness. "Is that what you're calling Lucy Ashton, an *inconvenience?*"

Resentment flashed in Sussex's eyes. "You needn't concern yourself with her, I'll manage her," he snapped, and Black felt the duke's possession in every word.

"You've fallen for Lucy."

"Of course I haven't."

"Your tone says otherwise."

"My tone is exasperation, Black. The young lady is far too intelligent and nosy for her own good," he grumbled. "I can't allow her to discover anything about the artifacts—or me."

"What makes you think she knows anything about the artifacts?"

"She's been plaguing me with questions about the Brotherhood and the Grand Lodge. She's enamored of its secrets and I'm afraid she might just uncover that our family has been using Freemasonry as a way to keep the secrets they found in Solomon's Temple buried. Miss Ashton has a hunger for knowledge, and it scares the devil out of me. She's started attending séances and spirit meetings, for God's sake. There's no telling what lengths that single-minded miss will go to in order to indulge her quest for answers."

"I'm sure you have charmed her out of seeking any further answers."

"She doesn't care for me."

Sussex sounded hurt—and defeated. Oddly, Black found he relished the knowledge. Misery did love company, for his desire for Isabella was just as hopeless as Sussex's for Lucy.

"She is only playing at the supernatural, Sussex. It's in vogue, after all, and Lucy Ashton is a forerunner in society. It is innocent curiosity and a cure for interminable boredom. Trust me, the girl hasn't stumbled upon anything."

"Oh?" Sussex reached into his jacket pocket, then tossed something into the air, which Black caught. Uncurling his fingers, he studied the gold coin that sat in the palm of his hand.

Facing up was the image of laurel leaves and a lyre. On the other side was a six-pointed star with the words The

House of Orpheus imprinted around the coin. Frowning, he stared at the image, wondering where he had seen it before. There was something very familiar about it.

"Still think we have nothing to worry about?" Sussex snapped. "I told you back in Yorkshire that someone was after the chalice and pendant. I could *feel* it."

Black looked up sharply. "What is this?"

"I found it in Lucy Ashton's reticule. So, you tell me, is it nothing to be concerned about?"

Black had no desire to question why the blazes Sussex was snooping in Lucy's purse, but he was curious about the coin, and its ominous nature.

"I've seen this before—not in the past, but recently," he murmured. "The image has been modified, but only slightly."

"So you remember the House of Orpheus, and its rogue leader?"

How could he not? Sussex's and Alynwick's fathers, not to mention his own father, had been the ones to shut down the club that had been created to mirror the old Hellfire Club of the last century. The leader had been a rogue Mason, but more importantly, he had been one of *them*. He had been the fourth Templar—the one whose ancestor had ambushed the other three while they lay sleeping before they left the holy city after stealing the artifacts. He'd been killed, or so they thought. All three Templars had believed their secret safe, buried with the body of the fourth. But then, after discovering the House of Orpheus, their fathers had been confronted with the fact that there was someone else out there, someone who knew of them and what they protected—and the prophesized powers they contained. Someone had wanted the artifacts twenty years ago—and someone wanted them now. Perhaps they even had them in their possession.

"Our fathers put an end to the infamous cult years ago. It cannot be the same one."

"Damn you, Black, because you wish it to be so doesn't mean it is. Whether you want to believe it or not, the club has been resurrected. Along with the coin, I found a piece of paper. On it was written, 'Now you have died and now you have come into being. O thrice happy one, on this same day. Tell Persephone that Orpheus has released you.'"

Black froze. "That was the initiation rite."

"Indeed. Someone knows of us—there are too many similarities to be a coincidence."

"Who?" Black growled. "Who could have learned of the club and resurrected it? Who could know of the relics besides us—or the fact that the catacombs beneath the Masonic lodge lead to the crypts of the Templar church? Our fathers made certain its existence was kept secret. Perhaps this new House of Orpheus has no connection to the relics."

"That is the answer we must discover." Sussex's eyes grew unreadable. "We must take every precaution, Black. No one can learn of us, or what our families are responsible for."

Black tossed the coin back to Sussex. "You think Lucy is involved, don't you?" And dear God, if Lucy was involved, there was every possibility that Isabella was, too.

Pocketing the coin, Sussex glanced up at the sky, to the moon that was being overtaken by a thick, black cloud. "I do not know what to believe. But if this club is returned, and the artifacts are missing, then we have much larger problems than I first thought."

"I'll go to the docks in the morning and search the ship."

"Alynwick will meet you there. I'll continue to research this coin. The next Masonic meeting we'll talk. We'll meet in private after it and discuss what we've learned."

He inclined his head and made to move past Sussex. Lamb was standing on the path, his huge tongue lolling out the side of his mouth. The dog was as ugly as a demon, and his name a bit of folly, but the canine gave him some amusement. He found himself wondering what Isabella would think of his pet beast. She was a kind and loving person; he was certain she would smother Lamb with a shocking amount of affection. It was strange how ordinary things suddenly made him think of Isabella. And after only one dance.

Sussex reached for the sleeve of Black's shirt as he went to pet the dog's head. "Find a way to keep Knighton close to you. I don't trust him."

The image of Wendell Knighton flashed before him. He was courting Isabella, a fact that made him see red. Black wanted to tear the young archaeologist from limb to limb, not take tea with him. One thing was certain, he would not attend Knighton while the fool was wooing Isabella. There were limits to what he could stomach, and Isabella falling for Knighton was not one of them.

"Your word. Keep him with you—*alive*."

"Of course," he drawled. "But you will remember that I'm cursed. Death has a way of following me."

Sussex's dark gaze met his. "He follows us all. Let us hope that this time, we have a head start."

"Sussex," Black said, "I've seen that very image on the coin, in the last few days. I can't for the life of me remember where, but I'll trace my steps and see where it leads me. I'll let you know."

Nodding, the duke raked a hand through his hair, then leveled his gray gaze upon him. "I have your word that if you discover any connection with Miss Ashton and this club, you will keep it to yourself. Lucy's—er—Miss Ashton's reputation must be protected at all costs."

Sussex disappeared amongst the shadow and the faint glow of the gas lamps that lined the street. Glancing down at his hand, Black lifted the bloom to his nose, and began to think of the coin and the familiar image. Where had he seen it? The scent of rose almost immediately made him forget about Sussex and the Templar artifacts that were missing, and instead, brought him back to the dance he'd shard with Isabella.

"The last rose of summer," he murmured idly as his finger stroked the velvety petals, and he knew just what to do with it.

"Miss Fairmont," Isabella's maid, Annie, announced from the door. "There's a gentleman here to see you. I've put him in the back parlor, for he smells like the Thames."

Isabella's brows raised in curiosity as she glanced at the clock on her rosewood writing desk. "It's only eleven."

"A trifle early for calls," Lucy moaned as she flung herself back onto the heap of pillows that lay on the bed. "Doesn't Mr. Knighton realize that there is a proper way to call, and it is not before a lady is breakfasted, or dressed?"

"Should I send him away, miss?"

"No," Isabella announced, rising from her chair in a froth of white sateen and lace. "Help me out of these bedclothes, Annie. It won't take me long to dress and be ready to receive him."

"I will return right shortly, miss. Just let me go and tell the gentleman that you are at home."

The door shut behind Annie, and Lucy groaned. "Men! They do know how to put a pall on a perfectly good morning, do they not? I was utterly enchanted by your story, Issy. Now I must wait to hear what happened when your heroine sat on the bench, suffering beneath Death's lascivious stare."

Isabella glanced at her open journal. There was much more there than her story of Death and his mysterious lady on those pages. There were her penned memories of last night, in the maze with Lord Black—which somehow had found their way into the newest writing of her novel.

Closing the cover, she shut the tiny lock with a click and wrapped the key around her wrist, which she held on a delicate bracelet of black jet. She trusted Lucy not to go prying into her personal writing while she was below, taking tea with Wendell. Still, though, she could not allow the events of last night to get out. While she knew that she was not yet in love with Wendell, she cared for him, would not want to jeopardize what might possibly turn out to be a marriage proposal. She also didn't want Wendell to discover that she had been out with Lord Black, allowing him unmentionable intimacies—and enjoying them. More than enjoying them, she finally admitted, but dreaming of another evening with him and perhaps allowing even more scandalous intimacies than a lady of good breeding and sound sense would ever dare think of allowing a gentleman.

But dream she had. All night, in fact. Her sleep had been fitful, the dream at times sensual, but then turning darker, dangerous. Black had featured in her dreams, and this morning she was paying for the hours of restlessness. She had the beginnings of a headache, the type that were brought on by her dreams. She didn't believe it to be one of *those* dreams—the sort that had plagued her since she was twelve.

"I'll come down with you," Lucy announced as she rolled onto her side and slipped from the bed. "I'll fetch Sibylla and meet you downstairs."

At the mention of Lucy's maid, Isabella felt compelled to ask, "Has Sibylla arranged for you to attend any more séances?"

Lucy's green eyes shone as brilliant as emeralds. "Sibylla has the same deep interest in mysticism and spiritualism as I do. I do not care a fig that she can't dress my hair for anything, for she can find the most diverting amusements. Where she hears of these things I'll never know—but I won't be the one to ask her, for she has kept me amused for a month."

"Lucy…" Isabella warned. "You're evading the question."

"Oh, all right then, yes. There's to be a séance tonight, and guess where? Oh, it's going to be so brilliant," Lucy cried as she ran to her and reached for her hands, squeezing them hard in her exuberance. "Imagine this, Issy, a séance in Highgate Cemetery! First we will do our séance, and then at midnight, and beneath the full moon we will walk amongst the headstones and see if we might not conjure up an apparition! The medium is to be Alice Fox, directly descended from *the* Fox sisters. So you know it's not going to be a sham. Oooh, I can hardly wait."

"Uncle will forbid it." And thank heaven for that, because Isabella had no desire to spend the night at Highgate Cemetery, with anyone directly or indirectly related to the three sisters who were considered responsible for making England crazed with spiritualism.

"Father is at his Masonic lodge meeting tonight. So he won't even know."

"Lucy—" Isabella began as her headache began to thump in her head.

"There's to be an initiation tonight, I heard father telling his valet this morning. You know he's out at the lodge all night whenever there is an initiation. He won't even know about me going out, and we'll be home well before father returns in the morning."

Dread suddenly consumed her, while her head pounded mercilessly. At first Lucy's interest in spiritualism had been amusing, and nothing concerning. Mysticism was fashionable, and Isabella had assumed that Lucy was following suit. But lately, Isabella had noticed a change in her cousin. She wasn't quite as jovial and laughing. Her conversation seemed focused solely on séances, and spirit meetings, and all other kinds of things that Isabella had

no desire to dabble in. Who, or what, was Lucy searching for when she went to these things? It was a bad omen
to court the dead—and Death, she added.

Isabella could no longer put aside her intuitive feelings. She could not help but notice that Lucy's increasing
hunger for séances had seemed to begin with the arrival
of Sibylla a month ago, which also coincided with Mr.
Knighton's courtship.

"Lucy," Isabella said softly, trying to find the right
words. "Are…are you by any chance…lonely?"

"Of course not!" her cousin gasped, but Isabella saw
the widening of her eyes. "I have far too much to do to
allow loneliness to get in the way."

"You would tell me, wouldn't you, if…if…"

"Goodness, Isabella, I'm just fine. Now, allow me to
dress and take tea with your Mr. Knighton. A rousing
rendering of the contents in those dirty old crates from
Jerusalem will be just what I need to liven up my morning."

"Lucy, please do not make a jest of Mr. Knighton. It
is only that he is very proud to be the one to have discovered the secret tomb beneath the temple. His treatise has
been published in all the history papers, you know."

"I know," Lucy drawled, "and really, I am rather excited to discover what he's brought back. Honestly," she
said with a laugh. But Isabella stuck her tongue out, and
Lucy let out a very unladylike snort. "All right, I'm wondering how I'm going to stay awake and not snore or drool
while he's enlightening us yet again with stories of his
Holy Land escapades. Really, Issy, how many times have
you heard them?"

"A few," she admitted, "but I take comfort in the fact
that Mr. Knighton can undoubtedly carry on a conversation. I'm quite certain that we will not be sitting across
the supper table staring at each other in stony silence."

"Issy," Lucy whispered. "I think I'd prefer Mr. Knighton's silence to another story of the Holy Land."

"Lucy!"

Her cousin stuck out her tongue and ducked before the pillow Isabella threw could hit her. Lucy, drat her, did have a point. It was rather difficult to keep smiling and laughing when she had heard the same story for well over a month now. Certainly something of import, or excitement, would soon come along to make Mr. Knighton's conversation not quite so…singular.

ISABELLA SENSED something was wrong. Wendell was pacing the length of the parlor with long, agitated strides. He'd removed his hat, and carried it in his hands, which were clasped behind his back. His dark chestnut hair was rumpled, as well as his suit jacket and trousers.

The air in the parlor smelled strongly of fish, seaweed and the musty hull of a ship. Three things that were not conducive to the temperament of a hungry morning belly and aching head.

"Wendell," Isabella murmured as she closed the door to the parlor. He stopped pacing and whirled around to look at her. With a laugh, he threw his hat onto the rose-colored settee and in three strides reached her, wrapped his arms around her waist and twirled her around in a rather uncharacteristic show of mirth and impetuousness.

"My goodness," Isabella gasped, then laughed. "It must have been quite a haul in those crates."

His brown eyes flashed as he set her back onto her feet. "You are looking at the newest recruit to the Masonic Grand Lodge, London."

Isabella's mouth dropped open. "Did my uncle—"

"Black," Wendell announced as he sat on the settee and crossed one long leg over the other. "I encountered Lord Black on the docks this morning. We chatted for a bit and he invited me to the lodge. He's sponsoring me,

Isabella. I can hardly believe it. A Mason. A member of the Brethren."

He clapped his hands and whooped in delight and Isabella couldn't help but notice how young and handsome he appeared, with the sunlight filtering through the windows, casting him in a brilliant glow. "My first meeting will be tonight. I can hardly wait. You know of my interest in the Templars, and it's no secret that the Freemasonry, or at the very least, Black's lodge, practices the Templar ways. Rumor has it, that this particular lodge was opened by members who could actually lay claim to being descended directly from Templar knights!"

"Something must be very exciting," Lucy announced as she breezed into the parlor, wearing a celadon-colored morning gown. "I could hear the enthusiasm from the hallway."

Wendell stood and bowed. "Good morning, my lady. Forgive the early hour of my call, but I could not contain myself."

"Well, I can understand why. Isabella does look astonishingly lovely in pale pink. Ethereal, wouldn't you say?"

Wendell's smile faded as he cast a glance in the direction of the chair where she was seated, pouring the tea. Her outfit was a lovely pink bodice made of pleated silk, adorned with an ecru high lace collar that was at once extravagant but beautiful. The bodice fit snuggly, emphasizing her full bust, and the overskirt of pink silk damask was edged in thick velvet. It was something a grand lady would wear, not a poor Yorkshire girl. She felt like a sham wearing such beautiful things, but Lucy had made it for her, another one of her particular designs. Her cousin certainly had an eye for fashion, and the sewing skills to match. Lucy was a forerunner of fashion, and every debutante and fashionable lady strove to uncover the modiste who outfitted Lucy in such wonderful clothes. Little did they know, the modiste was Lucy herself. A fact that would shock society. No society lady would ever deign to make their own clothes—that was for the middling classes. Herself, she didn't see what all the fuss was about, especially since her cousin's sense of fashion and ingenious designs outshone anything she had seen done up by the seamstresses that outfitted the cream of the ton. But then, she had never been able to afford to contemplate such things. She'd counted herself lucky if she possessed a cloak without holes in it. Which very rarely happened.

A masculine cough ended her rumination. "Oh, yes, yes," Wendell said hurriedly. "In my excitement, I forgot myself. You look lovely today, Miss Fairmont. Pink is a very fetching color on you."

She handed him a cup and saucer, made out of Wedgwood china, which was so fine and delicate she could see through it as the sun's rays sparkled through the salon windows. "Do not trouble yourself, Mr. Knighton. Really, my vanity can survive a morning without it being complimented."

She sent Lucy a warning glance, which her cousin, of course, ignored. Sinking onto the chair beside hers, Lucy reached for a cup of tea and brought it to her mouth for a delicate sip before replacing the cup in the saucer with a slight chink. "You must tell us what is so exciting, Mr. Knighton."

"I am to be initiated into the Brotherhood, my lady. The Masons," Wendell said with a mix of pride and awe.

"Are you?" Lucy asked. "Did my father offer to sponsor you?"

"In fact, no. Lord Black did."

"Black?" Lucy asked, her auburn brow furled as she glanced at her.

Wendell took a sip of his tea, then nodded. "Indeed, Black. Very amiable fellow. There is to be a special meeting tonight, an initiation which I will not be privy to. But before that, Black will offer to sponsor me."

Lucy slid her gaze to Isabella. "Well, then, I do believe you are free tonight, cousin."

Isabella hid a groan. Not that séance business again. Her head was paining her, and she felt queasy, and the thought of attending Lucy's morbid curiosity only made her feel worse.

"Oh, yes, please," Wendell said as he rose from the settee. "Please, Miss Fairmont, go out and enjoy the evening. There will be few nice ones left before the winter comes. Do not let my plans interfere with yours."

Isabella accepted Wendell's hand and allowed him to help her from her chair. With a chaste kiss, he kissed her hand, then reached for his hat. "Good day, Miss Fairmont. Please do enjoy it."

They watched him leave the parlor, and when the door closed behind him, Isabella sunk into an ungraceful heap onto the chair. She felt…let down for some reason, but why, she could not fathom. Wendell's visit had been like all his other ones, and she had never felt anything less then satisfied when he had left.

Lucy must have known her thoughts, for she kept her lips pressed firmly together as she toyed with an imaginary speck of lint on her skirts.

"I wonder what Lord Black is playing at, sponsoring Mr. Knighton?"

Isabella took a sip of her tea. "Perhaps he is just being kind, Luce. Not everyone has ulterior motives."

Lucy's gaze met hers. "Think back to our conversation last night, Issy. Did I not tell you that Black would not be deterred?"

"Deterred from what?"

Like a sly kitten, Lucy smiled. "You know very well from what."

"In fact, I don't. What is it you're trying to say?"

Isabella asked, irritability making her voice sharper than she intended. The mild headache she had been suffering under all morning became a loud and painful throbbing. Now she knew for certain, it was one of *those* headaches, she thought. Rubbing her temple, she tried focusing on her cousin.

"What I am trying to make you see, dear Issy, is that Black has just removed an obstacle."

Isabella dropped her hand from her temple. "I beg your pardon? I'm not following your line of thinking."

"He has removed Knighton from your side, and quite effectively, in fact, for Mr. Knighton will be studying for weeks to make it through the first degrees, thereby leaving you alone, and available for the evenings."

The door opened, thankfully relieving Isabella of the task of rebutting Lucy's wild suggestion. Stonebrook's butler, Jennings, appeared, his face austere and wrinkled. He was ancient and frightfully proper. Isabella had been terrified of him when she had first come to live with Lucy and her father. But since that time, she had softened to crusty old Jennings.

"For you, miss."

Jennings presented a silver salver with one perfect bloodred bloom, with an ivory card attached to the stem by a black satin ribbon.

"For me?" she asked, even though she could read quite clearly that the card had her name written on it, in bold, black lettering.

"Indeed," Jennings murmured.

"Thank you," she returned as she lifted the delicate flower from its resting place. Oh, it was perfect. And the sender had removed the leaves and thorns as well.

Jennings departed, and with a quick glance at her cousin, who was pressing forward in her chair, Isabella turned the card over and noted that there was no seal imprinted on the wax. The only thing keeping the edges together was a large blob of black wax.

"Well?" Lucy asked. "I can hardly bear the suspense, Issy. Open the blasted thing."

"Your language," Isabella reprimanded her, feeling every bit as anxious as Lucy.

"Oh, get on with it," Lucy commanded. "It's only you and I, for mercy's sake."

The wax seal broke, and she opened the card to more of the elegant black script.

'Tis the last rose of summer
Left blooming alone;
All her lovely companions
Are faded and gone;
No flower of her kindred,
No rosebud is nigh
To reflect back her blushes
To give sigh for sigh.
I dreamed of your sighs last night, Isabella—a most haunting,
    beautiful sound that I hope, most fervently, I might hear again
    very soon.
        Your servant, Black

Isabella tried to hastily fold the card before Lucy could read it. But her cousin was too quick, and managed to read Lord Black's missive before she could hide the card.

"Well," Lucy drawled with amusement, "how could Lord Black know that you have a fondness for Thomas Moore's poetry?"

Puzzled, Isabella looked up at her cousin. "I don't know."

With a smile Lucy breezed past her then stopped at

the door. With a glance over her shoulder, she said, "You know, Issy, I would bet my dowry that Lord Black would not command you to see to your own amusement in the evenings—not like Mr. Knighton. Something tells me that Black would keep you exceedingly busy, and delightfully amused, all night long."

CHAPTER FOUR

PALL MALL AND COCKSPUR STREETS were bustling with trade. Elegant carriages transported the rich and fashionable down the cobbles for an afternoon of shopping, while wooden carts carrying fresh vegetables and apples wound their way to Covent Garden where the goods would go up for sale in the market.

On the sidewalks, people walked shoulder to shoulder, some in a hurry to carry out their business, others at a more leisurely pace, stopping occasionally to peer into a shop window or to purchase a newspaper from one of the many young boys selling them on the street corners.

"Wolf escaped from London Zoo! Still at large!" called one such boy as Isabella passed him.

"Mystery in Spitalfields!" cried another. "Bodies found murdered! Read all about it in the *Standard!*"

Pressing on, Isabella ignored the chilling headlines of the day and continued down Cockspur Street to Jacobson's, the preeminent apothecary in London. Her headache would not give up, not even after a pot of tea and a nap. When she'd left the house, Lucy was still napping, so Isabella had taken a footman with her. The footman, Isabella noted, was lingering behind, talking to a buxom shopgirl who was trying to sell the young man a haunch of pork—and other wares, Isabella was certain. It didn't matter that she was getting farther and farther away from him, for her head was throbbing, and the smells of the city were beginning to nauseate her. She needed that medicine, the only tonic that had been able to cure the headaches and stem the dreams.

Oh, how she hated to think of them coming back. They'd been gone for months now. She'd thought herself cured. How very distressing to know she wasn't. She'd had one of those disturbing dreams that very afternoon, during her nap. It was upon awakening that she realized the dreams had only been on hiatus—not banished. She knew then that she must come to Jacobson for more of the tonic.

"Women gone missing from the Adelphi Theatre," a boy called as he rang his bell. A group of gentlemen stopped and clustered around the lad for a look at the day's headlines. The boy held out an issue of the *Times* to her when he saw her standing on the sidewalk, attempting to move around the group of men. "Read all about the Adelphi mystery in the *Times*, miss."

Reaching into her reticule, Isabella removed a shilling and gave it to the lad.

"Thank you, miss," he said, his eyes growing round. "'Ave a good day."

Nodding, she accepted the paper from the boy and unfolded it. Scanning the headlines, she read the blurb of the actresses who had gone missing from the Adelphi, the notorious music and dance hall.

The ladies were last seen in the company of a tall gentleman, his features concealed by the brim of his top hat. An eyewitness observed the ladies being ushered into a black town carriage driven by four black horses...

The Earl of Black had such a carriage, which was drawn by four magnificent warmbloods the color of midnight. The thought stopped her cold. Lucy had mentioned seeing Black leave his town house late at night...the very night, in fact, that the women were seen getting into the carriage.

Nonsense. Black was a refined gentleman. What in the world would he be doing with three women whose reputations were dubious at best? Women were always missing from the Adelphi, and more often than not showed up months later after a sojourn in the country and with a child on their hip.

Silly, overactive imagination, she admonished. At times it could be such a nuisance. And yet, an image of her and Black dancing whisked through her mind, paralleling the opening of her book. They shared the same eyes, Black and her image of Death. As well, they both embodied the blood-heating characteristics of mystery, danger and a luring sensuality. And that, she thought with a little shake of her head, was the most preposterous thought of all.

Folding the paper in half, Isabella tucked it under her arm and continued walking. The three actresses, if they could be called such, were probably listing away as mistresses to some rich man. Everyone knew that the music hall was as infamous for its debauches as it was its musical performances. Still, the streets of London were getting more dangerous…

She rounded the corner of Cockspur and crossed onto Haymarket where stood a short, round man on a box, soliciting interest in an illusionist. She glanced to where a crush of people were gathered around a man standing beside a coach that reminded her of a gypsy's caravan.

"Step inside and witness for yourself the mystery of Herr Von Schraeder. Come, come," he said, waving them closer. "For a crown you can witness all the magic."

Her gaze drifted over the crowd, then down the street that led to the Strand. The Strand was packed with tourists and young men vying for tickets to the numerous theaters and music halls that lined the street. The crowd was turning rowdy—this wasn't the fashionable part of Mayfair where everything was polite and orderly. This was the gray area of London where the posh West End melted into the slums of the East End.

With the days turning shorter and the nights longer, Isabella reminded herself that it would not do to stand idle and woolgather. She needed to retrieve her medicine and return to Mayfair before dusk. And by the look of the cloud-covered sky, dusk would be arriving far sooner than usual.

Turning away, she stepped onto Haymarket Street, stopping abruptly when she saw a tall man, dressed in black, leaning leisurely against an ebony-and-silver-inlaid walking stick, obstructing her path. He was watching her over the rims of his blue sunshades. She could not help but shudder at the intensity of that unblinking gaze. Or wonder why he was wearing them when there was no longer any sunshine.

"Good day, Miss Fairmont."

Lord Black.

"Oh, good day, my lord. I did not recognize you with your sun spectacles."

He smiled as he took her hand, his gaze catching hers over the silver rims of the lenses. "I will forgive you this time," he teased, bringing his lips to brush against her gloved hand.

"Are you enjoying the autumnal weather?" she asked. "Or are you by chance hanging about for a chance to witness Herr Von Schraeder's magic show?"

His pupils grew large, engulfing the pale blue of his iris. He blinked, then hid his eyes from her behind the dark lenses of his spectacles. His body appeared stiff now, and he seemed to be watching her curiously.

She was about to speak, when she was jostled by a pack of young men running past her as the Adelphi opened its doors for business. She was pushed into Black's chest, and he caught her, wrapping his arms tightly around her waist to keep her from falling.

When the ruffians had passed, he slowly released her, and she looked up into his face, which showed none of the lightness that had been there when she first saw him. He was back to being a mystery—a beautiful one.

Pulling back, she put distance between them. *Discretion,* she reminded herself. It would be so easy to find herself failing against him, and the seductive lure he cast—Isabella couldn't lie—she was already weakening. Her mother had been weak, and her father had taken advantage of the fact.

"My lord, you were saying?"

"Unless Herr Von Schraeder's magic is exceptionally potent, I believe the citizens of London have seen the last of him," he muttered, guiding her with a hand on the small of her back, to the safety of the apothecary's storefront.

"What do you mean, sir?" she asked. As she looked over her shoulder at the cart, she saw Herr Von Schraeder's assistant come flying out, bellowing something.

"I believe it was the apothecary you were seeking," Black replied as he pulled open the door and ushered her through. The bells tinkled, drowning out the rest of the assistant's words as he ran from Von Schraeder's cart.

"How did you know I was coming here?" she demanded, her gaze narrowing, just as a fresh flush of gooseflesh erupted on her skin.

"Jacobson's apothecary is most famous. I guessed that perhaps it was him that brought you to this side of the city."

"Oh." She flushed and looked down at her gloved fingers, which were wrapping around the braided cording of her reticule. "Forgive me, my lord, if I seemed short just now. I have a terrible headache, I'm afraid."

Pulling his spectacles from his face, he caught her chin in his gloved hand and angled her face to the waning afternoon light that filtered in through the large window of the apothecary.

"You're pale, Miss Fairmont. I don't like it."

"Well, I can't help it," she snapped, not knowing whether to be touched or embarrassed by his frankness.

"It worries me to see you suffering," he murmured, his thumb grazing against the apple of her cheek. "Is there anything I might do to relieve you of it?"

She was touched. Not only by his words, which seemed to be spoken without artifice, but also by the concern she saw in his eyes. "No, my lord. I've tried everything, and nothing seems to relieve it, except for Mr. Jacobson's wonderful bergamot tonic."

Two elderly matrons waiting at the counter were watching them with unconcealed interest. Black dropped his hand at the same moment Isabella took a discreet step back.

"I will drive you home," he announced.

"Oh, no, I've brought a footman with me. He's..." Isabella peered through the gold-foil lettering on the window, grateful to see that the young man was still flirting with the shopgirl. "He's right over there."

Black followed the direction of her hand. "He seems rather inept in his duty of watching out for you, Miss Fairmont. No, I will see you returned safely home."

"Ah, good day, Miss Fairmont," Mr. Jacobson's son, George, called from behind the counter. "What brings you here today?"

"Good day to you, Mr. Jacobson," she returned, even as she stole a glance at Lord Black. Who, she was startled to discover, was watching her intently from behind the rims of his spectacles, which he'd put back on.

She really rather liked him in those, she mused, despite the fact it was no longer sunny.

Wiping his hands on his apron, George asked, "Another sleeping tonic, by chance?"

"Yes. Please."

"A tincture of laudanum and bergamot, alongside a dose of the valerian herb?"

"That's right."

Black's expression was as dark as his name and he was watching her with unrelenting curiosity.

"That is a very dangerous concoction, Isabella," he whispered into her ear. "*Very* dangerous."

"I'm aware of that, but I'm very careful to measure it out exactly as Mr. Jacobson prescribes."

He turned her face to his, his fingers resting beneath her chin. "Do you know how many lives Death has claimed after taking tonics like this? *Thousands,* Isabella."

She shivered. "I know what I am doing. I suffered almost daily for nearly a year with these headaches, and… dreams," she whispered before hurrying on. "I'm quite able to follow a prescription, my lord. I'm not a child. And furthermore it is the only thing that has helped."

"Here ye are, Miss Fairmont. Two spoonfuls at bedtime ought to do the trick. And if you find you're not resting well, take one during the daytime."

Reaching into her reticule, Isabella pulled out some coins and set them on the counter. "Thank you, Mr. Jacobson."

He nodded and came around the counter, holding open the door to her. "Good day, Miss Fairmont."

Sweeping out onto the sidewalk, Black moved in to stand beside her. The sidewalk was bustling, and she was bumped from behind by a steely body. The bottle of medicine fell from her grasp, only to be caught in the palm of a black-gloved hand.

Black.

Straightening, he held out his hand where the bottle of medicine was cradled in his palm. "I should have let the bottle smash onto the street, but then you would only have gone back inside and ordered another one. Wouldn't you?"

"Yes, I am afraid I would. I am desperate after all. I've had this headache since last night, ever since I returned from the maze—" She stopped, embarrassed to have mentioned what happened between them. She didn't finish her thought, and instead shoved the bottle into her reticule.

He watched from behind his spectacles, and Isabella felt his eyes burning through her clothes and skin until they pierced the very soul of her. Was he also recalling what had transpired between them? Had he been as affected as she?

Ridiculous, she chided. She mustn't let her thoughts stray into that dangerous territory. Passion was for novels. Not her life. What was it about this man that made her forget her own mantra?

Taking a step back, she prepared to part from him, but he reached for her elbow and held her. "My carriage is just around the corner. Allow me to see you safely home. You, there, boy," Black called as the newspaper boy who had sold her a copy of the *Times* ran past them. The lad stopped, his cheeks bright red, his blue eyes gleaming.

"Did ye hear, me lord, that Herr Von Schraeder is dead! Dead!" the boy cried. "I've got to be the first to make it back to the offices. A whole pound if I's the first to break a news story, and it's no secret that the sham magician was not liked. What if it were murder?" the lad crowed with enthusiasm. "I bet they'd pay me more than a pound if he were done in."

Black pulled him back by his collar. "I'll give you a fiver if you would be so kind as to cross the street and give this to that man in the blue-and-white livery."

"The man talking with Sally?" the boy inquired.

"That's the man." Black handed the boy his calling card. "Tell him that I have Miss Fairmont and I will be bringing her home. She's not well. Be quick about it,"

Black demanded as he slipped the boy a five-pound note. "And see that the task is done before you go screaming in the streets of Von Schraeder's murder."

"Right away, my lord." The boy grinned, then ran as fast as his thin little legs would carry him.

"This way, Miss Fairmont," Black commanded, as he took her arm and walked with her around the corner of the apothecary to his waiting carriage.

"What did that lad mean that Von Schraeder was dead?" she asked. When he stopped beside her, Isabella was forced to glance over her shoulder. Black was staring at something, but what?

"My lord?" It appeared to her that he was staring at the Adelphi Theatre and his complexion had grown quite ashen. "Black, is something amiss?"

Shaking his head, she saw his gaze rove over the theater before he tore it away and looked down upon her. "Nothing at all, Miss Fairmont. Shall we?"

Reaching for the carriage door, he opened it, then motioned her forward. Inside, it was dark, the upholstery a luxurious black velvet that lent the carriage a rich, relaxing air.

"Lord Black," she insisted, but he put a finger to her lips, silencing her. "This really isn't necessary."

"Shh," he murmured. "You mustn't tax yourself."

"I'm neither a child nor an invalid," she chastised. "I merely have a headache."

"A devil of one if you've resorted to valerian and opium."

There was nothing to do but accept his hand as he helped her up the iron steps. His hand felt large and warm in hers—strong—and Isabella closed her eyes, allowing herself a brief moment of sensation to absorb his touch and the feel of his hand engulfing hers. She'd never felt her hand pressed strongly in another's. The experience was at once comforting and arousing, making her wonder where else on her person his hands would feel as wonderful.

"Isabella? Are you unwell?"

"No," she gasped, realizing she was standing on the steps holding Black's hand. "No, I…my hem was caught, that is all."

Ninny, she scolded herself as she sat upon the empty bench. What must he think of her? Did he think her a silly child? She was certainly acting like one.

Black shouldered his way into the carriage and took the opposite bench. His long legs stretched out, his thighs outlined in his trousers, his shoulders taking up most of the space on his bench. Dropping her gaze to her lap, she flatly refused to look at him, sprawled out in masculine lassitude.

With a rap of his walking stick on the ceiling of the carriage, the coach lurched forward, and soon they were making slow but steady progress back up the Strand and toward Grosvenor Square.

She felt nervous and fidgety. The silence was almost unbearable, yet she did not know how to begin the conversation. She could hardly remark upon the weather, for it was gray and dreary, the autumnal sky heavy with the promise of a storm. Nor could she mention anything about last evening, when she had been most unladylike to sit in the dark, all alone, with him.

However the silence affected her, it had the opposite effect on his lordship. He was a man who was at ease with silence—and solitude. Black did not feel the need to fill the quiet with useless chatter. She did not have to be well acquainted with the earl to know this about him.

He wore the quiet like a shroud—unmoving, soundless, becoming one with it as it blanketed the luxurious interior of the coach. It unnerved her the quiet that hovered between them. Not because she feared it, but because it felt too intimate. She could hear his slow, steady breaths, could hear her own. There was a sensuality to it, the resonance of air whispering past their lips. Without words, they were alone with their thoughts, the images in their minds. The picture in Isabella's mind was that of her hand in Black's, and how it would feel to experience the brush of his thumb inside her palm. The pleasure of awaiting his kiss as he lowered his mouth to hers.

No, the quiet was far too intimate, and her thoughts much too reckless.

His leg moved, his booted foot brushed against the hem of her day gown, and she swallowed—averting her gaze, allowing it to roam the carriage—anywhere, as long as it was not lingering on him, or the imagery her mind wished her to acknowledge.

She was a sinful creature to be thinking such thoughts! She had been given the opportunity that many of her sort never had. She'd been gifted with the chance to live as a lady, and here she was, thinking base, depraved thoughts and succumbing to the lure of pleasure just like her reckless parents.

She *must* put an end to this. Unable to withstand the silence—and her own wayward thoughts—Isabella said the first thing that came to mind.

"I received your note this morning." He glanced at her sharply, but said nothing. It was a dim-witted thing to have said. She should never have opened up this conversation, but it was done, and she was committed now. "Thomas Moore's poem is one of my favorites. I can recite it from memory."

"Can you?"

"The last verse of Moore's poem is, in my opinion, the best. 'So soon may I follow when friendships decay, from love's shining circle the gems drop away. When true hearts lie withered and fond ones are flown, Oh! Who would inhabit this bleak world alone?'"

Slowly he turned to look at her. "You're a romantic."

Isabella felt her cheeks flame scarlet. "Yes. But what woman is not, my lord? I think you're a romantic as well."

"And what makes you say that?"

"You removed the thorns from the rose you picked for me."

He inclined his head, then averted his gaze on the window, fixing on the scenery that was passing slowly by. He declined further comment, and it made Isabella wonder if he had grown uncomfortable with the familiarity of their conversation. For certain, his quiet contemplation unnerved her. They were back to silence, and the intimacy was a living breathing thing—a pulsation—that throbbed with each of their breaths, their heartbeats.

Isabella could hardly stand it. But Black appeared to be unaware of the rippling current that simmered between them.

Hands trembling, Isabella could stand the torture no longer. She would keep up a one-sided conversation because talking was the only thing that kept her thoughts away from the image of Black holding her hand…kissing her.

"Mr. Knighton came by this morning."

"Did he? Did you not inform him that etiquette states that calls are not made till the afternoon?"

"He couldn't wait to tell me that you had offered to sponsor him as a Mason. It has been his fondest wish for some time. But you knew that, didn't you?"

Again he inclined his head, but refused to answer. Damn the man. She was unsettled, at a disadvantage, and she didn't like it. She felt herself growing reckless, the calm she had striven for having long abandoned her.

"You seem to know a great deal about me—a rather disconcerting amount, some would say."

His gaze continued to stay focused on the window. He didn't blink, didn't move, but his voice in the silence was like a velvet caress that Isabella felt along her spine. "I would not have you disconcerted, Isabella."

That was it? All he would say? Indeed, she was very disturbed by the fact he knew so much about her—and the man who was courting her. But Black…his inexplicable knowledge of her past made her nervous. Nerves were not a healthy thing for those who possessed an active imagination. All sorts of notions could run rampant through one's head. Isabella couldn't allow herself to even think of the possible ways Black had discovered so much about her.

It really was rather unfair. His lordship seemed to know her rather well, and yet she, and everyone else in London, knew basically nothing of him. He shielded his privacy well, and no one got beyond the cool indifference, or the iron gates that protected his realm.

What was he hiding? she wondered. Who was he really? Was he playing some sort of dark game with her? He seemed the type of man—worldly and intelligent— who could easily become jaded and bored by his life of privilege. Maybe it was a case of ennui, and he was amusing himself by toying with her?

These thoughts again made her quite agitated. How in the world had the earl learned so much about her—she, a penniless, fatherless urchin from the crumbling Yorkshire coast? *How* was forefront, but *why* quietly whispered in the back of her mind. Why would a man like Black, powerful, wealthy, sophisticated, wish to know about someone like her?

The only way to ease her questing thoughts was to have answers. Although she doubted the earl would grant them. He seemed content to sit quietly, staring out the window, keeping his own counsel while blanketing himself in his cloak of mystery.

"How is it you knew where to find me today?" she demanded. "And about Herr Von Schraeder? And why did you go to the docks to find Mr. Knighton this morning? Why could you not wait to see him at the museum or at a ball to offer your sponsorship of him? What was so urgent that it needed to be done then, at the crack of dawn?"

"So many questions," he murmured, trying to make light, but Isabella saw the intense scrutiny in his eyes as he slowly slid his gaze to her face. "And for one not feeling well."

"My head pounds even more, my lord, wondering about the answers."

"Quid pro quo, Isabella?" he asked, his eyes flashing beneath long onyx lashes. "Do you wish to play? It is not a game for one, but two. It is hardly fair that you get to ask all the questions, and I am not allowed the same luxury."

She met his stare, willing, for now, to play by his rules. "How did you know about Von Schraeder?"

"He was an old man, and reported to be ill. Minutes before you arrived at the apothecary I witnessed him in his traveling cart. He appeared weak and frail, and not long for the mortal realm. He was clutching his chest, as one does when suffering a heart seizure." He looked her over—slowly, methodically, and she did not doubt that one thing escaped his notice. She could never hide anything from him—she knew that, deep in her belly. Black was a man that let nothing slip by him. "Tell me about your headaches, Isabella."

"There's nothing to tell. I started having them when I was twelve. They grew worse last year. Mr. Knighton." She asked, her fingers curling in agitation, "Why did you look for him on the docks?"

"It's no secret Knighton's been anxiously awaiting the boat's arrival. I knew he wouldn't wait patiently at the museum for it to be delivered."

"So you waited for him on the docks?"

"I did."

"But why?"

He smiled and pressed forward, capturing her cheek in his palm. "It's not your turn." His grin turned wolfish, and she trembled. Good Lord, he was mesmerizing in his masculinity. There was something about him that made her feel very safe and protected, and…womanly. For so long she had relied on her own wits to get her through, it was rather novel to feel like a damsel in distress being saved by a knight in shining armor.

"I wonder," he asked, "do you dream of things with your headaches?"

Gasping, Isabella pulled away, but he followed her to her bench, and forced her to look at him. He stared at her—deeply—and Isabella was shocked by the sensation of having him so close, his full attention upon her. It went straight to her belly, to the tips of her breasts.

His gloved finger brushed the apple of her cheeks and he moved closer, holding her gaze. "Tell me."

"That, sir, is none of your concern." Struggling, she was able to put a small amount of distance between them. It was not enough to restore her composure. "How did you know where to find me?" she demanded.

"I followed you. Now, tell me, do you dream of things, see things when you have the headaches?"

"Yes," she whispered, hating to admit it. But something in his gaze compelled her to the truth. It drew her in, wrapped her securely in its hold. Whatever passed between them, Isabella knew—bone deep—*soul deep*—that Black would never tell another person. Her secrets would be safe with him. But was she?

"And that's the reason for the medicine, so that you'll sleep so deeply you won't dream?"

She nodded, held his stare, and braved the question that was burning in her mind. The one she could not suppress. The one question she needed to hear—yet feared—to have answered. "Why did you follow me?"

He traced her cheeks with his fingertips; the soft

kidskin leather gliding along her flesh felt decadent and wicked. When his leather-covered thumb brushed her bottom lip, parting her lips with a gentle but seductive sweep she inhaled sharply, let her lashes flicker and absorbed the erotic swipe of his finger against her mouth. "Can you not guess why?"

She shook her head, intoxicated by the scent of leather and man, and the pressure of his thumb as he pressed on her lip, parting them farther until the pad of his thumb swept across the damp tissue inside her lip.

"I wanted you to myself. Even if only for a few minutes."

She swallowed hard, and shivered as his free hand came up, only to wrap gently around her throat, while his thumb brushed over her bounding pulse. Did he know how dangerous and seductive the leather felt against her? Did he know that behind her closed lashes she imagined how the black leather must look against her pale skin—darkness and light—sin and purity. Could he tell that she was even now imagining him pulling his gloves from his hands and putting his skin against hers—his mouth to her throat?

"And Mr. Knighton?" she asked in a breathless whisper.

His thumb swept over her rapidly bounding pulse, brushing, lulling as his voice dropped to a sinful huskiness. "I would be lying if I said it was out of the goodness of my heart."

"Then what would be the truth?"

"To part you from him for the next few weeks while he studies for his first degree."

Her lashes fluttered and she gazed up at him through a haze of sensation that felt the way it did when the effects of her tonic began to take hold—but only better. It was sensual. Euphoric. And utterly improper. "I must remind you that I am being courted, my lord."

"He has made you no offer of marriage, has he?" She flushed and looked away, but he bent his head to catch her gaze, and lowered his mouth close to hers. His thumb was now brushing the contour of her bottom lip. "Has he given you any indication of his desire?"

Her heart was beating hard, and her hand, good Lord, her hand had come up and her fingers were brushing through Black's long hair. His eyes closed, and then they slowly opened, the green flecks more brilliant than before, making his pale blue eyes more turquoise.

"Has he given you a taste of pleasure? A glimpse of what you might find in his arms?"

"No," she breathed, the word nothing but a husky pant.

He brushed her lips once more with his thumb, the leather sliding smoothly along her dampened mouth, parting her lips until she could feel the edge of his leather-encased finger on the inside of her lip. But this time it was not slow and sensual, it was more forceful, direct. *Dominant.* She shivered in response, not a reaction that was of fear, but desire—her body's instinctive response to his. "Do you know what I would give for a chance to show you what it could be like in mine?"

Looking deep into his eyes, Isabella licked her lips, her mouth suddenly dry, her breathing harsh behind her tight corset and the cuirass bodice of her gown. "My lord, this is reckless."

"Reckless, dangerous, irresponsible, yes," he murmured as he pressed against her, his chest slowly, inexorably pushing her backward till she was lying on the carriage bench and he was looming above her. "It is all those things, but it is also unavoidable, inevitable, inescapable."

Isabella watched as Lord Black's face came closer to hers. As if in a dream, she felt her arms go up, supposedly to push him away, but they betrayed her and she felt her hands slide up over his shoulders where her fingertips tangled in his hair. "Inescapable," she repeated, her voice husky.

"Yes." He lowered his mouth slowly to hers. "Wherever you are, I will follow. I will find you, Isabella."

"Like Death," she whispered, her lashes lowering as she awaited his kiss. "He knows where to find those who hide from him."

Cold air swept between their bodies, and Isabella's eyelids flew open, only to see Lord Black abruptly pull himself away from her. Before she could right herself, he was seated once again on the opposite bench, watching her with hooded eyes. "We have arrived at your home, Miss Fairmont," he announced, his voice no longer filled with the desire she had only seconds before heard. "I bid you good afternoon. May I extend my best wishes for a speedy recovery from your headache."

"My lord?" she asked, puzzled, still breathing hard from the kiss he had nearly given her. Had she done something? Been too bold? Should she have put up a fuss, struggled beneath him as she ought to have?

Their eyes met, and in a swift move, he was before her, his hands clutching her face. "They say that Death is a shadow that always follows a body, but Death will not find you. I vow it. But you will promise me that you will be very careful with your tonic," he whispered fiercely, "for I couldn't bear it if Death were called to pay you a visit and forced to steal the roses from your cheeks."

"I will," she whispered back, awed by the severe concern she saw in his expression and heard in his warning.

"Vow it," he whispered, angling his head as though he was going to kiss her. "Swear to me, Isabella."

"I swear to you."

And then Lord Black lowered his mouth to hers, his lips brushing softly, slowly—once, twice—each time they parted more overtop hers until she moaned and he opened her mouth, slipped his tongue inside, devouring her as though he was starved for her.

She did not know how to return such a kiss. She could not breathe, could not move. Could only luxuriate in the silken feel of his lips moving overtop hers and the sweep of his tongue curling around her own. How enthralling it was to think of him so intimately connected to her. She could feel him seeking, searching, discovering and she wanted to do the same to him, but did not want to end the kiss with her bumbling inexperience, so instead, she allowed him to tutor her, to kiss her, and let his tongue search the depths of her mouth, to lick and probe and listen to the sound of Black's kiss, his rasping breaths and her soft, wanton moans.

She had no idea how long he kissed her, but she protested when his kiss became less fervent, and he broke away.

"Bella," he rasped between drugging sweeps of his lips and the teasing wetness of his tongue tracing the seam of her mouth. "Reckless, irresponsible, inescapable."

"Unavoidable," she breathed as she kissed him back.

He clutched her body to his, his hand skating up her side to her ribs, only to rest beneath her breast. Like a wanton, she pressed into him, making him feel her body—the body he had made ache with desire. The body she seemed no longer able to control. He had made it his with this kiss, and now she felt as though she would die if he did not show her how to give her body what it was screaming for.

She was wound tight, restless, and he knew it, made the tightness more taut as he deepened the kiss, kissing her harder and hungrier then before. Yes, she chanted. *More...more...*

Breaking the kiss, Black was breathing fast as he rested his forehead against hers, while their gazes locked. With his fingertip, he brushed her lower lip, sweeping slowly,

erotically. "Inevitable," he whispered, and somehow Isabella knew that what had transpired between them was
only the beginning of the fall.

CHAPTER FIVE

Two HOURS LATER, Black was still ruminating on the carriage ride, and the kiss he'd shared with Isabella. His mind should be clear, focused on his goals—find the person behind the House of Orpheus and locate the relics. However, he couldn't still his thoughts long enough to focus on anything but Isabella and how he had wanted much, much more from her.

He could still taste her, feel her shape beneath his hands. Damn it, he was still semiaroused, and thinking of it was making it worse.

"Your usual table is ready, my lord," the butler announced as Black shed his hat and coat and passed them to the retainer. With a nod, he turned and walked down the dimly lit corridor. It was late afternoon, and the gas lamps had not been lit yet despite the fact that the card rooms and dining room were already filled. But then, this wasn't a club where aristocrats wiled away the hours.

He'd come to Blake's, a little-known gentleman's club in Bloomsbury, for a reason. Its clientele mostly comprised artists and poets, and the odd financier. Very few people of the ton were members, and that was precisely why he'd chosen to pay his membership here—beyond prying eyes and gossiping mouths. He loathed gossip. Especially since he'd frequently been an object of it. He did everything in his power not to subject himself to it, but he'd broken his self-imposed rule last evening by venturing out of his house to a ball and singling out a beautiful young woman by dancing with her.

Years of strictures shot to hell in less than five minutes. But there were some things in life that proved too great a temptation—even for him. And Isabella had proved to be one of them. She was most likely the only temptation he could not resist.

Turning right, he entered the small room at the back of the club. The gaming rooms and bar were up front, leaving the back relatively quiet—and empty. A roaring fire crackled in the hearth. Sitting at the table was Sussex, reading a paper and drinking a whiskey.

At Black's entrance, a servant placed a freshly pressed news sheet and a dram of scotch at the empty place, which Black immediately occupied. Once the servant was out of earshot, he took a sip of his drink and watched as Sussex lowered the paper.

"Well?" he asked. "I received your message."

Black glanced around, shifted in his chair, giving the air that he was settling in for a bit. "I have information on the House of Orpheus."

His Grace's eyes lit with interest. "Indeed? You've been busy, and for one who apparently doesn't give a damn about finding the relics."

Ignoring the taunt, he continued. "Last night I told you I recalled recently seeing the image for the House of Orpheus." He lifted the paper and pretended to peruse it. "It was on a billet at the front of the Adelphi Theatre."

The duke's dark brow rose in question. "The Adelphi is little more than a bawdy house—with its painted women and questionable productions."

"Which makes it a wonderful cover for such a club, don't you think?"

Sussex folded his paper and downed the rest of his whiskey. "I do. Brilliant, in fact. Are you certain?"

"I knew I had seen that image somewhere," Black

murmured. "It was only a matter of time before I recalled exactly where. I was out of my mind with boredom the other night and decided to take in a show."

The duke merely arched his brow. Black glared back. "I don't need your censure, Sussex," he snarled. "So what, I needed a few mindless hours of terrible singing and even worse dancing. At any rate, I noticed the billet when I left the theater. I didn't read it then, but after I dropped Miss Fairmont off at her home this afternoon, I had my driver return to the Strand, and I nicked this—it was posted on the front of the theater, by the doors."

"Miss Fairmont, did you say?" Sussex asked with interest as he took the billet from Black's hand. "What was she doing there?"

"The apothecary."

Sussex glanced up from reading the billet. "And Miss Ashton?"

"She wasn't there."

Sussex's gaze turned dark. "This is an advertisement for the club, but it gives no address, no means of making contact or anything about what this House of Orpheus is."

"I know. That must be part of its allure. I suspect it's one of those exclusive, elitist-type clubs that men trip over themselves to join—nothing like a mysterious club with initiation rites and secret ceremonies to draw members."

"Sounds like Freemasonry," Sussex said with a grin.

"I think the Adelphi is the place to start. By its size alone it's the perfect venue to hide such a club. Maybe after a night spent there, we might find out more about it. I hear that the theater is closed on Wednesdays—perhaps it's closed because the club meets then? Or maybe there's a special room—there are always those sorts of rooms set up for theatrics that these places tend to induce."

Sitting forward, Sussex passed him the billet. "I don't like this, Black. Every gut instinct I possess tells me that this club has something to do with Lucy. And God help me if it's some notorious club set in the Adelphi. I should be thinking of the chalice and the pendant, and what bloody mayhem might ensue if they fall into the wrong hands, but I confess all I can think about is Lucy and how she's gotten herself involved in something dangerous."

"I'll go to the theater, mingle, ask around about this House of Orpheus and see what I can learn, and in the process discover if it has anything at all to do with the artifacts. Do not worry, Sussex. Lady Lucy's reputation will remain intact, and we will find the relics. Good God, we don't want it getting out that the pendant and chalice have the powers to alter the world."

"You said you didn't believe it. You stated it was nothing but a medieval fairy tale."

Shrugging, Black sat back in his chair and gazed into the fire. "I lack faith, I suppose. But that doesn't mean that I can let it go. It has been my family's curse to look after the damn pendant and hide it away from the world for over five hundred years. I simply can't shrug it off now. I must find it, whether or not I believe it contains nefarious powers."

"All my life, I have been consumed with keeping the chalice hidden from the world, but with one glance from a green-eyed nymph, I've suddenly become sidetracked."

"Besotted," Black corrected his friend. "A moon-calved fool."

"Enough," the duke growled. "I'm merely trying to keep the girl out of it. For the sake of her father. Stonebrook doesn't need the aggravation or the scandal."

Black snorted. "You may use your arrogance and aloof, distant airs to fool the insipid members of the ton, Sussex, but I know you better. You're pining away for the girl."

His Grace refused to return his stare, and instead focused on the fire that blazed in the large hearth. "Yes," he murmured so quietly that Black wasn't certain he was supposed to have heard him. "Pining, perishing, bloody angsting over the girl, and she won't give me the time of day."

He'd known Sussex since the cradle, and had never seen him this way. Lucy Ashton was tying him in knots.

"Enough of this," Sussex snapped. "When will you go to the theater, and do you want company? Lord knows I would do well with a night out."

"I'll make preparations and let you know. As an aside, I met with Knighton on the docks this morning. There was nothing of interest to us in the crates. I don't think him a threat, but all the same, I offered to sponsor him into the lodge. I hold to the adage that one should keep their friends close, and their enemies closer."

Sussex smiled slyly. "You just said he wasn't a threat to us."

"Not to the Brethren Guardians," Black murmured. "But he is a threat to me."

"Now who's moonfaced?" Sussex said, and laughed when Black rose from the chair and retreated from the room. It was fine for him to tease His Grace about this affliction for Lucy, but it was quite the opposite to be the object of the duke's mockery.

SHE COULD NOT STOP THINKING of that kiss, or the feel of Lord Black's arms encircling her. She had felt wild, unbidden and in truth, he was just as wild as she. Which was shocking in a way, for Black always seemed so composed and self-contained. That he should possess such passion was both a surprise and a fright. The kiss had been hard, frenzied, as if both of them had been denying such a thing for eternity. Yet they had only just met. And therein lay the fear.

She should be mortified. Ashamed. She had kissed a man who was not courting her. She should feel at least a glimmer of remorse for kissing Black while courting with Mr. Knighton. Yet how could she regret the *event* of her life? For this was what that kiss was…the most exhilarating moment of her entire existence.

She could still taste him on her tongue. Her lips still red and swollen from the fervor of his mouth atop hers. Her body, which had been so tight and hurting, now dully ached. She was aware of a persistent restlessness inside her, something she had never felt before. An agitation that she knew could only be abated by seeing Black again.

It had been a mere twenty-four hours after their introduction, and here she was, pining for him. How could this be? After so many years of carefully guarding her passions. After watching her mother throw herself at any man that glanced her way, here she was just waiting for the opportunity to lunge herself into Black's arms.

He was a sorcerer, a beautiful, dark magician who had woven a spell upon her. It was the only way to explain her rash behavior—the way she had discarded her beliefs, her fears. She had sworn never to allow herself to be at the mercy of her desires. But here she was, on the threshold of desire. With one kiss, Black had opened the door to a room she could not allow herself to enter, for inside that beckoning chamber, Isabella knew her destruction lay within the hands of a most alluring master.

This attraction between them was inexplicable. Despite having only been introduced, Isabella felt as though she'd known him all her life. When she was with him, she felt the familiar agitation disappear, suddenly filled with the calm from the storm that had been her life. In Black's company, there was familiarity, as if he had somehow long been a presence in her life. But she had never seen him or talked to him until the night of the ball. There was no denying that there was something inside him that beckoned her. Whatever it was, her soul seemed to answer.

Was it fate? Destiny? She no longer knew if she

believed in such things. Could passion be fate, or was it nothing more than an impulsive human instinct that needed fulfillment? Was what she felt shimmering between them destiny pushing them together, or was it nothing but physical attraction of the most basic nature?

No, that afternoon in the carriage had not been base. It had been beautiful, and the way he looked at her…yes, a man could be anything, say anything, but his eyes did not lie. When Black looked at her, there was something there other than simple lust. His words tempted her, so, too, his looks. Even their silence was charged with a palpable undercurrent. With Black, she was another person. A woman not afraid of the passion that simmered just below her skin. It frightened her, how easily he coaxed that person forth.

He would ruin her, she reminded herself, if she didn't have a care. If she dared step even one foot inside the door he had opened that afternoon she would be utterly destroyed—morally and spiritually.

The sound of the shutter slamming against the bricks startled her, pulling her back to the moment. Isabella jumped, unable to hide her response. Here was not the place to woolgather and daydream about her kiss with Black. Now was the time to keep her wits about her. How had she allowed Lucy to talk her into coming to Highgate Cemetery tonight, especially since she wanted nothing more than to sit by the fire and write down every little nuance of that magnificent kiss?

Why was it that Lucy was so drawn to such things as séances and spirits? They were dark entertainments done in the night. Without light there was only darkness—evil. What was her cousin searching for in the darkness?

Pausing at the window of the tiny cottage, Isabella pulled the curtain aside and gazed out at the trees beyond. The wind was up, stirring the dried leaves, blowing them upward as the branches waved back and forth. The clouds were thick and heavy, the moon hung low on the horizon, its brightness illuminating the sky, which churned with an impending storm. Another gust of wind howled, and she shivered, the draft wafting in through a crack in the mullion. Beyond the trees lay the cemetery. She could make out the tops of the statuary, angels and crosses, and the peaked roofs of mausoleums and family crypts. In the darkness and the cool October air with its lamenting winds, the crosses looked ominous and the angels mercenary. The shadows…well, they were there, too, weaving beneath the moonlight and the tendrils of fog that wrapped like ghostly specters around the headstones. Never in the wildest reaches of her imagination could she have conjured up such an atmospheric setting for a séance.

How she abhorred the darkness and shadows, while her cousin coveted them. Unlike Lucy, Isabella knew that there was nothing good to be learned by shadows. But Lucy was past listening to Isabella's protests. It was as if Lucy had somehow become a shadow herself. There was no denying that Lucy was not the vivacious young woman whom Isabella had always known. She was a shadow of her former self. Oh, she tried to hide it, but Isabella saw through her cousin's facade. Shadows flickered in her cousin's green eyes, and darkness, of unknown origin, was slowly blotting out the light that had been Lucy. Like a destructive vine, the darkness had its tendrils wrapped tightly around Lucy's soul. If only her cousin would confide in her. If only Isabella could save herself—and her cousin—from the shadows that had always seemed to haunt the women of their family.

But Lucy would not let her in, and Isabella, still filled with her own darkness of dreams and shadows, let her be—for now.

Draping her mantelet tighter around her shoulders, Isabella glanced back at the round wooden table that was

prepared for their séance. Already seated at the table were
Lucy, Sibylla, the Duke of Sussex—who Isabella could
not believe had joined them—and the medium, Alice Fox,
who looked like a madwoman with her wild mane of dull
red curls and large, crazed eyes.

Sussex, Isabella noted, was watching Lucy with barely
restrained concern. He had appeared on their doorstep just
as they were leaving. When Lucy informed him they were
off to Highgate with her maid as their only chaperone,
Sussex had demanded he join them. Lucy had been livid
and made Sussex pay for his presumptive behavior with
her icy demeanor and cold retorts. Isabella, grateful for
Sussex's presence, had silently prayed that Lucy's hostil-
ity would not force him to abandon them that night—but
the duke had steadfastly stayed the course—and was now
here, seated opposite Lucy at the table, watching her with
a heartwarming mix of worry and desire. There was implacability in those mysterious gray eyes. He would not
let Lucy come to harm—or her. She was quite certain of
that. It was that knowledge, and the quiet strength of the
duke that made any of this tolerable.

Maybe together, they could rid Lucy of this absurd
liking she had taken for the supernatural. For Isabella
had no desire to spend many more nights likes this one,
waiting for some spirit to jump out from the gloom. It
was never wise to stare too closely into the shadows. One
never knew what was there, lurking, waiting to be seen.

"Let us begin. First," Alice said, her voice dropping,
lending the ambience in the room a more sinister tone,
"we will attempt to conjure a spirit here, and then, when
the clock tolls midnight we will walk amongst the graves,
and try there."

Lucy sent her a pleading glance to join them. Isabella
did not want to do this, to invite spirits to come and talk
with them. *Let them rest in peace,* she had begged her
cousin, but it had fallen on deaf ears.

She could have stayed home tonight if she had wanted. Yet she couldn't bear the thought of Lucy doing this alone. Something was driving her. She was searching for something, or someone, and Isabella was determined to find out what or who. As unbearable as the thought of walking amongst graves at midnight was to her, the thought of Lucy alone, struggling to find whatever it was she was searching for, was even more frightening.

Lucy had been there for Isabella from the beginning. Never questioning, never probing into her past, or the *unfortunate event* that had caused her uncle to come for her. She owed Lucy at least this.

"Come and sit," Alice commanded with a wave. She held her lit candle higher, the limited light barely illuminating the tiny room. Alice grinned at her, Isabella's reluctance obviously amusing to her.

"The dead prefer the dark." Alice blew out the candle, plunging the room into darkness.

"I, myself, would prefer a light, any amount of light," Isabella mumbled as she sat in a chair. Lucy giggled, and reached for her hand. At least she thought it was Lucy. It was so dark she could barely do more than make out shapes. Even the moon, which hung low and full, wasn't enough to shed any light on the murky room Alice had chosen for their communion with the dead.

The shaft of moonlight shifted, and on the wall, Isabella saw shadows of naked tree limbs dancing. The shadows shifted again, and a wide arch obliterated the image of trees with a dark shapeless outline. Oh, God, how she feared shadows and what came out of them.

Her dreams…more specifically those dreams were always preceded by shadows. She had come to fear them because of those dreams, and the power they had over her—and others.

"Quiet your thoughts," Alice commanded, "and still your fears. The dead will come when they're ready."

Closing her eyes, Isabella tried very hard to calm her breathing. It was only darkness and shadows, she reminded herself. Nothing to harm when one's heart was not filled with darkness. That was what her grandmother had always told her. But Isabella had never truly believed her. One day, she was certain that someone, or *something,* would creep from the shadows and claim her. It had been a recurring dream, a nightmare that had somehow turned into a destiny—or so she believed.

Oh, how she wanted to quit this place! Her head still hurt, and she felt sleepy still from the effects of the tonic she had taken after her return home that afternoon. Alice was mumbling, chanting, perhaps. The tone was rhythmic, lulling and soon Isabella felt her lids lower and her breathing settle into a quiet pattern, the shadows momentarily forgotten.

"Now, think of…nothing," Alice ordered. "Empty your thoughts."

Isabella tried, but she couldn't do it. The words seemed to come from nowhere, unable to be silenced, spilling through her subconscious just as they ebbed through her pen and bled onto the page.

Death was beautiful as he peered down at me. He held me in his arms as we danced beneath the starlight, his gaze never moving from my face. He kissed me, a soft meeting of lips. I felt his breath on my cheek, smelled the spice of his skin as his cheek brushed against mine. His words were dark, and alluring, calling to me…

"Isabella, do you know what I would give to be the one…"

Her eyes flew open, and she saw a shadow move along the wall. She stiffened, felt her breath freeze in her lungs as the shadow took on the shape of a man.

"Good," Alice rasped. "Someone's come."

A chair scraped against the wood, and Isabella shrieked. Something touched her hand, and she whimpered, only to feel a grounding hold on her palm. The shadow danced along the wall, moving like mist, or fog.

She had seen it before, on a night like tonight, only it had moved over the water as she walked into the rolling depths of the sea. *"'Tis not time, my love. You will not die this night."* Yet still she had walked farther and farther out, the waves crashing around her, the heavy weight of her skirts making it harder to stay upright. The water grew deeper, colder, as it steadily climbed up past her legs, her waist, her breasts.

"You will not die this night," the voice had pleaded.

Yet she had continued, knowing it was Death that spoke to her.

The fog turned to shadow then, and she had seen the form of a man take shape. She had seen him before, the familiar shape of him when he had come to take her mother, and her grandmother. She had seen the same silhouette while attending births with her grandmother—the shadow that took newborn babes, and their mothers.

Death.

She had always been able to see him.

The shadow moved farther along the wall, and she blinked, hoping she was lost in a dream of her past, but she saw the curtains of Alice's cottage, and the view of Highgate beyond the trees, which were leafless, and knew that what she was seeing was real. Present.

"Do you not see him?" Isabella asked, searching through the murky darkness.

"Who do you see?" Alice asked.

"That man. In the corner. He has his back to us, but he's dressed in a long coat. His hands are folded behind his back, his head is lowered."

"Go on," Alice encouraged, her voice dropping. "Tell me what you see?"

"Can you not see him?" Isabella cried, and the hand, which she realized must be the duke's, held her tightly. "I can see him very clearly, despite the darkness. He is… tall. Dark. He's turning around."

"Do not look upon him," Alice hissed, and Isabella pressed her eyes shut, trembling. On her left, she felt Lucy's slender fingers quake against hers.

What was she seeing? A product of her imagination? A hallucination caused by her headache? Good Lord, could it be real?

"Spirit," Alice whispered, "what is it you want?"

Something came sliding down the long length of the table, stopping before her.

"The spirit wants to talk," Alice said. "It's the planchette he's sent."

"Oh, I love the talking board," Lucy whispered.

"Silence," Alice ordered. "Now then, all hands together, and place them on the planchette. And keep your eyes closed."

They did as she demanded, and Alice began to ask questions that were barely audible above the sound of Isabella's pounding heart. "Who are you?"

They waited long seconds and suddenly the planchette began to move.

"Who is moving it?" Isabella's voice was nothing but a high-pitched squeal.

"The medium," the duke spat. "Who else?"

"My hands are not even on it, the spirit in the room moves it."

Isabella shivered as the planchette moved a total of five times then stopped altogether.

"Have you come for someone?"

This time, the planchette moved three places. *Yes.* Oh, good Lord, Isabella could barely breathe.

"Who have you come for?" she burst out, unable to control her fear.

Immediately the planchette moved three places.

"Enough of this nonsense," the duke demanded. "Light a candle this instant. Miss Fairmont is about to succumb to the vapors."

Her worst fears were confirmed when the candle flared to life, and the answers to Alice's questions were written hastily on a white piece of paper that sat in front of her.

Who are you?

D E A T H

Have you come for someone?

Y E S

Who have you come for? That had been her question, and the answer curdled her blood.

Y O U

Lucy caught her gaze, and then her eyes widened as she looked beyond Isabella's shoulder. Following her cousin's stare Isabella turned in her chair, and gasped, then looked down at the planchette and the hands that were overtop hers.

Black.

"Wherever you are," he whispered for her ears only, "I will find you, and you will be safe with me."

CHAPTER SIX

THAT FRENZIED SUCKING sound…was it her? An audible wheeze, followed by a strangled echo erupted the quiet. She knew it was her, her rasping, choking breaths. Isabella felt her chest squeeze tightly behind her corset, her breasts constricted, the bodice of her gown pulling tight as she struggled to get air into her lungs. Oh, why had she allowed Lucy to talk her into tight lacings—tonight of all nights?

Oh, God, she prayed. *Please let this moment of frozen panic pass.* But as she prayed, and the seconds ticked on, she witnessed the alarm—and horror—on Lucy's, Sussex's and Black's expressions. She was making a complete fool of herself, acting in such a dramatic fashion. But she couldn't stop. The panic had a choke hold on her now, and she was quite certain she was going to swoon.

It had been Death there in the room with them—at least it had been her image of Death. Nothing could convince otherwise. Alice Fox, with her wild eyes and witch's hair, had conjured him from his dark forest where he dwelt until he was called forth to claim his souls. He had not got her soul before, and now…now he was returned to claim it.

She gasped again, a most horrific and embarrassing noise, and she wanted to die. Wanted Death to come back and steal her away, because she could not bear to think of what Black must think of her and her silly, swooning behavior. However much she was mortified by her actions, she was a powerless victim to them—always had been.

"Miss Fairmont is ill." Lord Black's voice, deep and commanding, broke over her constricted breathing. "I'll take her outside."

"Smelling salts, my lord," Lucy cried. Isabella heard her cousin fishing through her reticule for the tiny vial, but she did not see if Black had taken them. All she knew was she was suddenly in his arms, being carried through the cottage as she struggled to breathe.

He jostled her only once as he opened the door, and then they were outside—the sharp sting of the wind slapping at her cheeks—giving her a brief moment of clarity. The air was thick and heavy, full of dampness and moisture, and it made her cough, but did little to restore the easy rhythm of her breathing. She felt faint, hot—yet her skin was cool and clammy, and her vision was tunneling, growing dim. Dear heavens, she *was* going to swoon, and in Lord Black's arms.

"Breathe, now," he whispered as he set her on her feet and steadied her back against his chest. His arm, thick and muscular, wrapped around her waist, holding her against him as she fought to make her way out of the state she had worked herself into.

Death had come…she had seen him. He had been there. Right before…she glanced over her shoulder, saw the earl staring gravely down at her. She had seen Death's shadow right before Black had revealed himself.

Imagination running rampant, she thought back to her book, to her waltz with Black and then tonight, to the shadow that snaked along the wall and then to the man who had been beside her in the dark.

"Isabella, you must take a slow, deep breath."

Black's voice was authoritative, and she heard it only in the distance of her mind. Her head was swimming, her vision blackening.

"Breathe," she heard. "Damn it, take a breath."

She had heard that command before, whispering to her from the recesses of her memories. She tried to block the voice, but it pulled her under, like the roiling waves of the North Sea, sucking her deep, tossing her up, only to be pulled into the seemingly bottomless frigid waters. And then she was back in the past, and the crushing weight of the sea, the violence of the waves, and the sea-scented air that swirled with the approaching gale. She was battered between waves, jostled beneath and above until she did not rise up into the frigid night air, but sank lower, her arms floating alongside her, her body heavy. Then she remembered all too vividly the disembodied feeling of sinking to the sandy bottom of Whitby Harbor.

THE MOMENT ISABELLA went slack in his arms, Black pulled her tighter to him and furiously unbuttoned her gown, revealing her corset strings. Pulling at them with quick, efficient tugs, he loosened them, allowing her chest to expand.

Curse whatever idiot had thought tight lacing imperative. No wonder she could not breathe—she was tied and pressed like a sausage.

"Breathe, damn it," he muttered again as he freed her of her corset. Her head tilted back and lay on his shoulder, her pale throat exposed through the thin shaft of moonlight. The mist was now drizzle, and it beaded on her cheeks, glistened on her eyelashes and the exposed flesh of her décolletage, giving her pale skin a luminescence that was at once mesmerizing and terrifying. This was how she had looked in his dream—pale, lifeless, her beautiful skin cold.

She should be breathing now, but she wasn't, held in a grip of fright and shock. Cool efficiency—his hallmark—fled, leaving a keen sense of fear, and a touch of panic.

Don't do this, he pleaded as he turned her head so that he could gaze down at her. *Don't you dare...*

Placing his palm alongside her neck, he felt her pulse, full, bounding—healthy. *Alive.* And then he felt it, the deep release of her breath, the weak inhalation that followed. Her lashes slowly rose, her gaze glassy as she stared up at him.

Relief replaced fear, and he brought her close to him, his cheek against hers, her breath whispering against his mouth. And then his lips were inching to her mouth, brushing, caressing—her breath against his lips, telling him she was well, unharmed, but he refused to believe it—needed to feel her body soften, to sink boneless into his. It was hardly helping her, he knew. But his worries, his fright, had replaced logic, and he was ruled by this absurd need to feel her—to know, bone deep, that she was truly well. In those seconds of foreboding, he experienced a flash—a fleeting moment of vulnerability in which he needed to reassure himself that she was his, even if she did not yet know it.

"You scared the hell out of me," he whispered, harsher then he intended.

She did not return his kiss, still slightly dazed, but she touched him, her fingers soft and cool against his cheek as her fingertips fluttered against him. "I could say the same for you."

"'Tis only a parlor game," he murmured, brushing his lips against her brow, feeling her tremble from the ordeal. "Nothing to fear—especially not from me."

"Is that true, my lord? I have nothing to fear from you, and how we might appear to anyone who may happen upon us?"

"I don't give a damn what anyone thinks. I'm not letting you go, not until I know for certain you're well."

She stiffened in his arms, tried to pull away, but he held her tight, his arms holding her beneath her breasts, where he could feel her breathe, see her décolletage rise and fall. She was innocent, he reminded himself, not a woman to be trifled with. But he had been too long without the physical pleasures of sex. And he was weak. But then, he'd not ever had to control his base thoughts and desires before. Innocents had never interested him. But Isabella did. She ruled his dreams. His fantasies that played out late at night when he was alone in his room, with only shadows to keep him company. In those, he had not had to restrain himself. In his dreams his seduction of her had been sensual and erotic—so vivid—that even now he could close his eyes and recall how his mind had painted her naked. All pale skin and deep, feminine curves. Above his hand were her breasts, and he imagined them full and heavy and he itched to move his palm upward and test them, to see if they compared to his fantasy.

But this was not the time to bring to mind his desires. Already he had moved too swiftly. She was as fragile as a doe, and he was like a cougar, scenting her, running her to ground. If he wasn't careful, he would find himself pawing her.

"I am not usually so…unnerved," she whispered, bringing him back to their present situation. "Pray forgive that scene."

"There is nothing to forgive. You were frightened, that is all."

"Nevertheless, I do not make a habit of indulging in theatrics such as the ones I just displayed."

"You are overly concerned, Isabella."

She was warm; her skin, which had been clammy and pale, was now heated and pink. Even through the shadowy light, he could see the rose color of her cheeks, the sweep of a flush covering her bosom. Her eyes, mesmerizing and intelligent, sparkled, too.

A gentleman would promptly repair her gown and send her on her way. A gentleman would not stare at the enticing view of Isabella's gown sliding from her shoulders, exposing even more of her breasts. A gentleman would not contemplate pressing her against the wall and capturing her mouth with his.

"My lord?"

Did she see the hunger in his eyes? Did she know his thoughts? He had always been so damn good at staying controlled, aloof. An enigma. Yet this woman tore down his defenses without even knowing it.

"Help me?" She motioned to the back of her dress. "And then I may return to the others."

He had asked for nothing in this world—until two years ago, when he had asked for one thing. To know Isabella as only a man can know a woman. To unveil her secrets, to know what resided in her heart, to feel that beautiful gaze on him and bask in the glow of her body. He must remember that he had seen her that long ago, but that they had only been introduced. He mustn't move too fast and scare her away. But not too slow, either, his instincts warned. He must move swiftly—but carefully—capturing her without any way of release before she discovered his past. Her actions tonight had firmly confirmed his suspicions, and his fears. She might very well run from him if she learned of his past before he had her firmly his.

"Lord Black?" she asked, stepping away from him, alarm in her eyes.

He reached for her, but a shadow stopped him from pulling her roughly against him and capturing her mouth with his.

"My lord?" Lucy's voice. "My lord, is Isabella well?"

"She is quite well, Lady Lucy."

Isabella's frantic gaze met his, and he turned her around, quickly lacing her back up. The corset strings were loose and the bodice of her gown did not fit quite as well as before, but he doubted the others would notice, for it was dark in the cottage.

"Oh, there you are." Lucy Ashton wheeled around the corner, coming to an abrupt stop just as Black finished buttoning up the back of Isabella's gown. It was dark in this corner, the moonlight didn't fully reach them. Isabella's cousin would have no idea what he had done—and still wanted to do.

"Lord, you gave me a fright, Issy," Lucy admonished as she stood before them. "If Lord Black had not been here, I have no idea what we would have done."

"I am well, Lucy," Isabella murmured. Black noticed how Isabella would not meet her cousin's gaze. "It was a rather convincing scene, wasn't it? I suppose that is the only explanation for my behavior—utter fear."

"Mmm, I wonder how Miss Fox managed it all? She must have had some help."

Lucy's gaze darted to his. Despite the darkness he could see the flash in her green eyes. "Do not tell me after what you witnessed, after what we all witnessed, that you believe it a hoax? Come, my lord, how can you? I vow, Miss Fox successfully summoned Death."

"Miss Fox," he snorted, "did nothing more than move a planchette and write on some paper while using the darkness and impending storm to set her stage. No, Lady Lucy, Miss Fox did not summon Death or any of his minions."

"My lord," Lucy challenged. "You deny what you witnessed with your own eyes? Impossible!"

"There was something in that room," Isabella murmured as a shudder racked through her body. "I sensed it immediately, even before I saw its shadow."

"Nonsense. Miss Fox is a most convincing charlatan, that is all. There was nothing in that room but shadows, and then my arrival. It was me you saw, Isabella. Nothing more."

Lucy gazed between them, and for the first time both

of them were cognizant of how cold it was outside, and how Isabella was trembling.

"I suppose now is not the time to argue the presence of the supernatural, Lady Lucy. Your cousin is cold and worn down by this trial tonight. I would not have her ill, for it will prevent her, and you and Lord Stonebrook, from dining with me tomorrow night."

"We would be delighted to accept your invitation to supper, my lord."

"Lucy!" Isabella gasped in outrage. It was then that Black knew Isabella was having doubts—about him. About them. Moving, he placed his arm around Isabella's elbow before she could offer up any excuses for refusing his invitation.

"We must get your cousin out of this dampness. Outside, in the dead of October in a cemetery of all places, is most certainly not conducive to one's health."

Lucy did not misinterpret his pointed gaze. He held the young and carefree Lucy responsible for this night. It had been her desire to attend a séance, her will that she had imposed upon Isabella. He didn't like it, and Lucy knew it. Still, it did not prevent her from sending him a haughty glance before she took Isabella's hand in hers.

"I'm sorry, Isabella. Indeed, had I known it would disturb you so, I would never have brought you here tonight."

She allowed herself to be steered back into the cottage, Black following behind them. For some strange reason he had wanted to lash out at Lucy. She had made Isabella anxious. It had been Lucy's egocentric desire to attend the séance that had directly contributed to Isabella's frantic fear. And all he wanted to do was protect her. To wrap his arms around her and take her home—to his house and hold her, lie with her in his bed. He wanted to offer her the comfort of his home, shelter in his arms, pleasure from his body. She'd had very little of that in her young life, and he wanted to be the one to remedy that.

From the moment he had first seen her on the bustling streets of Whitby, he'd been drawn to her. It was if his soul had recognized her as his. For two years he had thought of nothing but her, of how he wanted to care for her, protect her, love her. He had been merely existing, a shell of a man living out his days in preordained routine. He hadn't lived until he'd discovered Isabella, and the fact that he had somehow managed to give his heart to a person he didn't truly know still baffled him.

But from that moment on, he had known what it meant to truly be alive. To live for something—*someone*. And he wasn't about to let her slip through his hands. Souls had a way of finding one another. He believed that. Would Isabella? Would she understand that true lovers did not search for each other? But that they were in each other all along?

"It was very kind of you to offer to see me home."

Black's eyes were not discernible through the darkness. Only his silhouette, outlined by the moonlight that shone through the carriage window, made him visible. She could hear him breathing, though, sense his presence. He seemed to suck the very air out of the carriage, so that Isabella was only aware of him.

"It is no bother, Isabella. It was apparent that your cousin had no great desire to quit Highgate before midnight and her jaunt through the stones, just as it was evident that you had no desire to stay another moment."

"You're upset with Lucy, I can hear the censure in your voice."

"Of course I am," he snapped. "I can think of vastly more amusing entertainments then the one I was just subjected to."

She shivered. His voice was different somehow. Colder? More aloof? What had caused this change?

"I fear perhaps that I have ruined your evening."

"My evening?" His quiet laugh was sardonic. "I had no desire to stay and bear witness to such things. The supernatural may be in vogue, but I am not, and never was, a slave to fashion. Your cousin, however, seems hell-bent on pursuing the pleasure, to the detriment of anyone else. She deserved far more than my censure for what she did to you."

"Lucy could have no way of knowing I would react in such a way, my lord."

"Did she not?" There was a long pause, followed by, "I'm not so sure."

"What do you mean by that?"

"Nothing." His hand waved in the air dismissively. "I fear you must ignore me, Isabella. I'm in somewhat of a mood."

"I didn't want to disappoint Lucy, or put an end to her evening. She…she has a great fondness for this sort of thing."

"And you don't?"

Isabella wet her lips. "No, my lord, I do not. I do not believe in taunting the spirit world. What good could come of it?"

"I don't know. I've often wondered about that, what the dead would say if they could return to the mortal realm. I shouldn't like to face a specter from my past, that is certain."

"I fear it," Isabella said with a little shudder.

"As do I," he murmured, making Isabella wonder what Black had to be frightened of.

"I believe the dead are just that. There is no purpose in returning to the mortal realm. They are at peace in the afterlife and should be left as such."

"Are they?" he asked quietly. "I've regularly contemplated if there is any peace in death. Or if the pain of life spills over into the afterworld. It's one of the things I fear most—the question haunts me, in fact. Is there to be no rest in the eternal life?"

This was another side of Black. He was brooding, his mood suddenly morose, sullen. It should have frightened her, but the opposite seemed to be happening. She felt herself being drawn to him, to the tiny scrap of intimacy he was letting her glimpse. He was comfortable with desire. But this, this was the first of him she had glimpsed that had nothing to do with desire. This was the man—not the mysterious earl.

"Do you worry for someone, my lord?" she asked. "Do you fear that their soul is not at rest?"

He did not answer, but kept his head turned, his gaze focused on the window where he could see nothing but inky blackness and a starless, cloudy night. Minutes passed and she thought he would keep silent, but then he sighed, his body slouching as he slunk more comfortably onto the bench, allowing his head to lean back against the squabs.

"My mother," he answered, his voice quiet. "My brother. And…another…" He paused, shook his head. "I've wondered about them, lying cold in their graves. Are they at peace? Is there anger that they were forced from this earth so young? Sometimes I think my dreams of them are just their way of haunting me. You see…they did not die…naturally."

"Oh, Black!" Before she could think of what she was doing, Isabella leaned forward and reached for his hand. "I'm quite certain that both your brother and mother and…this other person are most certainly at peace, regardless of how they met Death."

"Let us talk no more of death tonight," he said.

"All right. What shall we talk of?"

"Does the quiet unnerve you, then? Do you feel you must fill it with conversation?"

He was studying her. Isabella could feel his cool gaze

boring into her. She wanted to know more of him—the passion, but the man as well. There was more to Black than what met the eye, and she wanted to peel away the layers until she discovered the true man lying beneath.

"Isabella?" he asked again. "Are you afraid of the quiet?"

"Yes," she whispered without thinking. "Amongst shadows in the darkness of night I do fear the quiet, and things I find lurking there, for it is never truly silent, is it?"

"Are you afraid? Even now, here with me?"

Fingers fidgeting with her reticule, Isabella swallowed and gazed down into her lap, unseeing in the darkness. He probed too closely—much too close to the truth. Yes, she was afraid. Afraid of her feelings and the reckless desire that seemed to rule her blood when he was near. Not once this evening had she thought of Mr. Knighton. Before meeting Black she had thought of Wendell every night, and now, he seemed nothing more than a foggy memory. Everything had been obliterated by Black since their meeting.

The carriage leaned slightly as it dipped and swayed over the uneven track of road, making its way to London. In the near distance the glow of the city blazed through the night. It was like a beacon, the safety of a light from a lighthouse in a storm. She craved the light, the security she would feel once inside her uncle's home. Perhaps then, away from anything that had to do with the dead and the dark, she would feel more at ease. Certainly she would be more herself once she was away from Black. His presence was much too unsettling.

Black's gentle touch on her chin surprised her, made her gasp and grow rigid, replacing her growing sense of ease with a sensual tension she could not fight. She was afraid, truth be told. And she desperately wanted to throw herself into his arms and have him hold her, just as he had outside the cottage. She wanted to be cocooned in his strength, wanted him to stave off the darkness and shadows, and in the quiet she would hear nothing but his heart beating as she laid her head on his chest and allowed herself to take comfort.

"You'll not be alone tonight, Isabella," he said. "I won't leave you in the dark. Tonight, I'll keep the shadows away."

CHAPTER SEVEN

THE FRONT DOOR closed behind Jennings and Isabella
sighed, relieved to be at home, where the gas lamps were
lit and the hall was devoid of shadows. She was weary,
worn down by the evening and the headache and dream
of the afternoon. She wanted her bed, but she didn't want
to climb the steps and know she was alone in the house.

The servants were there, of course, but they would all
be abed soon, in their quarters on the third floor while
she was alone in the family wing until Lucy and her uncle
arrived home. She didn't want to think of that, how lonely
and frightening it would be stay in this huge house all by
herself, with no one to talk to.

Her upbringing might have been humble and poor,
but at least the two-room cottage that she and her mother
had shared had been cozy and full of light. She'd had her
mother and grandmother to talk with. She hadn't always
been alone. Despite the fact her uncle had taken her in,
sheltered her and cared for her as best as an elderly man
could, Isabella still felt the sharp pang of loneliness.
Sometimes at night she would lie awake in bed and weep.
She did not belong in this glittering world of Lucy's, no
matter how hard she tried. She was a simple girl, looking
for a safe, secure life. She did not need jewels and man-
sions. She wanted only comfort—the sort of emotional
safekeeping that money could not always buy.

Sometimes she missed her mother and grandmother
so much it was as if an acute pain had seized her heart.

Her mother had been many things—she might have been reckless in her passions—but she had at least been kind and ready with a hug.

She exhaled quietly, hating that she was being melancholy. Her mother had been gone nearly two and half years now. And her grandmother nearly five. She should not still be so sad. Yet something told her it was not just loss that made her this way, but her life. It was lacking something, despite the riches she had been given. There was something inside her that had not been gratified by her uncle's largesse.

What would make her happy? She had thought Mr. Knighton's attentions would. And they had, but things had changed. In that moment in her uncle's ballroom, when her gaze had locked with Black's, everything had changed. She no longer saw the world—and herself—through the same eyes as she had before meeting him.

Casting a glance over her shoulder, Isabella stared at the man removing his hat, and felt her throat tighten. How strange. Black was only a man. Yet she knew that he was no ordinary man. He had cast some sort of spell on her, enchanting her. With one dance he had made her forget what she truly desired in life. He had changed her, and not for the better. Somehow Black had unlocked the door where she kept her tightly guarded passionate nature hidden. She had never wanted to see what lurked behind that door, never wanted anyone else to see, either.

Sliding her cloak off her shoulders, Black handed the velvet cape to the butler. "Would you be so good as to bring in a warm drink for Miss Fairmont? The night is chilly."

Jennings's gaze narrowed. Whether Black noticed the butler's impertinence or not was unclear. But Isabella saw it, and reached out to touch Jennings's sleeve. "We'll be in the green drawing room, Jennings." *With the door open,* she wanted to add.

"Very good, miss," he muttered before hanging up her cloak and heading to the kitchen. With a deep breath, she turned to face the man she had come to rely upon this night.

"Lord Black," she began, but he silenced her when he pressed his index finger against her lips.

"You're pale and tired. Let's get you into the salon where you can be at ease and rest."

"You must think me weak, the damsel in distress. But I assure you, my lord, I have a core of steel. I can take care of myself, and have done so for years."

"I know you can. I've seen that strength reflected in your eyes, but sometimes it is nice to have another to lean on. Sometimes, Isabella, it is nice to be needed, to offer comfrot and a shoulder to a soul in need. I want to be that person. That comfort. That shoulder upon which you may lay your head and rest."

"I don't think this is wise, my lord." She swallowed and licked her lips, trying to be brave about this, even though what she was going to say was the furthest thing from what she wanted. "I think you should leave. People may talk, they might even see your carriage and realize that my uncle is out tonight. It's…not done to be here with you without a proper chaperone."

"I'll not leave you alone, Isabella. I promised you that. I also promise that you're safe from me."

"My reputation—"

"Will come to no harm. I assure you. Come, is my company so very unpalatable that you wish me gone?"

With a flush, she looked down at her clasped hands, then back at him. "You know it is not. But—"

"But nothing, Isabella. I will stay and keep you company. Nothing more. Perhaps I have need of your company, as well."

Something inside her fractured. No one since her mother had needed her, and hearing Black's words, whispered in his deeply masculine voice, freed her. To be needed by someone like him was a balm to her soul.

"Is…is that true?" she asked, her voice quiet, almost hesitant. When he caught her chin on the edge of his fingers and forced her to look at him, she saw with clarity the sincerity in his eyes.

"Never have the words been truer, Isabella. Tonight," he murmured, his eyes darkening, "I do have need of you. A need so great that I know I could never make my feet move to that door—even if you asked it of me."

Her insides felt warm, and she smiled, relieved that he had refused her. "I want to give you my thanks, my lord. You've been very kind to me, and I've taken you away from your evening festivities."

"Nonsense. Here, with you, is where I want to be."

Isabella was flushing profusely as he led her to the salon. It was clear he had been to visit her uncle before, for he knew his way around the house without being shown. How had she never seen him here? she wondered.

"Now then, sit here," he said softly, and helped her to sit on the chaise longue. The fire was laid in the hearth, and the roar and crackle of the flames instantly heated her chilled body. It was a wonderful feeling to be warm again. To feel safe. Highgate seemed far away now and that afternoon's dream long gone. For the first time since leaving Black's carriage after retrieving her medicine she felt at ease.

They sat in companionable silence while the parlor maid carried in a tea service, and passed a steaming cup of cider to her. Black refused a drink with a brisk shake of his head.

"I can ask the maid to retrieve the whiskey if you'd like. Uncle keeps it in his study."

"No, thank you."

"Something to eat, then?"

"No, I'm comfortable. And I will help myself later if I need anything."

Silence descended once more, and sipping the warm, comforting drink, Isabella let the familiar taste of cinnamon and apples, with a delicate lashing of mulled wine, warm her insides and quiet her thoughts. It was really rather lovely sitting here in this cozy salon, which was the smallest of the public rooms in Stonebrook's mansion, the firelight glowing and crackling while the autumn winds picked up and howled outside. She really should excuse herself and find a mirror. She probably looked a fright. Her gown was loose around her bodice and she was certain parts of her hair had come unpinned and were hanging loose. Except, she could not make herself move. The chaise longue was much too comfortable, and all too soon her eyelids began to close, only to flicker wide when Black's voice disturbed the quiet.

"May I say that I'm thankful you wrote to me and requested I join you at the séance, Isabella."

"What?" She was certainly wide awake now. "Wrote to you?"

"Yes. I received your note during dinner."

"My lord, I realize that I might have acted…indiscreet in the maze last night, and this afternoon in the carriage…" She swallowed another gulp of her cider and tried to meet his eyes. "It may seem to you that I am rather…well…bold for a lady of my years, and perhaps I have been, but I may assure you, my lord, that boldness has not lent itself to writing you missives."

His gaze narrowed, and something very dark and alarming glittered in his eyes. "You did not pen this note?"

Rising from his chair, he strolled to her as his fingers fished in his waistcoat pocket. Sitting down beside her, he handed her the missive. She opened it, read it and gave it back to him. Her hands were shaking and her mind reeling with the implications.

"I don't understand this, my lord. I most certainly did not write that letter. Someone has forged my signature. Oh, I cannot believe it," she began, her anxiety spiking. "Someone must have seen us today, in the carriage, or last night. Oh, what will my uncle say if he learns of my behavior—after everything he's done for me?"

"Your uncle will say nothing, because he will not learn of anything that has transpired between us." He placed his fingers on her chin and gently turned her head to look upon him. "And as to the message, I will discover who has written it. In light of what happened, maybe the missive was well intentioned, hmm?"

Oh, she didn't want to think of those events tonight, when she had acted like a complete ninny with him. To be able to turn the hands of time back, she would not have gone to that ridiculous séance in the first place.

"I'm glad I was there." His voice was deep and luring, and she gazed up at him as he brushed his fingers along her cheek. "The roses are still gone from your cheeks. Your skin so pale. I can still see you, struggling for air."

She was positively humiliated by the memory. Her overactive imagination, her irrational fears, had made her act like a silly chit straight out of the schoolroom. And in front of Black who was suave and worldly, and so in control of himself.

A sharp pang of disappointment seared her breast as he released her and moved away. Their intimate moment was broken, and she had been half holding her breath, hoping that Black would kiss her once more, as he had that afternoon in the carriage. The slight hum in her body that had been present in the cottage was now a very real, very live current of need. It took only his nearness to make it flare to life.

"Tell me, Isabella, do you know of something called the House of Orpheus?"

"No. Why?"

"Have you ever heard the name?"

"No. I have no idea who Orpheus is."

"Was," Black muttered as he returned the missive to his pocket. "Orpheus was an ancient Greek poet who descended to Hades and returned. His lover, Persephone, who was forced to spend half the year in Hades, is the symbol of rebirth for those believers who follow Orpheus's teachings."

"I'm sorry. I do not know much Greek mythology." Her face flamed, and she knew the exact instant the roses returned to her cheeks. It was the moment she felt utterly humiliated in Black's presence.

"Understandable. Mythology is not often taught to girls, is it?"

"No, I don't think you understand, my lord. My education was rather lacking until my aunt sent for me the summer I was fifteen. I was tutored then, upstairs in the nursery. But my studies focused on more practical matters. Not philosophy or mythology. Before that, my mother taught me to read, but little else. Her attentions were focused elsewhere."

Mercifully he did not comment on her lack of education or the embarrassment of not having benefited from any formal training. She didn't think she could bear it if he did.

"Perhaps you've heard your uncle or…Lucy talk of Orpheus and his teachings?"

"No, I'm afraid not."

"Mr. Knighton, then?"

Isabella shook her head, trying to understand what he wanted from her.

"You see, the wax seal on the missive, it contains a lyre and a set of laurel leaves and a six-pointed star. Upon the seal are the words *The House of Orpheus*. I think if I could discover this club, then it might lead me to find whoever sent this missive."

"I can't help you, but I can most certainly question Lucy or Mr. Knighton if you—"

He grasped her hands in his warm palms. "No, you don't have to. Leave it to me. I'll discover this House and the person behind the note. There is nothing for you to worry about, Isabella. Your reputation is safe. I won't allow anything to happen to your good name."

It was either the cider or the way Black was looking at her that made her feel entirely too warm. She was feeling a bit cup shot, as well. Her eyes were slowly closing and she longed to fall back on the settee and doze off. But that would be rude, especially since Black had condescended to stay with her until Lucy or Stonebrook arrived home.

"You're exhausted."

"Mmm," she murmured. "I did not sleep well last night, and this afternoon I had another dream."

"Did you?"

Sipping again at the cider, she let the warm liquid soothe her insides. She really should stop drinking it, it was making her tongue loose. "I did."

"And what was this dream about?"

She shouldn't tell him—she never spoke of her dreams, especially *those* ones, but she was speaking of it before she could stop herself. "I am in a strange room—all alone."

"Yes?"

"But there is a presence there. I can feel it. But it will not come out from the shadows but rather sits there, watching me."

"Do you know where you are?"

She shook her head and closed her eyes. Exhaustion was taking over and she was hardly cognizant of what she was saying. "No, I've never seen this place before, but I think it is a man's room. It feels very masculine. Like a library or study."

"And you fear this dream?"

"Yes, because it is one of *those* dreams."

He moved closer, took her glass from her hands and set it aside. The touch of his fingers against hers made her body heat, and she wished that he had let his touch linger longer. She wanted to feel his hand in hers. That afternoon he had been wearing gloves; tonight his hands were bare, and she had the shocking realization that she wanted to feel his hands on her.

"Why do you fear this dream, Isabella?"

She wanted to sleep, not talk, but Black would not hear of it. He kept prodding her until she answered.

"Because he is there, of course. Death. I feel him as I have always felt him. I haven't dreamed of him in months. I thought I was cured, but then, this afternoon, the dream returned. It is him in the room with me. Him I feel watching me."

"It is only a dream," he whispered soothingly. "Go to sleep, Isabella. And have no fear that Death will come to mar your dreams, for I shall keep him away."

SHADOWS FROM THE FIRELIGHT danced and flickered along Isabella's décolletage and shoulders. Like a lover's tongue, the forked flames licked their way across her skin, and Black found himself entranced by the erotic image— wondering what it would be like—after all this time— to feel his tongue gliding along her luminous flesh, just like the shadows.

Isabella feared the dark and shadows, two entities that bound him. He was at home amongst the shadows and mist. After tonight, he wondered if Isabella would understand that. Could accept it.

It had been years since he had made friends with the dark. In the end it had been the only way to bury his past.

To grieve for what he had lost, and for what he had received, no matter how he had tried to refuse it.

Society thought they knew him, but the truth was, they didn't know a fraction of what made up the Earl of Black. He had always thought Isabella a kindred soul. They had both been wronged. Both left alone to face the tragedies that had befallen them. He had believed that Isabella clung to shadows, just as he did. But he was wrong. Isabella was light. With her milk-white skin she was everything ethereal and he wanted to partake of it. But her response to his kisses was something altogether different. Sultry. Impassioned, dark and comforting, her passion was the sort that would encompass a man. Black wanted to bury himself in it, to feel his body encased by her response to him.

That afternoon in the carriage had shaken him to his core. There had been vibrancy—life—crackling in the atmosphere. The air had been charged, heavy, and he had sat there in utter silence, absorbing it. Never had he felt that static pull to another human being. It was Isabella who drew him. Like a moth to the flame, the tides and the moon, birth and death—they were intrinsically wound together, two spirits who had at last found their way to one another.

He was thirty-three years old and had lived long enough, had seen enough to know that what had happened in the carriage was beyond mere lust. That moment of silence, the hum that vibrated between them had been an omen, a whisper of what was to come. The kiss had been but a prelude, a temptation of what they would find together.

Isabella would fear it. Instinctively he knew that. She feared what lay between them because she felt it every bit as strongly as he. Her passion simmered too close to the surface; he had felt it, heard it begging to break free when he deepened the kiss and brought her body up against his.

She hadn't known what to do with all that desire. But soon she would. And soon she would have no regret or guilt about sharing it with him.

Inevitable. He had spoken the truth to her. It was unavoidable. A certainty that he would have her, that he would introduce her to the pleasures to be found between man and woman.

One did not have to know a person for any length of time to be convinced of this. He believed that you could live with someone for twenty years or more and still not know them. One glance at Isabella—the meeting of their gazes—and he had known what sort of woman she was.

A sigh escaped her lips and her head tipped back, her eyes shut. He studied the delicate fluttering of lashes against pale cheeks. There was no fear in her now. Just a languid warmth he felt as he reached out and skimmed the backs of his fingers along her cheek. He watched her lashes flutter, then her eyes open. She yawned, covering her mouth with her hand.

There was no fear in those eyes. And the slow smile she gave him spoke of a dreamy lassitude that beckoned him closer.

"Sleep," he whispered as he took her hand and drew her down onto the chaise longue. She was malleable in his hold, and did not protest as he maneuvered her so that her head and shoulders lay on his lap. The silk of her gown draped over the settee. The firelight danced over the silk, making the dusky rose appear a pale copper. She was warm and soft in his lap, and her eyes closed, her lips parting on a slow breath.

"I shall stay with you, Isabella, and keep the shadows away."

Instantly she was asleep, and he gave in to temptation and freed a loose curl that was tumbling from its pin. Her hair was soft, like corn silk. Rubbing his fingers against the golden strands, he watched them tumble from his hand, only to land on her exposed shoulders.

Running his index finger along her shoulder, he traced the outline of the delicate bones, the winged tip of her collarbone. Her skin was smooth, like a pearl, and the same color. The texture was indescribable—like cream—he thought, and wondered what it would be like to lap at her. To see her lush lips part in pleasure.

How he wanted to hear the sound of her pleasure, to listen as her passion escalated. Higher and higher he would take her, winding her up until she grasped at him, pleaded with him—until her pants turned from little gasps to moans, to the feminine cries of release. And then he would bring her to the peak, finish her, pull back just enough to watch her as he listened to her come for him.

She would be beautiful in her passion. Wanton. And she would be his. He would not wait much longer to claim her. Every cell inside him screamed that he must protect her, that she was in some sort of danger, but what, he could not imagine. Who would wish to hurt her? Nonetheless, he heeded his instincts. They had always served him well. The one time he hadn't, disaster had befallen him. A woman had died. A woman he should have protected. He would not make the same mistake this time. Not with Isabella.

He would discover the author of this missive, would guard Isabella—and he would make her happy. Tonight, after he left her he would go to Sussex, and together they would investigate this House of Orpheus. Whatever web was being spun, Isabella, and perhaps Lucy, too, were being caught up in the silk.

In his father's time, the House of Orpheus had been an elitist occult club where secret initiation ceremonies and scandalous sexual rites had drawn the bored and debauched of London society. Black couldn't help but fear the same could be said for this new club. If Lucy had been drawn into the seduction, how soon would it be until Isabella followed in her cousin's footsteps? And if the club was connected to the missing relics? What sort of dangers were Isabella and Lucy involved in?

Gazing down at Isabella, he felt his chest tighten. She was so innocent, so afraid of the dark. He would keep her safe. He would not allow her to die. She would not become Death's next victim. She would not, he reminded himself, become another Abigail Livingstone.

THROUGH THE HAZE of smoke, the man who called himself Orpheus lounged back on a pile of silk pillows, basking in his creation.

Surrounding him were his minions, these disciples who were bored and jaded, and willing to part with their money for a chance to join his club. The House of Orpheus... He smiled at the nonsense of it all. Fools, all of them. But for a taste of exotic decadence—for opium and absinthe, illusion and sex and the magical, mysterious ceremonies he staged—they paid him for a chance to experience his decadent, debauched world. A world where secrets were encouraged, and the dark and the occult were embraced. It was a world for the hedonist, and for those who felt the world above this club had nothing new to offer. It was sin and passion, darkness mixed with pleasure. It was ecstasy and power.

How easy it had been to get what he needed, which like any man who had dredged himself up from the stews, needed—money. How depraved and desperate the elite of London were. How damn willingly they had parted with their money for only a forbidden taste. And now, each week, they came back to him, paying to be entertained, to be corrupted by sin.

Despite their masked identities, he could pick out every person, their names, titles and the predilections they enjoyed. Through them he could move through the ton, to hear and see his enemies. For the House of Orpheus was no mere secret society—no, its mission was far more sinister then the pleasure it promised.

The smooth shining onyx he cradled so protectively was cool in his palm. He could hear it whispering to him, as if it were a living, breathing thing. The pendant was now warm, vibrating. With his thumb he shaped it, feeling its oval outline and the raised gold lettering in the tongue of the ancient Hebrews.

Did the Brethren Guardians know it was missing? He smiled, thinking of Black, Sussex and Alynwick frantically searching the city for their priceless relic. Let them come, he silently hoped, for it was his greatest wish. Retribution. Annihilation, utter destruction.

Let them come....

"It is time, Orpheus."

Nodding, he acknowledged his servant. It had been this longtime servant who had helped him infiltrate the Brethren Guardian, through a green-eyed minx who had so easily fallen for the illicit taste of pleasure.

Rising from his darkened corner, he slipped his gilded mask over his face and rapped his staff against the marble floor. The conversation of his minions faded, leaving only the sound of excited breaths. The weekly dues had already been collected and now the assembled dilettantes waited breathlessly for the secret rites to progress and the planned debaucheries of the evening to begin.

Raising his arms above his head, he repeated the words of Orpheus. His minions joined him...

"Now you have died and now you have come into being. O thrice happy one, on this same day. Tell Persephone that Orpheus has released you."

He had died, and now he was being reborn into a power that would shape the world, and inside his pocket, he felt the pendant vibrant with excitement. He would take back what was his. He would create a new world, and never again would he die.

CHAPTER EIGHT

Alone in the forest, I turned in circles, realizing at last that I was lost. An owl hooted in the distance, and the full moon hung low over the trees, which were bereft of leaves. The path was thick with mud, the wind cold and harsh, howling through the grove.

I was in Death's world now. Summoned by an unknown force—a need so pressing and compelling in the deepest part of night. That force had been Death, beckoning me silently, pulling at my body until I obeyed his unspoken command.

He was an ever-present entity in my mind, my memory—and I fear for my soul. How could I forget him, the way he whirled me around the dance floor? How could I forget his kiss? I couldn't. My body couldn't. My body ached for more—it longed for Death and his dark embrace.

How sweetly Death had enslaved me. How quickly he had lured me here, to his domain, where most mere mortals feared to tread. With Death's kiss I had been consumed. I was consumed now, awaiting his arrival.

Even if I desired to run from him, I could not, for my feet would not move, my dancing slippers caked with mud, glued me to the spot. The earth surrounding me was dark, quiet. Between the veil of the living and the dead, the

*mortals slumbered as midnight drew near, and
I awaited my fate along with all the other souls
whom Death would claim this night.*

*Death would come for me tonight. I knew
that. I felt his presence as it clung to the grove.
I smelled him, a scent now so familiar to me. I
should be weeping, fearing the inevitable, but as
I waited for Death my heart began to race, my
body, which had been cold, was now warming
at just the thought of feeling Death pulling me
into his intoxicating embrace.*

When would Death come for me?

*The wind gusted once more—violently, send-
ing a rustle of leaves swirling, circling, like whirling dervishes. They brushed against my face,
clung to my hair, and I raised my arms to fling
them away. And then as suddenly as the vicious
wind came, it stilled, and my arms fell away,
and there, at the opposite end of the path which
I stood upon was a white horse—riderless. It
stomped and snorted, tossing its head up and
down, as its giant hoof pawed at the ground.
And then with one final snort, it began to run—
to me.*

*Where was Death? Would he not save me?
Would he not gather me in his arms and protect
me?*

*He had kissed me once—so kindly, so tenderly,
that I knew there was warmth in him. He was
not cold and callous, but quiet. Reserved. Yet
inside him, I glimpsed a soul, something I never
dared dream Death would possess. But it was
there, in his kiss, in the way his arms wrapped
around me and embraced me.*

Where was he now? How could he lure me

here, only to sacrifice me to the bounding hooves and the horse that was intent upon trampling me?

Unable to do anything but stare in horror at the beast who would run me down, I stood frozen, the warmth leaving my body, as cold dread filled me. The moment of my doom was here, and I was alone. Death had tricked me. He tempted me into his forest, even though I knew that good girls should not be tempted. But Death was beautiful, his hands soft, his mouth against mine even softer. No mere mortal could refuse such beauty—the promise of such sublime pleasure.

I had wanted that dance. The kiss, and the embrace that was certain to follow. I had wanted Death. How foolish I was to believe in him. What a fool I was, for I had shoved aside my morality for one night with Death, and he deceived me. Abandoned me.

And now, because I was sinful in thought and action, I was going to die. This very night, in Death's forest beneath the crushing hooves of Death's mount.

The earth thundered, and the sound of the horse's powerful hooves echoed in my ears. My last thought as I felt the heat of the horse, the mist from his muzzle as it bore down upon me, was of Death, and how beautiful he was. How, if given the chance once more, I would still choose that dance. That kiss.

In those last seconds, I closed my eyes and waited for the inevitable, and then it happened. Time stood still as the horse's heaving snorts shattered through the thundering ground. He was upon me, and I was thrown up, and the pain… it did not come as I thought it would.

*I was floating, and when I finally found the
bravery to open my eyes, I saw that Death had
claimed me, swooped me up in his arms and he
was carrying me away. Death, how beautiful he
was. How welcoming...*

*I clasped his cheeks in my hands and opened
my mouth to his. His pale eyes, those mesmerizing blue eyes with sea-green flecks, watched me.
I shivered in awareness, understood that look.
There was no going back.*

*"Wherever you are," he whispered as he low-
ered his head to claim my mouth. "I will find
you..."*

The ringing of bells pierced the dream, and Isabella
came awake with a start. The bells were the chimes of the
library clock, the hour midnight. She was not alone. She
sensed that. And when she opened her eyes, she discovered she was sitting bolt upright on the chaise longue. Her
gaze flew to the right, to the wall behind where she sat,
only to see that she truly was not alone. As the twelfth
bell of midnight sounded, Isabella saw in the reflection
of the mirror, the man in her dreams—Death. It was not
Death, but Black.

She wanted to scream, but the sound would not come
out. It was midnight, the moment when darkness was at
its height and light at its lowest ebb. The exact moment
when the mortal realm was linked to the other worlds.
It was the time of day associated with chaos, the under-
world and Death—and the creatures of darkness were
most potent. It was also a time when it was most dangerous to look in the mirror in case the devil looks back at
you.

And, dear God, the last chime had barely faded and
here she was, gazing into a mirror, and seeing Black

standing there, watching her, his pale eyes so reminiscent of the man in her dreams. The hero in her story.

"You've had a dream."

The sound of his voice broke through her silent horror, and she allowed herself to fall back against the settee. "I did."

"I tried to wake you when I realized it, but you couldn't hear me."

"Did I say anything?" Oh, how she would be utterly horrified if he had heard her sleep talking.

He shook his head, and came to sit beside her. He was sitting far too close, but his warmth, and the security she sensed in him, were welcoming.

"Tell me about it?" he asked. "Perhaps it might help to share what frightens you."

"It was just a dream."

"Not the same one from the afternoon?"

"No, as a matter of fact, it wasn't." It was a completely different dream, much more sensual. Even now she was trembling, remembering what it had felt like to succumb to Death—Death who looked so very much like Black.

But how? she wondered. When she had started her story, she had never met Black. In her mind Death was already formed; he possessed those sea-colored eyes, and the black hair. Death was sophisticated and enigmatic, just like Black. But Death had been a figment of her imagination, and the earl…he was a flesh-and-blood man.

Black stood near the settee, watching her with unreadable eyes. "I hear a carriage approaching. It should be your cousin."

Listening, Isabella could hear nothing above the din of her pounding heart. She was overwrought, was all. It was the effects of the séance and waking up to the chimes of midnight. Her imagination was running away with her, aided by her fatigue. She had always been rather imaginative and excitable. She wasn't superstitious, she reminded herself. Discovering Black looking back at her in the mirror at the stroke of midnight meant nothing. He was not the devil and he was most certainly not…Death.

"Will you be all right if I leave you now?"

"Oh, yes. Yes, of course. My lord, I cannot thank you enough, and must apologize for being such a reprehensible host. I was very poor company this evening."

"You needn't apologize."

"Oh, but I must," she said as she rose from the chaise longue. "I've been asleep for more than an hour."

"An hour and a half, actually," he said with a grin. A grin that played havoc with her mind—and body.

"Again, my apologies, my lord."

He stepped closer and caught her face in his hands. He looked deeply down into her eyes and watched her carefully as his thumbs stroked the apples of her cheeks. "If you would apologize, Isabella, then let it be like this."

His mouth caught hers in a slow, sensual melding of lips. His tongue slipped past and slowly danced with hers. It was a languid, lulling kiss, as if he had all the time in the world to savor her lips.

Just when she grew impatient, he deepened it, let his hand fall from her face to the back of her head where his fingers raked through her hair and anchored her for his kiss, which was now harder, more demanding than coaxing.

Her moan shattered the quiet, and did something to him. He was no longer controlled, but needy, frantic in the way his mouth sought hers. She gripped his waistcoat, pulling at him, bringing him closer. Their bodies brushed together, and she gasped, feeling his hardness pressed against her, while he groaned, pushing insistently against the softness of her belly.

The kiss lingered, slowed, until it was a seductive dance and Isabella clung to him, weak and needy, refusing to think of him leaving her in such a state.

"Black," she purred, kissing him, meeting his mouth with her own urgent one.

"I want you," he rasped as he brought her up close and held her tight. "I want to keep kissing you, to carry you up to your room and love you until the sun comes up, and then I want to make love to you and watch as the dawn creeps across the windowpanes, and over your body."

She felt wild with need, and she clutched at Black's hair as he kissed her neck and whispered those words between rasping kisses.

"Come to me," he coaxed as his hand slid up her waist, to cup her breast. "Lie down for me and let me see you, taste you," he whispered before curling his tongue behind her earlobe. "Let me be a part of you."

The sound of the front door opening shattered their embrace, and with a groan, they reluctantly parted, attempted to school their breathing, when Black reached for her once more and kissed her, softly, reverently, before sweeping his tongue inside her mouth one last time. When he pulled back, he cupped her chin and brushed his thumb along her kiss-swollen lips.

"No apologies, for there was nowhere on earth I would have rather been tonight than here with you. Good night, Isabella."

She reached for him, and he half turned, glancing at her over his shoulder. "I meant every word, Isabella. I want you to come to me, or let me come to you. Think on it," he whispered. "Please."

"Oh, good evening." Lucy came to a halt just inside the doorway. Her gaze volleyed back and forth between Isabella and Black. Releasing her hold on the earl, Isabella watched as he passed by Lucy, mumbling good-night. With a slow smile, Lucy took in Isabella's disheveled hair and gown and smiled widely as she half turned to watch Black's departure.

"Why, Isabella Fairmont—" Lucy beamed incredulously "—you have, at last, been properly seduced!"

BOOT STEPS RANG on the marble tile of Sussex House, echoing off the high walls and domed ceiling. Inside the massive ducal town house, the servants were quiet and still above stairs. Only Hastings, Sussex's butler, remained awake. It was well past midnight, but Black knew the duke would still be awake.

Black followed the young butler down the long gallery hall to the end where the glass conservatory lay dark and quiet. To the right was Sussex's study. Outside, the wind had risen, and Black could see the swaying of tree limbs beyond the conservatory windows. The moon, which had been bright and full while he was at Highgate, was now obscured by thick cloud cover.

From deep inside the study, a log consumed with fire could be heard sparking and crackling—the sound beckoning one to pull up a chair and gaze into the dancing flames. The door was opened a crack, and Black saw the duke seated in a wingback chair cradling a glass of whiskey as he stared into the hearth.

"Your Grace," Hastings called after clearing his throat. "The Earl of Black wishes an audience."

"Send him in. I'll see to the lamps and locks, Hastings. You may retire for the evening."

"Very good, Your Grace."

When the butler had disappeared down the dark corridor, Black let himself into Sussex's den and firmly shut the door behind him. The duke did not bother to look up from his contemplation of the fire, and Black went to the sideboard and poured himself a drink. A double. He needed it.

The last two hours had been a lesson in torture. How he had managed not to awaken Isabella and ravage her was beyond him. He'd been sorely tempted on more than one occasion. Only the letter, and the mysterious House of Orpheus, had been motivation enough to sever his attentions from Isabella's lovely sleeping form.

"I suppose you're here about this séance business," Sussex muttered. "Damn frightening seeing Miss Fairmont worked into such a state. I never thought she was the flighty sort, but she certainly was terrified."

"Miss Fairmont has an unpleasant past," he answered as he lowered his tall frame into a chair and made himself comfortable. He, more than any other soul on earth, knew that. He knew more about Isabella than she suspected, and if she ever found out, she would be mortified. In just one day, he was already learning how her mind worked. She would at first be frightened by the idea of someone having private knowledge of her life in Yorkshire, and then she would be humiliated—worried that perhaps he knew of her *unfortunate event*—which, of course, he did. But what she didn't know was, he had witnessed it. Had been a part of it. It was that moment that tethered him so securely to her. His life before that was gone, faded into nothing. He had started living that night as a wintry gale blew into Whitby Harbor. It had been her, Isabella, who had made him look at his life through new eyes.

"What is in Miss Fairmont's past that makes her so jittery, then?"

The duke's question pulled Black out of his reverie and the memories of that night, the sound of the waves crashing violently against the shore and the rocks. The howl of the wind, and the stinging of the sea mist on his face. The frigid waters surrounding him.

"She is not a fan of the dark," he answered, "or the speculative nonsense our Miss Fox was so successful at conjuring up."

"You certainly timed your entrance perfectly. How did you know where to find her? I myself just happened upon them leaving Stonebrook, with nothing but Lucy's maid for a chaperone, if you can believe it. Reckless, silly girl," Sussex snarled. "She has no bloody notion of what could happen to her."

"So you accompanied them?"

Sussex glared at him, his gray eyes the most turbulent he had ever seen them. "Of course. What would you have me do? Let them travel to Highgate alone? And then what? There was no telling what might have happened to them out there. They may have been robbed, or…worse."

"No, you needed to be there. I beg your pardon, but it seems I am not myself tonight, either."

Sussex blew out a ragged breath as he let his head fall back against the chair. He was looking up at the ceiling as he said Lucy's name aloud. "If this is what love feels like, then it's no damn wonder most rational men fear the state." He glanced at him, his eyes troubled. "Damn me, Black, what the devil is the chit about? This is not some fashionable passing interest that Lucy is dabbling in. This…*obsession* with the dead and conjuring spirits is damn unsettling. I can't fathom why it has attracted her so."

"Why don't you have a look at this."

Leaning forward, Black pressed a folded news clipping into his hand.

"What's this?"

Sipping his whiskey, Black gazed into the fire. "Something of interest, I believe."

He waited in the silence as Sussex read the clipping. It was eight months old, and he'd found it hidden away beneath Lucy Ashton's mattress.

"A man found dead in a burned-out house in Bloomsbury. What of it?"

"This was hidden inside the paper."

Fishing in his pocket, Black handed him a gold coin, an identical one to the coin that Sussex had found in Lucy's reticule—not to mention a calling card, with the image of the House of Orpheus embossed on it. Sussex sucked in a breath, and at last met Black's gaze.

"Miss Fairmont?"

Black shook his head, suddenly unable to look at the man who had been his friend for years. "Miss Ashton."

"Like hell," Sussex snarled. He jumped up, his glass tumbling to the carpet, the golden liquid spilling onto the hardwood floor. "You bastard! You were nosing about Lucy's room."

"And Isabella's," he drawled. "And if you must know, I find myself feeling quite dirty for it, but there it is. Isabella dozed off on the chaise longue and I set about searching the house, not only because you had showed me the coin that was in Lucy's reticule, but because I received this during dinner."

Snatching the missive out of his hand, Sussex noted the familiar seal, the same image that was imprinted on the coin and the calling card. After he read the letter, he slunk back into his chair.

"Damn it, what has she gotten herself into?"

"I don't know, but I'd wager the reason she keeps trying to summon the dead at séances is because that dead man had a connection to her. A rather personal one, I believe."

Sussex's face went molten, and in a most uncharacteristic moment of utter loss of control, picked up the glass and threw it against the mantel, smashing the delicate pieces into tiny diamonds that littered the floor.

"Goddamn it!" he swore, and Black held his tongue, letting the unsettling information sink in. If it had been in Isabella's room, Black couldn't fathom what he'd do.

"She loved him—must still love him," Sussex muttered as he wiped his hands over his face. "That is why she is so damn reckless. So damn persistent in going to séances. She actually believes she might conjure his ghost!"

Sussex's question needed no answer. They both knew why Lucy was suddenly so ardently pursuing the supernatural.

"And that's why she can't see me," Sussex murmured. "Christ, I'm competing with a ghost."

What could he say? There were no words to comfort his friend. The woman he loved did not love him—she loved another.

Sussex paced a path before the hearth. He was lost in the turmoil of Black's discovery and Black said nothing, only watched as the wheels of Sussex's mind turned. Finally he stopped and leveled him with a clear stare.

"And what has this dead man to do with the House of Orpheus? What does he or Lucy have to do with this letter that was sent to you? Is there any correlation to the Templar artifacts?" he asked, one question after another falling out of his mouth, as Sussex tried to make sense of it all.

"I don't know. But one thing vexes me, however, and that is the purpose of the letter. If their intent was to harm either Isabella or Lucy, then why give me notice? Surely they would know I would follow, if nothing more than to see that they were unharmed."

"Perhaps," Sussex snarled, "someone has reasoned out you have developed a tendre for Miss Fairmont and therefore hoped that you would set out for Highgate and wring her neck for being so damn reckless, and thereby save them the trouble of doing her in themselves."

"You've thought this through, Sussex. May I ask if you've thought of wringing lovely Lucy's neck?"

"All damn night and now more than ever after discovering this clipping. Where did you find it by the way?"

"Under the mattress."

He snorted. "Damn women, they're all the same. *The mattress.* Most predicable place to hide something."

Shrugging, Black took another sip of his whiskey. "It saved me time, Sussex. In the end, it was all I found. There was nothing in Isabella's room, save a journal."

"Did you read it?"

Black paused, and allowed himself a moment to formulate his answer. "Yes," he lied. "There was nothing in it."

He had found the key for the journal; it was hanging from a bracelet of jet. He'd opened the lock and stared blankly down at the pages. It was such an invasion of Isabella's privacy. It was a book with her most sacred of thoughts. Her story. He had been so tempted, so very much wanted to read it, to know her as intimately as she knew herself. What he had read that night at Stonebrook's ball was naught but a tease. He had desperately wanted more—still did. But in the end, he had shut the book, allowing her to keep her secrets.

If he thought that Isabella had anything to do with this, with the House of Orpheus, which may even be connected to the missing Templar artifacts, he would have bared her secrets. But he didn't. All evidence pointed to Lucy, and the mysterious man in the newspaper clipping.

"So it seems it's Lucy then," Sussex murmured, and Black heard the pain in his voice. "There is no denying that she has some sort of connection to the club. At the very least she knows of it."

"I would not have brought this to you if I thought there was another way."

"No," Sussex mumbled as he picked up the clipping and studied it. "You were right to. We have a task to do, and that is to find and protect the chalice and the pendant."

"I'll be having Stonebrook, as well as Lucy and Isabella, to dine with me tomorrow. I thought you might come along, make it feel as though it was just a dinner party. I was hoping…" He coughed discreetly. "I was hoping that perhaps you might find time to privately speak to Lucy. See what she knows."

"Oh, I will be there, and you may be assured that I will corner the little baggage as soon as may be." Sussex glanced up as Black rose from the chair. "You might consider inviting Wendell Knighton. My gut says that there is something with him. I know we've no evidence of it, but it's best to have him close, observe his behavior and such. As there is a lodge meeting tomorrow night, we can make the dinner appear more of a celebratory fete for his initiation. No one will be the wiser. I especially do not wish to arouse Stonebrook's suspicions. He's old, but not senile. He'll catch on if he suspects anything."

"Agreed." Sussex's gray eyes pierced him. "There is still the matter of the letter. It's strange, how did the writer know that Isabella would be scared witless by your entrance? All that talk of death, it scared the devil out of the poor girl."

"I have no idea," he murmured. "But I intend to find out."

"How much does Isabella know of your past?"

Black's heart dropped like a stone, plummeting to his feet. "I don't know. I had hoped nothing."

"I think that's it, Black. Either you have gotten too close to Miss Fairmont, or she has become too close to you. Either way, someone wants you separated from each other. Why? It can only be speculated upon at this point, but I think it's safe to say that someone is illuminating your past for Miss Fairmont's edification. Someone doesn't want you getting close to her."

"Then we must find this person before he or she can ruin me in Isabella's eyes."

"I'll begin with Lucy. I suggest you commence investigating that letter."

"I believe I will—tonight. Hopefully Miss Fox will still be awake and eagerly expecting another specter from the grave."

CHAPTER NINE

"WAIT HERE, I won't be long."

Black left his coachman and carriage parked outside the massive iron gates of Highgate Cemetery and made his way across the gravel paths to where the small cottage stood amongst the barren trees. A soft light beckoned, and he realized that the lamp was on in the room where Miss Fox had created her spectacle just a few hours before.

Determined to ferret out this business of the letter, he walked toward the cottage, his boots crunching the gravel beneath his resolute footsteps. He was not in a good mood, and certainly in no mood to indulge an eccentric such as Miss Alice Fox.

Stopping, he stared up at the dilapidated cottage, deciding which was the best way to enter it. Certainly nothing as benign as a knock on the door would do. Not at this hour. No, something far more supernatural should be employed.

Trying the back window, he found it locked. Smashing it seemed beneath him, and crawling through the shattered glass with his rather large body a bit too daunting, so he made his way to the back, to the door that he had carried Isabella out of. Lifting the latch, he tried it, smiling triumphantly when the lever raised and the door squeaked opened.

He could hear voices inside, a female and a male. A laugh, followed by a cackle. Miss Fox, it seemed, was entertaining and seemed to be in rather high spirits.

Slamming the door, he waited for the response.

"Who's there?"

He did not answer, but reached for the window and rattled the glass until he heard the scraping of chairs against the hardwood.

"Damn me, Alice, it's one of your ghosts," her male companion squeaked. "I knew it were bad to wake the dead."

"Oh, shut up, Albert," Alice hissed. "There's no bloody such thing as ghosts. 'Ow many times do I have t' tell ye that?"

For added effect, Black rattled the window once more and dragged the chain of his pocket watch along the glass, giving the effect that Miss Fox had found herself a visitor who came rather encumbered.

"Is that chains I hear?" Albert crowed. "God save us, Alice, nofing but criminals owr buried in chains."

"I told you, there ain't no such thing as ghosts rising from the grave."

Black saw Alice through the dim light. She'd taken hold of a broom and was gripping the handle tightly in her fists. Albert, a thin little scarecrow of a man, huddled behind her.

"Get the lamp," Alice ordered, "and me pistol out the drawer."

"Whot's a pistol going to do, the intruder's already dead?"

If Black were in a more sporting mood, he would have made a low moan and rattled his pocket watch once more, but he was done with this farce. He wanted answers and he wanted them now.

Stepping out of the shadows, he heard them both squeak as they saw him. Albert, the fool, made the sign of the cross and Alice, the more sturdy of the pair, lunged at his vitals with the broom handle.

"Mistress Fox," he drawled as he pulled the broom

from her hands and snapped the handle in two before tossing the splintered wood aside. "We have some unfinished business."

Albert's eyes were large as saucers. What he saw in the shadows, Black could not tell, but Albert crossed himself again and ran for the cottage door, leaving Alice all alone and quite at his mercy.

"You," she spat through narrowed eyes as he emerged from the shadows and into the light.

"Yes, me. You didn't think you'd seen the last of me, did you?"

"Whot do you want?"

"Answers."

Black walked into the small parlor where Alice had held her séance. On the table where the planchette had once rested was a bottle of gin and a bag of coins. On the table the coins were spread out, and a deck of cards lay in disarray.

"Your evening has been profitable I see," he commented as he took a chair and seated himself.

"Why 'ave you come back 'ere?" she asked suspiciously.

"Nothing too terribly difficult. I merely want the truth. Who put you up to this tonight?"

"Put me up to whot? I fleece the fancy with my séances all the time. Tonight was nofing special."

"Forgive me if I disagree. You put on a phenomenal show, so lifelike that one poor visitor was rather alarmed that you had, indeed, magically produced Death."

She chuckled. "Those fancy ladies always are so bleedin' soft and easily discomposed."

"You intentionally frightened my companion, Miss Fox, and I am not disposed to believe that you are that clever. Nor do I believe that you were successful in conjuring up Death." He fixed her with a cold glare. "I want to know how you planned it, and who put you up to it."

"I don't have to answer ye," she snapped. She reached for her money, and Black held her by the wrist. The pressure of his gloved hand was sufficient enough to send alarm to Alice's eyes.

"You may not have to answer me, Miss Fox, but I assure you Scotland Yard might be interested in your shenanigans. Fleecing aristocrats is a felony."

"Bah," she grumbled. "It's not."

"When you are very well acquainted with the chief of police, anything can be a felony. Am I making myself clear, Miss Fox?"

"Why…yer blackmailin' me."

"Call it strenuously persuading you. It sounds so much more polite."

"Told me you were a tricky bastard, they did. Said you would catch on if I wasna careful."

"Did they? I'm flattered they remarked on my mental prowess."

"Said ye were as sly and devious as the devil, they did."

"I grow tired of this game, Miss Fox," he growled. "Who told you?"

"The ones whot hired me to do the séance," she replied flippantly. "I don't know the names. I didn't ask. I got paid by envelope this mornin', and that was all right by me. Names 'ave no place in me business. Only cold hard coin."

"Let us start at the beginning, shall we?" he said, growing impatient. "Who came to you?"

"No one did. There was a note, taped ta me door there—" she pointed to the front of the cottage "—'bout three days ago, it was. I was to perform a séance for a fashionable lady and her companion. I was to make it look as though Death were come for the lady. But then, yesterday, I received another note saying a gent would be arriving, and I was to make Death 'imself appear with his arrival—I suppose you were the gent?"

He nodded and motioned for her to finish the tale.

"The lady, the note said, had to believe it was Death in the room. And that's the truth of it. I know nofing else about it."

"Do you have the letter still?"

"I burnt them when the fashionable lady and her maid left. The deal was done and I don't make it a habit ta leave incriminatin' evidence laying about."

"Damn it," he thundered. Striking the table in frustration, the coins that had been lying atop the scarred wood bounced and scattered on the floor.

"'Ere now," Alice cried, "there's no reason for that. I earned that money fair and square." Alice dropped to her knees and began picking up the coins. Black heard her breath catch, then saw her eyes go wide as she looked up at him from the edge of the table.

"That cuff of yours," she said as she motioned to his white shirt sleeve that had edged out from beneath his jacket. "Let me see it."

Black glanced at his gold cuff link. "What do you want it for?"

"Let me see it."

Placating her, he pulled the link from the buttonhole of his shirt sleeve and passed it to her.

"Yes," she muttered as her fingers skated over the raised etching of a compass and square. "Your cuff link 'as the same symbols as the letter that was taped ta me door. I thought 'em odd, then. There's somefing rather strange about 'em."

"The Masonic symbols, you mean?"

"Aye, and the same numbers, too, 128."

His lodge number was 128. Every Masonic lodge had its own chapter number. Damn it, someone from within his own lodge had sent that letter, or, he thought, someone who had access to the official lodge letterhead could have written the note. Only three people did. *Lucy*...Stonebrook was high enough up in the lodge to have official letter-head. As a third degree, or Master Mason, Stonebrook might very well keep Masonic stationery at home, in his study.

"Thank you, Miss Fox, your information has been invaluable."

She handed him his link back and he pulled a few quid from his pocket and placed it with the other coins she had picked up. She glanced at him, her head cocked to the side.

"The letter says that Death 'as a habit of following you."

"Did it indeed?"

"It said it wouldna be too 'ard for the young lady to believe you was Death."

"That's preposterous, Miss Fox, because if I were Death, I would have taken your soul on the spot for causing such trauma to Miss Fairmont."

"Yer a dark one," she whispered as she backed away. "No one needs ta be a soothsayer ta know that."

"That is quite enough, Miss Fox. I've had my fill of you and your caterwauling about the supernatural tonight."

"Does the lady know ye killed yer brother, and yer own mother?"

"That is more than enough," he snarled through clenched teeth, alarmed that this person might know of his less than stellar family history.

"I'd wager that pretty piece wouldna allowed ye to carry 'er out of 'ere like a knight in shinin' armor if she knew it was ye that drove yer fiancée to her death."

"You've learned much about me, Miss Fox. I'm impressed. But possessing certain information can be dangerous. You do understand, don't you?"

"I understand yer a blackguard and someone who is playin' dark-and-dangerous games. No doubt that young woman will be yer next victim."

"You will hold your tongue and keep your piece if you wish to continue with this charade of yours, Miss Fox. If I hear that you have spoken of me, or my visit here tonight, I will not hesitate to exact revenge."

And strangely, she nodded and backed away, all the while crossing herself. He smiled, and she reached for the cross she wore around her neck.

"I wouldn't put your faith in such trinkets, Miss Fox. Death, I'm quite certain, is impervious to such things. He's heard every prayer known to man, and seen many tears. I doubt seeing your cross would prevent him from taking what is owed him. Good night, madam."

As he strolled out of the parlor and opened the door of the cottage, he heard Alice Fox's voice, shaking with fear.

"Devil!" she hissed, and he laughed while closing the door.

Alice Fox would keep her tongue quite firmly in her mouth, with her lips shut tightly. He would make certain of that.

With the candelabras lit and placed at perfectly measured intervals down the long length of the mahogany table, Death studied me over the rim of his goblet of wine, while firelight cast part of his face in shadow.

He had brought me to his home, where I was a most pampered guest. Every pleasure was catered for, brought to me by unseen servants. His house was richly furnished, decorated in voluptuous jewel tones done in silk and velvet. Cushions and pillows were scattered on the floor, resembling something out of a sultan's harem. The carpets were thick and soft, and the furnishings dark shades of walnut. The stone hearths were huge, majestic in their size, and lit with a fire that crackled with heat and the smell of pine and cedar. On the table in a tall-footed silver bowl, fruit was piled high, spilling over the sides—such an exotic assortment—pomegranates, figs, quince and grapes. Oh, the grapes! Lush and round and the deepest shade of purple I had ever known. The cluster was full, loaded with fruit as it cascaded down the side of the bowl. I felt my mouth watering as I gazed upon them. I had never had grapes. They were as forbidden to me as the apple from the Tree of Knowledge had been to Eve. I had never seen such decadence, for it was late autumn and the contents of this fruit bowl must have been imported. At great expense.

But then he was Death. And Death could take whatever he wished.

Casting my gaze away from the beckoning fruit, I took in my surroundings, awed once more by what my eyes saw.

It was like a castle from a fairy tale, except there was not an air of innocence in this room. It was heavy with the ambience of sensual decadence. It spoke of forbidden passion and reckless temptation. There was a thick blanket of sensuality that shrouded the room, and even I, an innocent, could perceive it—wanted to reach out and grasp it, and bury myself in the cloak of pleasure and carnal sin.

In his domain, Death was even more imposing, more beautiful. He possessed an air of sexual danger, as if he would at any minute lunge at me and devour me as he had his dinner. Something told me that Death had a ravenous appetite, and that if I allowed it, I would be his next meal.

I could not help but glance at his hand that held the goblet, and stare at the ring that bore a gleaming black stone. He wore it on his index finger—silver and onyx, heavy and masculine. It was a ring that a great knight would wear—a prince of darkness. I could not stop thinking of that hand, bearing that ring, what it might look like against my flesh. As I drew my gaze away from his hand and toward his eyes, I noted the gleam that shone in that tempest-tossed gaze. He knew! Knew my impious thoughts, and his slow smile, so sensual and wicked, confirmed my suspicions.

As we sat in silence, me, in my bloodred satin gown, and Death, in his black velvet jacket, we were as opposite as any two souls could be. Yet there was a connection between us. An understanding that both seemed to understand and accept. There was a force pulling us together. We were incapable of denying it—denying each other. But he was Death, and I, a mere mortal.

"Why have you brought me here?" I asked, already knowing the answer to my question.

"You were lost in the woods—my woods. The time had come for you to die."

"Did I die then, in your arms?"

His stare flickered over me, and I felt the lingering heat of that impenetrable gaze on my throat, my bosom, which was so much exposed by my gown.

"No," he murmured as he set his goblet on the table. "You wept."

I could not remember weeping in his arms—if I had, it had been tears of relief that he had come for me. Not tears that were shed in fear.

"I could not bear it, to take your life when I could feel your warm tears against my cheeks."

"You spared me," I whispered. "You do have a soul."

His expression blackened, his gaze turning even more turbulent. "I am nothing but Death. I do not have a soul. No feeling. I do not know what it is to be human—to feel—to experience life and living."

"Then why am I still here?"

He sat back in his chair and steepled his fingers, his gaze staring, assessing, making me wish to squirm in my chair. "I want to know what it is to feel. I want to weep, to feel the warmth of tears on my cheeks."

"You want to be human."

His nod was brisk, almost imperceptible. "You will come to me for three nights, and tell me a story. If, during those three nights you succeed in making me weep, then I will release my claim upon you. If you fail, then you will remain here with me—for eternity."

What could I do? I had to accept. There was no alternative.

"But what sort of story do you wish to hear?" I asked.

His grin was slow, intoxicating. I watched as he slowly rose from his chair and walked lazily to where I sat. Then, he bent down, placed his hands on each arm of my chair, caging me. Lowering his head, he brushed his lips against my bosom, my throat and then my ear, where I could feel his breath, warm and scented of wine, whispering across my flesh. "I want to hear our story—the seduction of an innocent at the hands of the unyielding, unfeeling Lord Death."

"Oh, my heavens," Lucy gasped as she threw herself back onto the heap of pillows in a rather overly dramatic parody of a swoon. "Death is every woman's dream—so dark and intense, and utterly delicious."

She was rather fond of him, too, Isabella realized. His story had begun to consume her. She had stayed up last night writing, the words pouring from her pen in a stream of thought that had the power of water rushing through floodgates. Something had compelled her to write, then she had slept and had a most wonderful dream of Lord Black.

"But you still haven't given us your heroine's name. Oh, wouldn't it be wonderful to hear her name uttered in Lord Death's velvety voice as he was about to kiss her and have his wicked way with her?"

Frowning, Isabella glanced down at her journal. She had purposely not named her character because nothing felt right. More than once she had caught herself writing her own name and had scribbled it out.

"Well?" Lucy said with a giggle, "I for one would like to put in a special vote that you name her Lucy."

"Definitely not." She shuddered with dramatic flare. "I couldn't possibility write your name during a ravishment scene."

"What a spoilsport you are." Lucy laughed. "But, Issy, you must write more. I insist. Stay in this chamber all morning and write. And please, please make it a scene where Lord Death takes her in his arms and forces the most shocking embrace upon her person. Make him merciless in his pursuit of her."

Smiling, Isabella closed the cover of her journal and clicked the lock shut. "I shall try my best to please you."

Closing her eyes, Lucy let out a long sigh. "That was just mesmerizing, Isabella. How do you do it, when you've never even been kissed, hmm?"

Lucy was fishing again. She had pestered all night

after Lord Black had left, wanting to know what transpired between them. Isabella had denied everything, and Lucy, curse her, had not believed her.

"Is that what it was like last night, in the carriage with Lord Black sitting on the bench in brooding silence as he stared at you from beneath his black lashes? Was he like your Lord Death, watching you from beneath hooded eyes?"

"Lucy, don't be ridiculous," Isabella answered as she stood and rifled her brush through the tangles of her hair. She did not want Lucy to see her expression, or the high color in her cheeks.

"If not then, what about in the parlor? Did he capture and cage you and demand a kiss?"

"Lucy!"

As she rose from the pillows, Lucy's long red hair spilled over her shoulders as she sat forward, her green eyes glowing as she whispered, "Did Lord Black make you commit unspeakable acts on the parlor floor, Issy?"

Isabella flushed furiously and Lucy bounced on the bed. "Oh, he did! Tell me!"

"Lord Black is a gentleman," Isabella muttered. "It wouldn't be very gentlemanly if he were to take advantage of me in my own home, now, would it?"

"No, it wouldn't," Lucy admitted on a little pout. "But I daresay it would be vastly exciting."

"Lucy!"

"Oh, Issy, it is only you and I here. We can be honest with each other, can't we?"

Not about Black. Isabella couldn't even allow herself the truth when it came to how exciting it was to be in Black's company, and his kisses…exciting was not the right adjective to describe what havoc his lordship's mouth could have upon a woman.

No, Lucy must never discover how Black had nearly ravished her in the carriage and in the salon. As an innocent, Isabella was quite certain that *ravishment* was the only correct word to use for what Black had done to her.

He had robbed her of thought and speech. Had made her a slave to her own passions. In the darkness of night it had been thrilling, surrendering to the need that flooded her blood, but with the dawn of morning that thrill had ebbed into something more like shock. With a good night's sleep and a clear head this morning, Isabella was astounded that she had so readily released the reins of her control. Not once, mind, but twice.

"Oh, isn't passion wonderful?" Lucy said wonderingly.

"You wouldn't say that if you had been forced to live destitute because of it," she grumbled. In the reflection of the mirror, Isabella saw Lucy frown.

"I know your life was extremely hard, Issy, and I am truly sorry for what you had to endure. But really, do you believe that the sins of the parent become the sins of the child?"

"I do."

"Oh, good Lord, then I truly am cursed," Lucy moaned. "For my parents' sins were to be excruciatingly polite and…absent. I don't want that for my fate. I'd prefer to give myself up to a feverish ardor."

"Lucy, passion is all very well and I suppose it has its place in life, but nothing takes the place of security. There is no protection in passion. It is a volatile emotion that is ignited by a spark, erupts into a fireball of flame and then promptly explodes, leaving nothing but destruction in its wake."

"You certainly have a way with words. You've completely destroyed my image of passion."

"I simply speak the truth."

Lucy glanced at her. "I would rather walk through hell for the chance of experiencing passion than exist in a cold world with little affection."

"Because there is only a little spark between two people does not mean there cannot be affection."

"Is that it, then? You and your Mr. Knighton have a little spark of passion between you?"

Isabella felt the blood drain from her face. Oh, good Lord, she had not even given Wendell a passing thought all night. All she could think of was Black and the embrace, and his whispered words in the salon. How she had wanted more—to be consumed in a fireball of passion and lust.

What sort of woman was she? *Her mother's daughter,* came the reply, and it hurt. Oh, Lord, it hurt to have to acknowledge such a flaw. She was an inconstant woman, and she was mortified by what she had done. True, there was no formal offer from Wendell, and their courtship was just in the beginning stages, but he had intimated that he liked her very much, and Isabella had allowed herself to believe that perhaps Wendell might see her as a suitable wife. But last night…with Black. Oh, she had been selfish, and she had betrayed Wendell. Formal offer or not, she had been disloyal to him with another man.

"Issy, is that it? You've decided that your nice, if inattentive, Mr. Knighton will do because you want security, not passion, in your marriage?"

"Lucy, let it go."

"I can't, Issy," Lucy said as she punched a pillow. "I love you too well to see you make the mistakes my parents made. Their marriage was based on the same ideas that you have. Politeness. Companionship. After twenty-five years of marriage they were nothing but friends. There was not enough spark between them to light a match, let alone a fireball."

"I'm content with that. Not everyone has the constitution for such a marriage, but I believe I do."

"I don't. How can you be content with such an arrangement? How can you say you will be satisfied when you write with such yearning? No woman who writes of passion so beautifully could be content with a marriage that is anything less than a maelstrom of desire."

"How can you ask me that," she exploded, "when you've seen where I was forced to live? *How* I was forced to live and what my mother endured after she gave in to her reckless passions. Both my mother and I suffered because of her desire to experience passion and love. As I watched her destroy herself I vowed never to become a victim to base emotions. My mother's selfish desire to experience a man's touch, his physical affection, destroyed her, and in the process it ruined me. Do not look at me and say such things, Lucy, for in your heart, you know what my mother's wildness led me to."

Lucy paled and glanced away. Oh, yes, Lucy knew the truth of her *unfortunate event.* She would never dare say the words, for they were scandalous—the gravest of sins—but she knew even though Isabella had never told another soul the real truth.

"It always comes down to this, doesn't it? Our different outlooks."

Trying to give her comfort, Isabella smiled sadly. "Lucy, we come from two different worlds. Our worlds have shaped us into the women we are today. That can't be changed. But we can learn from each other. I can warn you to be more temperate in your search for passion, and you can occasionally remind me that it is quite all right to indulge in a most unseemly kiss in the parlor."

Lucy's smile brightened the room. "Oh, I knew it. You had the look of a woman who had been thoroughly kissed. I bet it was wonderful."

Nodding, Isabella admitted it was. "But it won't happen again. It made me realize that I didn't care for the reckless feeling it gave me." *Liar!* "In fact, it rather confirmed Mr. Knighton is the one I want."

"Really?"

"Yes. Really. Now, let us talk no more about this," Isabella said. Resting the brush back on the tray, she turned in her chair and watched as Lucy gazed out the bedroom window. She was pale today, with dark circles beneath her eyes. There was a sadness there that Isabella wished Lucy would speak of. But try as she might, her cousin remained steadfast in her refusal to talk of it. This discussion of passion had only made her more melancholy.

"How was the séance after I left?"

"Predictable," she said with a heavy sigh. "I vow, the most excitement was when Black showed up and we all thought him a specter."

Not a specter, Isabella thought. But Death.

"And the duke?"

Lucy groaned and fell back onto the bed, covering her head with the sheet. "I absolutely refuse to talk of His Grace. What a prig! Do you know," Lucy snapped as she shot up in bed and tossed the sheet aside, "he actually had the audacity to lecture me on the way home. In fact, he forced Sibylla to sit with the coachman for the better part of the ride so he could lecture me on proper ladylike decorum! Oh, the nerve of the man," she ranted as she slipped from the bed and paced the room. "Can you believe it? As if I would welcome such a lecture. And from him! Oh, he's insufferable," she seethed. "He absolutely ruined my night, and then…then—" She broke off and whirled around to face her. "Oh, Issy, after he was done lecturing me he sat back and glared at me and stated quite boldly that once I was his wife, he'd paddle my backside if I ever sought another séance. Imagine, being denied my hobby!"

"Imagine being a duchess," Isabella said.

"Oh, don't you smile like that, Issy. This is…this is absolutely *horrid*. I won't marry him! I told him so at once, and quite forcefully."

"And what did he say?"

"Oh, something very pompous and ducal. The dreadful man actually said that my opinions on the matter weren't of importance here. Imagine it, being married to such a man." She whirled on her then, and there was true fear in Lucy's eyes. "Issy, there is honestly not even the tiniest flare between us. Most especially on my part."

"That doesn't sound like the duke at all. I knew he was concerned for your safety, but from what you describe of him, he sounded…provoked."

"Oh, yes, he said that…that I would provoke a saint and such nonsense. But, Issy, I can't marry him. I don't even like him, and the way he insinuated himself into coming with us, why, the man was as stubborn as a bull."

"Did he kiss you…when he was provoked?"

Lucy froze, then her gaze dropped to the floor. "Yes. And it was perfectly vile."

"Oh."

"Yes, 'oh' is right."

"Well, I'm quite certain that your father will not force you to marry him if you don't wish it."

"Ha!" Lucy grumbled. "How little you know of Papa. He will positively salivate at the very thought of me being a duchess. You know, he's already thinking of how my son shall inherit not only the Stonebrook title but the title of his father. The very thought of being a man with two titles excites him beyond belief. To know that his grandson will be a marquis *and* a duke will definitely seal the deal, and then I will be whisked away and forced to live with a pious, passionless man for the rest of my days."

"Passionless?" Isabella questioned. How could that be, when the duke was so obviously smitten with her cousin? Isabella had seen him on more than one occasion staring at Lucy with fire and unrequited longing in his eyes.

"Yes, passionless," Lucy snapped. "A vicar would have kissed with better skill than the duke. It was like kissing a dead fish pulled out of the Thames."

"Oh, that does sound dreadful."

"Do not laugh, Issy. I am in no mood for it."

"I can see that."

"Oh, this weather. I hate autumn. It's raining and cold, and we will be forced to stay indoors all day which will do nothing to remedy my mood."

"It is rather gloomy, isn't it?" she answered as her gaze strayed to the window where lashes of rain pelted the window. "Not even a trifling drizzle, at least in that we could take a carriage ride."

"Well, I must get my mind off last night—and the duke. Sibylla has promised to find out where the next séance shall be, and I am determined to finish off a dress that I'm making."

"I think I shall write, then. Maybe this afternoon the weather will clear enough so that we might take some fresh air."

"Oh," Lucy moaned as she fell back onto the bed and covered her eyes with her arm. "I just realized something dreadful."

"And that is?"

"Do you think the duke will be at Black's tonight? I don't think I could face him again."

"Black's? Tonight?" She had all but forgotten.

Lucy lifted her arm and glanced at her. "You don't know? Black sent an invitation around this morning, and Papa accepted. It's all settled, we're dining with Black this evening."

"Oh." She had planned on never seeing him again. After last night, and her irresponsible behavior, she knew it was the only way. Any more time spent with the earl would be a hazard to her sanity—and her body. She'd had it all planned—avoid the earl and be free of temptation. How difficult would it be? He was a recluse after all.

"What are you going to wear?" Lucy asked. "I think I'll wear my purple silk. Purple tends to tone down my red hair. Sometimes when I wear purple I can even make myself believe my hair color is brown." Picking up a handful of red hair, Lucy groaned. "I loathe that I was cursed with red hair."

"You have gorgeous hair, Lucy," Isabella mumbled, trying to figure out how she was going to extricate herself from tonight's dinner. "And I don't see what it matters. Won't any of my gowns do?"

With an impish grin, Lucy jumped from the bed and reached for Isabella's hand. "Come with me, I have just the perfect thing."

"Lucy, really, I'm sure any one of the dozens of gowns my uncle has purchased for me will do to dine with the earl."

"Oh, Issy, just indulge me for once."

"Why am I suddenly worried by that very wicked twinkle in your eye?"

"Because you have no taste for adventure. Now, come along," Lucy said with a laugh as she dragged Isabella behind her.

CHAPTER TEN

She was beautiful reposed like this—sleeping innocently on a black velvet chaise longue. Her hair was unbound, the loose blond curls spilling over the velvet, a stark and arousing contrast.

He had come to her, to claim her, to feel her warm, pale flesh heat against his skin. His gaze tracked her pulse, the slow beating that gently pulsated in her neck. She smelled so good there, and her skin was always so soft—alive.

What was he waiting for? he wondered. She was there, in his library. This was his domain. His hour—midnight. His powers were at their greatest potency. How was it, this beautiful woman, a being of light and warmth, would walk alongside him, a creature of dark coldness?

He didn't know how, only knew that she intoxicated him. He was drunk with the ecstasy of desire. She wore a red dress, such a vibrant, deeply sensual color. It made her skin translucent, mesmerizing like moonlight on white flowers. He had watched her all night, mentally undressing her, imagining the pleasures to be discovered beneath that tight bodice.

He knew her body would be perfect, her breasts full and soft, the mound of her belly slightly raised, ideal for raining kisses upon. Her hips rounded—wide, perfect for his hands to mold and grasp. She would be lush beneath him, the softest, most decadent pillow he had ever laid his head upon.

Reaching out, he finally allowed himself to touch her, his hand smoothing along her shoulder, then sweeping across the swell of her breasts. She stirred, moved—and his fingers curled around the satin sleeve and tugged, lowering her bodice, exposing more of her.

Leaning forward, he nuzzled the valley of her breasts, inhaled the fragrance of her skin, licked the flesh that tasted faintly of perfume and salt— the taste of woman.

He had spared her once. He had tried to stay away, but fate always drove him to her. He could no longer resist. He had come to claim her—tonight.

Looming over her, he watched as her lashes fluttered and slowly rose. She was as beautiful now as she was that first night, when he had been poised above her, the color of her skin bluish, her body cold—lifeless in its portrait of death. Tonight, her skin was porcelain, her cheeks and the apex of her breasts crested with pink. She was warm—alive.

She was awake now, yet her eyes were still glistening with the remnants of sleep. With a dreamy smile she reached up and touched him, her fingertips skimming across his cheek.

"I was dreaming of you."

"Were you?"

She nodded and snaked her hands around his neck, her fingers raking through his hair. "Have you come to claim me finally?"

With his palm on her throat, he felt the flutter of her pulse in the center of his hand—he smelled

*her growing arousal, and he pressed forward,
brushed his mouth against hers and said, "Yes.
Finally. You will become Death's Bride."*

"My lord, will you wear the blue waistcoat this evening?"

Standing before the full-length looking glass, Black glanced at the silk waistcoat Billings held out to him. He saw in the reflection of the mirror that his color was high, and he wondered how long his butler had been standing there waiting for him to reply.

Poor old Billings, putting up with a master such as he. The man had to fulfill not only the duties of a butler, but a valet, and all while the master stood before the mirror reliving a highly erotic dream from the night before.

"Thank you, Billings, but I believe I'll take the gray with the silver shot through it."

"Very good, my lord."

Reaching for his cravat, Black tied the strip of white cloth in a simple knot. He did not care for the current style in neckware; he much preferred the old-fashioned cravat. It had a flair of bygone elegance, and besides, it aided his air of enigmatic reclusiveness.

"I assume you will be going to the lodge after dinner, milord, so you will want your Masonic cuff links?"

"Indeed."

There were very few people he trusted, Sussex, of course, and the Marquis of Alynwick, who made the third in the Brethren Guardians. The only other person in the world who had his complete trust was Billings. The old retainer had been with his family since Black's birth. Each male of Billings's line had served Black's family, almost from the time his ancestor had come home from Jerusalem, carrying the sacred pendant.

Billings knew of his family's duty, and he kept Black's secrets—all of them. Even the unsavory accusations that

Miss Fox had hurled at him last night. All of them unfortunately being true.

"Your waistcoat, milord."

Black took the silk and pulled his arms through as he watched in the mirror Billings taking the black velvet jacket from the hanger.

Shrugging into the jacket, he studied himself. He looked subdued in these colors, but they were what he liked best. He preferred not to stand out in a crowd. Black and gray suited him.

"Shall I trim a bit of this?" Billing inquired politely as he pointed to the ends of his hair. "It lies on your shoulders now."

"No, I like it this way."

He found himself wondering if Isabella liked it. Did she find him handsome? Some women did, but others found his dark intensity frightening. In his dream, Isabella had not been frightened of him. In his dream, he had ravished her quite thoroughly and she had welcomed him without fear. He'd awakened hard and throbbing and, unable to forget the vividness of the dream, he'd been forced to take care of his needs.

Things were progressing rather well, he thought as he glanced once more at his reflection. Soon, he would not have to dream of Isabella in his bed, for she would be there, beneath him, atop him and he could live out every wicked, indecent fantasy he had ever had about her.

Black knew without a doubt that Isabella could be a person he trusted with his secrets. She was loyal and he felt, bone deep, that she would never betray him. It wasn't in her.

There had been few women in his life because of this. He was a man possessed of a heavy sexual appetite, but he fed that appetite by not taking mistresses, but women who preferred to work in trade. He had never visited the squalid brothels of the East End. Mayfair had enough exclusive men's clubs for that sort of thing. The women were lovely, conversed with ease and did not ask questions. His transactions had always been satisfactory and he had been well contented with the arrangements until Isabella had haphazardly come into his life. Then, sex had been a frustrating exercise. Always left physically replete, he found himself more and more emotion-hungry.

He no longer wanted anonymous sex. He wanted a connection. An intimacy based on love. He wanted to pleasure not out of duty or money, but because he was desired by another. He wanted to give a piece of himself to a woman as he never had before. He wanted to make love. Not fuck.

He'd never thought to have that, not even with Abigail, to whom he had been betrothed since the age of sixteen. Even then, he knew he would never love her. Knew that what would happen in their marital chamber would be born of necessity.

But Isabella…he could love her. He likely already did. And he wanted her. Good God, how he wanted her. He hadn't been with a woman in months, and his body ached for it, the feel of sliding inside female flesh—Isabella's tight, virginal flesh.

"If we are done here, milord, I shall go downstairs to check on dinner."

"Cook should have it well in hand by now," he murmured as he tried not to think of sex, and how his body ached to show Isabella pleasure. He'd asked her to come to him last night in her uncle's salon. Would she? he wondered.

"Then the dining room. Polly, the new maid, still requires watching. And I'm certain your lordship is desirous to make a good impression this evening."

"How well you know me, Billings."

With a polite bow, the butler backed out of the room. "I thought perhaps, my lord, that an article in the *Evening*

Standard might be of interest to you. I've left it on the bureau."

"Thank you, Billings."

The door closed behind the butler and Black moved to the window, parting the heavy black drapes so that he could stand at the glass and look out upon the world. There was no reason for him to read the paper. He already knew what he would see in the headlines. The death of one Miss Alice Fox.

Across the street, Black could very clearly see Stone-brook's town house. The light was on in Isabella's room and he studied it, waiting to see a glimpse of her. He imagined her standing before the mirror, her maid putting the finishing touches on her gown.

He smiled, closed his eyes and imagined himself coming up to stand behind her. He would wrap his arm around her waist, flatten his palm over her belly and let it slowly glide up to rest between her breasts as he kissed her neck. He would watch her in the mirror, then turn her in his arms and capture her lips with his.

Fingers rapping on the window, he stood until the light went out, and he turned away from the window, preparing to welcome Isabella into his home.

"OH, ISABELLA."

The sound of awe in Lucy's voice made Isabella blush to her roots.

"How absolutely breathtaking you look."

Isabella stared at her reflection in the mirror, unable to believe it was truly her staring back. "It is only because of the dress, Lucy. How gorgeous it is. Your talent…it's really rather amazing."

Lucy smiled as she walked around Isabella, admiring her creation. "I just knew that crimson silk would be fantastic for you."

Oh, it was gorgeous. She had thought the gowns her

uncle had purchased for her were stunning, but this…
this was a piece of art. She never could have imagined
owning something this spectacular. "Really, Lucy, I
cannot accept—"

"Oh, hush. Yes, you can. It was to be your Christmas
present anyway. What is a few months early, hmm? Besides, you'll be absolutely stunning sitting at Black's table
beneath the chandeliers wearing crimson."

"Lucy," she warned, but her cousin waved away the
comment.

"I only meant that because Mr. Knighton will be in
attendance, of course you want to be at your most stunning then."

Arching a brow, Isabella severely doubted that her
cousin had meant what she said. Wendell was joining
them tonight, a fact she was both relieved and worried
about.

"Your hair looks lovely, too. Annie did a wonderful
job, and I adore how she's pulled it all up and secured it
with the string of black jet. Makes you look very womanly, Issy."

Isabella smoothed her hands down the formfitting
gown. The bodice was cut low, adorned with crimson
rosettes around the sleeves and neckline. The bodice fit
like a glove, molding to her breasts, indenting sharply
at her waist and draping in ruched layers over her hips,
which only enhanced their curves. The train behind was
swept up in a ruffled bustle, with the same rosettes sprin-
kled in amongst the heavy layers.

The color was magnificent. It was a deep, rich crimson with a hint of shimmer when the gaslight hit it from
the right angle. The shade reminded Isabella of the first
drop of blood that pooled when a finger was pricked by
a needle while sewing.

"Issy," Lucy said as she stood behind her, "you're just

a picture, and that bosom of yours, I'd give my dowry for one just like it."

"There is quite a bit of it showing, isn't there?"

"Nonsense. It's very elegant. How can you help it? You're amply endowed. Take heart, you could be like me and have two apples for breasts."

"You're very slight, Lucy. Delicate," Issy confirmed. *Just like a mischievous pixie.*

"I'm shaped like a pear. If only God had seen fit to take some of what he has given my bottom, and dispersed it up top."

Isabella gazed at her cousin, resplendent in a very becoming shade of aubergine. Lucy may be short, but she had a much bigger personality, one that virtually palpitated with vitality. There was an ethereal air about her that Isabella had long envied.

A knock on the door interrupted them and they both turned to see Stonebrook, with his stark white mutton-chops, peering into the room. "You both look very nice. Now, let us be off."

The door closed and Lucy grinned. "Papa is a man of few words, that is as close to a compliment of utter adoration as you are likely to receive. Now, then," Lucy murmured as she walked to the wardrobe. "I have one last gift, and before you say no, you must realize that this dress is just not complete without it."

Lucy pulled out a black velvet cape with a deep hood trimmed in thick fur. When she wrapped it around Isabella's shoulders and Isabella sunk into the sinfully luxurious lining, she made a loud groan of pleasure, which caused Lucy to laugh.

"What is it that is so warm and soft," she asked as she ran her fingers through the thick black fur.

"Black bear. I ordered it all the way from the Hudson's Bay Company. Isn't it decadent?"

"Oh, Lucy, it's beyond decadent."

"I'm glad you like it. Now, we shouldn't keep Papa waiting or we will have to endure a lecture on punctuality."

"We're already fashionably late."

Lucy snorted. "Have you not met your uncle, Issy? There is nothing fashionable about him, and he has never subscribed to the notion of females making a man wait. 'Balderdash,'" Lucy mocked in her father's superfluous accents. "'Utter rubbish, making men wait about all day as if we have nothing better to do than stand by with bated breath till the lady makes her appearance.'"

"Luce, it's uncanny your ability to sound just like Stonebrook."

"Well, I might have heard that lecture a time or two," she said with an impish grin. "Papa may not say much, and when he does it is usually all bluster, but I suppose it's his way of showing some measure of affection for the daughter he's been saddled with."

Linking arms, they left Isabella's room and headed down the stairs. She was nervous, the emotion a mixture of excitement and fear. It would be all right, Isabella kept repeating to herself. They were just having dinner and it wasn't as though she would find herself alone with Black. She could forget the kisses they had shared. She *would* forget, she confirmed. Not only his kisses, but the man himself.

BLACK WATCHED from the shadows as Billings slipped the black cloak from Isabella's shoulders. For a moment he was struck dumb as his gaze hungrily drank in the sight of her pale shoulders and neck as the black velvet slid away, revealing Isabella in a stunning crimson gown.

By God, she was the most gorgeous, voluptuous creature he had ever laid eyes upon. That gown…it ought to be outlawed for what it did to her body. It framed her figure perfectly, he could see every indent and curve, as though she were wearing nothing but a thin lawn night-rail and standing before a candle flame.

And her bosom... Black swallowed hard as his lascivious eyes raked over her breasts. What a sight it was. She had not worn any jewelry, nothing to mar the flesh that lay between her breasts and her gown. He had a sudden urge to see her in the family pendant—a four-carat black diamond surrounded by glimmering white diamonds. The black diamond would rest nicely in the cleft of her breasts.

He could not wait to get her alone tonight and kiss her lips, which appeared cherry colored and succulent; to press his cheek to that soft, swelling expanse of bosom that was going to tempt his gaze to stray for the remainder of the night.

"Take a breath, old boy," muttered a voice beside him. "You're wheezing away like a pair of ancient bellows."

Black glared at the man who stood beside him. Iain Sinclair, the Marquis of Alynwick and laird to the Sinclair clan, was a renowned rake—known for his sexual proclivities, not to mention his exceptional taste in women.

"She is stunning," Alynwick murmured as he took a sip of whiskey and continued his appraisal of Isabella. "Amply curved, just how I prefer them. Nothing compares to the feel of a soft, warm woman beneath you. And that smile, so sweet it makes you want to kiss it off her face. And all that innocent milk-white skin pressed against that sinful crimson gown. Makes a man wish to skip dinner and move straight to dessert."

"Keep your damn eyes off her," Black growled, but Alynwick smiled knowingly.

"A physically impossible feat. With a body like that, she commands the eye's attention—and something a bit lower."

"She isn't one of your dolly-mops, Alynwick," Black snarled.

"No, she's someone you might discover at the back of

the royal circle in the Empire Theatre. I can see her now, wearing that glorious gown, smiling and nodding as she walks up and down between the velvet-covered couches."

Black couldn't keep his gaze from straying to her. "You will cease speaking of her in that common, disrespectful way."

Alynwick smiled, but it did not reach his eyes. "Ennui, I'm afraid, it does make a man a trifle provoking."

"Provoking?" Black snapped. "It'll make you a dead man."

Alynwick laughed and finally met Black's mutinous gaze. "Look at you in all your puffed-up glory, Black. You look like an enraged rooster snuffing and wheezing because there is a new cock in the henhouse."

Black raised a challenging brow. "I trust the cock in question has enough sense to keep far away from the hen—and the resident rooster."

Alynwick laughed, a deep melodious chuckle that drew Isabella's gaze to where they were standing. "I know about your attachment to Miss Fairmont. I saw you dancing with her at Stonebrook's. You never dance. Besides, Sussex told me you're moonfaced for her, and I can see his claims weren't exaggerated."

"Sussex should talk," he mumbled.

Tossing his head back, Alynwick finished the contents of his glass. He'd let his hair grow long, and the dark locks were now loose curls that made him look like a romantic poet, not the blackguard he was.

"Ah, yes, poor old Sussex. In love. Personally I believe it was the very fine bottle of my scotch whiskey that induced such feelings. Sussex in love, I can't countenance it. It's lust, I told him. Bed the redhead, and see if that feeling stays around. I bet him my finest horse that it would not."

"You're a jaded, dissolute libertine, Alynwick, that's why you can't countenance any of the higher feelings.

How do you bear it? I wonder," Black asked. "Waking up in the morning and looking into the mirror."

"With one part equanimity and the other part humor. It is the only way to get about through life, to laugh at one's follies and then indulge in them again."

"There is nothing of substance in your life."

"And how would you know, you're a bloody recluse. At least I've made an attempt to take a stab at living. Which is more than I can say for you."

"You're not living," Black challenged. "You're merely pretending to."

"Well, you can make damn sure that Iain Sinclair will not be so stupid as to fall in love. Lot of rubbish love is," Iain mumbled. "There is nothing I detest more than the promise of love. There is nothing more depressing than a room full of it," he drawled. "It makes one eager to run screaming. Or wonder what one will do to make the night more tolerable."

"Alynwick, you're to be on your best behavior tonight."

"Aren't I always?"

"That's debatable. It depends on whether you're employing your English manners, or your Highland rogue persona."

"I haven't decided who I'll be tonight. I suppose it depends on which one the ravishing lady in red warms up to."

Black was about to bash Alynwick over the head, until Isabella smiled at him, propelling him forward, leaving the marquis behind to brood and stew and pretend to an ennui that the ladies thought most fetching.

"Good evening, Stonebrook, Lady Lucy." Black turned his gaze upon Isabella and reached for her hand, letting it rest in his palm as he lowered his mouth to her gloved hand. "Miss Fairmont."

With a deep curtsy that afforded him a magnificent

view of her chest, Isabella smiled, and said, "Thank you for the invitation to your home, my lord."

"You are most welcome."

A discreet cough behind his right shoulder informed him that Alynwick was lingering in the hall, waiting to be introduced.

"Stonebrook, you are acquainted with the Marquis of Alynwick."

"Indeed," Stonebrook said as he pumped Sinclair's hand. "It's been a while, though, you've been up in the north, I suppose."

"Aye, Scotland," Alynwick drawled in his exaggerated brogue that never failed to make the ladies swoon—*bastard.* "The Highlands—there is no match for the beauty and wildness of the lochs and moors, except p'rhaps the company of these lovely ladies."

"Oh, I love a Scottish accent," Lucy purred.

"Do ye now, lass? 'Tis good tae know."

"Alynwick," Black muttered, "this is Lady Lucy, Stonebrook's daughter."

"My lord," Lucy murmured as she curtsied deeply.

"Verra lovely indeed," Alynwick murmured appraisingly as he took Lucy's hand and helped her to rise.

"And this, Alynwick, is Miss Isabella Fairmont."

Isabella conducted herself as though she were a queen. The incline of her head, the straight back, the inflection of her curtsy were perfect. It was unbelievable to him that only two years ago she had been a poor Yorkshire girl living in a ramshackle room above the fishmonger's in Whitby.

He could see how dazzled Alynwick was, until the marquis caught a movement in the corner of his eye, and his attention was deviated. Not that Black cared. He was too relieved to give a damn that Alynwick might find himself uncomfortable tonight with the other guests. Served the bastard right for always being so smug and arrogant, and assured of his prowess.

"Miss Fairmont," Alynwick replied, his brogue not quite as thick, or charming, as before, "delighted."

"As am I, my lord. I am not from Scotland, but from the north—Yorkshire—and I do share with you your assessment of the moors."

"Yes, yes, lovely," Alynwick muttered as he turned to peer inside the salon where Sussex stood holding the hand of a young woman.

"You will forgive me?" the marquis muttered. "I forgot something in the library."

With a gracious nod, Isabella released him. Their gazes met, and Black offered her his arm, while Lucy took her father's. "Shall we go into the salon? Mr. Knighton is there, and the duke. And someone else who is most eager to make your acquaintance."

"Oh, yes," Isabella whispered. "Mr. Knighton. I must speak to him."

Her hand trembled on his arm, and he felt her body grow stiff and unyielding. The glow in her eyes had dimmed, replaced by caution. The minute they walked into the room, and her gaze landed on Knighton, he heard her breath catch, and then she looked up at him, her cheeks blazing crimson, and he knew then that she was afraid.

She didn't want Knighton to know what she had done with him. Anger was swift and unyielding, overtaking him until all he could think about was taking her shoulders in his hands and demanding to know how she could even glance at Knighton in such a way after what they had shared.

"My lord?" she asked with a tip of her head. "Are you all right? Your color is high."

Anger was not a novel emotion for him—he'd experienced it numerous times. But this raging jealousy was so foreign to him. It stole his breath, made him vibrate like a damn tuning fork. He didn't know what to do with the feelings; he wanted to bash Knighton, and he wanted to lift Isabella into his arms and carry her off to his room, ravishing her until she could no longer see, or think of any other man but him.

Not trusting himself to speak, he bowed to her, excused himself and quit the room.

Five minutes, he told himself. And then he would be fine. He didn't glance back at her. Didn't want to find her sashaying her way over to Knighton.

"My lord, is everything all right?" Billings inquired.

"Fine," he grumbled, and then whirled around. "Where did you seat Mr. Knighton?"

Billings frowned in thought for a moment, then looked up. "On the left of Miss Fairmont."

"Move him," Black ordered. "Put him beside Alynwick."

"Very good, milord. Then I shall move Lady Elizabeth, and put her beside Miss Fairmont. Would that be satisfactory?"

"Fine," Black hissed as he struggled to get a hold of his emotions. Five minutes he told himself as he felt the anger slowly subside, and then he could once more be in control.

CHAPTER ELEVEN

"WHO IS THAT with the duke?" Lucy demanded as they strolled side by side with Stonebrook in the salon.

"I have no notion," Isabella muttered. She had enough of her own problems other than worrying over who was talking with His Grace. What had Black been about escorting them into the room and then promptly abandoning them?

"She's very elegant," Lucy observed.

"Yes."

"He's holding her hand," Lucy hissed. "The rogue! He kissed me last night and now he appears at a dinner, knowing full well I will be here, with another woman on his arm. Just because he is a duke does not give him leave to act so churlishly. Issy…" Lucy stopped her with a gentle hand on her arm. The look in her cousin's eye was most strange. "He spoke of marriage last night, and now this? Is this his mistress, then? I've heard about men like Sussex and Black who when they entertain, their mistresses act as hosts and all the other kept women of the gentlemen guests attend. I would never tolerate something like this. What utter humiliation it would be for a wife to suffer such a situation."

"For someone who found the idea of the duke revolting this morning, you're certainly acting strangely."

Lucy sent her a murderous glare. "I don't care to play the fool."

"I doubt anyone does, Luce," she mumbled. "But really,

it's of no concern since you're quite determined not to marry him."

"Quite," Lucy sniffed.

Isabella glanced at the well-appointed room. The furniture was exquisite, straight clean lines, with none of the heavy ornamentation that had become so popular in the past years. The walls were painted a pale crème with white trim, the curtains were silk and a most fetching color of amber, giving the room a cozy atmosphere. In the large marble hearth a fire crackled, and oversize leather chairs sat on either side of the fireside, begging for someone to curl up in them with a good book.

There were objets d'art strategically placed around the room—all of exceptional quality, and many of them looked to Isabella like priceless antiques. The room held and delighted the eye, but stopped just short of ostentation. In all, the salon was classical and distinguished, a very good reflection upon the owner of the house.

Speaking of which, where had Black gone? He had not returned after taking his abrupt leave of them. Nervously, she fidgeted. Lucy was still prattling on about the duke, sending Sussex and the woman venomous glares. In the corner, Wendell stood chatting quite animatedly with Alynwick. Whatever they were discussing, they appeared in deep conversation, for Wendell had not even glanced up and noticed her arrival. A fact, Isabella had to admit, that stung.

He looked quite handsome tonight, dressed in a new suit of black. His hair was brushed back, his usual scholarly dishabille replaced by slick sophistication. He looked like a man born to be a Freemason. She wondered if he felt nervous about the initiation, but from what she saw, Wendell seemed rather comfortable talking to these men who were socially above him. From her vantage point, that fact didn't seem to deter Mr. Knighton. He was at ease here speaking amongst dukes and marquis as he was in the lecture room, or while discussing a new find with his scholarly peers.

They had not talked since yesterday afternoon, when he called upon her at her uncle's. He had been so happy to have been sponsored—by Black no less. Today there seemed a marked change in him. For all his awkward, occasionally inattentive ways he sometimes had for her, he had never downright ignored her before.

What had happened to cause this? she wondered. He had not even bothered to glance up, despite the fact he knew very well that she and Stonebrook and Lucy were invited.

Did a man who was courting someone not feel even the slightest bit of anticipation when his lady was expected to arrive?

Something strange inside her began to twist, and she thought of Black, who had seemed to watch her arrival from the shadows. His eyes had glimmered with appreciation when he saw her, and she had to admit, her body had softened, and her heart did the tiniest little flip when she saw him. Shouldn't she be feeling the same thing with Knighton?

"She's very beautiful, isn't she?" Lucy whispered as she appraised the woman hanging on to Sussex's hand. "The color of her hair is like burnished mahogany, and look how the gaslight reflects the deep auburn in it. And her body," Lucy said in what sounded almost like a whimper of defeat. "Her bosom puts even yours to shame, Issy. And that gown…oh, how lovely that sapphire blue is on her, and the peacock feathers trimming the shoulder is just the touch."

"Lucy, you're not…comparing yourself to this woman, are you?"

"Of course not," Lucy sniffed. "Why should I?"

"You shouldn't. You're every bit as beautiful."

"Ah, Stonebrook, Lady Lucy," the duke drawled as he

looked up from his tête-à-tête with the striking woman who still had a hold of his hand.

"Good evening, Your Grace," her uncle replied. "Damn fine night, isn't it?"

"It is indeed. Have you seen the moon? It is the beginning of a harvest moon. An auspicious event, to be sure, especially for being initiated into the Brethren, isn't that right, Knighton?"

Wendell paused long enough in his conversation with Lord Alynwick to glance up and acknowledge His Grace. His eyes darted to where she stood, widened a fraction and then with his glass raised, he saluted Isabella and returned to his conversation.

She heard Lucy's sharply indrawn breath at Wendell's disinterested greeting. Thankfully, the duke started for them, and Isabella couldn't help but hear Lucy's indrawn breath once more as he wrapped an arm about the woman's waist and maneuvered her across the room.

"Lady Lucy, Miss Fairmont, might I introduce Lady Elizabeth York."

The woman smiled and Isabella thought she might be glimpsing an angel from heaven. She was that lovely—and pure.

"Good evening," Lucy replied coolly as she curtsied. "A pleasure, I'm sure."

The woman frowned slightly and Isabella felt compelled to elbow Lucy in the ribs. Then it was Isabella's turn, and she hoped she made her greeting a bit more civil, although she couldn't blame Lucy for being taciturn. The duke had kissed her cousin last evening, and even had suggested the prospect of marriage, and here he was standing before them with a most striking woman, whom he was holding much too familiarly for a formal dinner party.

The woman stuck out her hand, and His Grace held her hand in his. "Which one is which?"

"Lady Lucy is to the left, and Miss Fairmont to my right."

"You will forgive my brother, ladies," Elizabeth said with a smile, "for I see he has quite forgotten to tell you of my infirmity."

"Brother?" Lucy choked, which sent a rather bemused smile to the duke's face.

"Indeed. I am the younger York, I'm afraid," he said.

Lucy promptly recovered. "Oh, yes, I do recall hearing that you had an older sister, Your Grace. But I assumed, well, that is, I have never had occasion to meet her."

"Thought I was up rusticating in the country with my husband and a parcel of children, and my mop cap?" Elizabeth teased, making Lucy blush furiously.

"Oh, no, if I insinuated—"

"I'm only teasing," Elizabeth said with a beaming smile. "The truth is, I find it such a trial to go about in society, and really, one can only hear the same gossip being repeated so many times before one feels as though they are a candidate for bedlam. Now then, the introductions? Adrian can be forgetful at times. Lady Lucy," Elizabeth said, and the duke helped her to hold out her hand to Lucy. "Miss Fairmont." The duke took Elizabeth's hand and moved it to the right. Isabella clasped her hand tightly.

"It is a pleasure to meet you, Lady Elizabeth."

"And you as well. I've heard so much about you, Lady Lucy, and your cousin who is newly arrived in London. And I can tell that my brother has not exaggerated your merits. One does not need sight to sense a person's virtues."

Lucy looked humbled, and began to blush. The expression that crossed her face was an array of shock, shame and…relief?

"Oh, dear, have I said something wrong?"

"Of course not, Lizzie," the duke responded.

"Well, it is always like this at first, isn't it? But rest assured, Lady Lucy, Miss Fairmont, that each meeting in the future will get easier. I am not troubled by my blindness, and I hope that you aren't, either."

"Oh, no, no," Isabella blurted out. "I hope I haven't offended you."

"Of course not, but I've four other senses that have been heightened since I lost my sight. There was an awkward pause, a lapse in conversation, and I knew that you had not been informed before our introduction and were left feeling broadsided. But then that is a man, isn't it? Occasionally they are rather careless beasts."

Sussex grinned at them. "My sister has a way of chastising with such charm, does she not?"

The little group laughed, and the awkwardness eased as quickly as it had come.

"I must say, Lady Elizabeth," Lucy murmured with obvious appreciation, "your frock is lovely. That color of blue is just so deep and rich, like the most exquisite of sapphires. And the peacock feathers look charming."

"Oh, is that what I am wearing? I asked Sussex to describe it and he said in his perturbed voice—" which Elizabeth parodied perfectly "—'It is blue, Lizzie, with feathers blowing about your shoulders.' I had no idea what sort of feathers, for all I knew, they could have been those horrible ostrich feathers they put on horses pulling funeral carriages."

Laughter erupted again, and Isabella marveled at the skill Elizabeth possessed at putting people at ease.

"I do believe I mentioned something about a sapphire if you will recall," the duke grumbled.

"Men are never eloquent with descriptions of colors and such," Lucy teased. "They underestimate the power of color to women when it comes to the importance in choosing a wardrobe. Why, I do believe they would not even notice if we spent our lives going about in shades of black and gray."

"Well, Lady Lucy, you may be quite certain that shade of aubergine is most fetching on you. I've never known a woman with such deep auburn hair to wear that dark purple before, but you carry it off beautifully."

"Oh, well done, Adrian!" Elizabeth laughed as Lucy gracefully curtsied to the duke. "Aubergine. How lovely that sounds."

"Oh, wonderful, you've met Lady Elizabeth." Black strolled up to them and took Elizabeth's hand from Sussex and placed a chaste kiss upon her knuckles.

"Good evening, Black."

"And how do you know it's me?"

Elizabeth chuckled. "Because I know your voice, and I can smell you. You're still wearing that awful spice-and-sandalwood cologne. I told you, pine and cedar would become you much better. It's woodsy and grounded, like you."

Isabella disagreed. Black smelled divine. And he looked startlingly attractive tonight dressed in black and gray. How interesting that Elizabeth should think pine and cedar would suit the earl. Pine and cedar had featured in her writing of Death. Isabella had never thought to link it to Black. They were woodsy scents, true, but Isabella thought the spicy aromas of the East were more suited to him. There was something very seductive about the Far East, which meshed perfectly with Black's mysterious and sensual aura.

"Well, then, shall we adjourn to the dining room? Dinner is about to be served."

"Yes, where is Alynwick?" Elizabeth demanded. "He can walk me in to supper tonight."

"Lady Lucy," the duke murmured as he offered her his arm. "May I?"

"Of course," Lucy announced as her gaze, which was

rather perplexed, volleyed between Sussex and his sister, and then Isabella saw it, the faintest flicker of something flash in Lucy's green eyes. Was it interest? Sussex did indeed look most striking this evening.

Black stood back waiting as the salon emptied. He was not standing on protocol tonight. By rights, it should have been the duke to enter the dining room first—he was the highest-ranking noble present—but Sussex was content to hold back and allow Alynwick and his sister to pass him by. It had taken Isabella months to understand the ranking of the peerage and all their little rules. In her somewhat limited experience, they were always strictly adhered to, especially when one was called in to dinner. Already, Isabella mused, this had the making of a most unconventional evening.

Wendell, she noted, brought up the rear of the group. She saw he was engrossed in something her uncle was saying, and Alynwick was already escorting Lady Elizabeth into the dining room. When Wendell passed by her, seemingly unaware, Isabella wanted to die of mortification, but then Black was there, taking her arm, pulling her tight against his body as he maneuvered them toward the dining room.

"Goddamn fool," he whispered. "He doesn't deserve you."

Shivering, Isabella refused to look at Black. She couldn't. Just could not bear to see his face. She had promised to forget him, and she must. She knew that if she looked up, she would once more be swept away.

DINNER WAS A GRAND AFFAIR. The dining room was enormous, and very masculine. The table was at least twelve feet long and gleaming in the candlelight. The chandelier was doused, as were the gas lamps. Candelabras were lit, and the glow of the flickering candlelight made the event seem that much more intimate.

Black had a knack for setting a scene, and this one was straight out of the history pages. She had never dined by candlelight alone, and the effect was quite breathtaking. Not to mention dramatic. She wondered if the others thought so as well, or if it was only her, and her imagination, that thought such fanciful things.

She was aware of how the candlelight flickered over the guests' faces, and how lovely Lucy and Lady Elizabeth looked in the light's warm glow. She wondered how she appeared, and glanced down to see the candlelight was casting warm, flickering shadows over her bosom. She should have been self-conscious that so much of her chest was exposed by the low-cut gown, but when she noted how the crimson satin seemed to sparkle in the candlelight, she was transfixed.

All too soon she became aware of Black's staring at her. He sat to her right, his eyes hooded, giving him the appearance of boredom, but she knew he was staring at her—she could feel the heat of his stare, and she began to blush, knowing the crests of her décolletage would turn pink. Hopefully, no one would notice in this light. With any luck no one was paying them any heed, or chancing to see Black's lingering heated stare as it roamed over her body.

With the candelabras lit and placed at perfectly measured intervals down the long length of the mahogany table, Death studied me over the rim of his goblet of wine, while firelight cast part of his face in shadow.

The dinner scene was very reminiscent of her book, and the words she had written somehow sprung to mind as she gazed quickly at Black, who was studying her over the rim of his wineglass.

In his domain, Death was even more imposing,
more beautiful. He possessed an air of sexual
danger, as if he would at any minute lunge at me
and devour me as he had his dinner. Something
told me that Death had a ravenous appetite, and
that if I allowed it, I would be his next meal.

Black smiled back at her. It was a slow, intimate grin,
and Isabella looked sharply down at the bowl that a footman had placed before her. She had already had a third of
her wine. It was the drink that was making her so warm,
not Black's gaze. It was the alcohol that freed her imagination and made her think to compare her book to this
dinner.

Chastising herself, Isabella focused on eating. She had
barely eaten anything yesterday due to her headache, and
as a result she was ravenous today. Concentrating on the
meal and using the proper utensil would take her mind
off Black and his luring sensuality that seemed to flow
out to her, even when she wasn't looking at him. It was
always there, that feeling. He made his presence known,
or maybe it was just her body that perceived his being
there. Whatever it was, she was very conscious of how
close he was. Even with her head bent, she could see from
the corner of her eye how he held his silverware, how
beautiful his hands looked. All that was needed to make
the picture even more alluring was a ring on his finger—
a black onyx one.

Stop it, stop it, stop it, she thought as she took a spoon
in her hand. She must cease this fascination with Black
before she became irrevocably enthralled by him.

The first course was a soup of marrow, made from the
very delicate butternut squash. It was liberally spiced with
honey and demerara sugar and a spice called cumin. She
had never tasted anything so exotic before, and the flavors
blended nicely on her tongue. When Black encouraged her

to sprinkle some ground almonds on top, she had been intrigued enough to try it, and discovered how much the nuts enhanced the flavoring, and how much she enjoyed trying different foods.

She was well fed at her uncle's, but traditional English faire was on the menu. But Black, she discovered, had made extensive trips to the East and India, and had brought back many of their spices and dishes. He enjoyed good food, and wine, and sharing both at dinner parties.

Reaching for her wineglass, she sipped at the bloodred liquid. The rich red wine that was being served was full-bodied and sweet. She was surprised the earl had chosen it, for he didn't seem like a man who would care for anything sweet, but when the main course arrived she knew why he had: the sweetness enhanced the pork and brought out the natural sugars in the accompanying sauce.

"By God," her uncle said. "The members of the lodge were not lying when they said an invitation to dine with you was better than an invitation from the queen."

Amusement flickered in Black's sea-colored eyes. "I would not go that far, Stonebrook, but I do thank you."

"Nor would I," Sussex grumbled.

"We're adversaries," Black explained as she looked startled by the duke's ungracious comment. "You see, we both enjoy food, and different ways of preparing it. We have a long rivalry, which the members of our lodge seem far too keen to keep alive. I believe it is so we will keep issuing invitations to come dine with us so that one of us may be finally titled the victor."

"Ah, I see," she said, smiling at him. "So you attempt to best each other?"

"Yes, as a matter fact, we do. Sussex, however, seems to have a special butcher whom he refuses to name. His meat, I'm afraid, is always that little bit better than mine."

"Ha!" Sussex grunted. "Flattery will not get you the name of my butcher."

"So you see, the rivalry continues."

"Well, I can understand why everyone wishes to have an invitation. The meal is lovely. Might I ask what the sauce is on the pork?"

"Red wine, mustard, prunes and Stilton cheese. Do you like it?"

"Very much."

Everyone nodded and proceeded to eat. It was the first dinner party she had ever attended where the conversation lacked. The food was that good. There was a wild-mushroom bread pudding and an excellent mash of potatoes. The pork with its prune sauce was remarkable, and Isabella kept telling herself that there was not enough room in her gown for her to eat with unabashed enthusiasm. But how she wished she could. If she had been in her old frock, back in Yorkshire, she would have shoveled it in, and asked for seconds—possibly even thirds. There was enough food on the table for thirds, and as a child and young woman, the ever-present sense of hunger had always been there. There was never enough money and, as a consequence, never enough to eat.

Despite this lack of food, she'd always been what she described as sturdy, but since coming to live with Lucy and Stonebrook, she'd gained nearly a stone—and had enjoyed every morsel that had contributed to the gain.

"Legendary these dinners are," Stonebrook said as he refilled his plate with more mushroom pudding. "I believe that men join the lodge just to sample Black's and Sussex's dinner menu."

"Yes," Elizabeth, who was seated next to her, said, "your cook has outdone himself tonight, Black. But I assume he cooked what you requested."

"I did indeed suggest the menu. I have a very great fondness for wild mushrooms, and I recall that you do as well."

Elizabeth placed her hand on the table. It was amazing

to Isabella just how refined and regal she was. She couldn't see, yet she ate so daintily. Nothing slopped or splashed; Isabella could not boast such a feat, for she was staring down at a piece of prune that had fallen onto her napkin.

"Well, I can attest that both my brother's and Black's houses are the finest places to eat in all of London. Look at me," Elizabeth said with a smile, "without a vigorous exercise regimen, I've become rather plump!"

Lucy gasped, and Alynwick scowled.

"There, there, Lady Elizabeth," Stonebrook soothed. "Take heart. The most celebrated of beauties in history have been known to be plump as raisins."

"Why, thank you, my lord."

"There is nothing wrong with the way you look," Lord Alynwick muttered before refilling his glass with wine and raising his arm. "A toast to the ladies, it's about damn time Black saw to livening up these dreary dinner parties with such lovely company."

Elizabeth slid her hand along the tablecloth, her fingertips delicately searching for the stem of her glass. Isabella was about to help her, when she caught Black's gaze, and noted the gentle shake of his head.

There really was no need to assist her, for when Isabella returned her attention, Elizabeth was already taking a sip of the wine.

"Excellent red," she murmured as she discreetly licked her lips. "Beyond the grapes I detect berries, and apples, and perhaps some spice."

"Yes," Black said.

"It's not French. Spanish?"

Black smiled and saluted her with his wineglass. "Lady Elizabeth, you are a vintner's dream come to life."

"Thank you, my lord."

"Well, I for one am just as pleased with a good meat pie and a fine ale," Alynwick muttered. He glanced up and caught her eye. "You mentioned you were from York-shire, Miss Fairmont. Which part?"

"Whitby, my lord."

"Ah, yes, lovely scenery. Positively moody at this time of year. I've been once. There was an excellent tearoom there that made the best steak-and-mushroom pie I've ever known."

"Elizabeth Botham's!" she cried.

"Do you know it?"

"Know it? Oh, I spent every extra pence I had there. The Sally Lunns are not to be beat. And the Yorkshire brack. Oh, it's been an age since I tasted it," she said wist-fully.

"There was a very fine plum cake, too, as I recall."

"Oh, yes," she said, remembering her home with such a heavy heart. While her childhood had not been happy or prosperous, she had very much enjoyed growing up in Whitby. The Yorkshire coast was a beautiful place, with the ocean, the heather-covered moors and the forest of Pickering. There was beauty to behold in every direction.

"I enjoyed mine smeared with butter," Alynwick said. "And they make a bracing cup of good Yorkshire tea."

Isabella had never been able to afford butter. But, oh, she could imagine it, a thick slice of plum bread slath-ered in butter. Oh, how wonderful it would have been. Even plum cake on its own was heaven. She had never been able to afford it, but occasionally her mother would come into money when a shipping vessel and the navy were in port, and magically a loaf of plum cake or York-shire brack would appear at the breakfast table.

As a child, she hadn't bothered to question it. As a young woman, she'd known how her mother provided the loaf. Her scruples had told her that they were ill-gotten goods, obtained via a passionate drive to be loved and adored. Her mother never could resist a man in a sailor's uniform, and with her looks, which never faded, the men who were new to town, or staying for a brief spell, fell easily into her bed. Every passionate encounter was purported to her by her mother "to be the one." Unfortunately, after all her mother's passionate affairs, not one of them ended up being close to what she had dreamed of. Her mother had died a heartbroken, destroyed woman.

Which brought her back to the past, when she had been standing at the small table they shared, gazing down upon a loaf of warm fruit-filled bread. Isabella had known she shouldn't partake of her mother's sin, but it had always seemed like such a waste, cutting off one's nose to spite their face. If she didn't eat the bread, then it would go to waste. Waste not, want not soon became her motto.

"Whitby Abbey is a magnificent place. Gothic and melancholy, it's a most inspiring spot for contemplation."

Her body tingled all over at the sound of Black's voice. "You've been, my lord?"

"Yes, two years ago. It's a charming village, and the abbey, how it stands so tall and proud even in its ruin, is quite awe inspiring."

"The abbey was my favorite place to go. I used to sit there and gaze down at the ocean and dream."

"It seems a most fitting place for one to search out dreams."

Lowering her head, she felt the eyes of the table upon them. The subject of dreams was far too personal for a dinner exchange.

The conversation lapsed once more, and Isabella grew conscious of her gown and, having no wish to pull at the seams of the tight bodice, glanced around the table. Her uncle sat at the opposite end, merrily eating away. She watched as his thick sideburns moved with his jaw. She always wanted to giggle whenever he ate. It was a silly notion, but then, Stonebrook's sideburns were silly themselves.

Lucy sat beside her father, hardly eating. Every once in

a while she would cast a surreptitious glance at the duke. Whatever Lucy believed, there was something there between them. Lucy, the dear, just stubbornly refused to see it.

Next to the duke was the handsome Marquis of Alynwick. Upon their introduction he had been so charming. He seemed to have eased up somewhat during their discussion of Yorkshire, but now he was morose and brooding once more. Whatever had happened to cause such an abrupt change she had no idea. But when she noticed the marquis scowl for the third time as he glanced at Lady Elizabeth, she reasoned that his ill humor had something to do with her. But she couldn't fathom what had caused his displeasure. The duke's sister was a delight.

Across from Lucy and the duke was Wendell. He had been particularly quiet this evening, hardly even joining in the conversation. He kept checking his timepiece and fidgeting with his napkin. He certainly hadn't spoken to her, and an ugly black thought began to form in her mind.

Had Black told him? Wendell had arrived before her. There had been ample time for the earl to inform Mr. Knighton that he had quite thoroughly ravished her in the carriage and then again in the salon.

She swung her gaze to the right of her, where Black was lounging in his chair, his wineglass in his hand, his gaze boring into her, studying her. When he arched a brow in question, she flushed and looked away.

Was Black the reason Wendell was ignoring her?

"So, Mr. Knighton," Elizabeth said, capturing the attention of the table, "I have heard that you are the man who found treasure buried in Solomon's Temple."

"Indeed, my lady. I am."

"How exciting to see Jerusalem. You must tell me about the city. Is it hot?"

"Very."

"And sandy?"

"Yes. And when the breeze kicks up, the sand and grit land everywhere. But the winds bring with it the smells of the East, cloves and cumin, star anise and saffron. The sway of silk rippling in the air in the open bazaars. The glare of the sea against the whitewashed buildings. The sound of a foreign tongue surrounding you and the bustle of the markets. It is a land of antiquity, of Christian and Muslim worship. There are memories of the West interspersed with the everyday East. I find that sometimes my descriptions lack luster, for it's hard to truly convey just how powerful a feeling sweeps over you as you stand in the city that has been the cradle of Christian civilization."

"You paint a vivid picture, Mr. Knighton, I can see it in my mind, and how bright your words make it. I can almost taste the spice, hear the music."

Isabella noticed that Wendell was blushing. Curiously, she did not feel anything. Shouldn't she feel at least a little enviousness that it had been Elizabeth pulling him into the conversation and making him blush?

"Everyone must at one time go to the East. It truly is another world."

"Oh, I would love to," Elizabeth murmured. "My family is descended from a Knight Templar. Did you know that, Mr. Knighton? His name was Sinjin York, and he was considered a brave and highly skilled warrior. I've long been captivated by the Templars. Such a romantic story theirs is, and tragic, too."

"The Templars are fascinating. I've heard of your ancestor, Lady Elizabeth. There are stories that three Templars escaped persecution from the French king, and made their way back to their native Scotland. With them, they each carried an object purported to be from the time of Christ. If the rumors are true, there is a chalice, suspected of being the Holy Grail, and a necklace, which contains the seeds from the apple from which Eve ate."

Isabella did not miss the fleeting glances that volleyed between Alynwick, Sussex and Black.

"Sussex is a long and noble Scottish title, my lady. Perhaps it was your ancestor whom the stories speak of?"

Elizabeth smiled. "Oh, I doubt that, Mr. Knighton. You see, Sinjin, by all accounts and family tales, returned from the Holy Land rather dissolute and depraved. He brought with him women from a harem he kept, and in the end, he died living the life of a sultan. I doubt he could have cared for any religious relic, for he was quite immoral."

"Well, it would be a most gratifying find," Wendell said, "to be able to prove or disprove such a thing. I've long been enthralled with the Templars and the mystery that surrounds them. They were warriors and knights, protectors of pilgrims, but they had a sinister side, and despite their religious crusading, they were quite…well, amorous."

"Yes. So the stories say. There is even a tale that Sinjin's daughter was seduced by a friend—another Templar—and left ruined."

"What happened to her?" Isabella asked.

"She cursed the line of her lover and then she killed herself," Alynwick said irritably, before addressing Wendell. "Did you discover anything in Jerusalem about these three Templars? I must admit to my own keen interest on Templar history, and I've never heard of this before."

"Conflicting stories, I'm afraid. Some say there were three Templars, but many more claim that there were four knights charged with the safekeeping of the relics. The fourth was murdered, and any evidence of him, and his association with the other knights, was buried along with his body. I attempted to make further inquiries, but didn't get anywhere. I'm planning another trip," Knighton said, to Isabella's surprise. "Perhaps next year, and then I plan to investigate this mystery. I do believe that where there is smoke, there is fire."

"Next year, Mr. Knighton?" Isabella asked. "You'll be returning to the East?"

"Yes. I'll be gone a few months."

And when was he planning on telling her? she wondered.

"My brother has been, and Black, of course, but I could not prevail upon them to take me," Elizabeth said. "But I do so long to see it. Perhaps when they plan another trip I shall be successful in convincing them to let me join them."

Alynwick's fierce scowl was something to behold. "The East is no place for you," the marquis announced. "With its lawlessness and black market for the skin trade, you would be ripe for the picking. Any man would be a fool to take you along."

Elizabeth ignored the marquis's outburst and addressed Wendell once more. "You're having an exhibition, I understand?"

"Yes. At the museum. I've nearly got everything catalogued and the exhibition is planned for four days from now. I hope everyone will come."

"Did you find Templar treasure?" Black asked.

Wendell stiffened and gazed down at his plate. "Limited."

"Ah," Black said knowingly. "What of Christian icons?"

Wendell gazed down the length of the table. "Very few. The items I found belonged to Solomon himself."

"I see."

"I plan to go back because I know—I just feel it in my bones—that there is something to the story of the three Templars. I want to discover if it is true. And then I want to find the treasure."

"You're obsessed," Alynwick observed. "Like any archaeologist, I suppose."

"There is a very seductive power to the tale, I will

grant you that much. I've been consumed with the story, and the prospect of finding the relics. Imagine discovering seeds from the apple that thrust mankind into a world of sin. Astonishing."

Isabella could hardly wrap her mind around such a fact. She was still rather astonished by Wendell's declaration that he planned to return to the East.

"I would not put much credence into the tale, Knighton," Black replied. "The Templars are as much noted for their love of weaving stories as their skill with a sword. They were rather self-important, and probably spread the story to make themselves appear more powerful."

"Respectfully, I must disagree with you, my lord. There is some evidence that this story is not just a fable. Evidence exists—a book, and I know of someone who has information on it."

"The devil you do!" Alynwick thundered.

"Indeed I do, my lord," Knighton challenged. "And it claims that when the seeds from the pendant are mixed with the blood of an innocent in the chalice, it brings universal knowledge and immortality."

"Balderdash!" Stonebrook mumbled around a mouthful of pork.

"Do you, by any chance, read the penny dreadfuls, Miss Fairmont?" Elizabeth asked in an abrupt change of topic.

"Indeed I do." She flushed, refusing to meet Black's amused gaze, or Wendell's disapproving frown. When he had caught her reading them, he had made his opinion of them known. He was not a fan of such amusements. Instead, he had given her a tome on Solomon and the building of his temple for her enjoyment. Isabella had dozed off after wading through three paragraphs.

Granted, it was not a medieval treatise, or scholarly paper on Jerusalem, but the weekly serials were vastly amusing.

"Oh, I adore them, too." Elizabeth laughed. "Before my sight was totally gone, I used to read the shilling shockers, as well. I adored those gothic stories. My companion reads to me now, and she's utterly averse to the shockers, so I must make do with the penny dreadfuls."

"Lucy and I indulge in them."

"Waste of good money," her uncle grumbled on cue.

"Oh, Papa, what is a shilling?"

"A shilling a week, for a year, is fifty-two shillings. In five years' time that's two hundred and sixty shillings, and a damn decent investment."

Lucy sent Isabella an amused smile down the length of the table. "Yes, Papa."

"As I have already mentioned to Miss Fairmont," Wendell chimed in, "her money would be better spent on a book that would edify her knowledge. But then, women are not always so keen to expand their horizons."

Isabella gasped and Elizabeth reached for her hand, squeezing it. "My dear Mr. Knighton, are you suggesting that women's brains are mindless fluff?"

"Of course not," Wendell spluttered. "Oh, my lady, I meant no offense."

"None taken. But, please, let us debate this matter. Women are generally denounced for spending money on these diverting and amusing weekly serials, is that not correct?"

There was general agreement around the table.

"But it's quite acceptable for men to purchase the *Reynolds Weekly*," Elizabeth said, raising her voice over the loud groans of protests, "which is nothing more than a tittle-tattle rag that repeats the most scandalous gossip and publishes the most detailed and titillating police reports. Can you deny it?"

Black met Isabella's astonished gaze as he swirled his wine around in his glass.

"Aha, silence!" Elizabeth charged. "Is there no rebuttal to be had?"

"There is no arguing with you, Beth," Alynwick murmured, and Isabella heard Elizabeth's breath catch. Her face flamed red, and Black glared at Alynwick before speaking.

"You are, of course, correct, Lady Elizabeth. Men will seek their own pleasures and amusement without censure or guidance. But for some reason we are unable to spare a female from our opinions."

"Why is that, do you think?" Isabella asked him.

"The nature of the beast," Wendell provided. "As men we are designed to protect the weak. It comes naturally to guide women down the path we feel is safe, and in their best interests."

"And reading *Reynolds Weekly* is not considered dangerous?" Lucy laughed. "Why, the gossip in that magazine has ruined many reputations."

"Yes, why is gossip so exciting? You cannot deny that it intrigues both sexes equally as much," Elizabeth challenged.

"It may intrigue us," Stonebrook growled, "but we don't repeat it like women do, over tea."

"No, we do it over port and cigars," the duke said with a laugh. Even her uncle laughed, and when she turned to glance at Black he was smiling, too.

What a strange dinner this was. Dinners at home were quiet, polite affairs. The conversation, if there was any, was rather tame. Her uncle asked about their day, where they had shopped, who they had visited and not much more than that. Certainly nothing as lively as this.

"We were speaking of penny dreadfuls and shilling shockers, Lady Elizabeth, and I hope it's not presumptuous, but I'm quite certain both Lucy and I would be thrilled to visit you and read to you the most gruesome passages of the shockers."

"Oh, that would be splendid. I shall send Maggie, my companion, out first thing tomorrow morning for a copy."

"Oh, Lord help us," Sussex drawled, "we will be up to our knees in gothic horror and spectral phenomena."

"Speaking of spectral phenomena," her uncle grumbled. "Anyone see in the papers about the death of the Highgate Charlatan?"

"Yes, as a matter fact I did," Wendell said, brightening. "A rather curious case. She was found dead, and whoever did the deed left a shilling over each eye for the ferryman. The police reports are speculating everything from a crime of passion to blackmail. Although I can't countenance the blackmail theory. Her death certainly can't be motivated by money, because the murdering thief would hardly have a care to leave shillings behind for the safekeeping of her soul to the hereafter."

Isabella swallowed hard, and met Lucy's pale gaze. Alice Fox was dead?

"Do they have any leads?" Alynwick inquired.

"The paper said that a black town carriage led by four black horses was seen around one in the morning."

Stonebrook snorted. "All the reports claim the same thing, a black carriage and a team of four. Wasn't that the precise description of the carriage those music-hall dancers from the Adelphi were seen getting into? Bah, it's just a generalization. And I ask you this, what eyewitness could have seen a coach outside a cemetery on a night like last night at that time of the morning? The only eye it could have been from was a ruffian up to no good!"

"That is a very good question, my lord," Wendell replied. "And a coach and team of four is a rather pricey bit of goods. I doubt a common murderer could afford such luxury."

Her uncle's eyes turned downright frigid. "Mr. Knighton," he stated, his chest puffing up, "you would not suggest that a man of title and rank would be responsible for this murder, are you?"

"No, my lord, I am merely pointing out an obvious fact."

"Obvious?" Stonebrook snarled. "I see nothing obvious about it at all. It's not a coach and four that marks a man of breeding, by God. Even the middling classes now have a team and a coach and country house. No, Mr. Knighton, it simply cannot be one of my kind. The middling classes, perhaps, they occasionally produce offspring capable of this sort of behavior, but there is no need to glance at a titled man."

The silence was heavy and deafening, and Isabella could see how angry Wendell was becoming. Isabella and he were the only common members at the table. Even her mother's blue blood was not enough to outrank her father's poor red blood. And her uncle knew it, and didn't hesitate to use it.

Breathing heavily, she tried to calm herself. Tried to look anywhere else but at her uncle who had resumed eating his meal.

"What of you, Miss Fairmont?" Black asked quietly. "What is your opinion on this matter?"

"My lord?"

"Do give us your view, Miss Fairmont," Black murmured as he watched her carefully. "Is it impossible that a man born into a title and wealth could have committed murder?"

She thought back to last night. To the scene of the crime and poor Alice Fox. She thought of Black, and suddenly her story of Death came to mind. Her image of Death was that of a gentleman. Refined, well spoken— charming. How very much Black reminded her of him— of Death sitting down to dinner, a wineglass in his hand…

"Surely you have an opinion, Miss Fairmont," Black taunted.

Well, of course she did, but generally women were not ever called upon to give their opinion at any time, let alone at a dinner party.

"Come, Miss Fairmont," Elizabeth said gently. "He is in earnest. We are quite at ease giving our opinions. Why should you not, too? It is a long-standing tradition with us, our families have been friends forever, and despite society's rules, we often break them and have a lively discussion. Why, I often debated with them well into the night, and I know the marquis is sitting across from me scowling away because he has never successfully proved his point against me."

She was correct. Alynwick was scowling.

"Yes, Isabella," Lucy said, despite the warning glare her father sent her. "Give us your opinion."

"Well, that is…" She swallowed, and caught Wendell's eyes. His expression was unreadable, but the slight shake of his head told her she should keep her opinions to herself. To her right, Black watched her, waiting with genuine interest, encouraging her.

How could both men be so different? They were as opposite as the poles of the earth. One so dangerous to her, and the other…so wrong for her.

"Come, let us talk of something else," Stonebrook grumbled. "The evening will be done and over and we'll be off to our lodge meeting before too long. You must be thrilled and excited, Knighton," her uncle said as he clapped Wendell on the back. "Tonight is your initiation."

To be dismissed so perfunctorily made Isabella see red. She owed much to her uncle, but at that moment she couldn't think of it. The slight he'd just given, in front of everyone, and Wendell, too, just accepting it and allowing it to happen made her spine stiffen and her fingers curl into fists.

"I do not see that anyone is above performing some sort of crime. Man, or woman, aristocrat or commoner.

Breeding is not a factor. Neither is sex. It is the circumstance, the environment, that has shaped the person. Defects and criminal tendencies happen for many reasons, but they are not excluded on the basis of birth."

The table was quiet, and then Black sat forward, looking so dangerously handsome.

"Beautifully said. They should let women into Parliament if the remainder of your sex is as well spoken as you."

Her uncle actually gasped at the suggestion.

"I happen to concur. Man is man, whether he is born to a title or in the gutter. It is the circumstances around us that forms our behavior. One can never truly know what it is like to walk in someone else's shoes. I have known many honorable men, both aristocrat and commoner. But I've known far more unscrupulous men, from both walks of life."

"Now, see here, Black," her uncle chastised. "Murder is performed by the lower orders. There is no debating that."

"It's not that cut-and-dried, my lord," Black countered.

"It most certainly is so. Don't tell me you're one of these radicals in Parliament who support such nonsense bills as the ridiculous health act that is being proposed… forgotten cesspits causing cholera and typhus," her uncle muttered. "Preposterous idea! And the Contagious Diseases Act, what of that?"

"I think it a good thing that prostitutes are able to go to a physician to see if they have contracted a disease. It's safer for them, and their customers, and society in general."

"Those women are harlots!" her uncle thundered, clearly losing control and forgetting himself. This topic was never one to be discussed in mixed company, let alone the dinner table. Harlots? Of all the dinner topics to be had. But it did beat out talking about the weather and the theater.

"Quite right," Mr. Knighton agreed. "These women are multiplying like flies in our city and they are spreading disease like rats."

"One might question where the disease stems from in the first place," Elizabeth stated.

"From one whore to another," Wendell said smugly.

"The point is moot," Lucy interrupted, "because the entire business could be eradicated if one simple thing happened, and that is, if men no longer went to these women for servicing."

"You, my dear, have had too much wine," Stonebrook grumbled and reached for Lucy's wine, placing it far away from her.

"Very well said, Lady Lucy," Sussex stated approvingly. "But if men no longer procured their services, where would these women go?"

Lucy opened her mouth, then promptly shut it.

"You see, the nature of the profession offers a sort of employment," Sussex said delicately. "Put aside the moral debate, and you'll see that many women have profited quite well, and have been able to open a tearoom, or save a brother or sister with the proceeds. There are only so many positions for shopgirls and maids, therefore if you take away the profession, you leave many women out of work."

"And many men in ill humor," Alynwick charged.

Black sat back and glared down the length of the table. "Now, you cannot have it said that this particular problem is one that only affects the lower orders, Stonebrook."

The clock in the hall chimed, signaling the hour of ten. With relief, her uncle sat back in his chair and tossed his napkin upon the table. "Girls, it is time to leave. I have my meeting in less than an hour."

"I'll see them home," Black announced. "You take Knighton now to the lodge."

"Very well, we shall see you shortly at the lodge. Lady Elizabeth, it has been…most educational."

"Why, thank you, my lord. Debates can be most inspiring, can they not?"

Black rose and left the dining room to see her uncle out. Wendell reached her, and allowed his hand to trail lightly over her shoulder.

"Shall I call on you tomorrow?" he murmured.

"That would be nice." She smiled, and he returned it, although not with the warmth he once had. "Good luck tonight."

With a nod, he left her, and when her gaze tracked his progress across the room, she saw that Black was watching her with his beautiful eyes. There was something there in his gaze. Something she had never seen before—anger.

"Lady Lucy," Sussex said as he rose from his chair and reached for Lucy's hand. "Shall we take a turn around the salon? There is an interesting portrait I'd like to get your opinion on."

Not giving Lucy a chance to protest, Sussex held on to Lucy's hand and all but dragged her from the dining room.

"Miss Fairmont—" Black's velvety voice cut through the silence "—if you would be so kind as to follow me to my study. I believe I have a stack of shilling shockers that may be of interest to you."

His tone was casual, but it brooked no opposition. She had no alternative but to obey, or to cause a scene before Elizabeth and Alynwick.

"If you will excuse me," she murmured as she moved away from the table. When she stood before Black, he took her hand, flipped it over and traced the lines of her palm with his fingertip.

"There aren't any shilling shockers or penny dreadfuls to show me, are there?"

His gaze met hers, and she felt her stomach flip and flop. Her throat was dry. Outside, she could hear the door of a carriage shutting, then the sound of horses' hooves clopping against the cobbles. Her uncle and Mr. Knighton were departing, leaving her quite at the mercy of Lord Black.

"No," he said as he pulled her to him. "There aren't. Come with me."

And like a sleepwalker, she followed him, willingly, even knowing it might very well be to her doom.

CHAPTER TWELVE

"WHERE ARE YOU taking me?"

"To my library, I thought you might like to see it." He smiled mischievously. "Don't all authors love books?"

She ought not to be charmed by him, but it was useless to put up a front. She was captivated and couldn't help it. She would follow him anywhere, and not just because he acknowledged her as an author, but because she adored books.

She knew she shouldn't follow him anywhere, and leaving her cousin behind and alone wasn't something she should do, either. "Lucy," she asked as she glanced over her shoulder, but Black pulled her along, down the darkened hallway, and around the corner.

"She'll be fine," he muttered. "Your cousin has the constitution to attend séances, I daresay she can handle herself with Sussex."

Opening the door, he ushered her through and Isabella forgot all about Lucy and Wendell, and the fact that she had vowed to put Black out of her mind and never again allow herself to be alone with him.

"Oh, look at this," she whispered in awe. Turning in a small circle, she stood, openmouthed, and looked at the walls that were covered in bookshelves from floor to ceiling, every inch of them housing books with different-covered spines with gilt lettering.

A massive desk with a large leather chair dominated the room, and she ran her fingers over the gleaming veneer thinking how lovely it would be to curl up in that chair and write her book at this very desk.

On the other side of the library were more chairs, all wingback, and a very beautiful black velvet chaise longue with gilt-scrolled edges sat in the middle of the room, with a thick carpet underneath.

The hearth was massive, the mantel constructed of marble with heavy Corinthian columns. The crest of the earls of Black dominated the center of the frontispiece, a Scottish shield with a cross and a dragon curled around it.

Above the fireplace was an enormous portrait of a knight who bore the white mantle and red cross of the Templars. His hair was long and black, his beard the same onyx color as his hair, and his eyes…she stared up at him, and imagined this man a little younger, his hair shorter, his face clean shaven… It was the very likeness of Black.

"Drake Sheldon, the first earl of Black," he announced as he stood beside her gazing up at the portrait. "He was known as the Dragon because, simply put, he was a beast both in and out of battle. They said that one could see the flames of hell mirrored in the metal of his sword as it came slashing down."

"You have his eyes. My goodness," she whispered. "It's uncanny the resemblance."

"Do you think so?"

"Oh, yes, it's remarkable. He was a Templar."

"Yes. Before he left on Crusade he was a knight for hire. He'd be considered a mercenary by today's standards, selling his sword and arm to the highest bidder. But back then, in the twelve hundreds, knights for hire were as common as girls selling oranges in front of theaters."

"This portrait is over five hundred years old?" she gasped.

"It is. In my country house, in…the north," he said,

"the portrait gallery is lined with my ancestors. There are all sorts of wily Blacks staring down at you as make your way down the hall."

"In the north?" she asked, not missing how he was purposely being elusive.

"Yes. The north."

"Where in the north?"

His flickered from the portrait to her. A muscle ticked in his jaw. "Just outside Helmsley."

"Why, that is not at all far from Whitby, my lord."

"Yes." He cleared his throat and swept his arm in a wide arc. "What do you think? An acceptable collection?"

"I think it magnificent," she said, and meant it. "How many books are here?"

"I haven't a clue."

"If I were so fortunate as to own a collection so splendid I would know exactly how many books I owned so as not to have anyone come in and steal them from beneath my nose," she announced.

Books had been a luxury they had never been able to afford. Isabella clutched what few books she possessed closely to her breast.

He saw that he was smiling at her. "This is my sanctuary. Only Billings comes in upon occasion to dust. The books are quite safe from thieves."

She could see why he called it his sanctuary; it was a dark, masculine domain, with wood paneling and emerald-green velvet curtains. The scent of lemon oil, leather books and Black's cologne perfumed the air. She could hide away in here for hours and just stare at the walls, and the fireplace, and the portrait of the first earl of Black and let her imagination take root and soar. Drake Sheldon, what a dashing name for a knight. How the ladies must have swooned over him.

"What is your name, my lord?" she asked, suddenly curious. He had ever only been Black to her, and it had always suited him, but now she was consumed with the need to know him in a much more intimate way. Did he have a name that was as debonair as his ancestor's?

"My family name is Sheldon."

"And your Christian name?"

He met her gaze, his long lashes casting shadows on his cheek. Behind those lashes his beautiful eyes appeared slightly more green in this light. "Jude."

"Jude," she repeated in a soft voice. What a lovely name. It suited him, that one syllable could at once be said in a hard voice, or uttered so softly, a whispered name in passion.

"Say it again," he rasped.

"Jude."

She saw that he closed his eyes, and his hands curled into fists at his sides.

"I have not heard my name in so long, and now, to hear your voice say it…it quite undoes me."

The energy that always seemed to hum between them suddenly crackled, sending Isabella closer to the book-case, anything to get away from him. Trying to gather her wits, she studied the titles of the books as she calmed her breathing.

Her gaze landed on a black leather volume with gold lettering. *Jane Eyre*.

"Oh," she whispered. "Is this a first edition?" It looked old enough to be, and the thought sent her blood pumping wildly.

Black watched her with his mysterious eyes. "Indeed. Do you like the story?"

"Oh, yes," she whispered as her fingers slid down along the spine of the book. "I like it very much. Lucy has a copy that she lent me. I read it in one night. It was so beautiful…so perfect. I could never write anything so… exquisite."

"I'm quite certain you could, Isabella."

"No, I couldn't. But I'll keep trying, and one day, when I am old and it no longer matters if I am published or not, I will create a masterpiece. Oh, how beautiful it is," she whispered as her fingers trailed along the wrinkled spine. "It's hard to believe that this book is nearly thirty years old—it's older than me."

"It was my mother's."

"A gift?"

"I don't know. My mother was forever buying books, I can only assume she purchased it. My father was never the sort to take notice of another's pleasures. I find it highly doubtful that he had purchased it for her."

"Oh." There was pain in his voice, and a hint of anger, too.

"Have you no copy of your own?" he asked softly, coming closer to her.

"No, I have not. I…have not used any of my pin money for books." Books would not feed you. Clothe you. She had spent too many years hungry, wearing wash-thinned clothing that had sometimes been little more than rags. The money her uncle so generously gave her went into a biscuit tin that Cook had allowed her to keep when it was emptied. The tin was hidden away beneath a floorboard under her dressing table. Beneath the mattress had seemed much too obvious to her and she was afraid of the upstairs maids coming into her room and stealing it. She was like a ferret, coveting her treasures. She had teeth; she could bite the hand that would take it from her very easily.

Try as she might, the events of her past would not simply vanish. The fear of being left destitute or a spinster made her very careful. The thought that something horrible might happen to her uncle sent a tremor of fear down her spine. She would be all alone again if Stonebrook were to die. Lucy would be taken care of, but Isabella didn't dare hope—or believe—the same would happen to her.

No, she was a frugal creature, while Lucy spent lavishly, but then her cousin had never known hardship. Her next meal had promptly arrived with the sounding of the gong. Isabella had never had that surety.

"What have you spent your money on, then?" His question was bold. The expression in his eyes even bolder, and Isabella was momentarily caught off guard by his closeness, by the frisson of awareness that was always, *always* present between them.

"Nothing," she confessed in a small whisper.

"A little magpie," he murmured as he reached out and trailed his finger along hers as they rested reverently against the book's spine. "You hoard it away," he whispered, and she realized how close he was, standing right behind her, touching her with his chest, with his fingers that slowly glided down hers in a sensual, almost unbearably erotic touch. She could feel the hardness of his chest, the heat of him, the scent of man and the lingering essence of the red wine.

She swallowed, closed her eyes, no longer able to watch his fingers atop hers, it felt too good, looked much too sinfully improper. And yet, the act seemed even more exciting with her eyes closed, because then she was left with only the sensation of touch, hearing—Black's slow breaths—and smell. Everything coalesced, and she was left struggling to keep from throwing herself at him.

"You must take this book, Isabella," he whispered, and she felt the brush of his hair against her cheek, then her neck. It was followed by the subtle sweep of his nose against her skin, and at last, the brush of his lips against the column of her neck. "I want you to have it, to open the pages and reverently turn them, to glide your fingers along the paper, tracing the words, thinking of me as you read."

"I…I…" Her head tilted to the side, even as she tried to prevent it. It opened her up, allowed Black's head to press deeper against her, his lips to sweep up and down her neck in a caress that stole her breath. His fingers, featherlight, like the wings of a butterfly, continued to trace across her hand.

"You know I cannot," she said, her voice cracking, belying the need that suddenly seemed all consuming. Her lips actually parted, seeking his mouth—but she would not follow them, would absolutely not turn her face to Black, and press her lips against his.

"I want to think of you in your room, in bed beneath the covers, reading this book, thinking of me. I want you to close your eyes, and remember this, this moment between us right now, where our desire and need is so palpable neither of us can resist—where we will just fall into each other's arms without thought or guilt, or fear of repercussions."

"I cannot," she rasped. "Not the book, not…what you're offering."

"You must, for if you don't take it, I will go out and buy you a copy and have it sent directly to your house, where everyone will see…and will know."

"Jude…" His name was broken, a deep sound part fear, but mostly need.

"Say it again," he ordered, his voice harsh against her throat. His arm wrapped around her waist, his palm, flattened against her belly, slowly slid upward, and his fingers, which had only seconds ago been lax against hers, curled tightly around her hand. "God, yes," he said, his voice a seductively, velvety caress. "Say it, whisper it, let me hear my name on your lips, let me feel your lips against my skin as you say it."

"We mustn't do this," she pleaded even as her fingers gripped his.

"Why mustn't we?" he asked as his palm slowly but

steadily climbed over her ribs to where it nestled between her breasts. Her eyes flew open and she saw that he traced the outline of one of the rosettes on her bodice with the tip of his index finger. Slowly he circled the fabric rose. Each time the circle became smaller and smaller as he worked toward the middle until he was very slowly, very erotically, circling the very center of the flower. It was a seductive innuendo of what he would do to her areola and nipple, and the image of his hand on her, his finger reaching out and touching her, circling her, made her stomach burn. Between her thighs she felt quivering, wet, aching—she could feel her body opening to him, and she was aroused and frightened by it.

No woman in the world could possess the willpower to withstand such beautiful torment. She was breathing much too fast, her breasts now hurt behind the harsh confines of her corset and the bodice, and despite all this she tried to fight it, the desire to know what it would be like to be held by him—ravished by his mouth and hands, the powerful body she felt crowding her from behind.

She couldn't continue like this. It was wrong. Deceitful. Dangerous.

"Did you tell him?" she asked on a gasp as he trailed his tongue behind her ear and over the delicate, sensitive shell.

"Tell him what?" He was back to toying with another rosette on her bodice. Behind her, she felt the hardness of him pressing into her backside. "How much I want you? How I haven't been able to stop looking at you all night in that gown? How now, I'm imagining what your body will look like beneath this red satin."

"Jude," she warned, but his name trailed off on a little moan as he slipped the tips of his fingers beneath the bodice and brushed the swells of her breasts with his warm fingertips. "You know what I'm asking. Did you

tell him about that afternoon in the carriage? Last night…
in the salon?"

"No. If Knighton wishes to know your activities he
should keep a better eye on you."

His fingers left her breast only to move around to her
back, and the little buttons that secured her gown. One
by one, he slowly undid them. "Please, don't. This…this
can't go on. You know that."

"Because of Wendell Knighton?" he asked incredulously. "Why would you waste yourself on a man like
that?"

*Because he won't break my heart when he leaves. Be-
cause there won't be this passion with him, and because
of that, I won't be afraid.*

"I don't know what you want from me."

"You don't?" The button came free and the bodice
gaped open in the back, the sleeves sliding off her shoulders. He pressed in, and she felt his lips against the bones
in her neck, then lower, as he pressed soft, silken kisses
along her spine above her corset.

"I want you, Isabella. Heart, body and soul. I want to
feel you beneath me, I want to know you—every inch of
this beautiful flesh. I want to see it turn pink from my
hands, the wicked words I want to whisper in your ear. I
want to learn your taste, the sound of your pleasure."

"Stop." But it was not a refusal that carried any weight.
It was a breathless sound, and he moaned, pressed his
forehead against her shoulder blade as he lowered her
bodice to her waist and returned his hand to the fleshy
mounds of her breasts that strained over her corset.

"Stop?" The word was pained. "That is like asking me
to hold back a new day, or the tide from rushing in. It is
like asking a starving man to sit at the table of a king and
watch as others around him feast. It is a feat that is impossible, Isabella. I can't do it." The words were breathed
against her, and she felt the hardness of him, now as hard

as ever, pressing relentlessly into her as he held on to her hand. With his free hand, he began to pull at her corset strings, and she kept her eyes shut in hopes it would settle her, but it only made it worse. In her mind were unbidden images, she heard the words—hers, and what she would later write in her book.

"Would you deny a starving man a little scrap?" he asked as the corset came undone in his hand. He turned her around, caging her body with the front of his. His arms were above her head, his fingers gripping the bookshelf as he peered down into her eyes. His gaze was devouring every inch of her.

"Tell me you don't want this." He pressed against her, let his head drop to her shoulder where he nuzzled his mouth against her throat and ear. "Tell me you haven't thought of this, wished for more than just kisses."

"Yes," she said, relenting. "I've thought of more. I've thought of your hands on me. My lips on you, learning how your skin will taste."

He groaned, cupped her face in his hands and lowered his mouth to hers. They fell into each other without thought, both meeting each other halfway, then melting into one as Black's lips took hers.

She had prepared herself for a physical assault, but was pleasingly, achingly aroused by his gentle kiss. It was slow, thoughtful, almost as if he was savoring her. His long fingers threaded tightly with hers while his other hand stroked the side of her face, down to her chin. His lips pressed once more against hers, then gently covered them, coaxing her to return his kiss.

It felt as though she were drugged, disembodied somehow. She was conscious of the moan that escaped her when he slanted his mouth against hers, encouraging her to open for him.

"Your tongue," he said against her lips. "I want to feel it."

She gasped at the same moment she felt his tongue slide along her lower lip. He parted her lips and slid his tongue into her mouth. She was left with the feel and taste of him as his tongue boldly swirled inside, mingling with hers.

It seemed like an eternity before he drew away. "You make me ache," he whispered, resting his face into the crook of her neck. She stilled her rapid breathing as his index finger slid down her throat to tickle the tops of her breasts. His breath came in short pants, whispering along her neck as he nuzzled the skin beneath her ear. "So soft," he murmured, burying his face farther against her neck. "So beautiful. Let me see you."

Her legs gave out as his long tapered finger circled her nipple through her corset. Her resolve was slipping, she knew it and was helpless to stop it. Every sensible thought was blown away on the breeze, despite the years and extensive experience of controlling her desires, of constantly reminding herself of her mother's hardships—which all stemmed from passion. A passionate nature that Isabella had inherited.

Moving barely an inch away, Black allowed the corset to fall to the floor, landing at his feet. She was naked to the waist. He did not lower his gaze, but looked her in the eye, watching her, and she was undone by what she saw. Stark need. Masculine arousal. He wanted her. She had never been wanted or desired by anyone and the feeling was euphoric, addictive.

Reaching for one of her hands, he brought it up over her head, held it with his other hand. Then reached for the other arm, made her fingers curl into each other as he held both her arms up with one hand. Her back was arched, her breasts lifted high toward him, and then his gaze slowly burned a path down her face, to her lips, to the bounding pulse in her throat, and then to her breast.

She felt that gaze instantly, and her nipples puckered, lengthened for him.

She waited for him to touch her, but he stood still, just looking, and she couldn't stand it, the pain, the need she felt to be touched—kissed—to be wanted. Just once, she wanted to feel someone's desire for her. To feel touch that was meant only to please and arouse, a touch meant only for her.

Please, she silently pleaded. *Oh, please, just love me...*

"JUDE!" IT WAS A HUSKY reply that did strange things to his brain, making him think of nothing other than hearing his name on her lips as he slid inside her. She would be hot and wet, and tight...so tight. She would be his.

Her breasts were arched forward, a perfect offering, and he could not resist just staring, letting the tempest of lust swirl inside him.

He wanted to touch, to cup and watch her breasts spilling out of his hands. He wanted to put the tip of his tongue to her pebbled nipples and taste the pink buds. He wanted to tease and toy with her, just as he had to the fabric rose on her bodice.

"You want this," he rasped. "Admit it, tell me, Isabella. Just this once. Give me the words."

"Yes," she gasped, breathless. She struggled in his hold, but he held her tighter. He wanted her like this, a supplicant for his pleasure. He would not hurt her, harm her, but he would awaken her slowly. To bewitch her with pleasure, to bind him to her. Wendell Knighton would be long forgotten by the time he fitted himself inside Isabella's body.

Pressing forward, he rubbed his cheek against the full swells, inhaled her perfumed skin. He could hear her heart beating hard, and he kissed her where her heart hammered against his lips.

"Little magpie," he whispered. "You clutch everything

to you, trying to keep it close, so afraid to lose it. But there is no fear with me. I'll stay close, and you can clutch me forever. I'll never let you go."

She said nothing, only gasped as he lowered his mouth and circled her areola, which was shell pink, with the tip of his tongue.

Her moan nearly unmanned him, and he pressed forward, seeking relief between her thighs. She felt so soft against him, so right. Her breasts were full and high and made for his mouth and hands, and her thighs, good God, they hugged and molded his erection as if she had been designed for him. Everything about her was perfect. But he wanted more. Needed more. To feel the heat between her legs, the honey of her on his fingers.

Carefully he tongued her once more, let the tip of his tongue press against her nipple as he reached for her skirts and pulled them slowly up her thigh. The sound of satin sliding upward was an erotic charge. The panting breaths—both hers and his mingled together. Her little whimper as she felt his fingers trace her garter only made him more crazed.

Their eyes met, and he watched her, then turned to her breast, kissing her, positioning her, and then, he took her nipple into his mouth, and simultaneously snuck his finger into her folds.

One long moan echoed in the quiet. It was both of theirs, and Black closed his eyes, feeling Isabella's body clamping down on his finger.

"Jude," she whispered, and he looked up, straightened, demanded that she look at him. How beautiful she was to him, her arms held high, her fingers clasping his, her green eyes ablaze with desire.

Carefully he stroked her, watched her mouth part, her tongue sneak out and wet her lips. She was cresting, building, and she tried to close her eyes, to shield him from watching her, but he stopped, toyed with her until she obeyed his whispered commands.

When she was looking at him, and he could see her, could watch her fall apart, and come in his arms, he pleasured her with slow intimate strokes of his fingers. He built her up, then set his fingers on her, circled the little bud of flesh and nerves, and watched her eyes go wide.

"I can make you feel this way when I'm inside you," he said as their gazes locked. "I can touch you, make you cry out, make you fall apart as I'm buried deep, loving you."

He had no idea she would respond as such. She was innocent, and this was her first taste of pleasure. So, when she cried out and began to tremble and shake in his arms, he was helpless to do anything but watch her, memorizing her, knowing she was going to look even more arousing when she was beneath him, his body deeply inside hers.

When the tremors subsided, she collapsed in his arms, and he went to the floor, taking her with him so that she sat in his lap. He held her, kissed the top of her head and closed his eyes, feeling her in his arms.

"The first time I saw you I wanted you this way."

"At the ball?" she asked, rubbing her face against his chest like a well-fed kitten.

Sighing, he held her close, wondering how much of the truth he should give her. Would she run from him if he told her that he'd first seen her almost two years before, in Whitby? She seemed a nervous creature when it came to her past, and the things she didn't want anyone to know. He didn't want this moment to end, to disrupt the intimacy that was now between them. She was softening, allowing herself to indulge, and he was afraid that honesty would ruin it all.

"Jude?"

"Yes," he lied. "At the ball."

The way she felt in his arms was sheer perfection.

He still ached with unspent desire, still wanted so much more, but holding her like this, having her curl into him for safety and comfort, was just as pleasant for now.

"My lord?" The sharp rap on the door made Isabella go stiff in his arms, as if she had forgotten everything outside this room.

"Shh," he whispered while he rubbed his hand up her naked back. "It is only my butler and he would never dare enter until I gave him leave."

Nodding, she kept her face pressed against his cravat, and her fingers buried in the back of his shirt. God, he couldn't give her up. Not now, not ever and especially not tonight. He wanted to sit here on the floor of his library all night long and just hold and caress her. He wanted to talk, to learn everything about her. He wanted to hear about her life, her book, her dreams.

"I've readied the carriage, my lord. It's nearly eleven. I thought you'd like to know."

"Thank you, Billings. I shall be there momentarily."

Tipping up her chin, he took in her face, her ruined hair that looked utterly captivating and her kiss-swollen lips. She had never looked more beautiful to him, a picture of ravishment, and he was the ravisher.

Smiling tenderly, he clutched her face in his palms and stroked his thumb over her lips. "How will I sleep tonight?" he asked. "When my arms will ache for you, and behind my closed eyes I will see you, shattering in my arms, a picture so beautiful and arousing, I will have to play it over and over."

She was shy, and she closed her eyes, avoiding him, but he placed a gentle kiss on each eyelid.

"Let me get you safely home."

"Yes, we've been in here much too long."

Tipping her chin up, he gazed into her eyes, losing himself. "Not nearly long enough, Bella."

CHAPTER THIRTEEN

"WELL THAT WAS THE MOST exciting dinner of my life!"

Climbing the huge winding staircase that led to their rooms, Isabella held on to the banister, her legs still shaking and her mind swirling with the memories of what she had done with Black not more than ten minutes before.

"Imagine, talking of such things! There was absolutely no discretion at the table, and how I loved it! I never knew it could be so liberating to be freed of social constraints. I thought Papa would have paroxysms, though, when Knighton and Black challenged him about the lower orders."

Content to let Lucy carry the conversation, Isabella stayed inside her mind, reliving those moments of sheer bliss in Black's arms. The way he had touched her, suckled her breasts. It was…rapturous. She should never have allowed it, of course, but she had been at the mercy of her own desires. One taste, the taunting demon inside her coaxed. She had thought it would be enough, just a little glimpse of what she would find in Black's arms if she allowed herself to fall. But like a sweet from the candy shop, she could not stop at just one.

"Wasn't Sussex's sister delightful? Imagine, his sister!" Lucy shook her head and smiled. "I was perfectly horrid to her, and I did find a moment to apologize to her in private. I…I don't know what came over me."

Isabella did. Lucy may not understand it, but she was, on some level, attracted to the duke. Seeing him there with a woman brought those feelings to the forefront, and she hadn't been able to control the swift sense of jealousy she was experiencing.

Isabella was happy for her cousin. The duke was an excellent choice. Perfect for Lucy, in fact. Unlike Black, who was the exact opposite. Where the duke represented safety, Black was danger. The duke would temper Lucy's sometimes flighty nature. Where Black brought out the absolute worst in her.

She had acted like a wanton in his arms. Everything she had told herself she must not allow was flown away with his touch.

"Elizabeth is so cultured, so very adept at conversation. I wonder why she doesn't come out into society?"

"Perhaps her blindness inhibits her," Isabella suggested. She more than anyone knew how harsh the ton could be to those whom they felt were inferior. While Elizabeth appeared to be well adjusted and content with her lot in life, Isabella knew that a woman wore two faces—the face she knew everyone wanted to see—and the face she hid—the one that was her true self.

"Elizabeth and I are going shopping tomorrow," Lucy prattled on. "You'll come, won't you?"

"Of course." She would love to see Elizabeth again, and the outing would keep her mind off Black and what had happened in his library.

The door opened to Isabella's chamber, and Lucy followed her in. Isabella had to admit that she was somewhat irked by her cousin's presence. She was not up for entertaining Lucy tonight. She was exhausted, both mentally and physically. As she lay in Black's lap, held in his arms, his scent and body heat enveloping her, she had wanted to close her eyes and sleep. Wanted to awaken in his arms. Whatever he had done to her made her feel lazy and languid, a boneless heap of quivering flesh. And his butler had knocked on the door, making the sensation of euphoria slip away, replaced by horror. What had she done?

"Lady Elizabeth's blindness does not bother me one whit, Issy." Lucy sighed as she flopped down onto Isabella's bed. "What of you?"

Perhaps spending a few minutes talking with Lucy was the tonic she needed to get her mind off Black and the feelings in her body. She was restless, and her body, now that it seemed awakened to passion, wanted more.

"No, of course her blindness is of no bother to me. I find her quite brave, in fact, and very beautiful."

"Yes, her eyes, how lovely they are, so gray and mysterious, like a steel-laden winter sky. I would never have guessed she was blind, for her eyes…well, you know what I mean."

"She wasn't born blind, I do recall that."

"Yes, well," Lucy said as she lay onto the pillows, "it doesn't matter to me. For I'm certain that Elizabeth will make us a most agreeable companion, and a wonderful friend. I don't have many friends," Lucy murmured.

Neither of them did. They were each other's best friend. And that had always seemed enough for Isabella. But suddenly she was thinking of her cousin, looking at her lying in the middle of the bed—so beautiful and fashionable. Rich, titled. She should be the belle of the ball, the favorite of the ton. She should have a hundred friends, and yet she didn't. There were few girls their age that could be described as acquaintances, but nothing more than that.

"And what of the duke?" she found herself asking. "Does he improve upon closer inspection?"

Lucy's face flamed as red as her hair. "The Duke of Delicious," she drawled, using the sobriquet the women of the ton had given the duke. "There is no denying he is a handsome man, but he is not what I want." Frowning, Lucy looked away. "He's too bland. Staid. I want someone more elemental. Someone at the mercy of his own desires, who would do anything, risk anything, to be with me. Like your Lord Black, Issy."

"He isn't *my* Lord Black," she muttered irritably.

"Isn't he? He certainly seemed like he was yours when you exited the library. Were you aware that your hair was not quite right, and that Black's hand was intimately and possessively pressed against your back? No, Issy, I fear he is yours, whether you want him or not. And, you'd be a damn fool if you didn't."

"How can you say that? You know nothing of Black! *I* know nothing of *him!*"

"What is there to know? He's an earl, he's rich and he's utterly besotted with you. And he desires you. His every look speaks of it. He can't keep his gaze off you. He was practically devouring you with his stare during supper."

"I don't know him, Luce. Not his past, his future, what his dreams are. I don't know what sort of man he really is. There is nothing between us but a strange, and rather alarming, flare of desire," she said while biting her lip. She was pacing. She couldn't help it. Lucy watched her from the bed, her head tilted with curiosity.

"Issy, I think you had better tell me what happened in the library."

Never! Oh, she could never admit to another living soul how brazen she'd been—she had not even pretended to rebuff his advance. He had touched her *there,* and she had never protested, just asked for more—encouraged him with her moans and the way she'd panted like a common dockside harlot.

He had gone slowly, the raising of her skirts had been gradual and seductive. He'd given her plenty of time to protest, but she hadn't thought of it. Not once. By the time he turned her to face him, her mental admonishments had ceased and the dangerous and unseemly behavior was being encouraged with the voice of desire. She'd wanted it. What he gave her, and that much more.

It had been liberating. She had loved the feel of being desired so fiercely by another living soul. But now, in the aftermath, she was mortified by her easy fall. But more than that she was afraid. Afraid of what she had become. Afraid that, like her mother, she was thinking of the next time she would see him, touch him.

"Oh, Issy," Lucy said irritably. "Look at you, wearing a path into the carpet. For heaven's sake, you're not going to hell because of a little kiss and caress."

Lucy's irreverence annoyed her. How could she make so little of the turmoil of what was eating away at her?

"Oh, do not look at me like that," Lucy said as she sat up, watching her. "You're allowed to be attracted to Lord Black. He's a beautiful, mysterious man. I daresay any woman's dream. And he wants you. How can you deny it? How can you refuse it? If I had a man desiring me with such passion," she continued, "I would not hesitate to take what was offered."

"Well, you and your kind have that ability. Others do not."

"What do you mean me and my kind?" Lucy demanded as she flew off the bed. "What an absolute insult!"

"It is the defect of the aristocracy, isn't it, to take whatever they want with little consequence. But an ordinary person like me cannot do so, not without consequence."

"Oh, do not use that excuse with me, Isabella. You've been living the life of an aristocrat and taking to it quite nicely. You cannot now look down your nose at us. Besides, this has nothing to do with me, but Black, and what he does to you. You're a frightened little mouse, afraid to reach out for what you want. I wouldn't be, not in a million years."

"That is because you are spoiled!" Isabella countered, unsure of just where this sudden rage was springing from. She only knew that it bubbled up, erupted like the force of the ocean pounding relentlessly against the rocks. "You care only for yourself, your own pleasures. You don't care what happens, or who gets hurt just as long as you get whatever it is you want!"

"Oh, how could you!" Lucy cried. "Is that what you think of me? You chastise me because I would follow my heart? You think I'm blind about Sussex? Well, you should have a look in the mirror, Isabella, because you're being just as blind. Black wants you, and you want him! You're just too frightened to allow yourself to take him. You're still that waif from Yorkshire, cowering in fear, making excuses to not enjoy life because of what your mother chose to do with her life!"

"And then what?" she demanded as they stood toe to toe baring themselves to one another. "I shall surrender to him, and he will tire of me and cast me aside. And then I will be soiled goods. No, I will not allow it. I don't want what he's offering. I'd rather be the cowardly waif from Yorkshire. At least I know her. I don't know this person you want to make me into—this creature who lives for pleasure. Who would offer herself to a man she barely knows."

"So, what Wendell Knighton is offering is something much better? He could not even be bothered to greet you properly or escort you in to dinner. You're wasting yourself on a man who only wants you because you further his social position and open doors to him that might have forever remained closed."

That stung. Even as it stabbed at her heart, Isabella knew it for the truth. In a sense, they were both using each other.

"Why would you throw away your life in such a way? God," Lucy raged, "you have been given what few others in this world have. You've been given a second chance at life, and you're going to toss it away for something cold and calculated and safe!"

"There is nothing wrong with longing for safety."

"There is everything wrong with settling," Lucy countered. "And selling your soul for comfort, instead of giving it freely to the man you want."

"You may think that way, Lucy, because you have never had to worry over anything more substantial than when your pin money will be increased so you can buy anything and everything you see. You can give your soul and body to whoever you damn well please because deep down you know your father has power and influence. He can make any man yours. But it is not like that for me."

"It is, you just stubbornly refuse to see it. You'd rather hide like a coward than to live. You almost died, and here you are, given a second chance and still you refuse to live. Your fears of your past rule you."

"Perhaps if you understood hardship, if you knew what it was like to be denied anything, instead of having everything handed to you on a silver platter, you would understand my feelings. But as is so typical of you, this conversation has turned into what you would do, what you would feel if you were me. Well, you aren't, and you can never, ever know what it was like to grow up as I did. What it is like to be me."

"And this is what you think of me, that I am a spoiled, indulged, pleasure-seeking ingrate."

"Yes," she gasped, then immediately wished to take it back. "No, Lucy, not exactly—"

The ravaged expression on her cousin's face made her reach out to her, but Lucy's green eyes suddenly blazed, and she brushed past her, running to the door. "Do you know something, Isabella, you don't know me, either. You're much more indulged and spoiled than I, because the one thing I've longed for my whole life is what Black is giving you. And do you know, I could almost hate you for tossing it aside for some lukewarm respect and barely feigned attraction from Wendell Knighton. You have been given the one gift that money cannot buy—true desire, and I daresay love. Dearest Papa," she spat, "won't be able to buy that for me."

Her body jolted as the door slammed behind Lucy. In a fit of despair, Isabella slid to the floor and gave in to a flood of tears.

Lucy was wrong. She didn't understand anything, most especially Black, and her fears of unbridled passion. They would ruin a woman who had nothing. She had seen it. Lived it. Lucy had been tucked away, richly clothed and fed. If she was cold, a servant was summoned to stoke the fire. When she had been cold, Isabella had had no choice but to huddle beneath threadbare blankets. Stoking the fire had not been an option, because more times that not, they had been saving the last piece of coal or two.

No, Lucy did not know what it was to suffer, to long. But as she wiped the tears from her cheeks, Isabella thought of her cousin, the hurt, the devastation in her green eyes. And then she realized that behind the haughty indignation was the look of a young woman who had suffered. It had always been there, although vague, and fleeting, she had seen it, on more than one occasion—but more of late.

Lucy knew what it was to be sad. To hurt. To long for something she could never have.

THEY GATHERED in the upper balcony where the candle-light could not reach, and where the shadows reigned. Ceremonial incense wafted in curling tendrils, the scent of frankincense cloying the air, coating their clothes and hair. Below them, members of the lodge surrounded the candidate who was applying to be initiated in the first degree.

The steward walked to where Wendell Knighton stood in black trousers and a white shirt. He had been stripped of his coat and neckcloth, and was in the process of being divested of all money. His shirt was pulled open, his chest bared, then he was blindfolded and a rope placed around his neck. Next, the tip of a sword was placed over Knighton's heart as he swore never to reveal the secrets of the craft, the mysteries, the handshake and password, the tools of their kind.

Black remembered taking his vows. His father had been the worshipful master, and had actually pierced the sword tip through his skin. Black could still feel the warmth of his blood running down his chest and stomach; his initiation had been more than the mere taking of the first degree. His acceptance into the lodge was symbolic of the oath he was undertaking. It was not just to keep the secrets of the craft to himself, but something else.

Later he had been taken below stairs, to the old crypt that had once been the place where the Templars had held their secret meetings. There, he had been stripped to the waist and placed on a stone slab. Surrounding him had been his father, the old Duke of Sussex and the Marquis of Alynwick. Beside the marquis had been his son, Iain, who watched with knowing eyes. He had already been initiated to his first degree, and branded.

As his father turned and reached for the handle of a brand, its glowing metal, orange at the end, Iain had pressed forward in a pretense of whispering the words of the sacred induction ritual of the Brethren Guardian.

"It burns like the devil's tongue licking your skin," he murmured. "Lay quiet and still and endure it. It will be faster. If you struggle, they'll only prolong it. They want us men, strong of mind and body."

He pulled away and Black watched him, his eyes fixed on the ice-blue eyes of Sinclair who, at sixteen, was already rough-hewn and hard. Black knew at that moment that Iain had struggled, maybe even cried out, and had suffered the effects of three old men and their absurd drive to carry out an ancient, barbaric ritual.

"The candidate is ready," Iain said, his voice deep. He

did not glance away, but held Black's gaze, giving him unspoken strength to endure. At fifteen years old, Black was a year younger than Sinclair, but he doubted he was stronger. There was something in Sinclair's eyes that was at once comforting and frightening. Black did not flinch or cry out when the brand sizzled against his chest. Did not frown or turn his nose up at the smell of burning flesh and hair. Sinclair did not, either, for he was inured to pain.

Black gritted his teeth, held Iain's gaze as, his anchor and endured the horrific pain of being branded.

"Again." It was the old Duke of Sussex's voice, the sadistic bastard. "He did not cry out. He acts above us, above the pain, above God."

It was the only time Sinclair's gaze ever wavered. Iain had cried out and was punished. Thinking to save Black such pain, he had warned him, only to discover that the three men standing above him in white robes adorned with red crosses would punish him for not crying out and surrendering to his pain.

He was branded again, only this time it was his father who pressed the searing metal into his skin, letting it stay for unendurable seconds. Only when he screamed and fought the bonds that bound his wrists and hands did his father lift the brand.

"He is humbled," his father replied.

"What is your oath?" Sussex growled, and Black could hardly speak, could barely see through the black cloud of pain.

"Never tell what you know. Never say what you are. Never lose our faith in your purpose, for the kingdom to come will have need of me and my sons."

The symbol of those words no longer burned his flesh, but they scorched his mind. He could not imagine giving his son up to this, this band of families. He could not imagine Isabella willingly giving her child over to him, to torture with heated brands—would she ever countenance her own flesh and blood as a Brethren Guardian?

"So easy for them, isn't it?" Alynwick murmured as they looked upon the initiation of Knighton. "Had they any idea of what we endured, they would run." Alynwick snorted with distaste. "Cowards, all of them. There is no loyalty amongst them, no faith. It has become a social club, a reason to meet and smoke and indulge in dinners. There is nothing of the old ways. It is only men of leisure who join now. Dilettantes."

"I think it's them that are the normal ones," Black muttered. "It is only the three of us who are crazed. A legacy from our fathers."

Alynwick snorted in disgust. "Knighton is the biggest dilettante of all. He's only here because we need to keep an eye on him, and it was right to do so."

"How has Knighton come dangerously close to the truth?" Sussex murmured.

"I don't know," Black replied as he listened to Knighton repeating his vows.

"You haven't been free with your tongue, have you, Black?"

"If you're insinuating that I've spoken to Isabella about this, then you can go to hell, Alynwick. I may not like what I am obligated to do. I may not believe in those damn relics, but I gave my word. And I do believe in my vow of honor. I have not spoken to Isabella about any of this."

"Then how does Knighton know?"

"I don't know. Who killed Alice Fox? I don't know. Who wrote the letters to Alice, on Masonic letterhead? I don't know," he growled.

"We must move fast," Alynwick demanded. "We have to find the chalice and the pendant. Damn me, I'd love to know how Knighton discovered so much about the pendant, how it contains the seeds from the apple of the Garden of Eden."

"What I would like to know more is how he knows the seeds, when mixed with innocent blood in the chalice, brings knowledge and immortality," Black murmured. "Just think of the consequences if they're found. Mankind will be forever changed, plunged into darkness and sin by the very serpent who seduced Eve into sinning."

"What did you learn from Lucy, Sussex?" Alynwick asked.

"Nothing. She vehemently denied even knowing about the House of Orpheus. She protects someone," he snarled. "Someone she must care a great deal for, because she is keeping his secrets close to her."

"At least the scroll is safe," Black reminded them. "That will buy us time while we search for who is involved." Glancing at the dozen of Brethren below them, he studied each one. Lords and politicians, doctors and barristers, they came from all walks of life and, unlike Stonebrook, Black knew that it could very well be an aristocrat behind the whole business. But why? What was the motivation? That was the crucial piece that was missing.

"I'm going to the museum," Alynwick murmured. "I have a feeling that Knighton has stumbled across something in Jerusalem."

"I'll go to Miss Fox's house," Black said. "She claimed she destroyed the letters, but maybe she was lying."

Sussex nodded. His fingers rapped against the marble balustrade. "I'll stay and follow Stonebrook. We cannot deny that Lucy has some involvement. Perhaps the old marquis does as well—perhaps he keeps Masonic letterhead."

"Then it's to the Adelphi to investigate the club."

"Knighton will spend the night here for his contemplation of the darkness. It's the best time for us to continue our investigation, knowing he'll be here and not following us."

Silent as wraiths and as unseen as ghosts, the three

of them dispersed deep into the shadows, their ancient order calling them forth to find the relics, and protect them from greedy humans who would use them for their dark powers.

"Tomorrow, in the park. We'll meet on Rotten Row, make it look like a coincidence," Alynwick said. "We must make sure we're not seen too much together. We may be being watched."

"I'll bring the carriage, and Elizabeth. It will look more natural if we're not all on horseback."

"Damnation, man, she doesn't need to be involved in this business," Alynwick growled. "She's too fragile, too…well, you must have a care with her."

"She was involved the day she was born. The day my father dragged her into this business of Templars. Besides, she did a wonderful job of ferreting out information from Knighton, and deflecting the conversation from our families when he got too close. Once she discovers where I am going and what I am doing, there will be no stopping her. I thought you knew how bullheaded she can be."

Sussex was talking to the air, because Alynwick was already gone. Black looked at him, shrugged and headed the other way, for the back exit of the building. He did not need anyone to see him. He wanted to be undisturbed when he searched Alice Fox's house. He knew now he was being watched by someone from inside the Freemasons. More than ever he should stay away from Isabella—for her protection, but she was already involved. His gut told him that it would not be as simple as staying away from her. If he thought it would keep her safe, he would try to give her wide berth until the matter was solved. But the murder of Alice Fox and Isabella's name being purposely written on that letter sent his instincts tingling. She needed his protection. His love could save her. In more ways than one.

IT WAS NEARLY OVER. The silence was deafening, his blindness disorienting. This was the final part of the initiation. The hours he would spend contemplating the darkness. When they came back for him, he would be unbound, reborn to the light. It was part of the ancient Templar practice, and Wendell Knighton breathed deeply, focusing on what he most wanted.

The door of the lodge echoed through the columned room, alerting him to the fact that he was now all alone in the lodge—bound and blinded.

"Up you go."

The shock of the voice behind him made him stiffen. "Who's there?" he asked, but silence answered him. He felt himself pulled from where he knelt and dragged along. Stumbling in his blindness, he struggled to keep up.

"Where are you taking me?"

"Keep your damn mouth shut."

Through the darkness he walked, blind, hands bound, the rope around his neck tightening as some unseen person guided him through winding twists and turns like a horse being led by the reins.

This was not part of the initiation ceremony. He knew that much.

"Where are you taking me?" he demanded. But he was met with silence, just as he had been the other dozen times he had demanded explanation for this absurd behavior.

He was nervous, he was sweating with it. He didn't like the feel of this. The danger. He had the sense it was Black. There had been a menacing air about him at dinner. More than once he had caught Black staring at him. Those strange eyes of his could unnerve a man, and in truth they had intimidated him. There was blatant dislike in those eyes…dislike, and a very great anger.

On the carriage ride over he had wondered about it, what had he done? Black had sponsored him, but left it up to Stonebrook to see him educated and prepared to take the first degree.

Isabella. Somehow he knew it had something to do with her. He'd seen Black's villainous gaze coveting her, devouring her in that low-cut gown. She had no reason to wear such a garment. She was lovely and pure, and tonight she had been dressed like a courtesan. He had been enraged when he saw her, so angry that he hadn't trusted himself to greet her.

That sort of gown was best left to the boudoir, for the eyes of a husband. She had flaunted her luscious body, the creamy swells of her breasts, and he had almost taken a hold of her and pulled her from the room. But Black had been there, assessing his every move. And then there was Stonebrook. He had made it very clear that he loved his niece and considered her happiness and safety vital to his own. He could not afford to become ill favored in the old marquis's eyes. Marrying Isabella would open many doors to him—more than he could have ever hoped for. And having Isabella for a wife would not be a hardship. She was beautiful and timid. So eager to please. She would be biddable and would not complain when he continued his pursuits for knowledge. She had looked surprised and perhaps a bit let down that he would be leaving again for the East, but she would not give him any fits of pique. She knew her place. She was the exact sort of wife he had always wanted. And bedding her wouldn't be a chore. His appetites, compared to those of other men, were rather subdued. But they had been suddenly aroused tonight, seeing Isabella in that harlot's gown.

It was all due to her cousin, the rash, impetuous Lucy Ashton. He loathed her and everything she stood for. She was the embodiment of the aristocracy that the middling class, as Stonebrook called him and his brethren, despised. She lived for pleasure and felt no guilt that she had so much, while millions had nothing.

He had risen from virtually nothing to get where he was. The thought of marrying a woman from the ton repulsed him, but then he had met Isabella. She was of blue blood, but with a humble upbringing and a past scandal that had been very tightly shut up. He'd decided immediately that he would have her as his wife. Isabella represented the blossoming of his career through gifts and introductions from Stonebrook, while making it possible for him not to compromise his principles. The very thought of placating a spoiled wife was anathema to him. Isabella had grown up poor and in harsh circumstances. She would be grateful—and happy—for anything he gave her. He would be kind. He would allow her—to a certain extent—to read the ridiculous gothic stories she liked so much, provided they did not taint her idea of what sort of marriage they should have. Often, those silly weekly serials gave women the wrong impression of what a man should be. *Silly love stories,* he thought as he tripped along.

He would have her to wife, provided he survived this ordeal. And if Black was behind this bit of business, he doubted very much he would live to see the morning light.

Death was no stranger to the Earl of Black. He had discovered at least that much about the reclusive earl. It was suspected that Black had murdered his brother in cold blood after discovering his brother's plan to run off with the woman the earl was intended to marry. After offing his brother, he'd turned his murderous intent to his fiancée. The police had deemed her death a suicide, but there were many who believed she'd died at his hand.

If he survived tonight, he would make certain Isabella knew of Black's character. Make her realize how much of a danger he was to young women.

They had stopped, and Wendell felt warmth on his bare chest, as if he stood in the glow of a hundred candles. He heard the hiss of candle flame as a draft swept through the alcove.

"Kneel."

He was forced to his knees at the command of a new voice, a familiar voice. There was an accent to it. A rather cultured accent. If he could only hear it again.

"Wendell Knighton, correct?"

"It is." That voice… He searched his mind trying to place it, but could not.

"You found something of interest in Jerusalem, did you not?"

He swallowed hard; the thickness of the air was saturated with danger. "Yes."

"An ancient text that tells of how three Templar knights were given three sacred relics to protect from the world."

How had they discovered such a thing? He'd said nothing about it, not to anyone. Unless they had been to his house and discovered…

"Bastards," he spat, thrashing about his bonds. The rope around his neck was pulled back and was choking him. Damn thieves! The bastards were everywhere. Well, they would get nothing out of him. That was his find, and he would die in silence and under torture, for he would never reveal what he knew. That find would bring him riches—greatness. It would be his claim to fame, and he would not see someone else take it from him, not after all the digging, the weeks of finding nothing! And then, when he had almost abandoned all hope, he'd come across the dusty, crumbling tome, and the story of the Templars and the relics they had taken from the Holy Land. It had long been maintained the Templars had been guardians of an ancient wisdom, and the text he'd found proved that fact.

"Release him."

The rope went slack and he pitched forward, gasping and coughing. He heard footsteps walk around him, the brush of a robe against his bound hand, and then he was brought upright.

"Who the hell are you?" Wendell rasped.

"Orpheus."

"Not bloody likely," he snapped. "You're a treasure-hunting thief."

"In a way, I suppose I am, but you need have no fear of me."

The voice was more familiar. He could almost place it…

"You found an ancient text that speaks of three Templars. You discovered that they have in their possession relics of significant religious importance."

He neither confirmed nor denied the accusation, but remained on his knees, head bent, and allowed his captor to talk. Religious importance, perhaps, but from what the tome said, it went way beyond that. It was a mixture of alchemy and black magic and the power of the devil himself—and with that came the darkness, the greatest gifts one could ever dream of.

"I want to offer you a chance to make your place in the world. I know the name of the three Templars, and their descendants—the Brethren Guardians."

"How?"

The sound of the laugh chilled him, even as he was intrigued by the very notion of this person knowing anything about his mysterious Templars, and even more, the artifacts.

"I have risen from hell, have seen Death and survived his grip—I have knowledge that you can only begin to guess at."

"Black," he gasped, suddenly seeing it quite clearly—remembering the earl's expression as he talked of his discovery at supper. "Black is one of them—these guardians."

"Well done, Knighton. Yes. Black is one of them."

"And Sussex, and Alynwick."

"Good," the man named Orpheus said with a laugh. "You have all the pieces you need."

"What do you want from me?"

"For you to join us."

"Why?"

"We need your skills, your ability to speak the tongue of the ancients—and the chalice and scroll. And as a gesture of good faith, I will give you this."

His hands were lifted and a thin metal chain was curled into his palm. His thumb caressed the metal, and swept over something egg shaped and smooth. Heat rose from the metal, and he swore he could hear the seductive siren song of a woman's voice calling to him.

"The pendant from the Garden of Eden?"

"Indeed. Take it, and in return you will help me."

"To do what?" he asked with suspicion.

"I need you to discover the scroll that is necessary to decipher the powers behind the pendant and the chalice. Think of it, Knighton, being able to bring this story to light. To take credit for such a monumental find."

He could hardly believe it, knew he should probably realize it was too good to be true, but the power of knowing he would be the first to expose the Templar story was too enthralling. He knew what he kept hidden in his workroom. Knew what he held in his hand was the monumental piece he needed.

"Have we a deal, Knighton?"

"Yes," he rasped closing his fist around the pendant. "Yes."

"My man will contact you when I am ready for you. Tell no one of this. Most especially do not alert the Brethren Guardians that you know anything about them."

"No," he whispered, "no, I won't."

"Do not make an enemy of me, Knighton," his captor said with chilling coldness. "You would not like what I would do to you if I find you have betrayed me."

CHAPTER FOURTEEN

UNABLE TO FIND Lucy in her chamber, Isabella cracked open the door to the sitting room where Lucy sewed. She found her there, sitting at the round table with a piece of emerald-green velvet in her hand. Surrounding her were the hundreds of dolls that had been carefully placed on shelves, and the dozens of dollhouses she had collected since childhood. They were all dressed in elaborate costumes—all made by Lucy's hand.

As writing was a solace to Isabella, these dolls, and the dresses she made, were a comfort to her cousin. Isabella should have known this was where she would find her.

"What are you doing here?" Lucy demanded as she held up the cloth to inspect her work.

"I came to see what you were doing."

"Acting spoiled and indulged, as you can see. I'm working on a new frock for Christmas, because I haven't enough already."

Wincing, Isabella said, "I deserved that."

Closing her eyes, Lucy bent her head. "No, you didn't." When she looked up, her eyes were shining with tears. "I apologize for what I said before, Issy. I've sat here all this time wondering how in the world I could have said such a horrific thing. No one is more relieved that you survived that November night. I don't know what I was thinking to accuse you of not living your life to the fullest."

Isabella took the empty chair beside Lucy and ran her fingers over the gorgeous green velvet that Lucy was embroidering with silver thread.

"I think we both made statements we regret, but the things you said to me were not without some truth."

Lucy reached for her hand, clasped it tightly in hers. "Issy, pay me no mind. I'm…not myself."

"I've noticed you haven't been for quite a while, Lucy. And it's gotten much worse this past month, since…Mr. Knighton began paying me attention."

She glanced away, but Isabella lowered her head, forcing Lucy to meet her gaze. "Won't you tell me, Luce? Maybe I can help you. Maybe I can't, but it is better not to keep these thoughts and feelings bottled up inside."

"Oh, Issy…" Lucy began to cry in earnest. "I am not a spoiled child, and whatever people think of me is not the truth. I can only say that I, too, have been hurt. And while I did not grow up poor like you, I was every bit as lonely as you. Do you think it is only your mother who has this family's share of passion? No, it is you and I that she has bequeathed them to."

"Lucy, what is this about?"

"Don't you see?" Lucy whispered as she dried her tears. "It is about you and me, and our futures. Issy," she cried, squeezing her hands. "You have a chance to live— truly live—with a man who feels so much for you, and you would throw it away for something cold and comfortable. I know what sort of life that is. I've lived it my whole life. I watched my parents endure it. And I would rather be dead than to suffer it—to see the vibrancy in your eyes dulled over time. I would give my soul to have that passion. I had but a taste of it, and it was taken from me. Gone, in a flash. I didn't cherish it the way I should have. Didn't care for it. And when it was gone I was left aching and alone. Despondent. Searching for something that will never come back."

"Whatever are you talking about?" she asked, suddenly worried by the hysteria she heard climbing in her cousin's voice.

"You don't understand."

Gripping her hand, she forced Lucy's gaze back. "Then make me understand. Tell me in plain terms, Lucy."

Lucy swallowed and Isabella noticed how much her hands trembled. "I've had a lover, Issy, and it was passionate and heady, and everything I could ever want, but he was taken from me—gone. Forever. I am left aching, searching for something that will fill the void he has left in my heart and soul."

"Lucy! A lover? When?"

Her cousin would not answer. "Don't throw this away, Issy. Black, don't push him aside because you fear what he makes you feel. Trust him."

"That is the reason for the séances, your consuming interest in the occult, you're trying to find him—your lover."

Bursting into tears, Lucy launched herself into Isabella's arms. She held her cousin, let her weep against her shoulder until she had cried all her tears.

"I would give anything to see him once more. We...we never got to say goodbye. I never told him I loved him."

"Lucy," Isabella whispered as she looked at her cousin through her own veil of tears. "What can I do?" she asked. "How can I make it better?"

"You can keep my confidence. And you can learn from my mistake. Don't let Black be a regret of yours. Regrets are unbearable to endure, Issy. Follow your heart, and passions. No one who writes like you, with such deep rooted passion should commit themselves to a life without it. Only think on it," she whispered as Isabella tried to protest. "Please, for me. Do not dismiss anyone yet. You know how I have been living since he—" she gulped and choked on a sob "—since he died. Can you say you want that for yourself, to be burdened with regrets?"

"All right," she said, but because Lucy was working herself up into a lather again. "I will try, for you."

"Thank you," she replied quietly. "I'm sorry to be such a watering pot, but it is…well, it's the first time I have spoken of him—Sibylla knows, of course, but it is not at all the same talking to my maid as it is to you."

"You can tell me anything, Luce."

"And the same for you, too, Issy."

Isabella knew that they were both holding back secrets. There was something in her past she'd never tell a soul because, looking back on it, she was utterly ashamed of it. Neither one would speak of it. The time wasn't right, but one day, maybe it would be.

Holding up the black leather book she had brought with her, Isabella said, "I brought my journal."

"An olive branch?" Lucy asked with a smile.

"I hoped so."

"It is accepted. Will you read to me while I sew?"

"Of course."

Rising from the chair, Isabella made her way to the window bench that overlooked the square. From the window she could see Black's townhouse standing tall amongst the trees. The moon was cast in shadow, but she could still see its bloodred glow between the black clouds.

Curling up on the cushion, she drew her knees up and silently stared at the house, remembering her encounter in the library with Black. The passion that had flared between them frightened her. The intensity of it, the unbridled need that would not be harnessed.

She was scared to death of that passion, and the need.

Glancing down at the book, she read the words she had penned…

Watching. Waiting. Hungering…the whispered words seemed to burn in my belly, filling me with a warmth that curled low in my womb, making it ache. Yearn.

Death was here, a beautiful vision—a feeling. I could not see him, but I sensed him, as I always did. I had come to him, this the first night of my task. He was not here to greet me, but instead I awaited him by the fire, curled upon a black velvet chaise longue.

And then I felt him, the power he held over my soul—my body. I was warm in his presence. My body tingled. The heat intensified, engulfing my neck. And closing my eyes, I savored the fluttering touch against my skin, hoping—praying—that I might once more experience the illicit sensation of being stroked by a strong, seductive hand. Death's hand, the one with the black ring that held me captive. How I wanted to see that hand against me.

Eyelids flickering slowly, as if heavy from sleep, I reluctantly raised my lashes, not wanting to wake from my dream state. Outside, the wind howled yet again, followed by a violent gust that thrust the window wide open. The blast of cold air immediately extinguished the candles and plunged the library into blackness. The sound of the rain angrily hitting the windowpane, the relentless, haunting howl of the wind as it wailed through the open window announced his arrival. Lord Death.

"You have come," I whispered as the current of cold air engulfed the room. It hovered in the atmosphere like a patch of wispy fog, then seemed to find its way over to me and wrap itself around me. Like a burial shroud it became part of me

as it slowly swirled around my shoes, up and around my ankles and calves, snaking up my skirts and petticoats and beneath my fine lawn chemise. It spread across my lap, winding its way between my thighs, caressing their inner faces. Involuntarily, my legs parted. I felt the air stroke me, high on the inside of my thighs, felt my flesh begin to quiver and grow moist where the coldness kissed the joining of my thighs.

Rising up, the sensation stroked my belly before it lingered over my breasts, which felt painfully confined behind the tight crimson bodice of my gown. Struggling for air, I began to breathe faster, felt my breasts rising and falling as the sensation all but engulfed me.

"Feel me," I heard him whisper. "Feel me now."

"My Lord Death," I whispered as my hand came up to rest against the swells of my bosom. My head seemed to tilt to the side of its own accord, exposing the expanse of my throat as my fingers gripped the rosettes that edged my bodice. Pulling the satin aside, I exposed the swollen mound of my breast. I needed him…I needed Death's kiss.

And he gave it to me. The cold turned to warmth as it covered my breasts like the breath of a lover. The warmth—now hot—washed over my bosom, to the deep valley, and then up to my throat where the vein in my neck throbbed. For seconds I waited to experience a touch, a kiss, a whispered word.

The rhythm of my blood sang in my ears until it was all I could hear; the rushing of my blood in my veins, the life soaring in. I could feel the warmth stroking over the vein that throbbed just beneath the flesh of my throat as if someone was *breathing against me. It was Death. I smelled him, and my lips parted as I tilted my head farther, desiring to feel more. And then I did—a mouth—warm and soft. A strong, wet tongue that repeatedly stroked the vein, priming it as if preparing to suckle the bulging length beneath the tender flesh of my throat. Is this where Death would steal my soul? Would he suck the life essence from me in an erotic kiss? Would I die in his arms, with his mouth clasped to my throat?*

The stroke of his tongue, the pressure of the lips increased as my hunger deepened. Wetness pooled within me as I lowered my bodice farther, silently begging for the caress to descend to my breast and nipple, which was beaded into a hard little bud, and which throbbed mercilessly against the satin.

"Kiss me, Isabella," I heard Death whisper, and when I opened my eyes, the vapor that had warmed me turned solid, and I was looking upon Death. His mouth lowering to mine as his hand cupped my breast. Death…

Black. That was who she saw when she had written that. It had been so clear. Somehow, her vision of Death had meshed with Black's beautiful face.

She also realized that for the first time she had written her own name. *She* was Death's mistress, his lover. And Lord Death was Black. And her dreams…they were of Death and Black, and herself.

Frightened by what she had written, and the dreams of lying upon that black chaise longue made her toss the book aside, as if touching it burned her fingers.

Glancing at her cousin, Isabella wanted to see what her expression was after hearing such an intimate tale of seduction, but with a relieved sigh, she saw that Lucy had fallen asleep. Her pillow the mass of emerald velvet. She looked like a sad little pixie, her face pale and awash with the glistening trails of her tears.

Isabella wondered how much Lucy had heard of that scandalous tale. Why had she written it, something so personal, so intimate…? What was happening to her?

Resting her head against the glass, she peered out at the dark, silent night beyond the window.

She had always been given to fancy, it had been her way of surviving the harshness of her world. But this… this felt different. It was too real, no imaginary tale. There was a story being unraveled here, and it was a triangle between her and Black and Death.

Just as she was closing her eyes, she heard carriage wheels coming closer. And then, as if by magic, the wind howled, and the previously still trees began to sway. A black carriage pulled by four magnificent black stallions came into view. It slowed before the house, and Isabella held her breath, noting how gleaming and shining the black lacquer was. The shades were drawn, and she saw them slowly rise. And there was a most familiar face in the window, looking up at where she sat. It was Lord Death. It was the Earl of Black.

"DEAR ME, you're very quiet this afternoon, Miss Fairmont," Lady Elizabeth exclaimed as they walked arm in arm along Bond Street. Behind them, Maggie, Elizabeth's companion, followed silently, watching the three of them like a mother duck. Beside her, Sibylla kept a sharp eye on them, though not quite as conscious of her charges as Maggie.

"Yes, Issy, you've hardly said a word since we left," Lucy said.

"A headache, I fear," she answered. "I beg your pardon. I know I'm not good company today."

"Then we must go back," Elizabeth announced and

pulled to a stop. "Bond Street is open all year for business. We can postpone our shopping excursion for another
time until you are feeling better."

"Yes, a nap will set you to rights," Lucy encouraged.

Oh, no, she couldn't do that. She didn't want to be left
alone. The dream would return, and she couldn't have
that.

"No, please," Isabella said while sharing a glance with
Lucy. "I'm already feeling a touch better. The air, you see,
it's clearing my head."

"It is brisk today, is it not? I can smell autumn in the
air, and the taste of winter is not too far behind," Elizabeth murmured as she raised her lovely face so that cool
air could caress her cheeks. "Tell me, what is the sky like
this afternoon?"

"Gray, like the shade of the sky in the bleak midwin-
ter right before the snow approaches," Lucy answered.

"Oh, yes, I can see it now. I remember that sky as a
child, how chilly and foreboding it looked."

"The clouds are heavy, shaded like charcoal colors.
Rain will come later tonight, I think," Lucy continued.
"I can feel the dampness."

So could Isabella. The sky was foreboding this afternoon, a moody visual that fit perfectly with the state of her
emotions. She had not slept well last night. After leaving
Lucy's room, Isabella had paced her own chamber, lost
in thought about what had transpired in the library. She
could still not comprehend how she had allowed herself
to disassemble quite so easily. She had been gelatin in
Black's skilled hands.

Once she had fallen asleep, she had been plagued by
the same dream she had the first night after meeting
Black. She was in a room, lying on a black velvet chaise
longue. She was wearing a crimson gown—the gown
Lucy had made for her, and she was sleeping. Someone
was watching her, she could sense the presence in the

room with her, but in her dream could see only shadow, the shape of a man—tall, broad, compelling. And then she had felt it, a hand caressing her face, slowly slipping down her neck where the fingers of that hand had slowly begun to squeeze.

She had awakened on a silent scream, her sheets tossed aside, her body sweating and chilled. It was the second time she had dreamed that particular dream and the importance of that number struck fear in her. So, too, did the mysterious note that had been awaiting her at the breakfast table. Jennings had put the missive beside her teacup, her name written in a highly stylized form of script, in very fine black ink. It wasn't Black's writing, she had memorized that. This was a different hand altogether.

In the end, the missive had not been signed, but that hardly mattered, for she had been rendered a mass of jumbled nerves anyway. It was fortunate she had been alone at the table then, since she had no wish for her uncle or Lucy to see her emotional state.

Even now, the missive had the power to make her shiver, and Elizabeth sensed it, and asked her if she was chilled.

"Are you chilled to the bone, Miss Fairmont?" Elizabeth inquired.

"No, indeed," she replied. "But the air is crisp this afternoon, isn't it?"

"You would let us know, wouldn't you, if you desire to end our excursion and return home."

Isabella smiled and tried to make light of the situation. "I'm of good hearty Yorkshire stock, I vow a little chill will not send me running."

They made small talk after that, and occasionally they would stop before a shop window, and Lucy and Isabella would take turns describing what they saw. Elizabeth's face was always in raptures over their descriptions, and as they came away from a milliner's shop, she laughed and told them how she occasionally dragged her brother on outings like this, and he proved utterly useless to her.

"He is a man of very few words, and his descriptions are sadly lacking. 'Brother,' I've often asked him, 'how do you fare with the opposite sex, for you have no knack of the language? Your compliments are sparse, and your talent for flattery nonexistent.' And do you know what his reply is?"

"No," Isabella said, because Lucy would not—she could not partake of any conversation that included the duke, and now Isabella knew why. Her heart was engaged elsewhere. However hopeless that was. "How did he respond?"

"With a grunt! Can you believe it? How easily he proved my point!"

Isabella laughed. She could see the duke responding as such. It was true that he did not speak all that much, and his comments were always very proper and direct. But she had seen the looks he sent Lucy when he thought no one was watching. There was such longing in his gaze—such passion, locked up behind an ironclad control and propriety.

"Shall we stroll to the dressmaker's, then? I could use a new gown. I was told that you, Isabella, wore a rather rapturous concoction in crimson last evening. I have a very great desire to have something done up in a brilliant shade."

"Oh, you should most definitely consider amber, Elizabeth, or perhaps burgundy," Lucy suggested. "I saw the most luscious of colors at Simon and Water's the other day. The softest silk, and the colors…so deep and rich it was like looking upon gems."

Soon the two were lost in a discussion of colors and fabrics, and Isabella was led back to worries of before.

The missive. Black. The strange dreams that felt less like dreams but like premonitions of her death.

Death comes in threes,
the mother, the brother and the lover who weeps,
the harlots, the charlatan and then, at last, to
thee.

She had memorized those lines, had been haunted by them even after folding the letter back up. What did it mean? On the heels of her dream, her imagination ran riot. She was being warned, by whom? About whom? *Death?* It seemed impossible, but it was a warning. Someone knew she had been at Alice Fox's séance, and now she was dead. And the women at the Adelphi, they were often referred to as harlots, and now three of them were missing. And then there had been Black last night, his carriage rolling along the street, coming to a stop before her house.

She shivered again, this time most violently, and Elizabeth demanded that they take a carriage ride to the park, and then back to her house for tea and cakes.

Isabella was most relieved that Elizabeth had mentioned no more about returning home. She did not want to stay alone. Nor did she want to walk any longer. Her head was pounding, and it had begun to rain.

"My brother is to meet me at the haberdashery. He's picking out a new tie and a pair of gloves for the winter and he wants my opinion. How I am to give it, I haven't any idea," she said with a smile, "but I do like to indulge him. He is all I have in the world, and one day I know that he will wed, and I will become something of a third wheel."

"Nonsense," Lucy scoffed as she led the way. "His Grace is the kindest man I've known in a long, long while. He would never cast you aside. Of that I am most certain."

"Oh, so you have noticed that about my brother," Elizabeth asked slyly. "What else has caught your attention, pray?"

With a groan, Lucy led them into the store and out of the rain, where the duke turned and greeted them with a smile.

"Ah, ladies, how lovely to you see. I'm quite perplexed. You see, I cannot decide between gray, dove gray or steel gray for my new gloves."

"Oh, Adrian, you always get gray," Elizabeth chastised. "Do try something else."

"What would you suggest?"

"Black," Lucy whispered as her fingers caressed a pair of fur-lined kid-leather gloves. "Such a mysterious color, don't you think?"

"Yes. And mysterious is good," Elizabeth concurred.

"Black it is," the duke quickly announced after tearing his gaze from Lucy's face. "Faircourt, pack those up, will you, and put them on my account. It seems I'm breaking with tradition and living dangerously. A man of mystery, I daresay you might be very close to the truth, Lady Lucy."

When he smiled, Isabella saw Lucy flush, and for the first time that day, Isabella felt a measure lighter, her worries gone—for now.

"Miss Fairmont," Elizabeth murmured, "perhaps we might wait for my brother and Lady Lucy in the carriage, hmm?"

Elizabeth had a hold of Isabella's arm and was dragging her out of the shop before she could protest.

The footman jumped down from the carriage and carefully handed Elizabeth up the stairs. Isabella promptly followed and settled back against the squabs, relishing the warmth that infused her chilled body.

"Tell me your worries, Miss Fairmont," Elizabeth demanded. "I won't give you a moment's peace until you do."

Isabella was relieved that the duke's sister could not see her expression. She was horrified that Elizabeth could so easily discern that something was bothering her.

"Out with it," Elizabeth demanded.

"Nothing but a poor night's sleep, I'm afraid," she replied.

Arching her dark brows, Elizabeth slipped her gloves from her fingers and rested them on her lap. "You're frightened, Miss Fairmont. I can feel the tremors of fear flickering along your body—and don't bother to deny it. Nothing will convince me otherwise. Why don't you tell me what it is."

"I couldn't," she whispered.

"Because it involves Black?"

Isabella gasped, and Elizabeth's face tilted upward. "I was right, then. You fear him."

"I…I don't know what to think, truthfully. I only know that strange things have been happening since we've been introduced."

"What strange things?"

"Letters that are a warning, but from whom, or about whom, I have no idea. They talk of death, and are most… disconcerting."

"Read them to me."

Isabella didn't have to pull the missive out from her reticule. She could recite it by heart.

"Death comes in threes,
the mother, the brother and the lover who weeps,
the harlots, the charlatan and then, at last, to
thee.

"I know it's about me, but who I am being warned away from…? I can only guess that it's Black."

"You have nothing to fear from Black," Elizabeth murmured, "but I cannot tell you more, other than he has secrets, and you must ask him for those yourself. I cannot tell them."

Isabella studied the duke's sister. "You know a great

deal about him. Were you…are you…" She swallowed hard, not knowing quite how to phrase her question.

"Have we been lovers?" Elizabeth smiled. "No. What I can tell you, and you must realize that this is not to be repeated, is that our families are quite closely connected. I've known him since childhood."

"And Alynwick?"

"Yes. But again, I must impress upon you that our connection with them must not be spoken of. I cannot say why, only that it is so. I trust you, Isabella, with this, just as you must trust Black."

"Tell me, then. Why does he hide in his home? What secrets does he keep?"

"I want to tell you," Elizabeth whispered, "but I cannot. That is his story to tell. You must be brave, Isabella, and go to him. He won't hurt you."

Isabella wasn't so certain he wouldn't hurt her. She already cared for him, and she was starting to worry that she might actually be falling in love with him,

God help her…the last thing she should do is go to him.

IT WAS TOO SUSPICIOUS to ride in the park. There was a deluge outside, and no one would be riding, which would raise questions, if anyone happened to see them, as to what the three of them were doing jaunting along Rotten Row in the pouring rain. That is what happened when a recluse was seen out and about, talking with others.

Black had a reputation to uphold. It had served him well, but it was moments like this, when his appearance was noted and remarked upon, that made things sticky.

So Sussex had decided to meet at his house. It was a risk, but then, they had to do something. The chalice and pendant had been missing for days, and there was no telling how long they had been gone before Sussex had noticed their disappearance.

Try as he might, his attention was not focused on the relics he had sworn to protect, but something else.

As Black paced the perimeter of Sussex's study, he listened to the murmurs of feminine voices, and the occasional laugh. Isabella was in the salon next to him visiting over tea with Elizabeth and Lucy. She had looked beautiful, if not a bit pale and withdrawn when he had arrived.

Something was wrong. He'd known it instantly; she would not meet his eyes, and when she stiffened as he took her hand in greeting he had felt a tremor run through it. It was not a frisson of sexual awareness, but of fear.

Was she feeling embarrassed about what had passed between them last night? Hell, he hadn't slept for thinking of it. How damn good she had felt in his arms. How perfect her arousal was clinging to his fingers. When he finally fell asleep he had thought of when he would make love to her. When he would open her, stretch her, making her his.

She would be passionate and wild beneath him—he would make certain of that. He would hold her in her his arms and watch her unravel. Would savor every nuance of her climax.

She had wanted him last night. But something had made her wary this afternoon. He had felt that wariness, seen it in her eyes. She had another headache. He could smell the licorice on her breath from the valerian herb and her pupils had been small, the effect of the opium. She had taken her tonic and that meant she had suffered a dream, and a resulting headache. How he wanted to know about those headaches, and why they held such fear for her.

He longed to take her in his arms, hold her, kiss her temples and lay her on his lap and let her sleep. He would watch over her. Protect her. Kiss her awake and then slowly make love to her.

"If Black here would cease attempting to eavesdrop on the ladies, then we might get started."

Alynwick's perturbed voice intruded on his thoughts, and he turned to the hearth to watch the flames, and thought of what it would be like to lay Isabella on the rug in his library and kiss her naked body, watch the flames cast shadows along her curves. He would chase those shadows with his mouth, his tongue...

"Poor sod, he's lost," Alynwick muttered. "I wager he didn't even make it to Alice Fox's place last night, but stood standing outside Miss Fairmont's window like a depraved Romeo."

"I found nothing there," Black announced, trying to think of anything other than the image that was trying to consume him—him chasing shadows, and his tongue dipping and darting into the most erotic places. "The police have cleaned out her house. There was nothing there. If the letter was not burned, then the police now have it."

"I doubt she kept it," Sussex said. "She was a fraud, she wouldn't want evidence to be found that she could be bought for a staged séance."

"Whoever wrote that letter killed her," Black announced. "And wanted me to look guilty. Or at least to cast suspicion my way."

"Yes, it's strange, that. Who have you managed to provoke, Black?" Alynwick asked. "Other than Knighton? You must admit you have made it quite clear you covet the lady he has been courting."

"Indeed," Sussex agreed. "The letter only referenced you and Miss Fairmont. The author has to be someone very close to her."

"Knighton does have the motivation," Alynwick reminded them. "And the background knowledge of Miss Fairmont. He must be intimately acquainted with her to know about her past."

"He doesn't know a damn thing about her," Black

snarled. Someone was trying to scare Isabella away from him and it made him wild with rage to think of it.

"Nevertheless, you must proceed with caution. If your name, and that black carriage and four, comes up one more time, you're bound to have Scotland Yard knocking on your door, and you—and we—don't need that."

No, they didn't.

"Perhaps you should leave the young lady alone until this settles," Alynwick suggested. "You know people are still talking about you even a decade after the scandal. This is bound to stir it up again if your name gets mentioned in the papers."

Yes, they were still talking, but then there was little the ton loved more than gossip. Black knew Alynwick was right. If his name and his carriage were linked with Alice Fox or, God above, the missing women from the Adelphi, then he would be questioned. And he might not get off this time.

But the thought of leaving Isabella alone—exposed— did not sit well with him. He could not in all conscience stay away from her.

"It's agreed, you'll stay away and we'll—"

"It is not agreed." The words were razor-edged, his voice gruff as he drank deeply of the whiskey he held. "I haven't agreed to this, nor will I. Isabella is vulnerable, and we have no proof that she is safe."

"Black—"

"I said no!" he growled and slammed the crystal glass atop the mantel. "You may make plans for our retrieval of the chalice and pendant, and I will go along with whatever those plans entail, but when it comes to Isabella I will do as I must. And I *must*," he stated emphatically, "protect her. And to do that, I must be close to her. Besides, it will allow me to investigate further. See if Stonebrook keeps Masonic letterhead in his study, that sort of thing."

Sussex and Alynwick looked dubious, and he suddenly

didn't give a damn. The chalice and the pendant could go to hell for all he cared. Isabella was his first priority.

"As you will, but if you get yourself arrested, do not expect us to vouch for you. Our oath states that we keep our family business secret and our connection to one another hidden. We are acquaintances, nothing more."

"Understood. Now, what did you discover at the museum?"

Alynwick's dark eyes gleamed. "I came up empty-handed at the museum, so I decided to search Knighton's apartments. I discovered in his desk an extract from a Templar treatise. It talks of the three Templars and the relics. And the scroll that is needed to discover how to use the ancient power contained in them."

"So, Knighton knows something after all."

"The extract did not list any names of the Templars who possess the relics. But it did speak of the pendant, and its powers."

"Do you think Knighton knows the pendant has the power to bring you what you most want? That you must only take the seeds between your hands and whisper the words in the text to make what you most desire in the world yours?"

There was a rap at the door, and all three turned their heads sharply to the crack where the door had silently opened. Sussex leaped from his chair, and threw the door back, but there was no one there.

"It must have been a draft," he said as he closed the door. "It's windy out, and these windows are old and drafty."

Alynwick glanced between them and sipped his whiskey. "You should know that someone knows of my family's involvement. When I returned home after searching Knighton's place, I discovered that someone had also been busy in my home."

"The scroll?" Sussex growled.

"Safe. But I moved it."

"Where?"

"Someplace they'd never look. The library at the lodge."

"Are you insane?" Sussex exploded.

Alynwick smiled. "Mad as a hatter, I'm afraid. But my choice of hiding place is really rather clever. I've planted the scroll right beneath their noses. It's too obvious, and if the thieves do take a mind to search for it there, there are over a thousand books in that library—it will take them quite a while to search for it. Well, I had to do something," he growled. "They hadn't gotten to the comely little maid's room where I usually hide the thing beneath the floorboards."

"Only you, Alynwick, would think of such a place," Sussex drawled.

"Servants' quarters are never of much consequence to thieves, and the maid is not snooping, she's far too busy entertaining two of my footmen to pull up the floorboards."

"So what now?" Black asked with impatience. He wanted to quit this room and find Isabella. How far he had fallen. His every waking thought was of her.

"I'm escorting my sister to a ball this evening. A few members of the lodge are going. They once had ties to the original House of Orpheus, and I want to see what I can learn about them."

"You're using Elizabeth," Alynwick growled.

"No, she wants to be of use."

Alynwick waved his hand. "Split hairs then. But do not come to me when she is hurt by this game you're playing. She has no business entering into this world of ours. She is—"

"*Blind,* Alynwick," Sussex said softly, "not stupid or useless. You would have me hide her in this house wrapped in cotton wool if you had your way—or perhaps you think I should lock her away in one of your homes?"

"Damn you!" Alynwick thundered. "You know I think no such thing. It's just that…well, with her infirmity, she's at risk. We don't know who this person is, and we can't child mind her all the time."

"Child mind?" Sussex laughed. "I would adore being there when you toss that in her face."

"Enough!" Black snapped. "We're arguing like children and accomplishing nothing. If Elizabeth wants to be involved, she should be. Had we had siblings, Alynwick—" and he felt a queer sensation pierce his chest, for he'd had a brother once, long ago "—they would no doubt have some involvement as well."

"Not my sister," Alynwick grunted.

Black ignored him. "I'll go over to Stonebrook's tonight. I want to search the marquis's study."

"I'll be staying in," Alynwick drawled. "I'm expecting my company to return and finish what they started last night, and considering my present mood, they will not find me a charming host."

"One more thing," Black announced, "I went to the Adelphi last night. There was talk of an exclusive club, and the man who runs it—Orpheus."

That caught both Sussex and Alynwick's attention.

"I have plans to go when the club next meets. My contact will arrange it."

"Good, we'll join you," Alynwick announced. Before Black could argue, Elizabeth appeared at the door, grasping the frame to steady herself.

"Is your business concluded?" she asked in a whisper.

"Yes, for now, I think," Sussex answered.

"Good. I've arranged for Black to take Isabella home. Something is wrong, and I thought you'd like to know."

ONCE MORE she found herself bundled up and packed away in Black's carriage like a fragile child. She was more than mildly provoked by Elizabeth's tactics. Apparently the sisters of dukes could be just as high-handed as the dukes themselves.

In silence the carriage rambled on, while Isabella studied the grain of the silk shades Black had drawn. She could not look at him. To look at him was to remember what she had done with him in his library last night. To think of that was to want more. And to experience more would be her downfall.

"Isabella, tell me what troubles you."

"Nothing does," she replied.

"Elizabeth—"

"Was mistaken."

He moved silently to her bench, pulled the strings of her bonnet loose and let it slide backward till it landed on the bench behind her. Cupping her face in his palms, he tilted her chin upward so that he could see her through the thin shaft of daylight that crept through the edges of the shades.

"Shadows haunt your eyes, love," he murmured, before brushing his mouth against hers. She stiffened and he pulled back, his eyes narrowing, his mouth turned into a deep frown.

"What is it? You're trembling."

Damn her weak constitution! She didn't want this, to be a fragile flower with Black. "It's nothing," she snapped and tried to turn from him, but he wouldn't let her.

"You're afraid of me," he said, following her, pressing closer to her. "What's changed? What's happened between last night and this afternoon?" he demanded.

"Nothing!"

BLOODY HELL, he swore as he reached for her. It was not nothing. Isabella feared him. He saw it in her eyes, felt it in her body, which trembled whenever he got closer.

What did she know? Suddenly he felt his iron control begin to unravel. His mind searched for possibilities. What had she discovered about him?

Suddenly, she whirled on him, a new Isabella than the one he had seen. "Someone has written me, warning me away from you. I'm sure of it."

"What the devil do you mean?"

She thrust a piece of paper at him, pressing it into his chest. He released her, opened the paper and stared down in horror at the words.

Death comes in threes,
the mother, the brother and the lover who weeps,
the harlots, the charlatan and then, at last, to thee.

His mind blanked and he folded the paper back up, and put a little distance between them. "You believe this?"

"I don't know what to believe."

"You obviously have questions. What do you want to know?"

"What that warning means! It's about you, isn't it?"

"Have you not heard the gossip, the rumors, the speculation about me, Isabella?"

"No." When she turned and looked upon him, he saw the truth in her eyes. She didn't know his secrets.

"I killed my mother."

She gasped and pulled herself away from him until she came up against the side of the carriage.

"My brother, too, and the woman I was to marry."

Isabella's mouth gaped open and he turned away, hating to the see horror in her eyes. Seconds ticked on as he gathered the words he would say to her.

"I don't believe it."

His world stopped, and slowly he turned his head to look at her. "You don't?"

"You're not a murderer."

He touched her, and she did not flinch. He moved closer, and she did not try to back away.

"I did murder my mother." The pain of that admission causing a catch in his breath. "She was dying from a cancerous lesion in her breast. She was in great pain— horrible pain," he whispered. The memory of seeing his mother like that ate at him. It had been agony to watch her wasting away.

"She had resorted to a tonic to ease her pain, a tincture of opium and valerian herb."

Isabella's eyes knowingly widened. "She asked me to help her die," he murmured. He could not look at her face, but instead dropped his gaze to her lap, where her hands rested, folded demurely. He lifted one of her hands, studied the trimmed nails, and brushed his fingertip along them. "She was in such great pain, but I couldn't do it. She pleaded for it, and I...denied her."

"Jude," Isabella whispered, and touched his cheek. He clutched her hand to his face and closed his eyes, willing himself to go on.

"She was in so much damn pain," he said, his voice ragged and breaking, "but I couldn't do as she asked. And then one day, when I was sitting beside her bed, she asked me to pour her tea. I did. She drank it down eagerly, the first she had to eat or drink in days. She asked for another cup, and I gave it to her. I was so damn thrilled to see her drinking. And then..." He shuddered, pressed his lips into Isabella's hand, held it there against him. "And then she closed her eyes and took her last breath. It was then that I saw the bottle of tonic was empty. I lifted the lid to the teapot, smelled the valerian and knew that I had caused my mother's death."

"It was suicide," she said, and he closed his eyes, not wanting to hear the word. "Oh, Jude," she whispered, clutching him, making him look at her. "You didn't kill her."

"My younger brother. We had a row—about a woman—he left to go hunting. I don't know what happened, but he was thrown from his horse and the rifle he was holding was loaded, it fired and killed him. Everyone thought I did it because he was in love with the woman I was to marry."

Isabella's eyes held such sympathy and understanding. He could hardly bear it. He didn't deserve it.

"She died, too?" she asked, and he nodded, kept his eyes pressed closed.

"We had been betrothed for years. I…forced the engagement to continue, and she…resented it. She loved my younger brother. She grieved for him when he died, and instead of marrying me, she killed herself on the eve of our wedding."

"Jude." Isabella's lips brushed against his. "You are not responsible for their deaths."

"Someone would have you believe it. Someone would make you think I am also involved in the disappearance of the women at the Adelphi, and the murder of Alice Fox. Someone," he charged as he held her face fiercely in his hands, "wishes for you to believe the worst of me. To take you away from me. Bella," he whispered as his mouth lowered to hers, "don't believe them. Don't go. Don't leave me, too."

Isabella went weak in his arms. Beneath his mouth, she softened, succumbed. How could she not? She wanted this man. This moment. He'd shown her his vulnerabilities, shared with her the secrets in his soul. Her heart ached for him, for the young man struck by such tragedy, for the burdens he had been forced to carry. For the pain that was still so evident.

"Jude," she whispered over and over as he kissed her, their mouths open and hot, and searching. Their tongues touched, and she felt him push her back, till she was pressed up against the side of the carriage and he was between her legs, which were bent.

His hand, hot and large, was snaking beneath the hem of her gown, slowly, surely, as he lips and tongue rattled her thoughts—stole her will. The only right thing to do was to put a stop to the kiss, to the embrace that was becoming far more than what it should. That was the honorable path, but she was selfish, wanted more, wanted to take what he would give her. *Little Magpie* he had called her, and she was, clutching everything to her chest so that she could steal it away—including the memories of him. One last time, the little voice inside insisted. One last decadent, pleasurable memory to take away, only to be brought out in the darkness of night, and the privacy of her thoughts.

She could never see him again. Deep down, she knew she couldn't, becuase she could no longer resist him and what he so readily offered. It was her only defense, to cut the string that drew them together.

Resolved, Isabella let her worries float away, her plan was set; this would be the last time and she wanted to absorb every touch, every breath, every heated second in his arms.

Closing her eyes, she listened to the sound of Jude's breath against her, how it rasped in uneven gasps as he pressed his arousal into her thigh. His hand, so large and masculine, gripped her and she felt him undulating against her in a rhythm that was not choreographed, but urgent, primal. There was a sense of frenzied need that permeated the carriage. She felt it in the taut strength of his shoulders, in the way her heart beat rapidly against her breast and the sound of his uneven, hurried breathing.

"I can't be more than this," he rasped as he pressed once more against her. "I can't be slow and luring. I need you, Bella, and we'll be home soon, and I can't wait another moment to do what I wanted to do to you in my study."

With a nod, she acquiesced. Her fall so easy.

Breathlessly she waited, and then her skirts were raised to her waist, exposing her to his gaze while his fingers searched through the slit of her drawers in a frantic motion that made her arch and writhe and capture his mouth with hers. The kiss was demanding, consuming, and she clutched at him, her hands raking through his hair, grabbing handfuls as his fingers slid possessively over her sex.

"Let me feel you," he breathed. "Taste you."

Before she could understand, he wrapped his hand around her calf, spreading her thighs as he lowered his head, scraped his chin against her thigh. She gasped at the sinful sight, gasped again as she felt his fingers parting her, studying her before he placed his scorching tongue to her folds.

The feeling was heaven, his tongue a mix of light flicks and firm pressure, and long, languid strokes. The previous urgency bled away, leaving her feeling hazed as Jude slowed his movement, brought her up, then down, only to build her higher and higher, until she was moving beneath him, and her hands were stroking his hair, tightening with every arch of her body.

"Jude," she cried. He was killing her, she knew. Felt her soul lift from her body and float upward as she felt her limbs quivering, and her heart stop, only to restart after a missed beat. She cried out, a strangled sound, and he looked up. Watched her fall apart beneath his ministering tongue.

"La petite mort," he murmured as he cradled her in his arms. "The little death. The next time," he whispered, "I will die right alongside you."

CHAPTER FIFTEEN

LATER THAT NIGHT, Black made his way across the street to Stonebrook's house. The marquis was out, he'd seen his carriage leaving. Lucy and Isabella were inside, and he decided that it was the perfect opportunity to sneak into Stonebrook's study, and to see Isabella again.

He had to see her again. He'd thought of nothing else all afternoon and what had transpired in the carriage. He felt at ease; the secret of his past was out, but there were other secrets he was hiding, as well. But the one he feared the most was out, and she hadn't believed it.

Where had she been ten years ago, when no one had believed him? When everyone, including the ton, believed he had murdered his brother and Abigail?

Maybe it was how it was intended. Ten years ago he could not have appreciated Isabella, and the gift she was. He would not have seen past her status, and the fact she was poor. It had taken years of pain and isolation to make him see the true beauty of life.

When he had dined, he'd glanced at the chair she'd occupied the evening before. Her image had so easily come to him, and he thought back to the library and how good she had felt in his arms, and today, when he had tasted her, put his mouth to her sex and taken from her. He could hardly wait to have her with him again.

The wind was high, and he turned up the collar of his coat to ward off the chill. Rapping on the door he waited till the butler swung it wide. It seemed like an eternity before Jennings, the marquis's haughty butler, opened the door.

"The Earl of Black to see Lady Lucy and Miss Fairmont."

"I beg your pardon, milord, but the ladies are not receiving visitors this evening."

Laughter resounded from the salon, and he heard Lucy's husky voice cry out, "Oh, well done, Mr. Knighton. Tell us another story of your magnificent discoveries."

Black's thoughts turned murderous. Knighton was there? The bastard. "Announce me now," he stormed, "or I shall announce myself."

"My lord, Miss Fairmont expressly—" The butler swallowed hard and moved his neck from side to side, as if his necktie was choking him. "Miss Fairmont," he uttered in superfluous superior tones, "has expressly requested that if you came to call this evening I was to decline you entrance. Good evening to you, milord."

The door slammed shut in his face and Black stood there for long minutes mute, confused and also enraged. What the bloody hell was Wendell Knighton doing here? And why had Isabella purposely shut him out? Damn it, didn't she realize that after that afternoon there was no going back?

He stood quietly shaking, contemplated kicking the door down, or smashing a window and letting himself inside that way. Both methods would not endear him to Isabella.

What was this game she was playing? he wondered. She had wanted him that afternoon. There had been no games between them then. Damn it, what had changed? Why did she fear him? Or was it the passion she feared? Whatever it was, it was preventing her from giving herself to him. But he would have her. He wanted her more than Knighton could ever dream of.

In a most unsavory thought, Black reluctantly admitted that Isabella had won this first round. But that was okay, because he would demand satisfaction for this. He would speak with her tomorrow, and he would deal with Knighton.

But three days later, Black was still wondering why he had suddenly and summarily been shut out of Isabella Fairmont's life. She had cut him off, refusing to see him, avoiding him at balls and routs, and even the theater. He had seen her in the park, and she had promptly turned around and headed for the carriage that had conveyed her and Lucy and Elizabeth.

Three days of wondering, of seething. When next he saw her, he'd corner her, run her to ground and she would not escape him.

Whatever it took, Isabella would speak to him.

Staring at the book in his hand, he traced the golden lettering on the title *Jane Eyre.* Isabella had no idea how damn persistent he could be.

So far, he had acted the gentleman—as well as he could—but now he was no longer eager to play by the rules of society. Now he was playing by *his* rules. Isabella would soon see a new side him. A very dark and dangerous side.

Black did not give not give up on his desires. And Isabella was his one and only.

"He's come."

Orpheus smiled and drew back into the shadows, allowing the silk curtain to conceal him. Around him, the smell of sweating bodies, feminine perfume and the heady incense of opium clouded his senses.

"He has nerve," his lover whispered to him. "Coming to your domain."

"Let them come," he said, patting her hand.

"How soon they have put the pieces together," she

purred as she kissed him. "They want the pendant. How did they know to come here looking for it?"

"Because I made my trap easy."

He felt himself rise, felt her hand slide down his body. She purred once more in satisfaction. "I want him," she murmured. "I want him to hurt, just as my sister did."

"I know, darling," Orpheus replied as he maneuvered her hand till her palm rested on his straining manhood. "He will. Black will be taken from his little paramour. And he will suffer," he vowed.

"But what of the pendant? You should not have given it away."

"Trust me to take care of my business," he said, growing angry, "and I will leave you to yours."

"You forget," she whispered as her clever fingers worked on the fastening of his trousers. "that our business is one and the same."

Yes, it was. The redhead. She was next on his list. His lover would take care of Black, but Orpheus wanted Sussex. Out of them all, he wanted that preening, righteous bastard the most.

"My lord," his servant said. "Lord Black has arrived, and is wishing entrance into the club."

Let them come... It had been his design after all. "Allow him in. And keep your eye on him. Does he bring the others?"

"He does, my lord."

Orpheus smiled and reached for his lover. "Good. See, pet, soon you will have Black at your mercy. I shall be in my room," he told his servant. "I trust you'll know how to handle Black and the Guardians if they should come by asking questions."

"Yes, my lord."

And then Orpheus retreated into the darkness. Now was not the time to confront them. He was laying a trap, and they were walking headlong into it.

"DAMN IT, Black, you're as staid as a nun."

Walking through the Adelphi, Black bumped shoulders with the crowd as he and the others made their way to the back of the theater. This was the direction his informant had pointed him.

"Why don't you just tell us what has you champing and stewing."

Like hell he would. It was all he could do to think straight. The last thing he wanted was Alynwick needling him because he was acting like a lovesick fool over Isabella.

"Damn me, man, get yourself another woman if that is the cause of your behavior."

He would if he could, but Isabella had ruined him for all other women. Bloody hell, he had sworn he wouldn't think of her tonight. He couldn't become distracted, not now. Not here.

As they brushed aside a crimson silk curtain, they stopped to take in the tableau before them.

"Looks like nothing more than an orgy!" Alynwick exclaimed.

"Good God, what is that stench?" Sussex said between coughs. "My head, I feel odd."

"Opium," Black stated. "Try not to take deep breaths."

As they walked through the clouded room, amongst the naked bodies and the sounds of pleasure, Black felt his face turn up with disgust.

"We won't learn anything here."

"Have faith," Alynwick demanded. It was then that Black noticed the hungry look in a blonde woman's eyes. She stood in the corner, her identity shielded with a mask. She was dressed provocatively, her shoulders bare, and the crest of her breast visible. "I think I'll see what I can do with her," Alynwick murmured.

Black snorted. "Trust Sinclair to make this more about pleasure than duty."

Sussex rolled his eyes. "He has a point. Maybe we should split up and see what we can discover."

Black hated the thought of spending hours in this place. His head was throbbing with the effects of opium, and the heat in the room was stifling. Tugging on his cravat, he loosened it, only to feel a set of arms snake around him, taking the task over for him.

"Let me do that," a feminine voice whispered in his ear. "You're new."

"Yes." He closed his eyes, tried to think about his duty to the Brethren Guardians. Tried not to think about how much his body ached from unspent desire. Tried to think of anything else but Isabella.

"Very nice," she murmured appreciatively as her hand slid down his back. "Have you come for sport?"

"Perhaps."

She laughed, one filled with feminine desire. "Mysterious. I like that. Why don't we move to the corner, it's more private."

The woman tugged him along, and brought him to a darkened corner. She was tall and willowy, her hair a dark brown, her eyes feline behind the opening of her mask. She perused him as if he were a prized stallion, and erotic intent flashed in her eyes.

"It's always strange when it's your first time," she said. "But it only gets easier."

"Does it?"

"Mmm," she murmured. "Have you been shown around?"

"No, as a matter of fact, I haven't."

"Then you should let me."

"I have some questions."

She slid up to him, wrapped a thin arm around his neck and let her fingers tangle in the ends of his hair. "Perhaps I could answer them?"

Black had never been good at games like this. He was

much too intense for subterfuge. This was Alynwick's domain, and suddenly he wished the marquis were here to rid him of this woman, and this insipid game.

"Ask your questions," she whispered, and he felt her press her body into his. She was too thin for his tastes. Immediately he had flashbacks of Isabella, and how she had felt in his arms. Soft and warm. Something to sink himself into. This woman was all bones and hard angles. There was nothing soft about her.

"This Orpheus, have you seen him?"

"Of course."

"Is he here tonight?" he asked, trying to act nonchalant as the woman ran her finger down the front of his shirt.

"Oh, he's not here tonight. Only comes on Wednesdays, when the initiations take place and the members' dues are collected."

"Oh." Black swallowed hard and looked around. "My friends and I thought we might come for a lark," he began. "We really don't know anything about the club, other than some mates of ours said it was good fun."

"Excellent fun," she whispered. "And completely anonymous."

"I've heard," he said, hoping he was doing the right thing, "that Orpheus has a pendant, something very special."

"Oh, yes. The Templar pendant. He proclaims its magical powers will gives us the greatest of pleasure. He also claims it is the source of his bewitching powers."

"Have you seen it?"

She frowned, leaned forward and brushed her lips against his chin. "Not for about a week. Come," she whispered as she pulled him closer. "Let us not talk."

"I'm afraid I'm married."

"I am, too. My husband is in the grotto with a girl half his age."

"I'm sorry," he said, "but my affections are engaged elsewhere."

"I'm not offering affection, darling, only pleasure."

"I'm not accepting, I'm afraid."

She huffed, then slinked off, searching for more willing prey.

Sussex found him through the opium smoke, and Black signaled Alynwick to leave.

"What did you discover?" Black asked Sussex.

"Not a damn thing. Everyone is too drunk, or too… occupied for conversation."

"This is it, the place we've been looking for," Black announced. "Orpheus only arrives on Wednesdays for initiations, and he has the pendant."

Alynwick looked shocked. "How did you discover that? And in less then ten minutes?"

"I have my ways."

The woman caught his eye, blew him a kiss before they disappeared in the smoke.

"Damn me, Black, you're a legend," Alynwick teased.

"Bloody hell, Alynwick, I'm not following in your footsteps."

"Pity. We could have some fun together, out prowling the streets."

Black gave him a perturbed glare. "The woman claims to have seen the pendant, but not for about week."

"Let's get out of here. I feel as though I'm going to pass out. I can't think with this smoke in the air."

Outside, all three took gasping breaths of air. When their heads were clear, they looked at each other. They were only slightly better off than when they arrived. What they needed was to discover who this Orpheus fellow was, what his connection to the Freemasons was and where he'd hidden the pendant.

"What now?" Black asked as he looked up to see the night sky lit over the city.

"We stay here until the theater shuts down, and then we break in and search the club.

"Agreed."

"It's damn cold out here," Alynwick grumbled. Black reached into his coat and passed him a flask.

"This will keep you warm."

"And what will you use to keep your thoughts away from your lovely lady in red?" Alynwick teased.

"Sod off, Alynwick," Black snapped, and the marquis's laughter filled the dank alley behind the Adelphi.

"God help me if love ever finds me. The look of the two of you…you're both so long in the face, it's comical."

Black turned his back and closed his eyes, thinking of how he was going to break into the theater. But the image of Isabella crept in and he groaned, then snatched the flask back from Alynwick's hand.

With a deep drink, he tried to push her out of his thoughts. But it wasn't working. Nothing worked.

CHAPTER SIXTEEN

ISABELLA HAD VOWED to steer clear of Black and his temptations, and thus far she had been successful. The memory of what had happened in the carriage was still fresh, and never far from her thoughts, but she refused to dwell on it. She had taken the coward's way and out and cut him dead, without any reason for her horrid behavior. The truth was, she just couldn't trust herself around him. She had to give him up because he wasn't what she needed. What she desired was right here. Mr. Knighton was back at her side, which is what she wanted—a proper courtship with a proper gentleman.

Wendell was as he always had been, perhaps even a bit more distracted than before by his work at the museum, but she accepted the fact that as a scholar he had many things on his mind—not just her. Truth be told, she was not one of those females who must be constantly entertained. She was quite content with her own company, and that of her imagination, but there were times, she admitted, when she felt as though something was missing. There were unexplained moments of utter despair that would grip her, and she couldn't understand from where it sprang, she just knew that it had arisen from a place deep inside her—a place she refused to look at.

She had Wendell now, she reminded herself. Here he was, at her side. Tonight it had been she whom he had asked to attend the unveiling of his artifacts at the museum. She was honored that he'd singled her out. This was a proud moment for him, and he had asked her to be a part of it. There was now no doubt to her, and to society, that Wendell Knighton was officially courting her.

She should be congratulating herself on her victory, but it felt hollow. Not a victory at all, but rather a defeat. Strangely, she felt the loss of Black so keenly. She had not expected that. Had no idea how hard it would be on her to forget him—or how often her thoughts would stray to him, or her gaze would look longingly out the window to where his gloomy town house stood tall and proud, and dark. It was during those moments of reflection that the melancholy was strongest. The despair she had felt ate at her, until she had been forced to find something else to do—anything that would take her thoughts away from Black, and the inexplicable link she felt to him.

How had he impacted her so much, and in so short a time? Put in perspective, she had spent but two full days with him—but in those days and nights she had experienced more than she ever had in her twenty-three years of life. In the private moments they had shared, she could not help but think that she had shared them with a kindred spirit. There was something about Black that mirrored her soul. Occasionally that happened in life, two souls would find each other and connect on a higher plane. There was no doubt that Black had been that person for her. But that didn't mean he had been the right fit for what she wanted in life. Sometimes love and passion were just not enough. It hadn't been for her mother. Her mother's love for Isabella's father had been a curse. A yoke she was forced to bear all the days of her life.

Isabella did not care to bear the weight of such a burden. No, it was far better that she continue, with her dream of a proper marriage—even a passionless one. Her deepest desires she would save for her novel. Wendell need never know of it. It would be her secret, and it would be enough. It would have to be.

"Here we are!" Wendell said excitedly as the carriage slowed before the imposing facade of the British Museum.

"Oh, look at the people," she whispered, and both Wendell and Lucy pressed closer to glance out the window.

"What a crush!" Lucy exclaimed. "Why, Mr. Knighton, you'll be famous throughout England before the night is over."

His smile was slow, and Isabella stared at him, startled by the transformation in his face. He looked different somehow—there was something about that smile. It was knowing, superior and it gave her a start. There was ambition in his hazel eyes, something that had never been there before. Certainly he had wanted to succeed, but what she saw now seemed beyond success.

"Mr. Knighton?" she asked. "Wendell," she said when he didn't answer her or look her way.

"One day, people will look at me and know that I am responsible for unearthing the most sought-after relics in the world," he said.

His voice was distant, hollow—eerie. Chills chased down her spine, and she watched as Wendell rubbed his temples. He murmured something, but Isabella could not make it out. Was he…talking to himself? she wondered. She'd noticed this behavior the past few days. He was always mumbling to himself, and rubbing his temples.

Perhaps the strain of this unveiling was having unhealthy effects upon him. He was not a robust man, but quite lean. He'd lost weight, too, she noticed.

"Wendell?" she asked, concerned. "Are you well?"

The carriage stopped and Wendell did not wait for the footman to open the door, but thrust it open and kicked out the metal carriage steps. He did not turn to assist them out, but walked up the lit pathway to the stairs, shaking hands and basking in the adulation of the crowd that gathered around him.

"Well," Lucy muttered as the footman reached into the

carriage and offered his hand, "Mr. Knighton has a rather high opinion of his dusty old relics, doesn't he? Really, Issy, he's become rather pompous."

Indeed he had. But Isabella could never admit to such a thing. Lucy and she had called a truce to their squabbling about what sort of man she should desire. The waters had been relatively calm, but she could tell from the flash in Lucy's eyes, and the way her spine stiffened, that she was sorely tempted to tell Isabella exactly what she thought of her suitor.

And to be certain, Isabella had a good mind to pull Wendell aside and question what the devil had gotten into him. She would do so, too, right after this evening was over.

Holding the footman's hand, Isabella descended the stairs, careful to ensure that her hem did not catch on the metal steps. She had worn a very plain evening gown, as was Wendell's preference. The color was crème, with little adornment or lace. Her shoulders were bare, though, and she had chosen to wear a four-strand choker made of black jet. Wendell had frowned when he had seen it, stating that the black stones were for mourning, but Isabella loved the piece because it reminded her of home— of Whitby where the jet was mined from the Yorkshire cliffs.

Standing side by side, she and Lucy took a minute to admire their surroundings. Patrons of the museum, scholars, lords and their ladies strolled up the lit path. Wendell was in the middle of the melee, talking animatedly and shaking hands.

"He'll be a busy fellow tonight by the looks of it."

It was the duke's voice, and they turned in time to see Sussex escorting Elizabeth over to them.

"Your Grace," Isabella gasped. "How good of you to come."

"Oh, I wouldn't miss it for the world, Miss Fairmont.

I'm intrigued to discover just what Mr. Knighton has unearthed beneath Solomon's Temple."

"Where is Mr. Knighton?" Elizabeth asked.

"Being adored, up by the doors," Lucy said with a sardonic smile. "He quite forgot us."

Sussex's gaze flittered over Lucy, and she looked away, trying not to notice how close His Grace stood to her. "I have an extra arm, if you would allow me," he offered.

"Well, then, I shall insist Miss Fairmont escort me," Elizabeth said as she held out her hand. Isabella grasped it, and wrapped Elizabeth's fingers around her forearm. "She promised to tell me of the book she is writing, isn't that right, Isabella?"

"Oh, it is nothing. Just a novel."

"I love novels," Elizabeth said. The duke and Lucy were ahead of them, and Isabella stood still, just for a brief moment, to gather herself. She was nervous. She wanted to be the sort of woman tonight that would make Wendell proud. Her education was sadly lacking, and she did not want to make a faux pas, or embarrass him.

Closing her eyes, she lifted her face to the cool breeze—the quiet was what she needed to get her thoughts in order—the solitude would lull her into relaxation. With her eyes closed she became aware of the change in her surroundings, the heaviness of the air, the earthy scent of the autumn night.

It was a subtle thing, like the calming of the wind, and the quieting of the rustling leaves. It was as if the earth had stopped turning for just one brief second.

And then she felt it. Or rather *him*. That inexplicable feeling of awareness whenever Black was near. She felt it in the atmosphere, in its changing current, in the tingling down her spine and the fluttering of her heart. The feeling was so close now, nearly palpable. She knew he had to be standing directly behind her.

Whirling around, she met him, his hand outstretched

as if he was reaching for her. His eyes were unreadable, his expression one of implacability.

No words were said, both stood before the other, silent, taking each other's measure, wondering how to get past the difficulties of the past few days.

"Shall we?" Elizabeth asked, and Isabella broke the spell of Black's stare, and gently raised her hem to walk up the long pathway.

"Yes, let's."

HIS GAZE FOLLOWED HER around the perimeter of the room. She felt it, that impenetrable stare burning into her back. Despite the crowd, the heat, the noise of excited chatter, Isabella could still make out his presence in the room. Quiet. Focused. Intent. He unnerved her. This... connection intimidated her. It was wrong. Mr. Knighton was courting her. She was happy with the situation. It was all she had ever desired—a good match and a proper marriage. Yet why did she feel the tentacles of sin reaching for her, enveloping her? Black was sin incarnate, a temptation that must be resisted at all costs.

"Ah, there you are," Wendell murmured. Grasping her arm, he held tightly onto her elbow. "There is someone I wish for you to meet."

Wendell was in his element. Isabella could not help but smile up at him. He was so immensely proud of his accomplishments, and so he should be. Finding the Templar relics in the Holy Land and bringing them to London was the highlight of his career. He was most sought after now, and Isabella couldn't be happier for him. There was a lightness to him tonight. He smiled more and his conversation was certainly more varied. Albeit he continued to talk of his work. But that was a man. And a wife's duty—to listen to his stories and support his efforts. It didn't matter that Wendell hardly knew her. She supposed that he would, in time.

"Come, he's waiting."

Isabella allowed Wendell to steer her away from the crowd, and to the back of the room where the gaslight did not quite reach. Seated behind a large desk was a man with long dark hair and pale skin. He wore sun spectacles despite the darkness and the dim lighting.

"The glare of the light hurts his eyes," Wendell supplied. "Make nothing of it. He's rather eccentric, and easily offended. But he's the museum's most devoted patron. And I've just learned that it was his anonymous donation that funded the majority of my research trip."

"Oh, then we must meet him," she said, and Wendell scowled.

"Make no mention of the donation. It's not done for females to mention such things."

"I won't embarrass you, if that's your concern."

Wendell glanced at her. "I didn't mean to insinuate such a thing, Isabella. I merely meant to guide you."

"I am not completely lacking wits or manners, Wendell."

"Shh, your voice is carrying, and you're frowning. Come, we do not want people speculating that we're having a row."

"But we are."

"No, we're not. Smile, he's watching."

"Ah, Mr. Knighton," the man announced as they approached. "A success, yes?" Isabella detected the faintest of French accents.

"Indeed, sir. And one I hope may grow over time."

"You are the foremost authority on the Templars during the Crusades, Mr. Knighton. I expect many more successful finds from you. Your career is just beginning, sir."

Wendell practically preened like a peacock. "My thanks, sir. But I suppose my interest is just as great as yours."

"It is," he murmured. "I have a very great interest in

the subject. And who, Knighton, is this charming young lady?"

"May I present Miss Isabella Fairmont?"

"Ah, so this is the Miss Fairmont you told me about. Delighted, my dear." The man reached for her hand and bowed over it. "The fairest of roses," he murmured. "Mr. Knighton was not profuse enough in his testament to your beauty."

Isabella blushed to her roots and glanced at Wendell, who turned a deep shade of scarlet.

"Miss Fairmont, this is Nigel Lasseter."

"An honor, sir."

"Mr. Knighton tells me you have a great fondness for the museum."

"Indeed, sir. I do. I grew up in the north, where museums are few and far between."

"Ah, the north. I detect a Yorkshire accent. Is that correct?"

"Indeed, sir. Have you ever been?"

He smiled, but it was not one of warmth, but rather distaste. It was not a smile, but rather a sneer. "Indeed, Miss Fairmont. I was once there and have no wish to ever go back."

"Oh!" She was rendered mute by the venom in his words.

"It has been lovely to meet you. Now, if you will excuse us. I have business with Mr. Knighton."

Dismissed. And so rudely, too! Who was this Nigel Lasseter anyway? Wendell gave her an apologetic smile and motioned for her to rejoin the others.

"I shall be along shortly," he murmured, and then he turned back to converse with the taciturn Mr. Lasseter.

Why should talk of Yorkshire change Mr. Lasseter from all that was complimentary to reticent? *Men.* She doubted she would ever understand them or their moods.

But then, she had never grown up with a male in her life. Perhaps this was what they were truly like.

Meandering through the throng, Isabella fanned herself. The room could do with an open window, for the air had grown stuffy and close. She was fighting the onset of another headache, and knew that any more time caught in this room would be her undoing. Deciding on a glass of punch, she made her way to the refreshment table, hoping a cool drink would help her. She wanted to find Lucy, who, the last time Isabella had seen her, had been promenading with Sussex and Elizabeth.

"You've been avoiding me."

The velvety timbre of Black's voice whispered over her, and she closed her eyes, savoring the sound, while steeling her wits. Black was the last thing she needed now. Wendell, she noticed when she opened her eyes, was casting anxious glances her way, and her head, which was suddenly pounding fiercely, was not clear enough to do battle with the enigmatic earl.

"I saw you in the park yesterday, and I know you saw me."

Yes, she had been strolling with Lucy and Elizabeth, and she had glanced him from afar, and purposely set out on a different path. "No, I'm sorry I didn't," she lied.

"And last night, at the Renfrew ball. You saw me coming toward you and you fled before I could reach you."

"I was merely engaged for that dance, my lord." *No, she had hid like a coward.*

"I sent you a letter this morning."

"Oh? I'm afraid I didn't get it."

She felt him press against her, his breath caressing the exposed flesh behind her ear. She wanted to shiver—in pleasure. But she stood firm, hiding any signs of her desire.

"Why are you avoiding me?"

"I have been rather busy, my lord."

"Busy evading me." He stood behind her, and she felt the barest touch of his fingertips along her spine. He was close, far too close. Someone would see, and she could not allow that. "But why? I wonder." His fingers glided softly, like the fluttering of butterfly wings, against her skin. "I have asked myself the same question these past seven days. 'Why would Isabella Fairmont be avoiding me after that magical night in my library, and that moment in the carriage when I tasted your pleasure, and you came for me?'"

"Please, someone will see," she hissed. "You mustn't… that is, you're much too close to me. And your voice… lower it. *Please.*"

"Then take a turn with me about the room. No one will talk then."

"No."

"The hall. Meet me there where we can be alone and unencumbered by roving eyes."

"My lord, you know I cannot."

"Cannot, or will not?"

Glancing over her shoulder, she met his gaze and was startled by the dangerous expression he wore. She had never seen him like this. He was always amazingly controlled, but tonight he was wild—feral. She could easily see how he could be the most dangerous man in England.

"Well?"

"I fear the answer is both, my lord."

"Why?"

"I think we both know the answer to that, Lord Black. Now, if you will excuse me, I see a few friends. Good evening, my lord."

She made to move away, but he reached for her wrist, giving her no opportunity to flee. She could struggle, but then that would cause a scene. She had no other option but to do his bidding—for now.

"Walk with me."

He moved through the crowded room, stopping occasionally to admire some object or another. They did not speak. After a few minutes, Isabella found herself staring up at a picture of a Templar knight. In the background was the Holy City, and Solomon's Temple. Behind them, the guests mingled and conversed, heedless of her standing beside Lord Black.

"I will quit the room now. In ten minutes, you will come to me. Walk through the doors to your right—no, don't look," he murmured. "There is a hallway beyond the doors. I will wait for you there. If you do not appear, I will be forced to come into this room and drag you out. Do you understand?"

She nodded. And she felt him soften the slightest bit as he stood beside her. He reached out, caught himself and forced his hand back to his side.

"Ten minutes," he whispered. And then he was gone.

WENDELL KNIGHTON CAST an anxious glance around the room only to discover that no one was watching him. Slipping into his workshop, he reached for a sulfur match and lit the oil lamp that sat on his desk. Fumbling with his keys, he fitted the skeleton key into the lock and pulled open the desk drawer, only to find it empty.

"Looking for something, Knighton?"

From the shadows, Black emerged, holding the tome he had been searching for. "How did you get in here?"

"That's irrelevant."

"And my book!"

"Also irrelevant."

"You bloody bastard, what do you want?"

"I want to know what you've discovered."

Wendell tried to make certain his gaze didn't dart between Black and the back cupboard. Black was a clever bastard. He would notice, and then he would be compelled to search for the chest. Wendell could not allow that.

"I don't know what you mean."

"You know damn well what I mean," Black thundered as he slammed the book on the desk. "You found something in Jerusalem, Knighton, and I want to know what it is."

"That book," he snapped, glancing at the tome.

"There's more," Black said, his voice lethally soft.

"That's it, I swear it."

Black watched him closely, his eyes roving over him. "We have unfinished business, Knighton, and it's more than just what you're hiding."

"Isabella," he replied, his body stiffening.

"Isabella," he answered.

"What is left to say, Black? You attempted to steal her away, and she wasn't interested in what you were offering. There is nothing left to be resolved."

"You little prat," he shouted, then reached for him. Wendell was forced to move behind the desk, but Black lunged across the wooden top and grabbed him by his jacket.

"Black, stop."

It was the Marquis of Alynwick's voice coming from the door. He ran into the study, shoved Black away from him, put his body between the two of them. "Enough," he said over and over until Black appeared to be once more in control. But those eyes... Wendell could very easily imagine he saw his own death in Black's eyes.

"Sorry about that, Knighton," Alynwick said, "Black here has had a bit too much. Always full of vinegar when he's in his cups."

Wendell straightened and smoothed his waistcoat. "Just get him out of here."

"We're not done, Knighton," Black growled. "I'll be coming for you."

The door slammed behind them and Knighton locked it, then hurried to the chest of drawers, emptying the sheafs of paper and the maps. Tossing them on the floor, he frantically dug to the bottom. His fingers came in contact with the smooth grain and silk and he sighed deeply, and pressed his eyes shut. In his hands, he felt his prize.

Gently he pulled out the ancient white cloth and lovingly peeled it back to reveal the glittering gold goblet in his hand.

The chalice. He smiled, his body soaring with energy. How fortunate he'd found it first. It had been a stroke of luck to discover that the passage that ran beneath the Masonic lodge led to the fourteenth-century Templar church. He had spent the night searching the catacombs, his fingers bloody from clawing away at rock and loose mortar. And then he had seen it, hidden behind a rock at the base of the floor. He wouldn't have noticed it at all if the white cloth had not been disturbed and the candle he held in his hand had not glinted off the gold, drawing his eyes.

He studied it from all angles and felt the pendant he wore around his neck begin to hum and vibrate against his skin.

He only needed the scroll now. And after Orpheus had informed him which of the families protected each relic, he knew where to look. Alynwick. He'd made an attempt before to search his house, but he'd been disturbed. Tonight he would try once more.

One step away, he though with awe. One more relic to claim and the world would kneel at his feet.

CHAPTER SEVENTEEN

ISABELLA FOUND HIM standing in the hallway before a large transom window. The glow of the moon outlined his tall form, and she stood there just drinking him in. The magnetic pull that she so often felt around him lured her, and she walked toward him, powerless to break whatever spell he was weaving. There had been an altercation between him and Wendell. Lucy had told her about it—she had heard the raised voices of both Black and Wendell when she had passed the office on the way to the ladies' retreating room—right before Isabella had left the gallery to meet him.

She could not fathom what Black's intentions were to corner Wendell in his workroom.

"You would tempt me into a seduction, and then a scandal," she said quietly as she came to stand beside him. "You would see me ruined."

"No."

His refusal was swift. Hard.

"Then what is this, my lord, this clandestine meeting in the dark—all alone?"

"Desperation."

"And meeting with Knighton a moment ago? Was that also desperation?"

"Yes." He turned to her, and lifted his hand to her face, where he cradled her cheek in his palm. "Sheer desperation, Isabella. I can't go on like this."

"You got on quite well before my uncle's ball."

"Do not tell me you don't feel this, Isabella."

"What should I feel?"

"This…this thing between us. From the first time our gazes collided in Stonebrook's ballroom there has been a force drawing us together. That night in my library—how can you refute it? What happened was inevitable—from the moment I first saw you, I knew that I would one day have you naked in my arms. In that moment when our gazes met, and we suddenly fell into each other's arms without thought or fear, I knew it was an inescapable fate. It was the only thing to be done—to taste the pleasure in each other. You felt it, I know you did. This connection between us…it crackles. It's a living, breathing entity of its own, and that night…what we did was not just about my desires. It was about yours, too."

"To deny this and pretend ignorance is missish. I will not do you the dishonor, and myself the disservice, of acting in such a way. Yes. I feel it. This force as you call it. It's called reckless passion, my lord. My mother succumbed to it and it left her disgraced and ruined. Her recklessness ruined my life as well, and I will not have it."

"How can you deny it?" The words were said in a deep, dark whisper that made her body heat. "Even now it is crackling between us. You don't want Knighton. You want me."

How she wanted him to kiss her. To draw her into his arms and hold her, taste her lips and touch her flesh as he had that night in his library. His hand left her cheek, and now his thumb was brushing against her mouth, rubbing her bottom lip, and she wanted to taste him. To touch her tongue to his skin and feel his flesh, taste the salt and maleness of him. But it would not stop there. She knew that.

She tried to think of her mother. The life of poverty and shame she had endured because of her mother's wild behavior. She summoned up every painful childhood memory and forced them to the front so that she would not think of this—would not remember what it was like to be in his arms, his mouth hungrily moving over her neck and bosom.

"My God," he rasped. "How can you deny it? I ache with it, Isabella. A week without you…the pain of it haunts me. You must know that."

"As much as you know that I feel the same way, my lord." The words were spilling out of her. She was baring her soul to him, but it was so easy to do. With hardly any effort he stripped her bare—emotionally she was exposed, when she sought never to tell him her true feelings.

"Then come to me," he whispered. "End this suffering—for both our sakes."

"I cannot. Feeling and acting upon such things are two very different things."

"Forget Knighton, Bella. He's not who you crave. Who you come alive for. You are so warm, so alive beneath my hands," he murmured as he swept his finger along her lips. "I can feel the heat from you, your breath on my finger, yet you wish to kill these feelings. To cut me dead."

"No."

He moved so swiftly, Isabella didn't see his intent until she was encased in his arms and pressed against the wall. The stone was cold against her back, and Black…oh, Black was hot against her breasts, and she was melting beneath those pale blue eyes that could see deep inside her.

"Seduction, yes," he said as he reached for her hands and entwined his long fingers with hers. "The most intense and pleasurable kind. The kind that will make you weak and satiated, unable to run from me. But scandal? Never."

"The sort of passion that has flared between us ends in one of two ways," she said. "It dies out as swiftly as it flared, or it is put to death beneath disgrace. Either way, it ends. I would rather it stop now, before it truly starts. I don't want any pain between us, Black. I…don't want to hate you when the passion wanes, and we are left with nothing but regrets "

"You fear it, this current between us."

"I fear the results," she whispered. Her body was weakening, her resolve waning. Isabella did not know how much more of this she could take.

"You are no naive little girl, Isabella. You know what you want."

She turned her face to look up at him, her mouth brushed his chin and she closed her eyes, absorbing the feel of his night beard abrading her lips. "There is passion between us, a desire that is strong, breathtaking in its intensity, yet it is all we have. There is nothing more than that. We don't even truly know each other."

He moved against her, brushed his long, hard body into her softness, and she bit her lip to keep from moaning. He was a master of seduction. He knew how to make her weak. She was a woman, and he used his body against hers—a perfect foil to make her give in to his masculine power.

Black dropped his head until she felt the brush of his lips against her ear. "There is a deep knowledge in intimacy, Isabella. Deeper, more profound than a hundred conversations. To be so deeply inside you, our bodies connected, to feel you pulse around me, is to discover you as no other ever could."

The vivid images of him atop her, his muscles gleaming in the firelight, consumed her. He would be magnificent naked, his strong arms caging her as he made love to her. She could see it, and it made her weak—wet— made her curse the imagination she had been born with. It had once been her salvation, now it was her damnation, for all she could see was Black looming above her, while moving lazily inside her. He would be beautiful, his lovely eyes trained on her every movement, her every sigh. He would love her long, and slow, even if she wished for something else. He would do as he pleased, knowing it was what she truly needed. No man would ever know her like that. Would be able to read her secret desires like Black.

"A month with Wendell Knighton, and how well do you know him, Isabella? How well does he know you?"

She squirmed, the statement hitting too close to the truth. She needed to quit this conversation, to remove herself from this space where all she could feel and smell and touch was Black.

"Does he know you like to kiss? That you have a sensitive patch of skin behind your ear that when kissed, or touched with the tip of the tongue, makes your knees weak? Does he know the sound of your surrender, as your breath leaves your lips and you give yourself up to a kiss?"

"Jude, please," she begged. "Don't do this."

"Have you told him you write? That you dream of being a published novelist? Have you shared a meal with him, and gazed at him across the table with desire in your eyes? Have you allowed him liberties in the library?" He moved forward, nuzzled her ear and let his voice drop into a devastating husky whisper. "Have you let him taste you, run his tongue along your folds and make you wet?"

"You know I haven't," she gasped. He knew it never would be so. No other man would even do such a thing as Black had done to her, most especially Wendell, and after Black, she was utterly ruined, for she would never experience that earth-shattering experience with another—didn't want to, in fact. Instead, she would lie awake and relive those times when Black had awakened her to her true self. Every time she closed her eyes, she saw him—it would forever only be him, and this fierce pull that was unrelenting in its grip.

"A month of conversation and you are no closer to knowing Knighton than you were before the introduction. But one glance at me, and you knew, knew there was something between us. Five minutes in my arms, and you knew what you desired."

She was weakening, her traitorous body brushing against his in an attempt for more. Not only could he seduce her with his touch, he seduced her with words.

"You know me, Isabella, the way I kiss, touch. The sounds I make when you arouse me. I know your sounds, the press of your breast, the silken flesh of your thighs against my face."

She moaned, pressed, brushed, felt hot and aroused, needing more. She could no longer think, just act, and damn her soul, she wanted this—what he was offering. She felt warm and alive, and different from any other time in her life.

"I still taste you," he whispered darkly. She moaned again, then purred as he brushed his nails over her bodice. "Your nipples are hard, perfect little points for my tongue—"

"Stop it," she cried, her voice just a sob of pain and aborted pleasure. "Please, just stop! My God, I hate what you are making of me."

He stilled, pressed his forehead against her cheek and kissed her closed eyelid. "What if I can't? What if I've tried and have not been able to keep myself from you? You're in my blood, Isabella, and that's a bond that can't be severed."

"Lust always weakens. Soon the bond will become dilute and you will no longer even recognize it."

"You fear the basis of this attraction is only lust, that it could never develop into anything more, but you're wrong,

Isabella. So wrong. Desire doesn't have to die, nor does it end in shame."

"You would make a wanton of me. A slave to my own desires. You're a man of the world, you've tasted your fill of such pleasures, but I have been starved for them. The taste is new and exciting, and I hunger for more—and you know that. You understand how intoxicating your touch is, how enthralling your whispered words. You know how to play this game of seduction. But what will happen when you have your fill? When the dish no longer tempts the palate? What then, when I am still left with a ravening hunger?"

"Then I will feed you."

"Jude…" His name was a pleading whisper that passed through her lips.

"I could never have my fill of you, Isabella."

"That is what my father told my mother. What the sailors who rolled into Whitby told her. It is the same line that men have used for hundreds of years to make a woman succumb. But I cannot."

"Come to me and I'll prove you wrong. I will tell you anything you wish to know about me. You already know my deepest secrets. No other woman has known what I told you in that carriage."

Cupping his cheek, Isabella smiled sadly. She would do anything to be with him. But it would be a short-term solution. No man with this amount of passion inside him could be content for long—and with someone as inexperienced and sexually gauche as she.

"I know the look in your eye, Isabella. Don't do it."

Raising herself on tiptoe, she kissed his cheek, allowing herself the temptation of brushing her cheek to his. "Goodbye, Jude."

He reached for her, shackled her wrist and swooped down to capture her mouth, but he stopped as soon as she said, "Please. Don't."

He released her, but Isabella knew it was not for long. This was not their goodbye. She could sense that much. As she walked away, she could feel his eyes watching her. It took everything she had not to run back to him and fling her arms around his neck and beg him to take her away.

When she entered the gallery, Wendell was there, waiting for her. His eyes were dark, his expression grim.

"I trust you severed all ties with him?"

It did not surprise her that Wendell had discovered she'd met with Black in the hall. Despite his aura of indifference, nothing seemed to get past him.

"Is it over?" he demanded as he shackled his hand around her wrist. "Damn you, tell me," he snarled.

When she glanced up at him, she was taken aback by the barely tethered anger she saw in his eyes. He was hurting her, and for the first time, she was truly frightened of him.

"Yes, yes," she whimpered as she tried to tug free of his hold. "It's over."

"Good. See that it stays that way."

CHAPTER EIGHTEEN

"Do you recall the night we dined at Black's?" Wendell Knighton droned on. With a yawn, Lucy pretended interest in her embroidery hoop.

"Of course," Isabella replied.

Lucy had no clue how her cousin tolerated Mr. Knighton's uninspiring company. His conversation always threatened to put Lucy to sleep.

"We spoke of the Templars and the mystery surrounding them."

"I remember," Isabella murmured as she poured Knighton another cup of tea.

Glancing at the clock, Lucy saw it was nearly ten and wondered when Knighton would take his leave. She was tired tonight and wished for a warm bath and her bed, but that would hardly do, for she was chaperoning her cousin's visit with her suitor.

"Well, I've come across something rather interesting. The Brethren Guardians."

Lucy took a sip of her tea and glanced at Knighton. He was itching to tell them something. She could tell. He always preened, and got this queer glittering look in his eye. If he began talking once again about his expedition to Jerusalem, Lucy did not know what she'd do. She wanted to pull out her hair, she'd heard the stories so many times. She could just imagine how Isabella felt. Poor dear, she mused as she took in Isabella's polite but distant expression.

He certainly was no Lord Black. Somehow, Lucy knew that her cousin missed the company of that particular gentleman. They had seen little of Black, but Sussex had been a frequent visitor to their home, along with his sister, Elizabeth. She had seen Issy's eyes light up with each visit, only to see the glimmer of hope die away when Black was not part of the party.

Lucy had no idea what had happened between the two. She only knew that her cousin was utterly miserable. She pretended happiness, but in her unguarded moments, Isabella would glance wistfully across the street at Black's town house.

She wanted to tell her to go to him, but she promised herself that she would no longer intrude in Isabella's life. After their argument, Lucy had bit her tongue, allowing her cousin to do what she thought was right. But thinking of her marrying the staid and somewhat pompous Mr. Knighton was not in Isabella's best interests, Lucy was sorely tempted to tell Issy that, and damn the consequences.

Setting the needlepoint aside, Lucy sighed and watched her cousin with Knighton. There was little passion on either side, and in truth, Issy's once good opinion of Knighton had faded, turning into something that could only be called polite disinterest. Lucy wondered if Knighton felt it, the slow withdrawal of Isabella's interest and affection.

Knighton droned on about the Templars, and Lucy glanced once at the clock. She wondered how to extricate herself for only a few moments, when something Knighton said caught her attention.

"You will recall the pendant I mentioned?"

Lucy's ears perked up.

"I do, yes," Isabella answered.

"It holds magical properties."

"What sort of magical properties?" Isabella asked with what Lucy was certain was feigned interest.

Knighton smiled knowingly. "The seeds from the apple Eve took from the Tree of Knowledge. The seeds, they say, when ingested, bring the person their greatest wish, and universal knowledge."

Suddenly, everything stopped, and Lucy found herself transfixed by Knighton's story. "Their greatest wish?" she asked, knowing what her wish would be—to be reunited with her dead lover.

"Indeed," Knighton replied as he reached into his pocket. "But there is a scroll to go with it. It tells how the seeds work, and what must be done to gain their power."

Lucy knew where the scroll was. Knew exactly where it was.

Her heart started to race as she recalled that afternoon at Sussex House, when she and Isabella had visited Elizabeth. She'd just returned from refreshing herself, when she walked past Sussex's study. Inside, the duke, Black and Alynwick had been talking. She stopped to listen, hoping to hear something from Black about Isabella—for she had been determined to see her cousin with the earl. But she had heard something else. Strange talk of pendants and scrolls, and then the marquis stated he'd taken the scroll to the library at the Masonic lodge.

She hadn't given it more than a fleeting thought at the time, but now her thoughts were churning, trying to recall every snippet of their conversation.

"Oh, Wendell," Isabella gasped. "It's extraordinary."

Lucy saw the glittering egg-shaped pendant shining in the firelight. It was made of onyx and embossed with gold symbols. It hung from a long gold chain, and it seemed to beckon, to beg to be touched.

"Yes," Knighton whispered as he lost himself in the beauty of the swaying pendant. "Simply extraordinary. And it's my find. *Mine*..."

"This will be such a coup for your career," Isabella said, but Knighton's eyes narrowed and he hurriedly stuffed it into his pocket. But he missed, and the pendant spilled out and thudded softly to the carpet.

All Lucy could think about was how she wanted it. Would it work? Could it be possible that the pendant did have powers? Would it bring back her lover?

"I'm not ready yet to share the find with the world," Knighton mumbled. "Naturally you won't say anything to anyone, will you?"

"Of course not, Wendell."

"Lady Lucy?"

"No," she murmured, unable to take her gaze off the onyx stone and the gold chain that was curled up like a snake on the carpet beneath Knighton's chair.

"Well, it's late, and I have more studying to do. My second degree," Knighton preened. "Good night, my dear."

Knighton bowed before Isabella, and Lucy heard her cousin say that she would show Knighton the door.

When they left the study, Lucy quickly moved out of her chair and fell to her knees as she reached for the locket. Once it was in her hand, she was surprised by the warmth of the stone as it rested in her palm. She could almost feel its power oozing into her skin.

This pendant was the only means of finding him again. Séances had proved futile and she had long given up on praying. No, this was the only way. And she knew the location of the vital piece needed to fully understand the power of the pendant.

God help her, but she was going to take it and use it, and find love once more. Where was the harm in it?

THE REALIZATION that they were no closer to finding the chalice or the pendant made Black's mood more foul. Orpheus had eluded them, as if he had somehow known they

were coming. The club's owner had literally vanished into
the smoke, despite the fact one of the Brethren Guardians
had gone nearly every night to the club. That vexed him.

After scouring every inch of the Adelphi, they had
found nothing, and the fact that they had uncovered nothing more of any value only further frustrated what little
sanity Black had left.

The longer the chalice and pendant were missing, the
greater the chance someone might discover their true purpose. And that he couldn't accept. It was his duty, his
sworn oath, to protect, and he'd failed.

Smoothing his hands over his face, he tried to think
through the small bits of information they had acquired.
Perhaps he had overlooked something? But he knew they
hadn't. Their search of the lodge had produced nothing,
and Sussex's investigation revealed that Stonebrook did
not keep Masonic letterhead in his study.

He groaned when he thought of Stonebrook, for it led
to only one place. Isabella.

Damn it! Two weeks without her. He could barely stand
it. He had spent it in a haze, a fog of whiskey and unabated
desire. His companion was the night, the fire that crackled in the hearth and Lamb, who dozed lazily at his feet.

He flatly refused to get up and glance out the window,
staring up at her window like a love-struck fool. But he
was. A fool. And love-struck, too. And he so desperately
wanted another glimpse of her.

He wondered if Isabella felt him when he thought of
her. Did she know he was moping about in this mausoleum of his? Did she know the only time his house had
felt like a home was the night she had dined there?

Did she even care? No, how could she? She had for-
saken him, and now he was drunk, and feeling dangerous.

How did he get around this, her paralyzing fear of passion? Goddamn it, he had not risked his own life to save

hers for nothing. She was tossing this second chance of life away, and he was enraged by the fact. To spend a lifetime with someone like Knighton, someone who would never know her true desires, even after a decade with her, was anathema to him. How could she want what Knighton offered, when Black could offer her so much more? He'd give everything for her, and Knighton would give her nothing that mattered.

He had watched them together at the museum, and detected nothing but the most mild of friendships. Knighton didn't look at her the way a man ought to look at his lover. And she did not look at him like a woman who had been awakened by a lover's touch. No, she had looked at *him* like that when she had experienced her first climax in his arms.

Angry, he picked up his crystal glass and fired it at the hearth, watching as the amber contents splashed into the flames, igniting them, sending them dancing viciously up the flue. Lamb barely stirred. His pet was used to the childish displays he had chosen to hide behind. He had been acting this way ever since Isabella had decided to cut him from her life. He was not used to such a thing. He did not invite closeness in others, nor did he invite them in, but he had offered Isabella a rare invitation to discover what lay inside the reclusive Earl of Black's soul, and she had rebuffed it. The fact still stung. She hadn't wanted what he was so ready to show her.

Resting his head back against the chair, he closed his eyes and laughed in pain and self-deprecation. He had never loved before—certainly he had experienced a familial love for his brother and mother—his father he'd never been close to. But he had loved his mother, and Francis, his younger brother. He had been engaged at the age of twelve. He had grown to like Abigail Livingstone, but never had he grown to love her. And the other women in his life…nothing had ever been close to love. It had been lust. Animal needs. There was no affection, just physical pleasure. And that had all changed when he'd dived into the ocean and swum the swirling depths to save Isabella.

Holding her in his arms, something inside him awakened. These feelings she feared were not sudden, he thought. They had been growing inside him these past two years, until he was so damn in love with her he couldn't see straight.

Perhaps she would believe him if he told her the truth, but then his secret would be out, and she would run from him, because he was a part of her past she didn't want to remember.

There must be a way, he told himself. Some way to make Isabella see that life with Knighton would be a disaster. If only he could make her believe in his love. Make her understand that love was like an endless ocean, with no beginning or end.

Opening his eyes, he glanced at the book he had left open on the table next to him. He picked it up, read the words and reflected how they resonated within his soul.

> I am your moon and your moonlight, too
> I am your flower garden and your water, too
> I have come all this way, eager for you
> Without shoes or shawl
> I want you to laugh
> To kill all your worries
> To love you
> To nourish you

Would Isabella find the words that Rumi had written centuries before as profound as he did? He could say nothing better than what the poet had written. Every word was how he felt about Isabella. He wanted to love her, nourish her, hold her until Death claimed him. Even in death he had the sense that he would still feel her. His soul, upon every rebirth, would always seek out hers.

"My lord," Billings asked. "A missive has come."

"Enter."

The butler stepped cautiously into the library, clearly noting the shards of crystal that glimmered in the dying glow of the fire.

"Shall I bring in a broom, milord?"

"No, I shall see to it in the morning."

Black flicked the letter open. Glancing at the words, he carefully folded it back up and slipped it into his jacket pocket. "I'm going out," he said. "Don't wait up, Billings."

"Very good, milord. Shall I set Lamb out again tonight?"

At the sound of his name, the mastiff lifted his head, his ears were up, alert. His huge tongue lolled out of his mouth, as if anticipating the duty before him.

"Yes," Black murmured as he rubbed behind the dog's ear. "Send him over to Stonebrook's. And you'll protect my lady from harm, won't you."

There was a keen understanding in Lamb's eyes, and when Billings called for the beast, Lamb loped across the floor and bounded out of the room. Strolling to the window, he watched the massive dog run across the street, only to hide in the side gardens, standing sentinel beneath Isabella's bedroom window. If she would not allow him to protect her then Lamb was the next best thing.

BLIND, HE KNELT before the fire. The flickering flames warmed his face, even as the draft of air wrapped around him.

"What have you learned, Knighton?"

Swallowing, he used the fleeting seconds to formulate his lie. "The text I discovered is in poor condition. It'll take time to decipher the tale of the Templars."

Something hard hit the stone, and he jumped at the

sound. He was normally not a brave, heroic man, but in this matter he would die for his cause. He was utterly consumed by the Templar story. By the seductive voice that spoke to him from the pendant.

The voice told him of the powers it possessed. Of what could be done if he could but find the chalice. His wildest dreams—his most coveted fantasy could come to life.

Thus far, he had learned that he required the blood of an innocent. A few drops on the seeds, and the powers would begin. He'd found the blood he needed. Had already set that part of his plan in motion. He had the chalice, but he needed the scroll. The pendant wanted to be reunited with the chalice. It chanted that, over and over, until he thought he would go mad at nights for hearing the words over and over again. But he needed the scroll in order to reunite them as the pendant needed.

"Damn you, tell me what you've learned, Knighton."

He knew he could not keep this up forever. Orpheus, as the man called himself, might decide to take the pendant back, and he couldn't be parted from it. He decided that he had to give up something in return. "The chalice is integral. We need to find it."

"I already know that," the man snarled. "Fool!"

Swallowing, Knighton tried to find a way to stall him. He wanted this find for himself. He was greedy. He wanted this power. The secrets contained in the pendant and chalice for himself.

Pain seared through his scalp as his hair was squeezed by a tight fist. "If you think to trick me, Knighton, you've got another think coming. I own you," the man snarled. "Don't think to keep a damn thing from me. You've got three days to discover what you can. Then we'll be coming for you."

Shoved forward, Knighton fell to the cold stone floor. The silence was deafening, and as he raised his shaking hand to the scarf tied around his eyes, he knew what he had to do. He must take the blood of the innocent and use what knowledge he had discovered—before the others came to him.

Tonight, he mused as he stood up on shaking legs. Tonight he would call upon the one he had chosen.

SHE HAD NEVER DONE anything like this, but desperate times called for desperate measures. Glancing at the missive in her hand, Lucy studied the directions she had written as her thumb brushed over her reticule. Tucked safely inside was the egg-shaped pendant she had found beneath the chair in the salon.

Damn Wendell Knighton for coming to her home with the prospect of Templar treasure. She had been smitten by the tale, just as Knighton knew she would be, but how had he known of her desperation? But he had known. She'd been too weak to resist. The story he had weaved had been so intriguing and hope inspiring that she had not even considered returning the pendant to him. From the moment it had touched her hand, it had become an obsession. The powers inside it spoke to her; she could hear the beckoning voice, even from inside the safety of her reticule.

As the carriage rolled along the cobbles, carrying her farther and farther away from Grosvenor Square, a deep-seated sense of apprehension invaded her soul. Breaking into her father's Masonic lodge was nothing she thought she'd ever do. But then, discovering a way to have her heart's greatest desire would make people do all kinds of silly things.

The hired hack slowed, pulling up before the darkened building that was off Fleet Street and the River Thames. It was well past midnight, and while Mayfair would be alive with people coming and going from balls and routs, this part of London was relatively quiet. Still, she would have to have a care not to be seen.

It was not as if this was the first time she had traveled alone, by hired hack. She was adept at sneaking away from the house.

"'Ere ye are," the coachman called from his perch.

Lucy heard him jump down from his seat, and the door swung open, revealing a lanky old man with yellowing teeth. Holding out her hand, she allowed him to assist her out. When she was safely standing on the sidewalk, she looked up at the imposing building through the rippling lace of her bonnet veil. The square-and-compass symbol, with the gold numbers 128, was clearly visible on the pediment of the building.

"Yes, this is the place."

"Told ye I knew of it."

"This is for the carriage ride," she said as she placed coins in his waiting hand. He wore a filthy glove with the fingers cut out to the knuckle. His long bony fingers curled around the gold, which shone in the moonlight. "This is for you—if you'll stay and wait for me."

"'Ow long?" he asked as his thumb moved over the coins, counting them."

"A half hour perhaps?"

"Aye, that'll do me. A 'alf hour, mind, or it'll cost ye more."

Lifting her skirts, Lucy ran up the steps and around the side of the building where the streetlights did not reach. She had chosen tonight because she had finally worked up the nerve, not to mention the fact the fog was thick, blanketing the city in shadows. The shadows were her friend tonight. No one would see her moving about the building or slipping in the back door.

Once around the back, she came to a door and fiddled once more with her reticule. Inside, she fished around for a key, just another object she had thought nothing of stealing. In the darkness she fumbled with putting the key in the lock. Nervousness, and perhaps anticipation, was making her clumsy.

"Damnation!" she muttered as she tried a third time. This time the key fit nicely into the opening, and turned, releasing the latch. Opening the door, she stepped into the hallowed halls of the Masonic lodge.

She'd brought a taper and match with her, and once inside, she struggled to light the match. She almost abandoned hope for it, when light flared, and the acrid smell of sulfur wafted through the air.

The candle cast deep, dancing shadows on the walls as she walked silently but efficiently down the hall, taking in the Masonic heraldry. She had always been intrigued by the secret society, and would have loved to explore more, but time was of the essence. She was not done hunting, and she could not risk the carriage driver's abandoning her here—all alone.

Heels clipping against the black-and-white-marble tile, she made her way to the back of the building where she could detect the faintest odor of must. The library, with its thousand tomes, must be back there.

Rounding the corner, she passed a door that had been left open, and raised her candle, taking in what lay beyond the flickering flame. Shelf upon shelf of books lay before her, and she stepped into the room, and found a candlestick in which to put her taper. Then she removed her gloves, and the necklace from her reticule. The second her hands touched the pendant, it seemed to come alive, warming in her palms, whispering to her to connect it with the book. Like lost lovers longing to be reunited, the pendant silently spoke, encouraging her to walk to one particular section of the library.

Was it her natural instincts that commanded her, or was it really the pendant guiding her? Regardless, she heeded its counsel, and moved to the section, looking in frustration at the sheer volume of leather-and-gilt spines that stared out at her.

Where to begin? But her fingers were already touching each book. She had no idea of the title, but suspected she might find it contained the same symbols as on the pendant.

In efficient silence, Lucy worked, listening to her instinct…cold, cool…her fingers kept moving as her belly grew nervous…warm, warmer…she could hardly breathe, and then she touched the book—the right one—for the pendant absolutely heated against her flesh, and her hand shook in eagerness as she pulled the old brown leather book—which appeared to be an illuminated manuscript out of its hiding spot. It had been rolled up, like a scroll, and nearly hidden behind another book. As she took the leather ties in her fingers and pulled, the scroll unraveled, and a cloud of dust sprung up.

Yes, the pendant whispered. *Yes, now hurry, open me, take the seeds into your mouth…*

Breathlessly, she stepped down the little stool and whirled around, her hood slipped back over her bonnet, and she heard a gasp at the door of library.

"Stop, thief!"

Her body froze, and she glanced up from the scroll, frightened as never before. Light flared, and the glare from a gas lamp being lit by the map table momentarily blinded her. When she could see, she looked up, and heard the deepest, most dangerous growl.

"Lucy Ashton?"

It was her turn to gasp in alarm. "Lord Black."

"Indeed."

"Wh-what are you doing here, my lord?"

"I would like to ask you the same question."

Numerous lies began to formulate in her mind. She fixed on one just as she saw how Black's gaze had dropped to her throat. He was staring at the pendant, and she let go the book, knowing she must protect the seeds inside.

Wendell had said, when he'd come to call on them, that the seeds were the power behind the pendant. It was the seeds that brought dreams—and untold power.

Yes, she heard. The voice in her head was all but screaming at her now, and she fumbled with the opening, trying to pry open the locket and take the seeds into her mouth.

But Black had launched himself into motion, and he was throwing himself at her before she could think. His large, leather-encased hand wrapped around her throat, and she swore she saw her impending death, but he only yanked the pendant from her neck and shoved it into his pocket.

She was enraged, and struggled against him, her hand searching deep inside the pocket.

"Lucy, listen to me," he growled as she struggled in his hold. "You're not in your right mind."

"Give it to me," she snarled. "Give it to me. It's mine."

"It's evil, Lucy. It brings only death, not pleasure."

"I want it," she screamed, clawing at him. "I want it, it's mine."

A part of her knew she was being hysterical, another part of her was at the mercy of the pendant. That voice, that hissing voice that seemed to scream to her, was relentless, gave her such incredible power to fight Black.

Raising her hand, she clawed at his eye as he tried to subdue her, raked her nails down his cheek until she saw a trail of blood rise to his skin and run down his cheek.

"Damn you," he seethed. "Listen to me. Did you take any of the seeds?"

Just one. The necklace had told her to. It was how she was connected to it, how she could hear its voice whispering to her.

"Lucy, damn it," he rasped. He was winded, struggling

with her. He would not hit her—Black was a gentleman, but suddenly she felt like no lady. An unholy strength seemed to infuse her. She would not lose this necklace, or this book. Her dreams depended on it.

"Sussex," Black roared. "Help me, damn you. I'm going to hurt her."

Arms suddenly snagged around her, and she craned her neck back to see who held her hostage. Sussex's face came into view, and he lifted her off the ground, pressed her back into his chest, and she kicked out like a screeching, hissing cat.

Black caught her feet, and together they carried her from the room and back down the hall. Slipping in behind them was Alynwick, who was bending down, retrieving the book, and she scorned with hatred.

"Come, Lucy," Sussex soothed. "You're frightened, overwrought."

"I hate you," she cried in a voice that no longer seemed to be her own. The two men paused, stared at her with horror, before gazing at one another.

"Now do you believe?" Sussex roared.

"I do." Black was gazing upon her with a mixture of sorrow and true fear. "The seeds, they really are poisoned with the venom of the snake that whispered to Eve."

Oh, God, she thought as the strength suddenly vanished from her body, leaving her limp and malleable in their arms. The snake had been Lucifer himself. What had she done?

CHAPTER NINETEEN

"BLOODY HELL," Black rasped as he fell against the velvet squabs. "Did you see her? She possessed the strength of ten men!"

Sussex gathered an unconscious Lucy against him. She was limp, and Black watched as his friend held her carefully in his arms. "She's not evil," he murmured. "She was under the spell of the pendant."

Alynwick climbed to the carriage box, his weight making the conveyance dip. With a crack of the whip, the marquis maneuvered the carriage away from the curb and into the street. Upon arriving, they had sent Lucy's hired hansom cab on its way. It had taken only an extra shilling for the waiting coachman to abandon poor Lucy.

"I'm not sure why you're surprised, Black," Sussex growled. "Your family has been in possession of the pendant for over five hundred years. You were weaned on the stories of it."

"I…I didn't know of its powers. I never felt the powers as keenly as Lucy did. But then, I never kept it on me. I… just never believed."

Glancing out the window, he could barely stand to see Sussex with Lucy, to watch as he held her, and as she lay trustingly in his arms. There was a hole in his heart, and Isabella had made it. Seeing Lucy tonight had only made his pain more acute. Isabella was home alone tonight, and likely frightened.

"Why did you not believe?" Sussex asked quietly, and

Black closed his eyes, not wanting to tread down that murky path. But the memories were there, and he replied.

"Because I lost faith." And he had. After his mother and brother and then Abigail had died and left him, he'd felt his faith slowly dissipate until he had been left with nothing but anger and rage and the fury of having to protect something he loathed.

"Does this prove it then? Have you seen how damn important it is to hide these relics from the world?"

He did. As he felt the heat of the pendant burning in his pocket, he realized that he did believe, that the horror of witnessing Lucy in such a state had reaffirmed what he always believed, that the relics were a curse upon their family, and that he had no desire to wed and breed for the purpose of perpetuating that curse. But looking at Sussex with Lucy made him realize he no longer wanted to live alone and isolated.

"God, I shudder to think of what might have happened to her if Elizabeth hadn't come to me with her suspicions."

"Yes," Black said, shoving aside his thoughts. "Thank God her instincts are sharper than most people's."

"How will we get her back into the house?" the duke murmured. "Stonebrook is home, I assume."

"No, I saw him leave. He very rarely stays in at night anymore."

"Well, that is a small grace."

"Sussex—" Black stared at the man who sat across from him "—this isn't the last. And Lucy hasn't acted alone."

"I know. What does your gut tell you?"

Punching the seat, Black felt a cloud of impatience wash over him. "Damn if I know. There are too many twists and turns, too many coincidences. I say we fight more than one person."

"I suppose you're right." Sussex sighed and leaned his head back against the carriage. "But, damn it, Black,

I can't think of that tonight. All I can think of is…her. What the devil was she doing there?"

"I think, Sussex, that you'll have to come to grips with the idea that Lucy is part of this. I think it's been her who has intentionally tried to part Isabella from me. Think of it, who more than Lucy would know of Isabella's fears? Lucy set up the séance."

"And Alice Fox's death? Lucy did that? No, I won't believe it."

"No, but her accomplice did."

"Rubbish. Lucy's involvement is true, but she's an innocent victim in some treacherous game."

"Your thoughts are clouded, Sussex, and your feelings for the girl are making you blind."

"Damn you, you should talk, Black!"

The carriage swayed and dipped, and Black let his body move to the rhythm. He was tired. And his mind and body were exhausted from two weeks spent tracking Orpheus, all to no avail, and nights spent awake, staring at the ceiling, thinking of Isabella.

"Here we are!" Alynwick called. "I'll bring us round back, and you can carry her in through the kitchen garden."

"Make certain the servants are out of sight. I don't want anyone seeing me carrying her in."

"Right," Alynwick agreed as he closed the hatch.

Stepping out, Black descended the stairs and took Lucy from Sussex. She was limp as a rag, and her hair cascaded over his arm. Sussex jumped down and immediately took her from him.

"Detain Isabella. Make something up about what Lucy was doing. Elizabeth is there with her. She'll help you."

"I won't lie to her, Sussex." There were already enough half truths that lay between them. Black had no desire to add more. In fact, he had the absurd notion to spill all to Isabella tonight.

ISABELLA PACED FRANTICALLY in the salon. Where had Lucy gone? Fear overrode her thoughts, and she was consumed with the image of Death claiming her dearest cousin.

"Sit, Isabella," Elizabeth encouraged with a gentle pat on the settee, signaling her to take a seat beside her. "All this exercise must be most tiring."

"I can't. My mind is racing with every possible thought and my body must move, or else the panic will set in."

"My brother has gone after her. She'll be safe."

"Oh, Lucy," she chided. "What the devil is she about?" She had been so desperate for passion, to search for anything that might remind her of her dead lover, that Isabella feared she might have gone and done something truly dreadful. She knew the sort of ends despair could drive a soul to. And she feared Lucy might have discovered them, too.

"I cannot thank you enough for coming to your brother with your worry and suspicions," Isabella said. "Had you not, Lucy might have ended up…" Oh, she didn't want to think of it.

"She said a few things that made me worried."

"What things were those?" Isabella questioned. Surely Lucy could not have shared her confidence with Elizabeth. She'd hid them above eight months from her, for heaven's sake!

"You understand, I'm not at liberty to discuss them, but suffice to say, I was alarmed. As I'm certain you're aware, my brother has developed a tendre for Lucy, and I knew that I would only have to mention my concerns, and he would go after her."

"I owe you—and the duke—for this."

And then, as if the heavens parted, His Grace came stomping into the house, his boots ringing off the marble tile. Isabella ran from the salon, forgetting to reach for Elizabeth, and skidded to a halt as she saw Lucy draped in Sussex's arms. Her first thought was she was dead, and her hands flew to her face, and she cried out, only to feel Black's arms go around her.

"She lives," he whispered, then pulled her back.

"Where is my sister?" the duke demanded.

"In the salon," Isabella murmured, unable to take her gaze off Lucy's pale face.

"Alynwick, get her. Black, see to Miss Fairmont."

She was gripped by the arm, tugged along by Black. She allowed it, took comfort in his hold, in his command.

"What is wrong with Lucy?"

"She's had a fright," he answered as he pulled her into her uncle's library and slammed the door. He helped her to sit on the settee and poured her two fingers of whiskey, and demanded she drink it.

The liquor burned, and she felt warm, languid, her nerves calming down.

"A fright? Do you mean she swooned?"

"Yes."

"I don't believe it. Lucy is not that sort at all."

Black frowned, evaded her gaze and dread filled her.

"Tell me all of it."

Black paced the room, and she followed him, her gaze never leaving him. He was pale. A muscle worked in his jaw, and she saw that he was not himself.

"We caught her in the Masonic lodge. She had broken in."

"That's impossible!" she gasped, and stood up, enraged. "Lucy is an honest person. She would never break in anywhere, least of all the Masonic lodge. For what purpose?" she demanded.

The muscle ticked, and he seemed to war with himself. "Isabella, you must believe me."

"Well, I do not!"

He whirled on her then, and she saw his eyes narrow, grow accusatory. "No, you believe people like Wendell

Knighton who seek to use you to further their purposes.
You believe Lucy, who has done nothing but lie to you,
but people like me, who seek only to keep you safe—
to…" His voice dropped to a dangerous whisper, and the
storm in his eyes blazed. "To love you, you don't give a
damn about those."

"Jude!" His name was a harsh sound coming from her
lips. It sounded like a reprimand, but it was not; it was
shock, surprise. Fear.

"My God, do not say it," he thundered. "Do not look
at me and tell me I shouldn't say such things. Such things
have been brimming inside me for two years, Isabella.
Two damn years," he roared, heedless that someone upstairs might hear him. "These feelings have seethed inside
me. I've been consumed by them, but you don't want to
hear it. You want the lukewarm attentions of Knighton.
You want it easy and clean, you don't want to have to
trust. To believe. To give a little piece of yourself to another."

She didn't know what to say, and when she finally
spoke, her words were nothing that she should have said.
"We were talking about Lucy."

"Lucy!" he barked, then he breezed past her, his anger
palpable. She reached for him, and something inside
him fractured. She saw it, the pain, and the rage, and he
reached for her, whirled her around, and she gasped at
the way he touched her—possessively, giving no thought
to her worries.

"Damn you," he whispered. "You make me lose
all control. I shouldn't be here like this with you. You
shouldn't even be here, tormenting night after night."

"What do you mean by that?" she gasped.

"Leave it," he demanded.

"I most certainly will not! This is my uncle's house! I
have every right to be here."

He sighed, raked his hands through his hair and hung

his head. Something like terror gripped her, and she asked, her voice shaking, "What did you mean, when you said I shouldn't even be here?"

"You know damn well what I meant."

And then she felt it, a warmth, a soothing comfort engulf her from behind and then he was there, pressing her bodice against the wall as he covered her back with his chest. Her thin gown did nothing to conceal his heat and she felt him, hot and hard, pressing against her back.

"Don't!" she cried, struggling against him. "You always do this, immobilize me with passion. Well, it won't work this time, my lord. Because I won't let it. We...we... don't even know each other, you know nothing of me."

"Jesus, Isabella, don't shut me out. Just let me in. You accuse me of not knowing you, of you not knowing me, but it's only because you won't allow it. You won't let me into the place where you hoard all your secrets."

"Don't," she commanded, and then she thought to play on his sensibilities, to return him to his purpose here. "Lucy—"

"She'll be all right. She's safe with Sussex."

"I need to know what happened tonight. What is going on?"

His hands reached for hers and entwining his fingers with hers, he raised her arms so that they were above her head and she was resting her brow on her clasped hands, which pressed against the wall. She could feel his heart beating beneath his skin and her own heart skipped with forbidden excitement.

"What is going on?" he rasped. "Me, here with you. Touching you. Taking from you. Two weeks, Isabella, you have denied us this, and it's not because you want Knighton. It's because you're too afraid to reach for this. To take what I've offered."

"What has gotten into you?" she asked, the question sounding more breathless than scathing.

"*You* have gotten into me. You're in my blood. I want you beneath me, the scent of you on my body, the taste of you on my tongue."

She would have given him a set down, but his mouth pressed against the curve of her neck and her mind went blank. Untangling one hand from hers, he trailed his fingers down her bare arm, over her shoulder and down her back where he grazed his fingers, featherlight, along her spine. His mouth, warm and soft, was pressed against her skin, continually nuzzling her neck, and her knees went weak, but he kept her standing with his hard body against hers for support.

Unable to stop herself, she sighed. Closing her eyes, she tipped her head to give him greater access to whatever it was he wanted. He growled appreciatively then flicked his tongue along the vein that pulsated wildly.

"I've missed your taste," he whispered. "Sigh for me, Isabella, and let me know you want this."

She couldn't help but moan when his hands roamed to the front of her gown and crept ever so slowly to her belly. She felt his fingers slide back up the silk until they pressed into the tender flesh beneath her breasts.

"Black, you're out of your mind," she murmured. "You're playing with fire by doing this."

"I know. I can feel the heat even now." He lowered his hand so that one long finger circled the indent of her navel. "Singe me, Isabella, for I care not." He kissed her cheek, his finger now sliding down the valley of her breasts. "You want this fire, too, if you would only be honest. This slow flame that is flickering to life inside you. You are not averse to these feelings I stir in you, are you? Your mouth doth protest, but your body belies your words. If you hated me so much you would have run from me. You would not be standing here, restless with longing, waiting with bated breath for me to lower your bodice and thumb your nipples."

Oh, she had never seen him quite this way before—so much more intense and demanding than he had been before—and so masculine. He would take what he wanted tonight, and she would let him if she didn't get control of her emotions.

But their absence had been too long. Her mind warned her about the perils of succumbing to him, but her body refused to listen, it craved every one of his touches, his words.

When she should have been worrying over Lucy, she was here, softening. But she knew Lucy would be fine. She knew that in the morning she could discover everything when Lucy awakened. But there might not be another night like this—with Black. The morning would come, replacing the night, but this…this moment with Jude was irreplaceable.

His touch, his hands on her body, ignited something so powerfully addicting that she could not forget it, or resist reaching out to capture it.

He palmed her breast and dipped his finger beneath the edge of her bodice and her body unconsciously pressed farther into his hand when his thumb flicked along her nipple.

He pulled her bodice down then, and her breasts bobbed free. He captured them from behind and cupped them in his hands. "Soft and large and exactly how I like them," he said in her ear. "I haven't stopped thinking of them, haven't stopped desiring them."

Then he turned her around and brought her breast to his mouth. He sucked, a slow rhythmic tug that made her whimper and want to clasp his head to her chest so he could deepen the embrace. But she resisted touching him and instead brought her hands above her head in a show of power. She could not submit to him.

He growled and clasped her wrists in his hand and sucked at her breast, alternating with little bites on her nipple. There was something about Black holding her captive like this that made her hope he would not stop until he had taken what he wanted.

He circled her nipple with his tongue then blew on it, hardening the tender flesh further. Curling his tongue around the nipple, he licked it while he rubbed his engorged erection between her thighs.

She gasped when she felt his free hand raise her skirts. A beautiful, stunning, sinful man, and she wanted to explore him, to discover everything he would show her, she was just too cowardly to take it.

"You make me reckless, Isabella. I am trying to be the gentleman, but you provoke me at every turn. My cock aches to be inside you. Can't you feel it?"

Her lips parted on a silent plea when his finger slid along her wet sex. Then she felt his hand between their bodies, through the layers of silk and chemise. She heard the buttons of his trousers being freed from their fastenings, felt her body being pushed against the wall and her thigh being raised and hooked around his waist.

Arching her back, she thrust her hips and breasts forward and he stroked his tongue along her nipples. She was rocking against him and she could hear his breathing, harsh and rapid, and she didn't care. She didn't care that they could be discovered and her name would be tarnished for life. She didn't care about anything save for what her body was crying out for.

His mouth was against her ear, his chest, muscled and firm, was pressing against her breasts, the silk threads of his waistcoat rubbing against her nipples and making them throb.

"Bella," he rasped. "Tell me you feel this, too. That you come alive in my arms."

"You know I do." Her mouth sought his, and he brushed his lips against hers; the feel of him back, kissing her, was soul filling. She moaned and opened to him, absorbing him. The hollow piece of her was filling, and she feared it, even as she recklessly plunged forward.

She felt her arm being raised, felt the contact of his face beside hers, the warmth of his breath caressing her cheek.

"Touch me."

Before she could protest or even move, Isabella found her fingers grazing his cheek, the skin warm and covered with the faintest dusting of stubble. His hand guided hers to his chin, which felt strong and angular.

"Isabella," he said against her fingers. "Touch me," he whispered again. This time need replaced the masterful tone of his voice. "Make me come alive beneath your hands. I've been dead these past weeks."

He placed her fingers over his lips and she startled at the softness of them. She swallowed hard and closed her eyes, almost whimpering when she felt him softly kiss her fingers.

"I need to touch you." His breath was harsh against her ear, and she felt the tips of his fingers glide down her throat and along the tops of her breasts. His finger dipped low. He stroked her nipple with his finger and she squirmed, her fingernails digging into the silk of his jacket. "*I* want this, Isabella. Do you?"

She couldn't think, couldn't agree or protest. She could only concentrate on the feel of his touch against her nipple that was now painfully taut. Her breasts were full, throbbing, waiting for the feel of his hand.

Swallowing hard, she nodded. He blew hot breath across her nipple before his tongue came out in a slow, tantalizing lick. Grasping his head, she moaned, bringing his mouth closer, holding him to her.

"Bella, come to me." His mouth moved across her breasts. "Be with me."

"You know I can't. It's not that I don't want to…it's…I just can't."

His expression turned dark—stormy—and he thrust himself away from her, looking very much like a ravaging knight.

"You forget, I know what your cousin was doing tonight."

"Yes," she said as she slid her sleeves back up her arms.

"I could ruin her."

She froze, lifted her face to his, which was dark and utterly unreadable. "I could go to Scotland Yard right now and tell all, and by morning her reputation would be in tatters."

"But you won't if I what? Sleep with you?" she shrieked. "Is that the sort of man you are, Black?"

He reached for her wrists, bent over her, caging her, and she was reminded of her story, when Death had huddled overtop her, his eyes dark and storming.

"You will come to me, Isabella. For three nights. And you will read to me from your book."

She gasped, her fingers flew to her mouth, trembled against her lips. Three nights for his silence. Oh, God, it was her book coming to life!

"Tomorrow night. Midnight. Be there. Or I will come for you."

She watched him storm away, and her gaze caught the journal that sat on the table. It was impossible to credit, but the story of her and Black was unfolding like that of Death's tale.

CHAPTER TWENTY

"I NEED THE PENDANT… Oh, Issy," Lucy moaned as Isabella mopped her sweating brow. "Please," she implored. "Black has it. Beg him, Issy. Give him anything he wants, if only he'll return the pendant to me."

"Lucy, you must calm yourself."

"Listen to me! I want the pendant—I need it. My soul relies upon it returning to me. Oh," Lucy growled in frustration. "Why will you not listen to me?"

"She's raving," Isabella murmured to Elizabeth who sat in the corner. "She's out of her mind with the fever. She keeps talking of a pendant."

Elizabeth sat quietly, listening. She did not respond to Isabella's fears.

"The doctor will be here shortly," Sussex said as he paced before the hearth. "I've done what I can, purging her of the poison, but she's not better. I cannot understand it, there can be nothing left in her stomach."

"What poison?" she asked, aghast, only to be met with silence. What the devil was going on here? Why was Elizabeth and her brother being so secretive, and how in the world was Black involved?

"Lucy," Isabella said sternly. Taking Lucy's pale face in her hands, she shook her cousin gently until her heavy eyelids opened. "Tell me what is going on."

"The pendant. It will bring you your greatest wish…"

"What pendant?" Isabella demanded. "Lucy, answer me!"

"Black's."

Glancing over her shoulder, she narrowed her eyes at the duke. "What the devil does she mean? Explain this, Your Grace."

"I cannot. She's…she's fevered. Talking nonsense," he muttered as he paced the floor. "I have no notion what she speaks of." But Isabella knew it was a lie. The duke knew exactly what her cousin was talking of.

"The voice is calling to me…calling," Lucy whispered as her head tossed on the pillow. "It wants to be reunited with the chalice and the book. It's chosen me to do the task…then I shall have…my greatest wish."

"Lucy, please," she begged. "Open your eyes. Tell me where you are."

"In hell," she whispered. "I am in hell, burning alive. I'm dying. Dying…"

"No!" she cried, gripping Lucy. "No, you're not."

"I want to," Lucy replied as she went limp against the pillows. "I want to be where he is…"

Sussex pounded his fist on the hearth, making Isabella jump. Lucy was raving, and the duke should not be present to bear witness to the demons that tore at her soul.

"Your Grace, you should remove yourself. I…I can care for Lucy now."

The glare he sent her was glacial. She had never seen this side of the duke, this dark, menacing air that came upon him like a thunderstorm. "You won't be throwing me out, Miss Fairmont," he snarled.

"I think it is better this way, Adrian," Elizabeth murmured as she carefully rose from the chair. "It is best, I think, to remove ourselves before the doctor arrives, don't you agree?"

Something played out across the duke's face, and Elizabeth, despite her lack of sight, seemed to sense it. She reached for the duke's hand, and he grasped it, held on to her tightly. "You'll send word to us if you need us, Miss Fairmont?"

"Of course. And please," she said, not wanting to sound imperial and autocratic. "We are deeply indebted to both of you. Your Grace, you saved Lucy tonight."

He said nothing, and with one last longing glance at Lucy lying in the bed, he left, leaving Isabella alone with her cousin.

"Lucy, what have you done?" she asked while pulling the sheets up high around her neck. "Whatever possessed you to do something so rash?"

"The pendant," Lucy whispered, her lips barely moving. "Issy...please... Black...Black has it."

"I have no intention of taking anything that belongs to Black."

"He'll use it," she cried. With a twist, Lucy was sitting bolt upright in bed, her eyes wide and wild, her voice deep, frightening. "Don't you see, he'll destroy everything."

Goose bumps covered her body as she gazed into Lucy's crazed eyes. Perhaps it was she who was slowly going mad. First her dreams, the story of Death, Black and his mysterious ways, and now Lucy, raving like a madwoman.

"Lucy, you're out of your mind." Perhaps all these séances were responsible for her behavior.

"Shall I stay with her?" Sibylla asked as she stepped around the door with fresh towels and a pitcher of water.

"No, I'll sit with her," Isabella replied as she watched Lucy's maid go about the room, tidying things up. She had never really cared for Sibylla. There was something about her that did not sit well with her. Ever since her arrival at Stonebrook, Lucy's mood had sunk even further. And there was no denying that since Sibylla's arrival, Lucy's interest in the occult had dramatically increased.

"Has she said anything?" the maid asked. She stood at the side of the bed, her long black hair pulled back in a plait. She was exotic, with her dark skin and even darker eyes.

"No."

"Nothing?" Sibylla asked, surprise in her voice. "I thought I heard her voice."

Isabella waved away the maid's concerns. She did not trust Sibylla with any information. Long years of self-preservation had taught Isabella to allow her instincts to guide her, and her instincts told her that Sibylla need not know anything of what had transpired this night.

"She has the fever," Isabella supplied. "She was talking nonsense."

"Oh." The way Sibylla looked at her let Isabella know that the distrust Isabella felt was mutual.

"Miss Fairmont, the doctor."

Turning, she saw Jennings usher in an elderly man carrying a black leather bag.

"I have taken the liberty of sending for Lord Stone-brook. He should be here shortly."

"Thank you, Jennings."

The doctor placed the bag on the bed and opened it, drawing out numerous bottles filled with medicine.

"She's fevered," he stated as his hand rested on her forehead. "His Grace said something about poisoning."

"Did he?" Isabella asked archly.

"He's waiting in the salon, he met with me on my way up. This is charcoal," he stated as he poured a vile-looking concoction onto a spoon. "It will induce vomiting and rid her body of the effects."

"I shall prepare more towels and bowls," Jennings said quietly.

"Yes, do," the doctor replied. "The vomiting will last for quite some time. I shall stay with her, of course."

"As will I," Isabella announced.

"It will not be easy, young lady," the doctor drawled as he spooned the medicine down Lucy's throat.

Stiffening, Isabella raised her chin. "My grandmother was a midwife, and I joined her many times. I've been awake the night through more times than I can count."

"Is that right?" the doctor muttered, although Isabella thought she saw a fleeting smile on his sober face. "Then you will be more than welcome here. Reach for that basin, will you? It looks like the tonic will take quickly."

MORNING LIGHT BROKE through the curtains, and Isabella, drained and exhausted, finally collapsed onto the bed beside Lucy, who had at last rested quietly. She barely heard the conversation that took place at the foot of the bed.

"Is it done?"

It was Sussex, and Isabella stirred, struggled to open her eyes. The duke's image was fuzzy, but she made him out, standing beside the doctor.

"She'll live."

The sigh that escaped His Grace warmed Isabella. He cared so deeply for Lucy.

"Well, Doctor," Stonebrook announced. "What did it? What made my Lucy so ill?"

"Poison, my lord. I'm not sure which, but the effects of it have been purged from her body."

"Poison? By God, what is poison doing in my daughter?"

"That is a very good question, sir."

"Perhaps we should remove ourselves from the room," Sussex said.

Stonebrook's voice broke. "She looks little more than a child, lying there pale and helpless."

"She will make a full recovery, my lord."

"Yes, well," Stonebrook grunted, and coughed, as if trying to hide his emotions. "I thank you, Sussex, for coming to her aid."

"No thanks are necessary, my lord. I am only happy that my sister and I happened to visit."

A lie. Sussex was lying to her uncle!

"When she is better, I will sort out this business. I have no notion where my daughter would acquire poison, and in her own home."

"I think it might be several days before Lady Lucy is feeling up to snuff. Normally purgatives drain a body of its energy and vitality. It may take days before your daughter is her old self."

"Well, then, I'll let her rest. I'll see you to your carriage, shall I?"

The men left, and Isabella dragged herself up from the bed and wiped her eyes, which burned from lack of sleep. Glancing at Lucy, she saw her cousin rested peacefully. She slid from the bed and made her way to the window and parted the curtains, watching as Sussex entered his carriage. The coachman cracked the whip, but the carriage did not make its way down the street. Instead, it turned and headed for the black iron gates that stood high across the street.

Black. Sussex was going there. Why, she asked herself, was everything come back to him?

Instincts were guiding, and Isabella knew what she had to do. She had to go to him, just as he commanded. Or he would come to her.

An image of Death riding his horse, sweeping her up in his arms, invaded her mind. Her instincts warned that the earl was not what he appeared. He was dangerous, and he had proved as much last night. But if she was to have answers, she would have to meet with him tonight—meet with Death in his domain.

TAKING THE BREAKFAST TRAY away from Lucy, Isabella frowned when she saw that her cousin had taken only a few sips of tea, and nothing to eat.

"You need your strength, Lucy," she said, trying to cajole her cousin. "You really must try something."

Frowning, Lucy turned onto her side, where she could not see the tray Isabella held. "After casting up my accounts all night long, you can hardly expect it. My stomach has been purged, and just the look of that food makes me want to retch."

"Well, then, perhaps luncheon will be met with greater success."

Sitting beside Lucy on the bed, Isabella began to brush out the tangles that had begun in her cousin's long red curls. "What do you remember from last night?"

"Very little, I'm afraid. I do recall setting out to retrieve a book from the Masonic lodge, but why, I have no idea. It was a relentless burning desire that would not let go. I can't even remember what I wanted there."

"You spoke of a pendant."

There was a beat of silence and an awkward pause before Lucy turned onto her back and gazed up at her. "Oh, yes, the pendant. I found it lying on the salon floor beneath the chair that Mr. Knighton had been using when he came to call. You remember, don't you? He was telling us of the Knights Templar and how the story goes that three of them were entrusted with the safekeeping of sacred artifacts. He showed us the pendant."

"But Black has it now?" she asked, perplexed about how Black featured in the tale. The points of the story were a little vague. Isabella was having a difficult time recalling exactly what Wendell had been saying. Her thoughts had been turning to Black. As a consequence, Wendell's story was lost to her.

"Miss Fairmont," Jennings said beyond the door.

Isabella rose and met him in the hall, closing the

door behind her. "Cook was wondering about luncheon, madam."

"I think a broth and toast is all we can expect Lady Lucy to eat today."

"Very good, miss. And might I say that staff is very relieved that Lady Lucy is on the mend."

Smiling, Isabella glanced up at the old retainer. "That is very kind, Jennings. I shall inform Lady Lucy when she awakes."

"And, miss?" Jennings said before he turned to go. "Staff is very grateful that you were here to care for her. The marchioness would have been very happy that you were there to care for her daughter."

It was the most human she had seen the man. She had thought him a cold, unfeeling cog in the wheel of the Stonebrook mansion, but this morning it was apparent that Jennings did have a heart after all.

"I believe, Jennings, that is the nicest thing anyone has ever said to me."

With a bow, he took his leave. She returned to the bedroom and saw that Lucy was resting easily. She moved to the window so as not to disturb her cousin, and gazed out at the dull sky. It was late autumn and the skies looked more like November than October. Few trees had leaves left, and the wind continued its relentless howl. Across the street, the iron gates that shielded Black's town house remained closed.

There was no other recourse. She must discover what she could of Black, and the mysterious pendant. There was no other way. She would have to go to him—tonight.

"His lordship is awaiting you in his study, madam."

Black's butler slipped her velvet cloak from her shoulders and hung it on the rack behind them.

"Shall I show you the way, miss?"

She was nervous, more than she had ever been in her

life. She was acting like a silly heroine from one of the penny dreadfuls, she reminded herself, but she could not stop it—no matter how hard she tried.

Following the butler, she tried to at least appear in control, even though every little nerve inside her jangled and flickered. She needed answers—answers to questions she feared to ask.

"Miss Fairmont," Billings announced loudly before opening the door. He ushered her through, and Isabella stepped into the darkened study. Her eyes took several seconds to accustom themselves to the dim light. Only one small oil lamp atop the desk glowed in the dark besides the fire in the massive hearth.

"Good evening, Miss Fairmont."

She saw Black sprawled out in a wingback chair, jacketless, the white shirt he wore unbuttoned to the waist, revealing an enticing view of his chest and the fine black hair that was hidden beneath. "I was beginning to wonder if you would come tonight. It is midnight after all."

On cue the large pendulum clock in the hall began to chime out the hour. Isabella met his gaze, marveled at the dark layers in his eyes. He appeared at once indolent, yet supremely masculine, and in his state of dishabille he was utterly breathtaking.

Shifting his weight, he swung one leg over the arm of the chair. Something glinted around his neck, and she saw it was a silver chain with a large black stone surrounded by diamonds. Beside the chair was a table, laden with a decanter of wine and a peregrine of the most luscious purple grapes she had ever seen. They were enormous, succulent and frosted with sugar, making them appear as though they had come in from a winter's ice storm.

She had never had grapes. They were a luxury she and her mother had never been able to afford—especially up north. She didn't even realize that one could have grapes at this time of year.

He caught her looking longingly at the fruit as he pulled one from the stem and popped it in his mouth. Her mouth watered, desiring the taste of the juicy fruit on her tongue.

Her uncle had never gone to the expense of serving grapes.

"Please," Black said as he slid the peregrine toward her. "Help yourself."

She wanted to, but there was something rather ominous about his offering, rather like the reversal of Eve tempting Adam with the bite of an apple.

Watching her, he took another grape and bit into the dark purple globe. Juice trickled onto his hand, and she looked away, trying to school her thoughts.

She had entered his lair, frightened; that fear had swiftly been replaced by a burning desire—a fire deep in her belly.

"You requested my presence," she said coolly. "I am here."

"To save Lucy's reputation?" he asked while watching her closely. "Or because you wanted to?"

"What does it matter? I am here now."

"It matters a great deal to me," he murmured as his gaze slid from her and over to the hearth. "I was rash last night. I should not have coerced you. It was wrong of me. I release you from this bargain. Lucy's reputation is safe, Isabella. You needn't barter your soul to save her."

"Was that to be the cost, then?"

"Very likely," he muttered.

Her gaze flickered along his body, over his chest, and she felt her insides begin to melt—to churn. She wanted to run her fingers through the black fleece, to press her lips to his chest, which looked so hard. Would he like her mouth on his nipples as much as she loved having his mouth on hers?

Would he moan? Cry out her name? Plead for more?

"You are still here," he said quietly as he pinned her once more with his unreadable gaze.

"I am."

She could not seem to make her feet move. She wanted to stay, she realized.

"What of your Mr. Knighton?" he quipped. "You are standing in the middle of my study at the hour of midnight."

"Black," she pleaded, but he was ruthless, his eyes narrowed and penetrating.

"Quid pro quo, Isabella? It seems the only way we can converse. A question for an answer. It's the only way we can let each other in."

She stiffened but held his gaze steady. "Very well."

"Do you fear me?"

"Yes." He flinched as if he had been struck.

"And yet you are here. In the devil's lair."

"I fear my reaction to you. The feelings you create inside me."

"And do you not think that I am also afraid?" He rose, and came to her, reached for her hand and lifted it into his. "I am well acquainted with passion. With base desires. But I am not familiar with this…these feelings I have for you."

"You said last night," she began, then paused, swallowed hard. "You said that you loved me."

His gaze flickered, yet he said nothing, but instead brought her to the middle of the floor and helped her to sit on the rug. He came down beside her, took her journal from her hand and tossed it aside. Slowly he leaned over, pressed her back until she was lying on the floor, and his hand was cupping her nape, his finger was tracing her lips.

"Lust I know, but this overwhelming need to have you, to make love to you, to keep you with me forever is something I've never felt. Pleasure I've experienced, but never with one I love."

"Jude," she whispered as she touched his face. "I'm so frightened of this. This bind that links us. It whispers to me to take what you're offering, but I fear the consequences. I have lived the consequences."

His fingertips traced the column of her throat down over the swells of her breasts where they lingered until her breath caught. "I am not your father, Isabella, and you are not your mother."

"I know, but—"

"There are no certainties in life," he murmured as he lowered his head and kissed the apex of her breast where her heart hammered so hard. "But I can give you this certainty. I love you. And I want you. I have wanted you for so long, and that feeling has only grown. There must be trust between us, Isabella. Passion is not enough for me. I want more from you."

"You ask for so much," she said, then trailed off.

"Not any more than I am offering you."

He slipped the necklace he wore around his neck over his head and placed it around hers, where the black stone nestled between her breasts. "The Sheldon diamonds. They belong to you. I cannot imagine another woman wearing them."

"Oh, I couldn't."

His lips, brushing against hers, cut her off. "Think about it, Isabella. Trust me enough to just think of what I'm offering. Marriage. Security and passion that I know won't fade over time. Little love," he murmured as he kissed her lips, the notch of her collarbone, "I didn't save you so that you could hide away from the world and slowly die. I risked my life so you could live. Love."

He was leaning over her, a lock of his hair had fallen forward and she brushed it back. When he looked down at her, his gaze boring into her face, she was transported back in time, to a memory that hadn't faded. Clutching his face, she peered up into his eyes, those gorgeous sea-tossed eyes, and imagined him looming over her with wet hair hanging down over his face. His body hard, reassuring her with his strength as his arms caged her.

She had opened her eyes, saw him as his mouth lifted from hers. Heard his voice above the din of the roaring waves and the howling wind.

"It was you," she murmured. "All along I thought it was Death I saw, but it was you."

His eyes closed, only to slowly open. He touched her, his fingers skimming shakily over her skin, but he said nothing, just let her talk. But there was worry in his eyes.

"You…you called to me. Your words—I heard them, as if in the distance. Your voice—it brought me back."

It is not your time, love. You will not die tonight.

All this time she thought herself in love with the notion of Death. His gallantry, his beautiful soul. She believed he loved her because he had spared her from his grip. But it had not been Death, but Black.

"Why?" she asked, and her body shook, knowing his sacrifice, knowing he knew her most guarded secret.

"Because I loved you," he murmured. "I couldn't let you go, because I knew I could no longer see you, I couldn't live, either."

Black had risked his life to save her from taking her own.

He rose, helped her up and clutched her in his arms. "It is too soon for you to make your decision," he said. "Come to me when you know what you want. My wishes will remain unchanged."

"What do you want?"

He kissed her, pressed her body into his hot, hard one. "To be inside you. To lay you out and touch you with my hands, my mouth and tongue. I want to slip deep inside you and never leave. I want to wake up in the morning and open my eyes to find you lying there next to me. I want to look at my children and see you in their little faces."

"Jude," she whispered, holding him, weakening.

"But I want you to want that as much as I do, Isabella."

"We have too many secrets," she began. "Our pasts…"

"Secrets, like passion, are meant to be spent. I will bear all my sins, all my secrets, when you come to me. It's all I can offer. You see, little love, I'm afraid, too, but the difference between us is that I believe it's worth it to face that fear if it means that I'll have you."

Death was hovering over me, his stormy eyes full of emotion. There was desire there, but there was fear, too. What would happen this night would be the start of a new world. A new beginning for me. My old life would cease to be, but I would be reborn into a new world; one of love and pleasure.

"I love you," Death whispered as he took my lips in his. "I love your beautiful, human soul. I want to claim it, to hide it away from the world so that no one can see it."

Death would smother me, but I did not fear his ardor. I reveled in it. His strength, his passion. His devotion.

"How is it you can love a creature such as me?" he asked. The look in his eyes was naked and exposed and I brushed his hair aside and kissed his lips.

"Trust me," I whispered, and I felt him tremble in my arms.

"You ask too much," Death whispered.

"Nothing more than you can give," I replied.

"I trust you, Isabella," Death said. "But the question is, do you love me?"

Isabella came awake with a start. The ormolu clock on her desk quietly ticked in the silence of her room. It was dark outside, and she slipped from the bed and padded to the window. She saw a shape, a flickering of light across the street, and imagined Black standing there, studying her window.

She thought back to her dream, to Death. To trust and desire.

Black would trust her with his secrets. He would protect hers. But did she trust him with her heart? Could she?

She thought of Wendell, and no longer felt any remorse for her feelings. She did not love him. Her heart had been taken two years ago, by a stranger she thought she had conjured up in the atmosphere of her imagination.

He had asked her to trust him—and there was only one way she knew how. She reached into the wardrobe and pulled out the crimson gown.

No regrets. No seduction. No scandal. Only love.

CHAPTER TWENTY-ONE

BLACK LOOKED UP from the flames flickering in the hearth. The clock had long struck past midnight, and he saw her walking to him, like a ghostly specter. She wore a red gown and he watched as she soundlessly padded across the carpet.

Lamb saw her, too, for she stopped and petted his head, smiling as the dog licked her arm. When she looked up at him, his breath froze.

This was no vision. This was Isabella. In the flesh. Come to him of her own volition. He studied her, just as he had that night two years ago when he had followed her to the water. It had not been fit weather for man nor beast, and he could not help but feel the ominous atmosphere as it surrounded the little harbor. Death was close by, he smelled it, the same lingering essence that haunted him after all these years.

He had walked to the beach, silently tracking her, but he needn't have tried. The wind was so loud he could barely hear himself think, and Isabella was lost in her thoughts. She stood too close to the water's edge, but he had thought she wanted to watch the waves, how violently they crashed against the rocks. The surf pounded in a fierce frenzy, and then she had begun to walk...to put her booted feet in the foaming water. And then he had realized with dawning horror that she was walking out, the drag of her gown and her cloak sinking into the water. He had shouted at her, but the wind drowned out his voice. And then a wave crashed over her, and he saw her go under, and then nothing. He had run then, without any thought. And for the first time in more than ten years he had prayed.

"I felt him, you know," she murmured as she came to stand before him. "He had a hold of me, and then I felt your hand grasping my wrist, tugging, pulling me from the sucking waves, but Death did not want to give up his hold. He dragged me down once more, and you fought him."

Her eyes were brilliant, shining with tears.

"I couldn't do it, you see, live alone anymore. I had just received a letter, a refusal of a post. It had been my last hope, that job of governess. And when the rejection came I knew I had no prospects. I could move where no one knew who I was, where they did not know my mother and her pathetic existence. But I would still be alone. Unloved."

Her breath caught, and she folded her hands before her. "So I did what I thought best. Death had been a part of my life. I was twelve when I saw him, with my grandmother. He came to take the life of a new mother and her infant. He has haunted me from that time. He took my grandmother who was the only comfort I had, and then my mother. He left me alone, and I thought he might as well claim me, too, rather than forcing me to live my meager existence."

He reached for her hands, parted them, then brought one to his mouth and kissed it, squeezed it as he looked up, encouraging her to talk.

"There was no pain, just a feeling of rightness, until you pulled me out and dragged me to the shore. You forced me to live. You risked your own life so that I might."

Closing his eyes, he pressed her hand to his mouth and held it there.

"You kissed me, and I opened my eyes and thought

you were Death. You were the most beautiful thing I had ever seen, and I clung to the memory of you because it gave me comfort—the only bit of happiness I had ever had. You were my secret fantasy, my lover. My story... Lord Death is you, and the woman he stalks...is me."

"Why have you come," he asked, "when you now know the truth?"

"Because when you saved me, you forged a link between us. I don't believe it will ever break."

"Bella," he whispered, "I couldn't allow you to take your life. Couldn't bear the thought of existing in a world that you did not."

"How did you know? Did you just happen upon me?"

He smiled, pulled her down into his lap. "No, love, I had known you quite well, if only in my dreams. The first time I saw you it was amongst the ruins of the abbey. You were writing, and I stood there watching you. I thought you beautiful, and there was something about you that made me think we might be kindred souls. After that, I would see you around the village. I asked about you."

"There was no end to the people who would talk about me and my mother, I suppose," she said with a frown.

"That's true. But I have my own mind, and I haven't the patience for gossip. I only wanted to know your name. If you were married. You see, I wanted you. But I knew that I couldn't come to you, not," he said as he placed his finger over her mouth, "because of your circumstances, but because of mine. Scandal followed me. I wouldn't allow you to find out."

"Your mother, your brother and the woman you were to marry."

He nodded.

"Jude, how awful. The pain of losing everyone you loved."

"I didn't love Abigail, Isabella. It was duty, nothing more. I have loved only one woman. You."

Jude tilted up her chin and peered into her eyes. "I have dreamed of you every night since I first glimpsed you. I thought never to have you, but I could not resist that one dance. I want you, Isabella. Dear God, how I want you."

The prolonged anticipation, the impatience, only heightened his arousal as he waited for Isabella to say the words he longed to hear. "I want you, too."

Lifting her from his lap, Black said nothing, but came up on his knees, facing her, and lowered his mouth onto hers. He swept his tongue inside and Isabella, for the first time, allowed herself to stop thinking—to only feel.

Jude took his time exploring her mouth, delighting in the weight of her resting atop him. Slowly he kissed her, savoring her lips, coaxing her into kissing him back. Patiently he waited, entering, retreating, entering, until she mewled softly and let her body go limp against him.

Weeks of suffering were near to consuming him. Her body grew restless against his and, struggling to refrain from ripping the gown from her shoulders, he lay back on the floor, taking her with him, holding her so that she was cradled in his arms. Their eyes met and he grinned when he saw her luminous blue eyes widen in wonder.

Her lips parted on a small smile and she shyly pressed her face into the crook of his neck. He itched to undo the satin buttons of her gown and bare her body to his gaze, but he forced himself to slow—to take it gently and love her as she so needed.

Pressing her back, he slid the bodice from her shoulders, catching his breath as the candlelight illuminated her body beneath the gown that he could tell she wore without a chemise or corset. She had come to him to be seduced.

His finger reached for the first button on her bodice. With a flick he opened it. He reached for the next, and then the next, heard her inhale and hold her breath when the satin gaped teasingly open.

The fourth button came undone and still she held his gaze, her breasts rising and falling, her breathing increasing every time he loosened one. He reached a bow and pulled at the string, unraveling it. The gown was undone to her midriff and it would not take much effort to slide the sleeves down her shoulders, to part the material over her generous breasts to reveal her silken belly.

Without a word, he rose to his knees, straddling her legs before reaching for the sleeves of the gown. Their eyes were locked as he revealed her fully. He let his fingers glide up and around the soft mound of her belly. A fine flush covered her skin, and he looked up to see her blushing.

"My God, you're every bit as beautiful as I imagined."

Her eyes were misty when she looked into his, and her lips trembled a fraction. "Truly?"

"I could not have conjured up such loveliness." Threading his fingers through hers, he squeezed tightly before straightening from her, letting his hands glide down her throat and breasts. His fingers lingered mere seconds before skating along her belly, to grip the satin and drag the gown along her hips till it rested at his feet. He knew he was staring—devouring her with his gaze, but he was helpless to stop.

Brushing the back of his hand along her downy curls, he delighted in her soft intake of air before he motioned for her to lie on her belly. His gaze traveled down her back; the faint dusting of down on her skin was illuminated by the candle's glow. He traced the length of her spine with his fingertips and watched as gooseflesh erupted and feathered along her back, down to her rounded bottom.

She stirred restlessly beneath his touch and he watched as the muscles of her derriere clenched and loosened. He couldn't help but stroke her soft cheeks, cupping them in his hands and stroking his thumb along her supple flesh. She moaned, the sound muffled against the Turkish carpet.

Isabella felt the air stir behind her, saw his corded forearms on either side of her shoulders. She knew he was straddling her, she could feel his muscled thighs riding against hers, could feel the heat of his body cocooning her. Yet he kept himself above her, his arms bearing his weight. Whimpering in anticipation, she sucked in her breath as his chest, the hair crisp and curling, grazed her back. His lips were nuzzling the nape of her neck and she felt her hips move restlessly, trying to ease the ache she felt between her thighs.

His tongue came out and raked her flesh, trailing along her spine, and she curled her fingers into her palms, shivering with the heat of his tongue, then the coolness that was left behind when he moved his mouth lower.

"I want my mouth on you," he whispered darkly as his tongue licked along her spine.

She could not say a word, only tighten her fists and wait, wait with bated breath to see what he would do next. He pushed away from her and ran his palm along her back and over her bottom. His hand came around her waist, his fingers pressing into her belly as he raised her slowly to her knees.

She was trembling now, not with fear or embarrassment, but desire. She wanted this, this illicit passion with Jude.

She felt his finger atop her bottom as it lightly traced her cleft, down to the slick petals of her sex. Parting her with one hand, he ran his finger along the edge of her wet folds, only to trace the opening of her body.

"Let me taste you, Isabella, as I have dreamed about all these nights."

His tongue flicked out and Jude closed his eyes, savoring the taste of Isabella's arousal. She squirmed, made a strangled sound deep in her throat. He didn't know if it was shock or delight, but he didn't care. He could not stop. She was wet, her sex pink with desire, hot with blood that rushed beneath her silky skin. He raked his tongue along her from the bottom of her folds to the top, where he flicked the nubbin of flesh and felt her body go taut. He repeated the action again, this time ensuring that her pleasure would be increased by swirling his tongue in slow circles around her swollen bud.

She moaned and he tasted the rush of arousal from her body. She was so responsive, so hot in his arms. "A thousand times better than what I have dreamed," he whispered, kissing her swollen sex and bringing her back to him so that he could lower her to the carpet and gaze into her passion-glazed eyes. "You have the sort of body that lures a man to his doom, Isabella." She smiled then, a dazzling, womanly smile that temporarily blinded him. "Touch me," he begged in a voice he could barely comprehend was his.

His plea, needy and haunting, pierced her fuzzy mind. She did as he asked, sliding his shirttail from his trousers and running her hands up the wide width of his back. The muscles tensed, flickering as her fingers traced each contoured ridge. He helped her remove his shirt and Isabella couldn't help but marvel once again at the sight that greeted her. Chiseled chest and abdomen, the muscles bunching, reminding her of rough-hewn stone. A sprinkling of black, silky hair swirled around his nipples and down his belly, intriguing her, so that with her index finger she followed its path to where it disappeared below the waistband of his trousers.

He groaned deep in his throat, only to have him capture her hand in his and place it against the buttons of his fall front trousers. Pinning her with his stormy gaze, he helped her to undo the buttons. "I want your fingers touching me. I've waited too long to feel your touch."

She must be crazed to be doing this, surely this was

beyond sinful. But when he brought her hand into the opening of his trousers and placed her fingers around his rigid length, Isabella could feel nothing but wonder. How could something so forbidden feel this right?

"Move your hand up the length of me, Isabella."

His voice was gruff and commanding and she found herself responding to his mastery. Her hand slid up the silky length of him, and he jutted out his hips, pushing his erection farther into her hand. His eyes flashed to her face before he focused them on where her hand stroked him. She studied the way his hips moved, slow, assured, an ancient rhythm she knew she would soon be part of. He pulled away and stood beside her, stepping out of his trousers, his erection finally freed from behind the black cloth.

Before she could touch him, he came down atop her, covering her body with his, his lips, soft and nipping, roamed over her throat and shoulders before skating along her breasts.

Gliding her hands through his hair, she tousled it, watching as the shining threads slipped through her fingers. Her breath hitched and her fingers tightened in his hair when he slipped her nipple into his mouth. His tongue darted out to lave and flick, hardening the sensitive flesh to an almost painful peak, making her forget her every thought.

His fingers trailed down her belly, where they circled her navel, his lips followed, then his tongue. "Let me make love to you," he whispered. "Let me show you how well we can know what is in each other's hearts."

"Yes," she answered. This is what she wanted. What she had always wanted.

He coaxed her to open her thighs for him and slowly pushed his fingers inside her. Oh, God. She cried out, covering her mouth with the back of her hand when she felt more wetness pool deep inside her. What was he doing to her?

"You like that, don't you," he asked, his voice deepening with passion. "I like to hear your cries, Isabella. I want to feel your desire on my hand."

His fingers continued to stroke her sex and she allowed him to widen her thighs. She was exposed and she could feel his hot stare on her. "I want to put my tongue to you."

The flat of his tongue raked hot along her, teasing and licking. Her back instinctively arched when his tongue circled her in short, firm strokes. She cried out again, smothering the sound with her hand when his mouth covered her fully, drawing out a moan that sounded foreign to her.

He refused to stop and instead continued to lave and build her up again to a peak that was almost painful in its intensity. Her hips began to move and he no longer had to hold her still, she was grasping him to her, greedily taking all he would give her.

"Jude," she panted, gripping his hair. "You must stop."

"Not yet," he said, drawing his tongue up the length of her sex and pressing it against her swollen clitoris. "I want to make you come this way."

Raising her shoulders from the floor, Isabella looked down to find Jude's black head between her pale thighs. A strangled sound escaped her throat and he looked up, his eyes wickedly gazing back at her as he slowly licked her. Another muffled cry whispered past her lips and he grinned seductively, still holding her gaze as he continued to pleasure her. Unable to help herself, she reached for him.

He licked fiercely until she felt her body tighten, poised upon a foreign precipice, when he eased himself up on his knees and bent between her thighs, his fingers dancing along her wetness. She thought she would surely die of pleasure as he slipped his fingers deep inside her, watching while he stroked her, his eyes blazing as she unconsciously whimpered, her body undulating as he rubbed his finger at the crest of her curls.

Then something far thicker and firmer began to stretch her. Closing her eyes, she fought to relax, to savor the feel of him sliding, inch by inch, into her body.

"You're incredibly wet, so extraordinarily beautiful."

"Jude." His name was ripped from her throat.

He groaned, filling her further, his fingers biting into her hips. "Open your eyes, and say my name again."

And she did, just as he thrust his way deep inside her, imbedding himself fully.

Jude could barely move, could hardly even think, save for luxuriate in the exquisite feel of Isabella's body clamping tightly around him. It had never been like this, never this slow and sensual, a feast for his senses.

His hips began to push and, gaining in confidence, Isabella's began to move against him, matching his rhythm. He was totally imbedded inside her, yet he couldn't get close enough or stroke deep enough to satisfy his craving for her.

He watched her arch beneath his strokes, her lashes fluttered closed, fanning against her cheeks, her breasts moving in time to his thrusting. He inhaled her scent— soap and feminine arousal. He felt her rounded hips rotate beneath his hands, felt her thighs encase his waist, could almost taste the sweet nectar of her breasts, could still taste the muskiness of her sex against his tongue.

He cried out, long and deep, and with a rough shout and a final deep, penetrating thrust, his seed splashed deep inside her.

For minutes they sat, clinging to each other, arms clutching and hugging—faces buried in each other's necks—a fine sheen of perspiration trickling down her back and his chest. Slowly he came back to earth, and saw that Isabella was still secured in his arms.

She was satiated, replete. The faint chiming of bells from the hall clock signaled an hour had passed since he looked up and found her there. She had come to him. And he wasn't letting her go.

"Where are we going?" she mumbled as he covered her with his jacket.

"To bed."

"Oh," she said through a yawn, then snuggled up to him as he lifted her in his arms. "But I should be going home, the hour."

"It's early enough that we have hours yet to love one another."

She was still satiated, still flushed from his lovemaking, and his heart swelled again.

"Will you tell me your story, then, Isabella? Tell me what you've dreamed of Death doing to you."

"No." She squirmed in his arms, embarrassed.

"I have wondered about it, you know. Tell me."

"No."

He kissed her and whispered, "I'm going to make you."

"Oh, no, you're not!"

"Will you not tell me more?" Black asked as he lay with her in his bed.

"There is no more to tell."

"So the maid comes to him for three nights and tells him a story. And he releases her?"

"Yes."

"And do they make love?" he asked. And she blushed, and he kissed her.

"Well…I suppose so, but I didn't write that. It's sort of…implied."

"Are you afraid of words, little love," he asked wickedly. "I could help you write it, help you to know what Death was thinking as he was watching his lover."

"Could you?"

"Mmm," he whispered as he kissed her ear. "I could. This is how I would start…

Passion hot and scorching rushed through his veins as his hungry gaze took in the picture of his lover, her pale limbs outlined against the black velvet while shadows cast by the fire danced across her creamy skin. The crimson silk hugged her luscious body and he stared at her, wondering how her breasts would look. How they would feel, taste…

Swallowing hard, Death approached the chaise longue, his eyes roving every inch of her, admiring her lush thighs, the roundness of her hip, the full, heavy breasts that strained against the ties of her gown.

He wanted her.

It wasn't merely a need to make love to her, or to kiss her senseless. He desired her, craved her, with a possessive passion that frightened him.

Resting his thighs against the curved arm of the chaise longue, he looked down at her, her glorious curls in disarray, her blond lashes fanned lightly against her cheek…he could think of nothing other than waking her slowly with passion.

"Jude," she moaned, now thoroughly aroused. But he continued, whispering in her ear as he began to act out the love scene with Death.

Unable to resist temptation, he leaned over the arm of the chaise longue and stroked the hair from her face. When his fingers trailed down her cheek she instinctively curled into his hand. He smiled as she mumbled something unintelligible.

His fingers continued to trace a path to her neck, where they, he was chagrined to admit, shakily reached for the fastenings of her gown, parting the lace ruffle to expose the pale globes of her breasts. His breath caught as he realized she was completely naked beneath.

A log cracked and sparked in the hearth, sending a flicker of light shadowing along her thighs, illuminating the curls that lay nestled between her legs. He itched to part her and taste her. To waken her with his mouth.

Forcing himself to take things slower, Death concentrated on removing the gown from beneath her. Once she was naked, he untied his cravat, his appreciative gaze traveling up and over her as the starched linen slipped from his fingers, landing on the floor. He hardened further when he saw how the bloodred silk evocatively contrasted against her milky skin, outlining her curves.

His demons were screaming to be fed, and tonight, he promised, he would sate them. He was powerless, both mentally and physically, to control them—and for tonight, he had no wish to.

His shirt landed atop his cravat while his eyes once more moved up the length of her legs. He remembered the way they had felt against his waist—soft, welcoming, infinitely feminine. He imagined his hands pressing into their softness while he plunged into her, her husky moan welcoming him, telling him she needed him as much as he needed her.

Sighing heavily, she turned onto her back, her breasts bouncing with the movement. Trailing his hands up the length of her waist, he stopped to cup them. They were full and heavy, the nipples already peeking out from between his fingers. Unable to resist, he pressed her breasts together, kissing each firm bud before circling the areola with his tongue.

Death's lover moaned sleepily, arching her back, thrusting her breasts farther into his mouth. He groaned when he felt her hands steal behind her head, her fingers busy clenching his hair.

"I've been waiting for you."

"I couldn't stay away," he murmured against her mouth before sliding his tongue inside. Indulging himself, Death opened his eyes as he kissed her, watching his hands, the skin much darker than hers, cup and squeeze her breasts. She moaned, angling her hips invitingly. His hand stole down her belly where he kneaded a path to her curls. It was powerful visually to see his large hand stroke her. It was a feeling of ownership, of possession. She was his, and he wanted her to want him as fiercely as he wanted her. Damn it, he wanted her to moan and writhe for him. Right there on the chaise longue, her smooth skin rubbing mindlessly against the velvet.

He said not a word as he tore his mouth from hers and walked to the side of the chaise longue.

He captured her wrists in his hands. Pressing them together, he held them above her head. "I need you, Bella." Her fingers gripped his hand and her legs clamped tightly together when his finger slid into her. She whimpered as he parted her and slid his finger along the length of her sex.

"I've longed for the taste of you, aching to be inside you. I will not deprive myself of the pleasure any longer."

Death could feel his demons nipping at his heels, driving him to satisfy his needs. He wanted to brand her with his passion. To leave his mark so that she would know that she belonged to him, and only him. Mine, *his brain screamed.*

Isabella cried out when he raked his tongue down the length of her. "So sweet," he murmured, his finger slipping inside as his breath caressed her wet flesh. "So damn sweet. And mine, aren't you?"

"Yes," she breathed, lost in his touch, in the story he weaved. And then he began to move his fingers inside her, and he whispered again, making her more aroused as he continued with his story.

She began to pant and twist beneath his ministrations. Death loved how she raked her hands through his hair, tightening her grip as he increased the pressure and the rhythm of his tongue. She moaned for him again, and this time he couldn't help but look up at her while his mouth loved her. She was beautiful in her passion, writhing beneath him, searching for fulfillment. The fulfillment only he could give her.

It was more than he could have ever hoped for. But then this was Isabella. His match in every way.

He pulled her up to straddle his hips, his fingers sinking into her thighs as he slowly lowered her onto him. Her body arched as she accepted his thrusts. He loved watching her body move in time with his. Loved how her hair glistened in the firelight, the ends rubbing against the velvet in time to his strokes.

Kneeling on the bed, Death placed her back against his chest, twining her arms around his neck so that her fingers were grasping his hair. He brought her atop his lap and slid inside, rocking slowly as he moved his hips in a rhythm that was both slow and seductive.

His finger stole into her curls and she whimpered in appreciation. "Now," he whispered into her ear as he felt her bottom still and tense as he stroked the nubbin of sensitive flesh. "Take all of me inside you."

She sunk farther on him, totally impaling herself on his length. He heard her suck in her breath, and he nipped at her ear as his finger continued to tease her sensitive flesh. She tightened then jerked in his arms, her bottom provocatively grazing his thighs. He smiled into her hair as the soft cries of her release splintered the air, and he watched as her face softened into exquisite bliss.

Isabella was still limp in her climax when Jude pressed her forward until her breasts grazed the sheets. He stroked his fingers down the length of her back to her bottom. He repeated the action, this time working up from her buttocks to her neck, his erection stiffening further as she quivered beneath his touch. Gooseflesh rippled along her spine, sweeping along her back and down to the soft globes of her perfect bottom.

"I love you," he said, stroking her damp flesh. Bringing her hips back to him, he filled her completely in one fluid thrust. She moaned deeply as he pulled out, filling her again, his fingers biting into her hips as he repeated the movement.

Jude was mindless now, watching and listening as he made love to her. The bed creaked and groaned under his thrusts, the sound of skin against skin heightened his senses, driving him to the precipice. An almost primal surge of possession engulfed him.

His seed spilled forth as he continued to rock against her, her warmth enveloping him, caressing and tightening around him.

"I won't ever let you go, Isabella," he said against her hair. "No matter what happens, you'll always belong to me."

CHAPTER TWENTY-TWO

"Black, we have to talk."

"I thought we had shed all secrets."

"No, I meant Lucy. Last night. This pendant she keeps raving about."

He groaned and fell back, and it was then that Isabella saw the brand on his chest that was obscured by his silky hair. It was the shape of a Templar cross.

"Knighton mentioned the Brethren Guardians. Does it mean anything to you?"

He watched her. "Yes."

"You're one of them, aren't you?" He glanced away, but she wouldn't let him evade the question. "It's true, isn't it?" she asked. "The story of the three Templars who were entrusted with three artifacts."

"Yes."

"Your family carries a pendant. That's what Lucy had."

"Yes. It contains the seeds from the apple that Eve took from the Tree of Knowledge. They're cursed with the venom of the snake who tempted her."

"Lucy?"

"Thank God I stopped her before she could take them all."

"How did Wendell get it?"

He went rigid underneath her. "How did you know it was him?"

"That night he visited us, he was telling Lucy and I

about the Templars, I don't think he knew who they were. But he had the pendant."

"Go on."

"Lucy, well, she has been searching for a lover, and she believed the pendant had powers." She paused, then glanced up at him. "Sussex and Alynwick, they're the other two Templar descendants, aren't they?"

"Yes."

"And Elizabeth?"

"Merely Sussex's sister. But she knows of the tales, and she aids us when we need it."

"Jude, you must be careful."

"I am, my love. But you must know that this isn't over. The pendant while returned to me, is simply not enough. We need to find out who is behind this. The chalice that Sussex is in possession of is still missing."

"Wendell never mentioned a chalice."

"Then you won't mention it to him," he murmured as he kissed her neck. "Our secret."

"There's more you're not telling me."

"There is, but it's grown late, Isabella, and you need to get back home, unless you're so eager to bring that scandal you fear so much upon yourself."

"You're right." She sighed as her fingers drew little circles on his chest. "But promise me you'll tell me everything tonight."

"I will. As long as you promise me that you'll let Knighton know in no uncertain terms that his attentions are no longer welcome."

"Jude, you're jealous."

"Insanely, and if the sun was not attempting to peek out over the horizon I would take you to bed again, just so you won't forget me while you sleep."

STANDING AT THE WINDOW, Black watched Isabella run across the street. It was still dark, although daylight was not far off. She was safe enough at this hour. Far safer than if she had been discovered with him beside her early in the morning.

Smiling to himself, he watched her run, remembering how she had felt all soft and womanly in his arms. He'd wanted her again. He feared he would want her every night for the rest of his life.

She disappeared around the house, and he waited for the lamp to be lit in her room. It was the agreed-upon signal that she had made it there safe and sound.

When several long minutes lapsed, Black's body grew taut. When a carriage careened around the corner from Isabella's house, fear assailed him.

"Billings!" he roared. "Send for Sussex, I'll be on horseback."

His butler, tired and disheveled, presented himself. "Where shall I direct His Grace, my lord?"

He had no notion. Only knew he had to hurry if he was to catch up to them. Whoever had taken Isabella would die this night.

"My lord?"

"The lodge," he said, more out of instinct than any real thought.

Then he lunged out of the room and ran to the stables. Lamb was hard on his heels.

"Follow them," he ordered the dog, and it was only minutes before Black had saddled his horse and was galloping after Lamb who had thankfully scented the carriage.

"AT LAST," a voice rasped from behind her at the same time a gloved hand covered her mouth. "About time you pried yourself away from Lord Black."

Isabella twisted violently, trying to see who the perpetrator was, but a steely arm reached out, slamming her hard against his chest. "Be still," the voice hissed in her ear, "or I will bind you." Isabella continued to squirm, her voice muffled by the stranger's hand. "Now then," the voice crooned. "You will come nicely and silently if you know what is good for you."

The villain turned her around to face him, his familiar face shocked her into speechlessness.

"Come now, my dear, you didn't think I'd let you get away that easy, did you?"

"What are you doing here?"

"Taking what belongs to me."

"Wendell, you're mad!"

"Furious," he said as he pushed her along. "You've cost me, Isabella. Now, I want to know what you've done with it."

"What the devil do you mean by abducting me from my home?" Isabella grunted inelegantly as she was pushed up into a carriage.

"Silence! I have had enough of your saucy mouth. If you cannot keep it shut, then I'll do the job for you. The only words I want from your lips are the whereabouts of the pendant."

She froze. Her first instinct was to protect Black—and the others.

"I don't know what you're talking about."

"Stupid bitch," Wendell growled, "you know what pendant I'm talking about. The one your lover is to protect. He's one of the Templars—it is the Sheldon family who has housed the pendant for half a millennium."

Pushed into the carriage, Isabella settled against the squabs, straightened her skirts and glared at her kidnapper. "What do you think you're doing? What the devil has gotten into you?"

He looked at her as if she'd lost her mind. "I told you, I'm taking what belongs to me. And you, Isabella, belong to me. So does that pendant. Now, be a good girl, like you

were when I first met you, and tell me where the blazes
that pendant is."

"I don't know."

"The hell you don't. Lucy, that bitch, got her hands on
it first, when it should have been you. Then what?"

"I've no notion what you're talking of."

His hand struck her face and she cried out, holding
her cheek. "The pendant I showed you, or were you day-
dreaming of Black when you should have been listening
to me?"

Dear God, she had to protect Black. Had to.

Gripping her chin, he forced her to look at him. "I grow
weary of this game, Isabella. Tell me where the pendant
is."

"I don't know."

"Does Lucy have it?"

"No."

"Then who does?"

"I don't know!"

Cruelly, his hand gripped her hair. Sweet heaven,
he was hurting her! Never had Knighton treated her so
roughly, or spoken so disrespectfully to her. This wasn't
the Knighton she had met, this man was far from the rational male she'd once known.

"Tell me now," he enunciated, tugging once more on
her hair.

"Get your hands off me," she yelled, letting her anger
get the better of her, despite the fact her instincts told her
it would only infuriate him further.

"You little bitch," he seethed, jerking her face up to
greet his. "You have the nerve to talk to me in such a way,
after you've let *him* treat you like a common whore."

"Wendell…" She reached for his hand in her hair.
"Stop, you're hurting me."

His hazel eyes darkened with anger. "Jesus," he swore,

his eyes raking boldly over her. "There's probably not a place left on you that isn't tainted by his touch. I'm right, aren't I? He hasn't left one inch of you unmarked."

"Knighton, you're out of your mind."

"Yes." He smiled coldly. "I'm afraid I am. You were so close to being mine, you see. But you threw it all away to play the whore for him."

"It isn't like that."

"I saw you," he roared, his hand once again fisting in her hair. "The both of you, rutting like animals." His mouth twisted into an evil grin. "To think I thought you innocent. But you're not. I'll spill all your blood now," he said, his lips curling. "You're of no use to me. Used, soiled goods," he spat.

"No!" She tried to twist out of his grasp.

He slapped her again, his face filled with rage. "You've cost me and I'll make you pay. You'll talk," he said. "I'll make you tell me where the pendant is."

His voice had gone dark, disturbing, as if someone else—something demonic had invaded his soul.

"I want that pendant, and your blood filling the chalice. That's the only way to get what I need."

Brushing her hair from her face, she winced at the throbbing pain in her cheek. If the swelling was any indication, her eye would soon be swollen shut. Gingerly, she probed the side of her face. The puffiness was firm and, she suspected, grotesquely bruised.

What had provoked Knighton to such violence? He'd never once raised his voice to her let alone his hand.

She stole a look at her captor from beneath the veil of her hair. He looked pale and nervous. His hands were clenched in his lap and his eyes fixed firmly out the window. He looked so different now, haunted, brooding—utterly dangerous as he rubbed his temples.

"Christ, look at your face."

She lowered her head, shielding her bruises with her

hair, hating how the anger in his voice made her shake. Never had she felt submissive before a man.

"Why did you make me hit you? Look at me," he commanded, tilting her chin up with his finger.

She whimpered when her eyes met his in the waning light. She was terrified of him, frightened to death to be alone with him—to be so far away from Jude.

"If only you would have listened to me and just told me where to search for the pendant, I would not have had to do this." His finger traced her lips, which were puffy from the blow.

"Wendell, you're frightening me."

"Good. I'll stop when you tell me where the pendant is."

"It has an unholy call upon you, doesn't it?"

"Shut up," he snarled, but Isabella saw the fear in his eyes.

"You can't stop it, can you? Don't you see how evil it is? It's making you mad."

"No," he said, shaking his head. "It'll make me famous. Rich. The most powerful archaeologist in the world."

"You'll bring nothing but evil upon the earth."

His gaze widened, and he gripped her chin once again. "You know much, Isabella, for someone who claimed she had no idea of what I was speaking."

"You're ill, Wendell," she pleaded as she held on to his wrists. "Please, let me go. I'll help you to get better."

He was mad. Utterly deranged. Had he always been like this? Why had she never seen this side of him before?

He was dangerously demented, and she had to think of a way to escape him. She shuddered to think of what he would do to her once he had her locked away, solely to himself. She had to think of a plan, she couldn't afford to waste precious time until Jude could find her. Perhaps he hadn't yet even realized she was gone.

Would Jude come for her? Bile rose in her throat as

she thought of losing him, and she gagged on the acidic taste.

She had to think—had to be logical about this, she couldn't let her paralyzing fear prevent her from planning her escape.

"I will tie you up and beat the information out of you," he growled as the carriage slowed and finally came to a stop. The door opened and Wendell shoved her out, but kept a cruel hold on her arm. Something hard pressed into her side as he pushed for forward.

"Scream and I'll put a bullet into you, do you understand?"

Nodding, she allowed Knighton to lead her up the stone steps. He was taking her to the Masonic lodge and no doubt to her doom.

What sort of torture awaited her inside?

On the steps, she faltered, her hem catching on her boot. "Damn you," Knighton hissed as he fell down to his knees.

"My hem," she pleaded. "You haven't allowed me to hold it up."

But she saw an opportunity and took it. While he was on his knees, she kicked him and he fell to the side, the gun spinning and falling down two steps, which made Knighton lunge. Isabella took that opportunity to run.

Raising her skirts, she ran up the steps and around the side of the building where she was grabbed by a steely arm.

"Lady Isabella." His shocked tone told her how awful her wounds must look.

Sussex.

"Good God, what are you doing here?"

"I was just leaving after searching the lodge. What is Knighton doing here?"

"He attacked me. He's gone mad looking for the pendant."

"So Black has told you everything?"

"As much as I need to know. Knighton wants the pendant and he's going to do whatever he has to do to get it."

The sound of pounding hooves echoed off the buildings. Black and his huge ebony stallion, and Isabella tried to scream out a warning, but Sussex clamped a hand over her mouth.

"No noise. Black can handle himself."

A pistol fired, the horse reared and Isabella pushed forward, but Sussex held her still. She watched as Jude's large body fell from the horse.

"I've got you now," Knighton taunted. "You're as much as dead, Black, and when I am done killing you, I'll turn to Isabella. I'll drain her blood, spill it all and I'll keep the pendant."

Rolling beneath the carriage, Black reached into his greatcoat, just as Wendell came running down the steep steps, pistol in hand.

Isabella could only hope that Knighton wasn't a crack shot, because Jude was vulnerable. He was too big a target, and beneath the carriage, he was essentially trapped.

Panicked, she felt Sussex's arms clamp tightly around her as he tried to remove her, but she refused, kicked out, connecting with his shins.

She managed to free herself, when Wendell turned and aimed his pistol at her.

"No!" Jude roared as he jumped up and ran around the carriage with his open pistol raised. Torn between which one to shoot, Wendell aimed high, and shot at Jude. Jude fired back, but it was too late, Jude was falling to the ground, blood like a crimson stream flowing from beneath him.

Crying out, heedless of her own safety, Isabella ran to him, praying she would get to him before it was too late. When the next bullet sounded, she froze. She heard

Sussex's roar, the pounding of her own blood in her ears as she waited to feel the bullet tear through her flesh.

Her gaze met Black's. Saw his lips move, his gaze raise up to where Sussex was standing, and then higher.

As she waited, the pain never came, and the body before her, Wendell's body, crumpled to the steps, a red stain saturating his shirt.

"Sussex, the roof!"

Her hearing returned just in time to hear Jude call out the warning. She whirled around, saw someone in a black-hooded robe run from the rooftop. Sussex chased him and Isabella ran down the steps to Jude, pulling him into her arms.

"You little fool," he murmured as he kissed her. "You could have been killed! My God, I will never forget the sight of Knighton pulling that pistol on you."

"Never mind that," she cried. "We need to get you home. You're bleeding."

"I'm fine."

"Jude, don't argue with me. You're ashen, you've lost too much blood."

"Isabella, I'm fine."

With her help he stood, wobbled a bit and then pitched forward. The hackney that Wendell had brought her in was still there, the coachman taking in the scene with astonishment.

"You there," she called. "Give me a hand."

The coachman actually began to shake his head.

"I'll make it worth your while," she grunted beneath Black's weight.

"'Ow much?"

"Get us home quickly and I'll give you twenty pounds. Tell no one what you witnessed and I'll give you fifty."

The coachman was down from his perch and running to her in no time.

"My lips are sealed," the man said. "And you had better have that fifty quid at the ready when we arrive."

CHAPTER TWENTY-THREE

ISABELLA STRUGGLED beneath Black's weight. The metallic tang of blood reached her nostrils as the same moment she felt Black's warm blood seep through her cloak.

"Billings," Black ordered as he struggled out of the carriage. "Get me to him."

"I promised the driver I'd pay him immediately," she whispered. "And I don't want you home alone. Come to my uncle's. We'll send a footman for his physician—"

"Billings," he insisted. "He'll arrange payment. No doctor," he hissed as he stumbled and banged his shoulder up against the carriage. "Damn," he gasped, and Isabella saw how pale he was.

"Our butler shall be out momentarily," she called to the driver, and she heard Black chuckle, then grunt in pain.

"*Our* butler? You've decided to make an honest man of me, then?"

"How can you jest at a time like this?"

"I'm not jesting, little love. I only want to know that you'll be my wife."

Just then he faltered again, and she thought she'd never get the black iron gates opened. A dog barked, and suddenly Billings and a footman were there to catch him.

"My lord!" the servant exclaimed in alarm.

"Shot. I need patching—and the damn driver needs paying."

"You there," Billings shouted to the hackney driver. "Wait a moment and you'll have your payment."

The footman and Billings took Black's arms and legs and carried him up the drive, while Isabella lifted the hem of her gown and ran behind them.

What seemed like only seconds later, Black was lying on the settee in his library and Isabella was on her knees, tearing his shirt from his chest, and viewing his wound for the first time.

"Jude," she whimpered as she saw the flow of blood that pulsated from his shoulder. "Oh, my God!" Her voice was rising, and panic and fear set in.

Warm fingers grazed her chin, and she looked up into his pale face. "There is nothing to fear, Isabella. It's not deep."

"But there's so much blood…"

"Miss Fairmont," Billings said as he pulled a table closer. "Might I request that you stand at the foot of the settee while I work."

She didn't want to move, but Black nodded. "I think it's best. Billings is a master of sutures, my love. There is nothing to worry about."

Mutely she obeyed, but she did not move away from him. She couldn't. Instead, she moved to the arm of the settee where his head lay. She knelt down, placed her cheek to his temple and raked her fingers through his hair. "Don't leave me," she whispered. "Please."

Closing his eyes, he said, "I won't. Never."

Nervously she glanced around the study. It was dawn— the sun just peeking around the clouds. The city was just stirring from its slumber, the night giving way to day. But it was still possible to see shadows, and Isabella could not help but look into every corner of Black's library. There were no shadows. Death was not there.

"You're lucky, my lord. Another inch or so and he could have got you in the neck." Black gave his butler a chilling glare. "Prepare yourself, my lord. I've found the bullet and now I'm going to remove it."

Jude looked up and stared into Isabella's face. "I'm ready, Billings."

Holding him, Isabella stroked his hair, pressed kisses against his brow. If Billings was amused by the two of them, he gave no indication, but instead focused on his work.

As Billings pulled the bullet out, cleansed the area with antiseptic, then began pulling the needle and thread through Jude's torn flesh, Isabella realized there were a thousand words she wanted to say to him—all things she should have told him when they were lying safely in each other's arms.

To think that she might not have had the chance to speak of her heart—after he had offered her his—made her tremble. So much wasted time. So much fear.

She would never be afraid again. Not of Black and not of her passionate nature. Her mother's lot would not be her lot.

"My lady," Billings said as he finished winding a white gauze sling around Black's arm. "Shall I take a look?"

Quizzically, Isabella looked down, wondering if she was bleeding. There was some dried blood on her arm, but it was Jude's. But then she saw that Billings was staring at her face, his expression a mixture of concern and anger.

"Yes, do, Billings," Black answered. "The bastard, it should have been me who killed him for what he did to you," he growled.

She had forgotten that Wendell had hit her—forgotten all about her eye stinging and pulsing with pain. After seeing Black fall to the ground, bleeding, she had forgotten everything but him—even the fact that Wendell lay dead on the steps of the Masonic Temple.

"You've been struck very hard," Billings murmured as he wiped at her eye with a clean cloth. "Does your head pain you, do you feel ill—or faint?"

"No, Billings. I'm of hearty Yorkshire stock, it'll take more than a cuff on the head to make me swoon."

The butler smiled. "You'll do well in this house, my lady." He dipped his fingers into a jar of salve and wiped her bruised skin gently. "One needs the constitution of a Yorkshire lass to brave the world of the Earl of Black."

"Nonsense. Ignore him, Isabella, he's prattling on."

Smiling, she watched Billings pack up his medical kit and rise to his feet. "I assume His Grace and Lord Alynwick shall arrive shortly. I will direct them, my lord. For now you must rest, and I shall return with a poultice for your eye."

The door closed behind the butler, and Isabella stood, helped arrange Jude so that she could sit down with his head on her lap.

"What an invaluable butler you have," she said thoughtfully.

"Mmm, yes, and he can be all yours if you consent to be my countess."

"That's not much of a proposal, is it?"

He turned to look up at her. "No, it's not. But I'm not eloquent. I only know what I want, and that's you in my life and my bed. It's thousands of nights, and thousands of mornings with you. It's children and grandchildren, and you reading to me—and me making love to you. It's you and me and a future I want so badly I can taste it."

"Now, that is the proposal of dreams, Jude," she murmured. "Yes, I will be your wife."

How she adored this man, how perfect he was in every way. He had risked his life to save her—he could have been lost to her—just like Lucy's lover had been lost to her.

"Jude," she began, stroking his cheek. "I could not bear it, to be parted from you. When I saw Wendell shoot you, the blood—" she shuddered "—my heart shattered."

"He was aiming for you, and when I realized that, my heart stopped."

Isabella opened her eyes and looked down upon him. "No one has ever loved me like you," she whispered, awed.

"No one ever will. I won't allow it."

"I didn't speak the words, Jude, but they were there all along. I love you. Oh, how I adore you. I have loved you since the moment you pulled me from the ocean and made me come back to life. The second I opened my eyes and saw you leaning over me, your hair dripping and your clothes sodden, and your lips, so warm and inviting, pressing against mine. It was you all along, my Lord Death. You were the hero of my story, because I loved you even then. I thought you Death—and my rescuer. But now I know that you're my life, and my savior."

"Isabella," he whispered as he pulled her down to him for a kiss. "You undo me."

He was weeping and she caressed his face, brushing away the tears from his cheeks. There was no more darkness in those beautiful tempest-tossed eyes, only tranquillity.

Smiling, she thought of her story, how Death had only wanted to feel, to know what it was to weep. It was a fitting end to his story, and a fitting end to theirs.

"I have something," she said. The recollection of her story and of Death reminded her of the small package in her reticule. "I bought it a while ago, and have been keeping it hidden, afraid to give it to you."

"My love," he whispered. "There is no need to bring up the past."

"You told me I could trust you. To believe in what we had, that it wasn't just lust that flared between us. The words didn't seem enough. You had given me so much, and I had given you nothing."

"Not nothing," he said. "I have been given the honor

of being your first lover—and last," he added in a deeply erotic tone.

"Words come easy for me, Jude. I can write them, I can search my soul and let them pour out. But I feared you'd think them too easy. You see, I wanted you to trust me, too. To know that I wasn't merely besotted with my first taste of pleasure."

"I did worry over that. The first pleasure can be intoxicating, and I feared that perhaps you were enamored of what I could give you physically."

"So it was right for me to do this." Pulling the black velvet box from her reticule, she handed it to him. He was forced to let her help him, as his left arm was bandaged and utterly useless to him for now.

The crimson satin lining gleamed in the firelight, and so, too, did his eyes. When he looked up at her, there was a mist to them once again.

"Little magpie," he whispered as he looked at the black onyx ring. "You gave up everything for this, didn't you?"

She nodded. "That is how much I trust you. Everything I had hidden away in that biscuit jar went to this. All my worldly goods are in that ring, Jude."

"Then I will take it and hold it close, and never give you cause for regret." He put the ring on his index finger, and Isabella grinned. How perfect it looked—how utterly sensual. She wanted that ringed hand on her body, comforting her. Loving her.

Raking her hands through his hair, she bent to kiss his forehead and commanded him to rest. Just when he was going to argue, the study door opened and Sussex strode in, followed closely by Alynwick.

"Knighton's dead."

The statement hung heavy in the air, and all eyes were upon her, gauging her reaction. She would not have had him die. Wendell had been kind—until he had let his greed and lust for power poison everything he was. She felt only deep sadness, and perhaps pity for the man he had once been. The Wendell of almost two months ago, not the monster who had abducted her that night.

"The body?" Black asked.

"We thought it best to leave him there. The authorities will make what they will of his death, but there is nothing to implicate us. It's better this way."

"How the hell was Knighton involved in this?" he asked, his voice sounding exhausted.

"I think we can only assume the culprit is someone from within the lodge. It has to be." Alynwick answered.

"Our rogue Mason?"

"Indeed."

"What did you discover about the shooter?" Jude asked as he struggled to sit upright.

"Once I spotted him on the rooftop, I ran up the back stairs to follow him. He was long gone, but he left something behind," Sussex said.

"Oh?"

"Yes, I'll take it upon myself to investigate it."

Jude opened his eyes, his stare focused on the duke. "Do you need my help?"

Alynwick snorted. "A soiled dove with a broken wing," he drawled. "What use would you be?"

Jude grumbled, "I'll be fine by the morning."

"You most certainly will not," Isabella gasped. "Now, Jude—"

Her reprimand was interrupted by a commotion in the hall, and the sound of Jude's deep voice. "Who the hell could that be?"

The library door swung open to reveal her uncle.

"Isabella!" Stonebrook's white muttonchops twitched as his eyes grew round with shock—then anger.

"Stonebrook," Jude said, holding out a hand. "I can explain."

"You'll explain over a set of pistols," her uncle

thundered as he charged into the room, but Sussex reached for him, and held him steady.

"By God, you're covered in blood and my niece has been injured! Isabella, have you lost your mind?"

They tried to answer, but Stonebrook kept blustering, interrupting them before they could talk. "I come here to inform you, Black, that someone has broken into the temple, and that Wendell Knighton is lying dead on the temple steps—terribly sorry, my dear," he said to Isabella. "And here I am confronted by your betrayal and the evidence that you have abused my beloved niece."

"Knighton is responsible for that. I'm only responsible for seducing her, and causing this scandal."

Isabella groaned. Black was making a hash of this.

"Damn you, sir, get up from that unseemly position!"

"I would," Black said, and Isabella saw his lips quirk upward, "but it seems I am a soiled dove with a broken wing." Jude held up his arm, where shadows of red were beginning to seep through.

"Compliments of Wendell Knighton, and before you can accuse me of murder, no, I did not kill the bastard, but I wish I did after I saw Isabella's face."

Her uncle looked between the three men, unable to make sense of the tableau before him. "You have precisely two minutes to make your case, sir."

"I am in love with your niece, my lord. Very much in love, in fact. I have offered marriage, and Isabella has accepted. Unfortunately, Knighton had other plans, and seemed hell-bent on having her. He abducted her tonight and I followed, and ended up taking the bullet meant for her."

"And Knighton? Who put the bullet in his chest?"

"A mysterious third person," Jude murmured. "From what you have just said about the temple being broken into, I can only assume it was his accomplice."

"Mmm," Stonebrook mumbled, then looked to her. "Is this true, Isabella?"

She could feel the weight of the stares from Sussex and Alynwick, but Jude's hand only tightened in hers. "It is, Uncle."

Nodding, he straightened his jacket and waistcoat. "Very well. Black, you'll see to the special license, and Isabella, you will find your way back home immediately. Do you understand?"

"Perfectly, Uncle."

"And there are to be no more shenanigans like this until you are well and truly married. Do you comprehend me?"

"Yes, my lord."

"Good. Sussex, Alynwick, I trust you can keep this to yourselves?"

"Naturally."

Stonebrook went to leave, but Alynwick stopped him with a question. "What were *you* doing at the lodge in the middle of the night, Stonebrook?"

Her uncle could not disguise his discomfort at the question, nor could he hide how he tried to conceive of a reason for his appearance at the lodge. "Paperwork and a matter of Masonic business," he muttered in supercilious tones. "And I don't need to answer to you, Alynwick. Insolent pup," he muttered as he left, slamming the door behind him.

"An interesting development," Alynwick said thoughtfully.

"He suffers from insomnia." Isabella felt compelled to explain. "He frequently goes to the lodge at night. I doubt there is anything more behind it."

With a shrug, the marquis glanced away.

"Alynwick and I have made plans," Sussex announced. "I will continue to research this Orpheus business, and Alynwick will continue his probe into the Masons.

Hopefully we'll find the chalice—and discover who is behind all this. When you're healed, Black, you will join us."

Isabella stiffened, but Jude put a calming hand on her own. "Of course."

It was then that she realized that Black had to do this. Had to save others from the horrible fate Wendell had suffered. There was evil in that pendant, and however this Orpheus person they spoke of was, he was evil incarnate, too.

With Jude's hand on hers, Isabella could feel his warmth, his strength, his inner convictions flowing into her body. She had let fear rule her life for so many years, she knew she could no longer give her fears so much power. She would be concerned for Black, would pray for his safety, but she would not allow her worries to change what he was.

He was a Brethren Guardian—and would always be.

"Where will you start?" Black asked.

"The shooter," Sussex declared. "The man on the rooftop. Orpheus himself."

THE SALON DOOR OPENED, then clicked softly closed behind him. Seated on the window bench sat Lucy, dressed in an unadorned white day gown. Her hair was loose, pulled back with a pink ribbon. She looked young—and sad. How his heart bled to see her like this.

Clearing his throat, Sussex sought to capture her attention, but she kept her gaze trained on the window. Dark circles rimmed her eyes, and the early-morning sunshine made her look pale and frail.

"Your father said I would find you here."

She would not look at him. Would not turn her green eyes upon him. He was not who she wanted to see. "I suppose you have come to ask me something?"

Yes. No. Christ, he wanted to ask her to be his wife.

Ask her to love him as he loved her. Wanted to see some flicker of excitement, or at the very least, of welcome. But there was nothing like that in her eyes, or in the tone of her voice.

"I came to give you this."

Two steps forward, he was beside her, the delicate white lace was in his hand and he pushed it at her, making her grasp it. Her gasp of shock and alarm seared his breast. Confirmation. A sword to his heart.

"You gave this to *him*."

Slowly she looked up. Her eyes were glistening, with tears—with hope. That tiny flare of hope in her eyes killed whatever hope remained inside him.

"You don't have to answer. I see the truth in your eyes."

"He's…still alive?"

"I don't know. I assume by now your father has told you what has occurred at the lodge. Knighton's dead, and he knows of the break-in."

Her eyes went wide and he had to steel himself from taking her in his arms. She did not want him.

"Don't worry. He believes it was Knighton who broke in, and I will not disabuse him of that notion."

"Thank you."

"I found this on the rooftop of the lodge. The man who shot Knighton was there. I went to chase him but he was gone. The only evidence of his presence was that."

Biting her lip, she looked at the lace that she held in her palm.

"Why did you bring this to me?"

Why? He'd asked himself that a dozen times as he left Black's house and crossed the street to Stonebrook. Why give this to her? She believed her lover dead. He was the only one who knew about that scrap of lace she held. But he had enough secrets, and didn't want this one. Besides, he wanted her to come to him without coercion, or subterfuge. Sussex wanted her to choose him, even knowing the bastard might very well be alive.

Pathetic as it was, he wanted her all to himself—without having another man there—always between them.

"You're playing some game," she accused, and he could not refute it. This was no game. This was real and dangerous, and the bastard he hunted was a murderer, and a hundred other things he didn't want to think of.

"Admit it," she demanded.

"You should know," he said, not relishing what he had to say, "that if you pursue him, if indeed the man you long for is the man I hunt—the man who killed Knighton—"

"Then I will be your enemy," she finished for him.

He nodded. Thankful that she at least had the strength to admit what he couldn't. He didn't want to think of Lucy enmeshed with this business. He didn't want to hurt her, but he had taken a vow, and his word was all he had—all he'd ever had. He was a Brethren Guardian, and it was all he would ever truly be.

"So cold-blooded," she murmured as she looked up.

Oh, how little she knew of him. He was burning with heat and longing, and the urge to pull her up from the window seat and crush his mouth atop hers. Inside him was a need so scorching he was nearly shaking from it. But she would never allow herself to see that. Or to let him show her.

"If he has returned, I will protect him at all costs," Lucy murmured. "If we are to be enemies, then so be it. Even if I must be the one to stand between you. I will not let you take him from me."

With a bleeding heart, he bowed before her. "Good day, Lucy."

Lucy watched as Sussex stepped up into his waiting carriage. The lace he had returned to her still felt warm from his body where he had carried it in his waistcoat pocket. The scent of his cologne, earthy and masculine, infused the air around her.

She watched as the carriage lurched forward, then closed her eyes, wishing the image to come to her eyes. But it was not the image she wanted—it was Sussex, with his gray eyes that spoke of deep mysteries and dark secrets that she saw.

In a moment of sheer panic—and anger—Lucy realized that she could not quite recall what color *his* eyes had been...

EPILOGUE

That night I dreamed of Death. His arms were strong and warm, possessive around me. I absorbed his strength, the feel of him. And as I turned in his arms, I saw that he was watching me, his eyes so beautiful in their intensity.

I was Death's bride now. His for eternity.

He pressed me back, following me until he was leaning over me, the firelight casting shadows over his shoulders as his gaze licked over my naked body. His hand, the one with the onyx ring, slid down my belly, lingering over my womb, before brushing against my wet sex. His eyes glittered, darkened, when he discovered that I was already slick for him.

"Open to me."

His command was dark and erotic, and I responded to him—giving my body and soul up to him. He thrust inside me, connecting us, giving me once more the raptures of la petite mort— *the little death. As he watched me, those beautiful eyes singed my skin, and I felt his breath in my ear, heard his heart beating—for me.*

"I love you, Isabella," he whispered, and I died in his arms, complete, overtaken by his body. I was floating on a cloud of indescribable peace, my body languid, my mind awash in pleasure. Darkness ebbed, and I gave myself

*up to his embrace, but then I came back, slowly,
like a feather flittering to the ground. Death's
kiss brought me into the light, back to life, and I
opened my eyes only to find him looking down
upon me.*

*"'Tis not your time, my love," he whispered.
"You will not die tonight."*

*"Never," I said to him, "for I have been blessed
by Death's Eternal Kiss."*

Closing her journal, Isabella smiled in satisfaction.
Beside her, her husband stirred. She glanced at him, but
she saw he was no longer sleeping, but watching her.

The sheet had slipped to her waist, and Jude reached
out, circling her nipple and areola. His gaze flickered to
hers. "A man could become rather jealous of his wife's
heroes. How fortunate for me that your hero is the embodiment of me."

"How right you are. Death has always had your face."

"Come then," he said in a husky whisper. "I want some
of what you've been giving Death."

With a small cry, Isabella found herself dragged on top
of him, her hair sliding along his chest. He made love to
her long into the night, and Isabella knew at last what it
was to be truly loved.

* * * * *

Dear Reader,

Seduction & Scandal is the first in my new Guardian Brethren series, and I hope you enjoyed reading about Isabella and Lord Black as much as I loved writing about them. You probably noticed some unfinished business, however, such as what happened to the chalice that Wendell Knighton had? What is Lucy's connection with the House of Orpheus, and just why was Stonebrook at the Masonic lodge the night Knighton was killed? These questions will be answered in Lucy's upcoming story, *Pride & Passion*. I hope you'll watch for it!

Happy reading,
Charlotte Featherstone

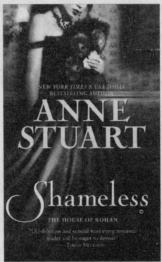